Kate Ellis was born and brought up in Liverpool and studied drama in Manchester. She is the author of the Wesley Peterson murder mysteries as well as the Joe Plantagenet mysteries and the Albert Lincoln trilogy set in the aftermath of the Great War.

Kate has twice been shortlisted for the CWA Short Story Dagger and for the CWA Dagger in the Library award.

Visit Kate Ellis online:

www.kateellis.co.uk
@KateEllisAuthor

Praise for Kate Ellis:

'A beguiling author who interweaves past and present'
The Times

'A powerful story of loss, malice and deception'
Ann Cleeves

'Haunting'
Independent

'Ellis skilfully interweaves ancient and contemporary crimes in an impeccably composed tale'
Publishers Weekly

Dead Man's Lane

Kate Ellis

piatkus

PIATKUS

First published in Great Britain in 2019 by Piatkus
This paperback edition published in 2019 by Piatkus

1 3 5 7 9 10 8 6 4 2

Copyright © 2019 Kate Ellis

The moral right of the author has been asserted.

A CIP catalogue record for this book
is available from the British Library.

ISBN 978-0-349-41828-5

Typeset in New Baskerville by M Rules
Printed and bound in Great Britain by
Clays Ltd, Elcograf S.p.A

Papers used by Piatkus are from well-managed forests
and other responsible sources.

MIX
Paper from
responsible sources
FSC® C104740

Piatkus
An imprint of
Little, Brown Book Group
Carmelite House
50 Victoria Embankment
London EC4Y 0DZ

An Hachette UK Company
www.hachette.co.uk

www.littlebrown.co.uk

For Ivy Rose

***And many thanks to Jane Webster who kindly
allowed her name to be used to help a very
good cause (CLIC Sargent)***

1

Linda Payne knew how to die convincingly. She'd yielded to the strangler's rope so many times that it had become second nature. She'd perfected the look of innocent terror as her executioner approached with the noose in his outstretched hands. She'd even mastered a brief display of final defiance, showing the ultimate triumph of virtue over evil obsession.

She knew her lines off by heart after reciting them to herself for weeks while she made up the bouquets she sold in her little florist's shop opposite Tradmouth Market. Her assistant, Jen, probably thought she was mad but when you'd been entrusted with the title role it was vital to get everything right.

It was dark by the time she'd said farewell to her fellow actors and left Tradmouth's Arts Centre, glad she'd managed to bag a parking space nearby. She hadn't eaten since lunchtime because she'd stayed late in the shop to deal with the flowers for a funeral the following day so she was hungry and eager to get home. But food wasn't the only thing on her mind.

As she drove she muttered her lines to herself. Even so, it was another character's speech from Act Five that echoed around her head; words so fitting for her situation that Webster might have written them with her in mind.

'I suffer now for what hath former been: sorrow is held to be the eldest child of sin.'

At one time, many years ago, Linda had known plenty of sin and sorrow and she'd been trying to forget about them ever since. But who had really sinned? The answer to that question had once seemed so clear but now she wasn't so certain.

When she arrived at her cottage just outside Neston she noticed a small dark car parked a little way down the lane, tucked into a passing place with its lights off. For a brief moment its presence struck her as strange but she put it out of her mind as she pulled into the gate and brought her little florist's van to a halt by the front door.

She had first seen the cottage in the kinder weather of midsummer and she'd fallen in love with the place. Now, fifteen months later, the windows were letting in draughts and the place felt damp. Autumn was here and the branches of the green trees would soon be reaching naked to the sky like grasping skeletal hands. At this time of year she regretted her home's isolation, especially in the hours of darkness.

Keys at the ready, she opened the front door but as she crossed the threshold she sensed a movement to her left. Someone was there, waiting in the shadows, and she wondered whether the moment she'd dreaded for so many years had finally arrived. The moment when she'd be called upon to pay the price for another's sins.

'Hi. This is Tradmouth Community Radio broadcasting to you this chilly Monday evening. Still, the weather's not too bad for October and, according to the forecast, there'll be no rain and a gentle breeze till the weekend so for all you yachting types out there it's sailor's delight.'

The presenter took a breath as he fumbled for the correct switch.

'I see we have another caller on the line. Hi, caller, tell us your name.'

There was an awkward silence.

'We have a shy one here. What's your name and where are you calling from?' the presenter said, hiding his irritation behind forced jocularity. It wasn't the first time a caller had lost their nerve at the prospect of being on air and it always annoyed him. Didn't they know he was trying to make a programme – that if things went well he might get a chance to make it to BBC local radio?

'Are you still there, caller? Don't be coy. We're all friends here.'

'Hello.' It was a man's voice. Gruff and local.

This one needed a little coaxing. 'Where are you calling from?' A direct question usually did the trick.

'I don't want to say. It's just that I've found a body – bones, like. He told us not to say anything but—'

The line went dead but the presenter broke the silence, feeling pleased with himself for his quick thinking. 'Well, it looks like we've got a mystery on our hands, folks. Perhaps we should all be "Watching the Detectives" – and here's Elvis Costello to help us do just that.'

He started the track and called the police. The caller had sounded frightened so it was something he felt he couldn't ignore.

From the first diary of
Lemuel Strange, gentleman

30th August 1666

I was sorely vexed by my wife's complaints when I rose from my bed this morning.

Yesterday came another letter from my cousin Reuben's widow Frances begging me to make haste. Yet my wife has little sympathy for the unfortunate woman whose husband was done to death in such a grievous manner. My wife has the toothache and I told her to have the tooth drawn if it causes her pain but she says she is afraid and that her maid will prepare a poultice of cloves. I told her she must do as she wills but I will delay my journey to Devonshire no longer.

From Frances's letters I fear much is amiss. And I suspect she has not told me the worst of it.

As I was waiting for the carriage to be brought to take me to St Paul's my wife fainted to the ground, saying I should not leave her on the morrow. My cousin Reuben is dead, she said, and is beyond any help I can give him. I said it was my Christian

duty to go to Frances's aid and told the maid to look
to her mistress for I will go whether or not her tooth
troubles her.

2

'Someone's handed this in at the front desk. Says he found it on the steps outside.'

Detective Inspector Wesley Peterson looked up from his paperwork to see DS Rachel Tracey standing by his desk holding a dirty green plastic bag at arm's length so it wouldn't soil her crisp white shirt.

'Don't keep me in suspense. What's in it?'

'You did archaeology at university so it could be right up your street.' She looked round. 'We'd better put something on your desk before I . . .'

She spotted an unused exhibits bag on a nearby filing cabinet and cleared a space on Wesley's desk for it before donning a pair of crime-scene gloves and lifting the skull carefully from its carrier bag as a cascade of dried soil trickled down. She placed it on the desk with exaggerated care and looked at Wesley expectantly, awaiting his verdict.

He studied it for a while before he too put on a pair of gloves and picked it up to examine it more closely.

'Judging by those brow ridges, it looks female to me, although I could be wrong. Possibly youngish. No dental work. It could well be old and none of our business but it'll take an expert to confirm that for sure. Was the person who left it caught on CCTV?'

'I'll ask someone to check,' said Rachel, suppressing a yawn.

'You look tired. You're not overdoing the wedding preparations, are you?'

'I'm fine.' She wasn't going to tell him that the mention of her coming wedding filled her with apprehension, especially when that reminder came from Wesley. 'Have you heard the latest? Someone rang the Community Radio station last night to say they'd found a body – or rather bones.'

'Could this skull be connected?'

Rachel shrugged. Anything was possible. 'They've sent over a recording of the call. Caller doesn't say much, mind you.'

'Man or woman?'

'Man. Sounds local. Wonder why they didn't call us.'

'Could be someone who doesn't like the police for some reason. We should play it to the boss. He might recognise the voice,' Wesley said, knowing DCI Gerry Heffernan's encyclopaedic knowledge of the area's criminals, petty and otherwise. 'I want this skull taken to Dr Bowman at the mortuary and the bag it was in sent to Forensics for thorough examination. If I'm wrong about it being old, we need to know.'

However, by the end of the day Wesley was none the wiser. The call to the radio station had been made from an unregistered pay-as-you-go mobile and even though Gerry said the caller's voice was vaguely familiar, he hadn't been able to place it.

'The line "he told us not to say anything" interests me,' said Wesley as he sat down by Gerry's desk. 'It suggests more than one person found these bones, if they exist. And who told them to keep quiet?'

Gerry looked up from his paperwork. 'Could be someone's idea of a joke.'

'The skull's real enough.'

'Didn't you say it was old?'

'That was my first impression, but it would need to be examined by an expert.'

'Then let's hope you're right and it's not our problem.'

Wesley left Gerry's office wishing he could feel so confident.

Whenever Grace Compton remembered her distant teenage years she thought of Wesley Peterson. Growing up in Dulwich she'd seen him regularly at the local church attended by her family and his; a church popular with the West Indian community. They'd been members of the same youth club and Wesley's mother had been her GP back then. Although the Petersons hailed from Trinidad and her own parents from Barbados, the two families had been close and Wesley's sister, Maritia, had been one of her best friends while they were at school. Then, like a lot of youthful friendships, they'd grown apart once they went their separate ways: she up to Manchester University to read architecture; Maritia to Oxford to read medicine and Wesley to Exeter to study archaeology.

She was still in occasional touch with Maritia who, like Wesley, had settled in Devon and was now married to a vicar. Maritia had a young son but whenever they communicated Grace rarely asked after the child, preferring instead the subject of her own glittering career as partner in a top London architectural practice. Over the past couple of years she'd persuaded herself that she pitied Maritia; that it was a dreadful shame that such a talented woman doctor was shut away in some rural backwater working as a part-time GP when she could be carving out a brilliant career in some metropolitan teaching hospital just as her father, the distinguished cardiac surgeon Mr Joshua Peterson, had done.

As for Wesley, she'd been astonished when he'd chosen to study archaeology at university and even more surprised when he'd decided to join the police force. The Petersons were clever and, in Grace's opinion, they hadn't made the most of their gifts. Even so, there were times when she wondered whether they were more content with their lot than she was.

Grace had dated Wesley for a short period during their adolescent years and whenever she contacted Maritia she could never resist asking about him. In fact she had a nagging suspicion that Wesley was one of the reasons she'd kept in touch with her old friend – but Grace had never been one to acknowledge her own weaknesses, and Wesley Peterson might have become a major weakness if things had worked out differently.

Then two years ago something had happened to make her realise that her feelings for Wesley had been little more than a schoolgirl crush. Someone else had entered her life; someone who'd shaken her ordered professional existence to the core. But when tragedy had struck she'd worked hard to convince herself that her former instincts had been right all along. Love only causes pain and you're better off without it.

Once what she termed her 'moment of madness' was over, she'd poured her energies into her work creating new buildings – her contribution to posterity. The Compton Wynyard Partnership had grown in size and prestige and had recently been awarded the contract to design an exclusive new holiday village nestling in the rolling countryside two miles outside the port of Tradmouth; a project that would keep her and her staff occupied for quite a while to come.

According to the plans there were to be twenty-five luxury cottages, each blended into the landscape with glass frontages and curved turf roofs, all clustered around a Jacobean farmhouse that was to be refurbished to provide seven luxury apartments – an attractive historic centre-piece to the development. No expense would be spared by the developer Hamer Holdings and the model on public display in the local planning office looked extremely impressive, even though she said so herself.

The Strangefields Farm development was Grace's baby and she felt protective towards it, wounded by every objection and annoyed by every interference by the local Planning Department – and by the County Archaeological Unit which had become involved because of the historic nature of the site.

Courtesy of the developer, she was staying in the Marina Hotel in Tradmouth and, as Maritia – and Wesley – lived in the area, she knew she ought to seize the opportunity to catch up with the brother and sister who, at one time, had played such a major role in her life. It had taken her a couple of days to get round to making the call and now, as she tapped out Maritia's number, she realised to her surprise that she felt nervous.

'Hi Maritia. It's me ... Grace.'

'Hello, Grace. How are you?' Maritia said, clearly pleased to hear her old friend's voice.

'You're not going to believe this but I'm in Tradmouth working on that new holiday village on Dead Man's Lane. I don't know whether you've heard about it but it's been keeping me incredibly busy. Having said that, I'm hoping to have some free time over the next few days so do you fancy getting together?'

'How about tomorrow?'

Maritia sounded keen, something Grace put down to a longing to escape her humdrum existence for a few hours.

'I'll check my diary. I've got to meet one of the sub-contractors but ... ' She paused, not wanting to seem too available. 'Lunchtime tomorrow's OK. How about grabbing something to eat in Tradmouth? My treat.'

'Perfect. I've swapped my day off tomorrow with one of the other doctors but Dominic's still booked in at the childminder's so I'm free all day. I can recommend a lovely little Italian place.'

'Italian sounds good. How's Wesley?' she asked, trying her best to make the question sound casual.

'He's fine. Busy as usual.'

After more pleasantries Grace heard a toddler shouting for attention in the background – then a scream and a howling cry.

'I'll have to go,' Maritia said. 'See you tomorrow. Twelve thirty.'

Grace heard the dialling tone and felt unexpectedly irritated that her friend's priorities had so clearly changed. She suspected that when they met the following day they might have little in common – apart from Wesley. They'd always have him.

That night in her well-appointed hotel room Grace didn't sleep well. She was turning over in her mind the questions she was planning to ask and rehearsing how she was going to bring up the subject at the forefront of her mind.

She kept telling herself she was a professional woman at the top of her game, not the sort of person who saw things that weren't there. But when she met Maritia the next day she knew she would be tempted to tell her what she thought she'd seen.

As she dozed she saw herself leaning over their restaurant table and whispering the words: 'You're not going to believe this, Maritia, but I've seen a dead man.'

3

The CCTV footage from the police station entrance showed a dark figure in a hoodie dropping the plastic bag on the steps and scurrying off as though the devil himself was after him. Gerry thought it was probably a man but beneath that hood it could have been anybody.

The fingerprint results from the bag containing the skull proved more helpful. When Wesley arrived at the station first thing the next morning he made himself comfortable and scanned the message that had just come in. Clear prints had been found on the bag – and those prints were on record.

Gerry Heffernan was already in his office. When Wesley had first transferred to Tradmouth from the Met, the DCI's timekeeping had become erratic in the aftermath of his wife Kathy's death. But now Joyce Barnes had moved in with him he usually turned up before the rest of the team. Rachel reckoned Joyce had been a beneficial influence and Wesley agreed. She'd put a stop to the gnawing loneliness the boss had tried so hard to conceal while he'd been on his own.

He gave a token knock on Gerry's office door which he usually kept open so as to hear what was going on in the main office.

'Tell me we've got a lead on this bastard, Wes,' Gerry said, looking up from the paperwork that seemed to have multiplied on his desk overnight.

'Which particular bastard are we talking about?' Wesley said, sitting down opposite Gerry. 'We have quite a few on our books.'

'This burglar who's been targeting the elderly. Nine cases, all within a ten-mile radius of Neston. No prints or DNA and nothing on CCTV. Mind you, he likes to take jewellery which means he'll need to get rid of it sooner or later,' Gerry added with a note of optimism.

'We're keeping an eye on all the pawnbrokers and jewellers in the area.'

Gerry rolled his eyes. 'Unless he goes further afield to get rid of it.'

'He's bound to slip up eventually,' said Wesley, eager to change the subject. 'You know that skull someone left on our doorstep?'

'What about it?'

'The bag it was found in has been examined for fingerprints and there's a lovely clear set belonging to an old friend of ours. Glen Crowther.'

Gerry snorted. 'Glen "someone must have fitted me up" Crowther. I presume he's out.'

'Yes, and word has it he's kept his nose clean since his last stay in one of Her Majesty's hotels. You've always had a soft spot for Glen, haven't you?'

'Me?' Gerry squirmed in his seat, as though he'd been caught doing something shameful. 'Well, I admit I couldn't help feeling a bit sorry for him. While I was stationed in Morbay I had dealings with his old mum and she was a nightmare: booze, drugs, dodgy men – you name it, she did it. And Glen's never used violence, which is a point in his favour.'

Wesley was only too aware that the boss tried to hide his softer side from both villains and underlings. But it was there alright. 'I've heard he's working on a building site. When I track him down would you like to come with me . . . renew old acquaintance?'

Gerry shook his head. 'No, Wes, I'll leave it to you. Take Rach. She's looking a bit peaky these days so the fresh air might do her good. Any news on the skull itself?'

'It's with Colin Bowman at the moment. There were traces of soil attached to it which suggests it's been buried at some point. An osteoarchaeologist or a forensic anthropologist will be able to tell us more once Colin's finished with it.'

'Think we should start going through our missing persons files?'

'Let's see what the experts say first.' Wesley paused. 'I'm wondering if it could be connected to that phone call to the radio station. The caller said bones. What if someone's sent us a sample? And where's the rest of the body, that's what I want to know.'

From the first diary of
Lemuel Strange, gentleman

31st August 1666

Up pretty early at seven of the clock, roused by the necessity to leave for Devonshire on the morrow which, I am told, is a wild place.

My wife's tooth is a little better, thanks to the poultice, but she desires somebody to bear her company while I am away. I say she shows too much familiarity towards our servants and she complains this is because she lacks other company.

I hear there is fresh sickness in Deptford and Greenwich so I begged her to accompany me to Devonshire, but she says she has no wish to travel there for when she met my cousin Reuben she had no liking for him and his Puritan ways. I said that if Reuben is dead as they say this will not matter as she will not have to converse with him. She made no reply then when I packed my things she began to cry and begged me to stay, saying my journey will be in vain for I have no prospect of inheriting my cousin's estate which will go to his young son. I told her that although my efforts will bestow no monetary benefit upon us, I feel obliged to put all in order for Reuben's widow and his fatherless child.

There is also the matter of ensuring the guilty are punished for Reuben's savage murder as the law demands.

4

According to Glen Crowther's probation officer he'd found himself a job at the new holiday village development about two miles outside Tradmouth.

He was driving up the hill, heading out of town with Rachel in the passenger seat, when she broke the amicable silence. 'Strangefields Farm. That's where that serial killer, Jackson Temples, used to live.'

A distant and unpleasant memory emerged from the hazy recesses of Wesley's mind. 'That's right. I remember now.'

He'd first heard the name Strangefields Farm while he was working in London, a brand-new fast-track graduate in the Met's Art and Antiques Unit, fresh from university and still wet behind the ears. The media had made much of the fact that Strangefields Farm stood on 'Dead Man's Lane'. The name had been a gift to many a sub-editor at the time and now Wesley recalled the headlines – THE KILLER ON DEAD MAN'S LANE.

The circumstances of the case had appealed to journalism's more lurid side. The victims had been teenage girls lured to an isolated farmhouse by an artist called Jackson Temples who'd set up a studio in the house he'd inherited from his late parents. The unfortunate girls had become household names for a few short weeks until the press moved on to some fresh horror.

Temples had persuaded them to model for him and they'd been flattered at the prospect of being immortalised on canvas. But when the images Temples had created of his victims were revealed to a horrified public in court, the strange and, in the opinion of the prosecution, perverted paintings had helped to secure his conviction.

A number of girls had gone to the farmhouse and had come to no harm, posing for their portraits and emerging unscathed. Four girls, however, hadn't been so lucky and by the time Wesley had joined Tradmouth CID, Jackson Temples was safely behind bars and his exploits old news.

Wesley knew Rachel would have lived locally at the time and when he asked her what she remembered about the case she gave a visible shudder.

'I was only fourteen when it happened and my parents still thought of me as a child which, looking back, I was. They thought the subject of Jackson Temples was too unpleasant for my delicate ears.'

Wesley couldn't help smiling. The Rachel he knew was anything but delicate.

'Anyway, I remember reading in the local paper that a girl called Carrie Bullen had been attacked and left for dead. Then about a week later the body of a girl called Nerys Harred was found washed up on the river bank near the castle. At first they thought the killer came from Morbay because that's where the girls had last been seen. The Strangefields connection wasn't discovered until much later.'

'You remember a lot about it.'

'It was the talk of my school. You know what teenagers are like.'

Before Wesley could ask more questions they'd turned into Dead Man's Lane, a winding road lined with tall hedgerows, just wide enough for two vehicles to pass. He slowed down, driving at a crawl, looking for the entrance. To his left he noticed an old cob cottage with lichen-stained walls, half hidden by the greenery that had grown up around it, like a witch's house from a fairy tale. Half the roof tiles had gone, revealing skeletal rafters beneath, and a pair of pigeons, presumably the only living residents, flew out of their nest by the crumbling chimney. The side facing the road was windowless as though the little house was hiding itself from passers-by and a few yards away a white post protruded from the narrow grass verge, the name Dead Man's Lane painted in stark black against the clean white background.

He brought the unmarked police car to a halt beside a pair of large gateposts, each topped by a stone lion, so worn down by centuries of Devon weather that the once-impressive beasts now looked more like domestic cats.

He turned to Rachel. 'You OK?'

'Course I am. Why wouldn't I be? In fact I'm curious in a gruesome sort of way. The girl who survived, Carrie, led the police here and if she hadn't lived who knows how many more he'd have killed. A fisherman found her on the river bank at Derenham with a severe head injury and suffering from hypothermia. Temples had tried to strangle her like the others but he hadn't made a good job of it. Still, she was the first so ...'

'He hadn't perfected his technique?'

Rachel gave a grim smile. 'You could put it like that. She was in a coma for a couple of months but when she eventually came round she gave the evidence that led to his capture. In the meantime Nerys was found dead and a couple more girls had gone missing. Their bodies were never found but there was evidence he'd killed them too.'

'What evidence?'

'Their clothes were found at the house.' She paused. 'Funny how some girls came here and left unharmed. Some even gave evidence for the defence at Temples' trial; said they hadn't seen anything suspicious.'

'Maybe they just had a lucky escape. Wonder why he chose those particular victims?'

'There was a theory going round that they were all the same type but I don't know how true that was. From the photographs in the papers at the time three were really stunning with long dark hair but one was quite ... ordinary, so that theory could be rubbish. Another story went round that he only killed when the moon was full, which meant girls were safe if they went there any other time.'

'Sounds far-fetched but you never know. Do they know what happened to the girls who were never found?'

'At the trial it was said that he dumped the last three victims in the river at high tide in the hope that their bodies would be washed out to sea. He'd once been in a sailing club at school so they said he knew about tides. The final two victims were never found, although a skull was caught in the nets of a trawler about ten years ago and dental records confirmed that it belonged to one of them – Jacky Burns. The rest of her'll be down there somewhere. Who knows, she might be found one day – along with the last girl he killed. Gemma Pollinger her name was.' She paused. 'Unless the skeleton the caller to the radio station said he found is hers. And the skull ... '

'I'm pretty sure it belonged to a young woman so you

could be right. We won't know for sure until the lab con-ducts tests. How long did Temples get?'

'Thirty years minimum. He always refused to admit his guilt so he won't be getting out any time soon.' For a few moments she said nothing, then 'I think the boss worked on the case. But he never talks about it.'

Wesley switched on the engine again and drove slowly up the potholed drive. He could see signs of construction all around; the foundations of small rectangular buildings dotted around a large Jacobean house. He'd expected a humble farmhouse but at some point in its history this building had been more than that – the home of a prosper-ous yeoman farmer, perhaps, or even a small manor house.

He climbed out of the car and stood looking at the house.

'Do you think some places are evil, Wes?' Rachel said softly.

'They demolished Cromwell Street and Rillington Place, which is understandable. But this place is Grade Two star-listed so you can't just go knocking it down. Even so, I can't imagine anyone wanting to live in a house associated with something like that.'

'Someone obviously does, or rather they'll be spending their holidays here. No expense spared by the look of it.'

'Better find Glen Crowther,' said Wesley, feeling they were getting sidetracked by the old case, although he knew there was a chance the two matters were connected.

There was a notice by the studded oak door saying in large white letters against a blue background that hard hats must be worn at all times. Wesley could hear hammering and drilling in the distance so he shouted at the top of his voice and waited. Eventually a small man with a wizened face appeared and Wesley held out his warrant card.

'We're looking for Glen Crowther. Is he here?'

The man rolled his eyes. 'I told the gaffer he'd be trouble. What's he done?'

'Nothing as far as we know. We'd just like a word, that's all.' Wesley suddenly felt guilty, hoping Crowther wouldn't lose his job as a result of their visit. For ex-cons employment could be hard to come by.

The man disappeared into the dusty depths of the house and a couple of minutes later a lanky young man in a stained sweatshirt appeared, his hands thrust in the pockets of jeans that looked as if they were about to fall down. He paused to hoist them up before approaching the two detectives warily, as though he feared they'd come to arrest him.

'What is it?' he said in a smoker's rasp.

'Glen Crowther?'

The man looked as though he was considering denying it. Then he nodded.

'We'd like a quick word. Nothing to worry about,' said Wesley, aware that he sounded like a doctor reassuring a patient that it wasn't bad news. Because his close family were all doctors he suspected he'd absorbed the bedside manner in his formative years.

Crowther stepped outside the building. 'Will this take long? The gaffer's on my back the whole time and he won't like—'

'We won't keep you longer than necessary.'

Rachel was carrying the green carrier bag, protected from contamination inside a transparent evidence bag. 'This was found on the steps of our police station with a human skull inside. Do you recognise it?'

'What makes you think it's got anything to do with me?'

'Your prints are all over it.'

A look of terror passed across Crowther's face. 'I didn't do nothing. Honest. I just found it. It was hidden in an old cupboard in the cellar. The door was all sealed up with paint – hadn't been opened for years by the look of it – but when I got it open I saw it sitting there grinning at me. I didn't tell the other lads 'cause I know what the cops are like once they start sniffing around and taping things off.' He swallowed hard. 'No offence.'

'None taken,' said Rachel.

'I put it in a bag and I didn't know what to do with it. Then I was passing the police station on my way home so ...'

'You thought you'd leave it to us to sort out.'

Crowther nodded eagerly, as though he was relieved that Wesley understood.

'Can you show me where you found it?'

After he'd handed them the regulation hard hats, Crowther led them into an entrance hall dominated by a wide oak staircase which must have been impressive in its day – and would be again once it had been cleaned up and a layer or three of beeswax had been applied. The rest of the hallway, however, had been stripped back to the bare brick. If the developer knew about the house's history, he or she was making every effort to ensure that no reminder was left of the time when Jackson Temples had committed his crimes there.

Crowther led them across the uneven oak floorboards to a door beneath the staircase. Here a set of worn stone steps led down to a cellar and once at the bottom Crowther pointed to an old built-in cupboard in the corner. 'That's where it was. You'd think it would be crammed with stuff

24

but the skull was the only thing in it. Cupboards are useful. My mum says you can't have too many cupboards.'

Wesley couldn't help smiling, remembering what Gerry had said about Crowther's mum. She might be a nightmare but her son was clearly fond of her even so. 'Your mum's right. You haven't found any more human remains?'

'I would have said if I had.' Crowther frowned as though something was worrying him. 'Mind you, we haven't finished in the cellar yet.'

'So it wasn't you who rang the radio station?'

Crowther shook his head vigorously and Wesley was sure he was telling the truth. Then he gave a theatrical shudder. 'This place used to belong to a murderer so I wouldn't be surprised if he buried lots of bodies down there.'

Wesley caught Rachel's eye. 'Might be worth having a look.'

5

When an old friend calls out of the blue and asks you out for lunch, it's normally a cause of delight. But when Maritia Fitzgerald sat opposite Grace Compton in the Maria Bella Italian restaurant on the embankment, at a table with a river view, she suspected she had more on her mind than catching up with the latest gossip. Grace looked worried and Maritia's instincts told her something was wrong.

The strange confession that Grace had made once they'd finished their starters stuck in Maritia's mind throughout the meal. 'I saw someone I recognised in Tradmouth yesterday. Only it couldn't have been him, because he's meant to be dead.'

Then Grace had changed the subject and started chatting about their mutual past, their families and work, but Maritia could tell that the encounter with the 'dead man' was at the forefront of her friend's thoughts.

Being inquisitive by nature, she tried to dig deeper. Who was the man Grace thought she'd seen? And how had he died? Grace's replies, however, were annoyingly evasive at first. It was someone she'd known in London; a former client of her practice who'd died in a maritime disaster a couple of years ago; a ferry had sunk in Thailand

and over thirty people had lost their lives, including this man. He'd been on holiday, she said; and he'd never come back.

'They say everyone has a double somewhere.'

Grace leaned towards Maritia and lowered her voice as though she'd made the decision to share a confidence. 'I'm sure it was him. I'm very good at faces.'

The intensity in Grace's words told her she wasn't talking about a casual acquaintance. 'Were you and this man ... close?'

Grace looked away. 'It was just sex. It wouldn't have lasted.'

Maritia, the vicar's wife, suspected that Grace was trying to shock her. But Maritia was unshockable and she knew her friend was lying.

'Are you sure that's all it was?'

Grace refused to meet her eyes. 'He owed my practice money. A lot of money. We had to borrow from the bank and we're only just getting back on an even keel.'

'Could that be why he chose to disappear?'

Grace didn't answer.

'Is there anybody else in your life at the moment?' Maritia asked, curious.

'There's a barrister I see sometimes. His family's from Ghana.'

'You don't sound keen.'

Grace's expression gave little away as she shrugged and tucked into the tagliatelle that had just been placed in front of her.

After they'd eaten in silence for a while Grace began to ask about Wesley. How was he? As an ethnic minority officer how did he fit into the police force in such a pre-dominantly white area? She knew he'd married a white girl. What was she like? How was his marriage? The anxious note in this final question told Maritia that the answer mattered to her.

'You know Wesley, he gets along with most people. And he and Pam are good. You know she was diagnosed with breast cancer a while ago?'

'You told me.'

'Well, she's had the all-clear, thank God. She still has regular checks of course but for the moment it looks as though everything's fine.' She paused, looking Grace in the eye and seeing a flash of disappointment there. 'You always fancied my brother, didn't you?'

Maritia's wicked side, the part that as the wife of a clergyman she was supposed to suppress, enjoyed seeing Grace squirm.

'He was a good friend.'

'First love. We always have a soft spot for our first love.'

'Nonsense.'

Grace glanced round, fidgeting with her napkin. 'Fancy sharing a bottle of wine?' The question sounded almost pleading.

So that was it. Grace's high-powered job in London had driven her to the bottle, unless Maritia's work as a GP, having to read between the lines of her patients' statements about their drinking habits, had led her into the habit of thinking the worst.

'I'm driving. Can't risk it, I'm afraid. Look, why don't you come round for dinner one night? I don't have much time to cook anything fancy these days so it'll just be a casserole. You can take a taxi and we can make a night of it. You can meet my son.' She saw Grace's expression freeze. 'Sorry, you're not into the baby thing, are you? And you haven't met Mark yet. It's time you and my husband got acquainted.'

Grace gave a feeble smile. 'I don't go to church these days.'

'In that case I'll make sure he leaves his dog collar off. He's nice. I'm sure you'll like him.'

'I'm sure I will. Sorry I couldn't make your wedding. Pressure of work.' Grace hesitated. 'Will you invite Wesley?'

'If you like,' Maritia said. 'And Pam of course if they can get a babysitter,' she added, fearing things might be awkward if Pam's presence came as a shock.

Grace focused her gaze on her food and pushed it around her plate. 'I'd like to see Wesley. I need to ask his advice.'

'About your dead man? You can always contact him at the police station if you're worried, you know.'

'I know but I don't want to make a fool of myself. You're probably right. It must have been his double.' She straightened her back, suddenly businesslike. 'I haven't told you about the new holiday village I'm working on yet.'

The subject of the dead man was closed.

6

In Wesley's opinion Glen Crowther's story had the ring of truth about it. For one thing Crowther was too unimaginative to have made it up; for another the discovery of the skull had obviously frightened him.

As he was driving back from Strangefields Farm he received a call from Colin Bowman at the mortuary to tell him that he'd handed the skull over to a forensic anthropologist for examination and was awaiting the verdict. Wesley had been wondering about the call to the Community Radio station but now he'd met Glen Crowther he was as sure as he could be that it hadn't been his voice he'd heard on the tape of the brief conversation, which meant that, unless it was a hoax, someone else had discovered human remains; possibly in a different location altogether.

When he arrived at the station he was told that Gerry was in a meeting with the chief superintendent so he seized the opportunity to check out the details of the Jackson Temples case, only to find that when the body of Nerys Harred had been found washed up on the rocks below the castle a Detective Sergeant Heffernan, then based in Morbay, had been one of the first on the scene.

Ten minutes later when Gerry returned to the office,

Wesley brought him up to date with the latest developments and saw the colour drain from his face at the mention of Strangefields Farm, the reaction telling him that the case had brought back disturbing memories. But the matter needed to be dealt with so he couldn't afford to be squeamish about Gerry's feelings.

Pressures on the police budget were such that Wesley was inclined to leave it to the builders to report anything untoward they came across in the cellar. Gerry, however, was of a different opinion. One of Temples' victims had yet to be found, he said, and, as the skull belonged to a young female, they couldn't say with any certainty that it wasn't Gemma Pollinger's, especially as, according to records, Gemma had looked after her teeth in life and had had no dental work. It was amazing, Gerry said, how the small details stay with you even after two decades. Burial didn't fit with Temples' known MO but it was a possibility they couldn't ignore.

If the skull was found to be recent they would have to halt the work at Strangefields Farm immediately and, although Wesley thought he could rely on Glen Crowther to report anything else he discovered, he didn't trust the developer to hold the project up voluntarily just to oblige the police. However, there was a way around the problem. Strangefields Farm was Grade II* listed which meant the local conservation officer could poke his or her nose in whenever necessary. And there was someone else who would be able to help out.

His old university friend, Neil Watson, worked for the County Archaeological Unit. Neil had mentioned a while ago that he was responsible for making sure that any archaeology discovered during the Strangefields Farm development was dealt with properly. If he could keep an eye on things it would cost the police budget nothing and put Wesley's mind at rest at the same time. He felt a glow of satisfaction, pleased that he'd come up with such a neat solution to his problem.

As luck would have it Neil was in his Exeter office when Wesley rang, complaining that he was up to his ears in paperwork. He seemed keen to meet Wesley at Strangefields to have a poke around in the cellar, as he put it. The house dated back to the seventeenth century, he said with an eagerness that suggested a desire to escape the office, so it would be an interesting exercise even if they found nothing more gruesome there than an old Victorian mangle.

Happy that the matter had been sorted, Wesley sat back in his seat, wondering whether to fetch himself a cup of tea from the machine in the corridor outside. He made the decision and as soon as he stood up Rachel appeared with a desolate expression on her face.

'What's up?'

She looked round as though she feared they might be overheard.

'I've been trying to get in touch with the florist who's doing my wedding flowers. Her name's Linda Payne,' she said, perching on the edge of his desk. The short black skirt she was wearing had ridden up to reveal an expanse of thigh and she pulled it down absent-mindedly. 'According to her assistant, Jen, she hasn't been in work for the last couple of days and no one knows where she is.'

'She might be ill?'

Rachel shook her head and a few strands of fair hair escaped from her ponytail. 'Jen's been trying to phone her but there's been no answer.'

'There's probably an innocent explanation.'

'Jen hasn't worked there long and I'm afraid she won't be able to cope with the wedding flowers on her own.'

The Rachel he knew was a good detective who would have wanted to know why the woman wasn't answering her phone rather than worrying about flowers, so her words surprised him. But he'd heard that brides – even normally level-headed ones – could develop tunnel vision as their nuptials approached.

'Let's get this straight, Rach: your florist's disappeared and you want to report her missing.'

Rachel hesitated, dragging herself back to her usual role. 'It's not like Linda to let anyone down, that's why I'm worried.' She frowned. 'Why would she go off without telling anyone when she has my wedding to prepare for?'

Wesley relaxed a little. 'Your wedding's six weeks away. There's plenty of time for her to turn up.'

'These things need to be decided well in advance,' she said as though she was explaining to a child. 'We had a meeting arranged at the shop yesterday evening to discuss the bouquets. Jen had to deal with it but she admits herself that she hasn't much experience.'

'Maybe Linda's been called away on urgent family business and she's not had a chance to let anyone know. I should stop worrying if I were you.'

Rachel sighed. 'I know where she lives so I think I'll go round. She might be ill . . . or . . . '

'OK. If you're worried it won't do any harm.'

Rachel gave him a grateful smile and returned to her paperwork. At least someone didn't think she was overreacting.

*

Bert Cummings enjoyed listening to the Community Radio because the presenters spoke of things he could relate to. But whatever its virtues, it was rarely exciting; that was why he'd been so surprised when someone had called the phone-in programme claiming they'd found a skeleton, although he thought it had probably been a hoax. Some people had a strange sense of humour.

He liked company, even that of the carers who came in three times a day to help him, and he'd been feeling a lot more cheerful over the past couple of weeks – ever since his grandson Kevin had turned up on his doorstep saying he'd decided to move back from Canada to live in Neston, which meant he'd be able to visit regularly from now on. Whenever he came he stayed a while and brought biscuits with him. Bert could never resist biscuits.

When Bert spoke to his carers about Kevin they didn't seem particularly interested, apart from Suzy. Suzy was the best of them and he was fond of her because she reminded him of his daughter who went to Canada with her family and died of cancer three years ago. Canada was supposed to be nice so he was surprised Kevin had chosen to return to Devon – and he hadn't acquired a Canadian accent either.

But that wasn't the strangest thing. Bert's memory was hazy about many things but he was sure he remembered someone telling him that Kevin had been in a serious accident. He'd been sure he'd heard Kevin was dead.

From the first diary of
Lemuel Strange, gentleman

4th September 1666

The coach lacked comfort as did the inns where we stayed
on the journey. The wildest and most uncivilised country
is out of London and worst of all in the North I hear,
although I have never ventured so far. They do say that
Devonshire is a fair county though I have not visited
since I was a child so I have little recollection of it.

I left the coach in Tradmouth, which is a busy port
with a handsome church named for Saint Margaret. So
many vessels were on the river there and so many sailors
on the quayside that for a moment I thought myself
in London.

The quay stank of fish so much that I was obliged
to hold my nose against the stench and it was with some
relief that I found the Star, which is a good inn beside
the church and the town pillory, where I was met by
my cousin's servant. The man who asked for me had a
cadaverous face and there was no smile of greeting from
which I surmised that the household still grieves for
its master.

I enquired of this servant, whose name is John, about the circumstances of my cousin's death and he told me in hushed tones that Reuben's corpse has yet to be found.

7

Wesley heard his phone ringing and hurried to his desk to answer it. The voice on the other end of the line sounded familiar but for a few moments he couldn't place it.

'Hello, Wesley. Long time no see.'

Light suddenly dawned. 'Grace?'

'Amazing Grace as you used to call me. Remember?' There was a flirtatiousness in her voice that made his heart beat a little faster. 'I've just had lunch with your sister. We've been doing some catching up.'

'She never told me you were here.'

There was a long pause before Grace spoke again. 'She might have had her reasons.'

Wesley suspected he knew what those reasons were. Maritia knew that he and Grace had once been close and she felt loyal to Pam, her sister-in-law. 'What are you doing in Devon? Holiday?'

'No such luck. I'm working. I'm responsible for the design of a new holiday village near Tradmouth. It's going to be a real asset to the area in terms of jobs and revenue.'

She sounded like an advertising brochure but he remembered Maritia saying a while ago that Grace's work had become all-consuming.

'Strangefields Farm? I was up there today. Looks as if it's going to be impressive.' He decided not to mention the skull for the time being – not until he knew more about its origins.

'My partnership only does high-end these days. How's crime fighting?'

'Keeping me busy,' he said, anxious to get the preliminaries out of the way. 'It's nice to speak to you, Grace, but I'm sure you didn't just call me at work for a chat. Can I do something for you?'

There was another long silence before she replied. 'I think I've seen someone from my past, someone I never thought I'd ever see again. I need your advice. Can we meet? Lunch tomorrow?'

Wesley hesitated, suspecting this was a ruse; an excuse to get in touch.

'My lunches tend to be a sandwich at my desk. Like I said, I'm busy. We're investigating a spate of burglaries and—'

'Surely you can spare an hour.'

In the face of her determination he gave in, telling himself that a quick lunch would do no harm. 'OK. Tomorrow. How about one o'clock? Will fish and chips on the embankment do you or are you above that sort of thing these days?'

'Fish and chips might be fun. Remember when we used to eat them out of a newspaper on our way back from youth club?'

'We were fifteen.'

'Those were the days. I'll see you tomorrow then. I'll meet you outside the police station.'

Grace sounded bright, almost brittle, as though she was trying to hide something beneath a veneer of artificial confidence, and as he ended the call he felt uneasy. Grace had never been a worrier and he'd sensed anxiety in her voice. But there was only one way to find out what this was all about. That was to keep their appointment.

It was unusual to see crows perched on a floating log like that. At least it looked like a log from where the bird-watcher was standing on the bank of the nature reserve's freshwater lake. The jet-black birds were pecking at the log just beyond the reed beds with single-minded determination, unbothered by the flotilla of ducks gliding by with their beaks in the air.

The man raised the binoculars that hung around his neck. According to his fellow birders a great egret had been spotted there but it hadn't yet made an appearance. Just the black crows, gathered like mourners around an open grave at a Victorian funeral, jostling for position on their small bobbing island.

He focused his binoculars on the birds and watched them for a couple of minutes with a growing sense of unease. The log seemed to be a strange colour; the colour of green-tinged flesh, and he'd never seen one with hair before. He tried to persuade himself that he was imagining things; that it wasn't a human body and that he'd look foolish if he involved the police.

What if he was wrong? What if his fellow birders cursed him for causing a disturbance? What if some rare species was about to take advantage of the thoughtfully provided facilities only to be frightened off by the arrival of hordes of police officers and forensic scientists?

But after a while he bowed to the inevitable and made the call.

8

Neil Watson had already visited Strangefields Farm several times to make sure the developer wasn't trying to conceal anything archaeological that would hold up the work and eat into his profits.

He'd seen the model of the new holiday village in the local Planning Office, complete with miniature trees and tiny people strolling through the landscaped grounds and lounging by the open-air swimming pool. The model of the Jacobean farmhouse that was to be transformed into luxury apartments with all mod cons was remarkably accurate, even down to the derelict barns at the rear of the building, converted in the architect's imagination into leisure facilities – whatever that meant.

The desk-based assessment he'd made of the area surrounding the house had thrown up no potential archae-ological problems; no lost buildings or evidence of earlier occupation. The only intriguing feature on the ancient maps he'd examined had been a tiny square building just inside the gates which was marked 'chapel' on a map of 1598. By the early eighteenth century the building had vanished from all maps and records, which Neil also found intriguing; but according to the plans he'd seen, that part of the land was to be left untouched which meant that, even if the foundations of a chapel were still beneath the earth, there was no immediate threat to anything of potential archaeological interest.

From the research he'd carried out back in his Exeter office Neil had learned that the house had been built by a family called Strange in the early seventeenth century. However, by the time Queen Victoria ascended to the throne in 1837 there was no trace of them in local records.

Strangefields had begun life as a high-status home but over the years it had changed hands many times and for much of its history had been occupied by tenants. More recently it had been owned by a family called Temples, and Jackson Temples, the convicted killer, had inherited the farm when his father died in 1993. He'd lived there until 1996 when he'd been imprisoned for the murders of three women and the attempted murder of a fourth. Since Temples' arrest the place had lain empty, its notoriety putting off potential purchasers, until it was acquired eighteen months ago at a knock-down price by Joe Hamer, a developer, who would presumably be careful to conceal the house's dark history. In a less enlightened age the Jacobean house might have been demolished to banish whatever imaginary demons might lurk inside, but fortunately the place was now listed and protected for future generations.

The narrow road leading to the gates was called Dead Man's Lane, a name that had whetted Neil's curiosity when his team had first acquired the contract for the archaeological investigation. The lane had been known as Hall Lane up until the late seventeenth century, presumably because Strangefields Farm had been known as Strangefields Hall in more prosperous days. Then a tithe map of 1690 had showed the change of name, although there was no hint as to the reason.

Neil was sure the developer would try and ditch this name for something more appealing. And the name of the house – with its disturbing recent associations – would be bound to go too.

He'd promised Wesley that he'd have a look in the cellar where the skull had been found, which gave him an excuse to pay another visit to the house and to check the area near the gate for evidence of the mysterious chapel while he was at it.

When he arrived in Dead Man's Lane he parked on the grass beside the ancient gateposts and as he walked through the gates he was surprised to see a large yellow digger standing twenty yards away, hidden from the lane behind the tall Devon hedge like a predator lying in wait for a victim. Because there were no plans for this particular location, Neil wondered what it was doing there. Then he noticed a patch of bare soil about twelve feet square scarring the ground that had previously been an expanse of rough grassland. The area had clearly been excavated and the soil piled in again with no attempt made to replace the turf as any archaeologist would.

He felt a stab of irritation. This was something he needed to ask the developer about as soon as possible because he didn't want him to get the idea he could take liberties with the site's heritage.

Still angry, he returned to his car and drove towards the house, taking the pitted drive too fast, and before approaching the front door he put on the hard hat and hi-vis jacket he always kept in the back of his car, knowing the builders would give him a better reception if he looked the part. The tactic worked because the builders, who were drinking tea in the hallway when he walked in, greeted him with 'Hiya mate. You from the scaffolder's?' When he introduced himself they looked wary but the connection had already been made.

'Is the boss about? Mr Hamer?'

'He's in Exeter.'

'Anyone know anything about that digger by the gate?'

There were blank looks all round. Perhaps they'd been told to play dumb.

'I understand Inspector Peterson has been here about the skull.'

The answer was a cautious nod.

'He's asked me to have a look in the cellar in case there are any more unpleasant surprises waiting down there.'

'There's still a lot of crap down there but you can go down if you want,' said Glen Crowther, looking at his mates. 'You know who used to live here, don't you? That serial killer, Jackson Temples. I reckon that skull belongs to one of his victims.'

'I'd better make a start then.'

'Rather you than me, mate,' said Crowther with a nervous laugh as he emptied the dregs of his mug onto the dusty floorboards.

9

'A call's just come in, sir. Birdwatcher at Bereton Nature Reserve thinks he's spotted a body in the lake.'

Detective Constable Trish Walton had hoped to leave work at a reasonable time so she could look for an outfit for Rachel's wedding before the shops shut their doors. She and Rachel shared a house just outside Tradmouth and although she was looking forward to the wedding she wasn't looking forward to having to find another housemate, or to staying alone in the cottage in the meantime. Her colleague DC Paul Johnson wasn't happy in the flat he was renting in town because of a noisy neighbour downstairs, but she and Paul had once gone out together so she feared that asking him to share would give him fresh hope of resurrecting their relationship. On the other hand, Paul understood the demands of police work, which was important in a housemate.

Wesley looked up. 'Has a patrol been sent?'

'A car's on its way. Do you want me to ... ?'

'Let's wait to see what they have to say. Hopefully it'll be a floating log.' Wesley gave her a reassuring smile. Her shift finished half an hour ago and he could tell she was anxious to leave. 'Why don't you get off? I can always give you a call if you're needed.'

'Thanks.' Although she knew she should accept Wesley's generous offer, she was suddenly reluctant to go. 'Something the matter, sir?'

Wesley's conversation with Grace was still on his mind but he didn't think he was so transparent. 'Nothing that can't wait till morning,' he said, not sure whether he was telling the truth. A skull had been found at the home of a notorious killer and then there was Rachel's errant florist, Linda Payne. But he told himself that Ms Payne was a grown woman and it wasn't illegal to make yourself scarce for a while.

He watched Trish go, stopping at Paul Johnson's desk to exchange a word before putting on her coat. With luck the birdwatcher's report would come to nothing, but he had an uncomfortable feeling about it – like the feeling he had about his imminent meeting with Grace.

When half an hour had passed with no word from the patrol, he convinced himself that it must have been a false alarm. Floating debris had been mistaken for human bodies before; he'd known it happen several times in the river. He walked into Gerry's office and when the boss raised his head he looked like a man with the world's troubles on his shoulders.

'I've been going through the reports on these burglaries again to see if I can spot anything new.'

'Any luck?'

Gerry shook his head. 'He does a neat job – no prints and no sign of a break-in. If the stuff wasn't missing you'd think he didn't exist. Money and valuable jewellery – it's happened too many times for some old dear to have imagined it.'

'The victims are all elderly and live alone. Whoever it is seems to know when their carers are visiting.'

Gerry flung up his hands in despair. 'We've been through all the care companies' records and there's no common denominator. Nothing. Zilch. Any news on our birdwatcher yet?'

As if on cue, Gerry's phone rang and after a few seconds he signalled Wesley to take a seat and hit the speakerphone button. It was the patrol and they had news.

'It is a body, sir,' said the disembodied voice. 'A woman. No clothes. You don't go skinny-dipping at this time of year so I think we can rule out an accident.'

'I'm on my way,' said Gerry. 'Alert the team and the pathologist, will you?'

He stood up, his leather chair creaking with relief. 'You heard, Wes. I'll give Joyce a call – tell her I don't know when I'll be home.'

Wesley left a similar message for Pam. *Suspicious death. Be home as soon as I can.* He wondered whether to mention Grace. Then he decided against it.

The patrol had left the body *in situ*, although the two uniforms who'd attended the scene had done their best to scare off the scavenging crows by waving their arms about in what would appear to the casual observer to be some sort of strange ritual dance.

After the officers had dealt with the birds they'd been needed to fend off the press, who'd somehow got wind of the police activity and were now gathering as near as they dared to the action, being shooed back from time to time like a herd of curious cattle.

When Wesley and Gerry arrived they saw a man, presumably the birdwatcher who'd reported it in the first place, standing some distance away looking awkward and fidgeting with the expensive binoculars slung around his neck. The man had been instructed to stay where he was until the detectives arrived but Gerry, assuming that he'd merely been in the wrong place at the wrong time, told one of the uniforms to obtain the man's full name and address then tell him he was free to go.

As the man was walking away, glancing back over his shoulder nervously from time to time, Dr Colin Bowman, the pathologist, arrived carrying his crime-scene bag. A few minutes later the CSIs turned up and Colin asked for the body to be brought ashore after the necessary photographs had been taken. Wesley suggested that the uniforms obtain waders and boathooks from the warden's lodge which stood a quarter of a mile away near the main road. The warden would have to be informed and interviewed along with any other birders they happened to come across, something to keep them occupied while Colin and the CSIs went about their work.

Once the crime-scene tent had been erected to shield the activity from prying eyes, the body was brought onto dry land and Wesley watched while Colin made his examination. Colin was an affable man, cheerful by nature, but as he probed the body and took his samples his manner was solemn and respectful. Like Wesley, he never forgot that the cadaver in front of him had been a human being: someone's daughter, mother, wife or sister.

'She's been dead a couple of days but that's all I can tell you at the moment,' Colin said once he'd finished. 'Post-mortem first thing tomorrow morning suit you?'

'That'll do nicely,' said Gerry. 'Cause of death?'

Colin didn't answer. The mortuary van had just arrived and the CSIs were bagging up the corpse's head and hands to protect any evidence that might remain.

While they worked Wesley took the opportunity to study the dead woman. She was blond, probably in her late thirties or early forties, and her figure was good although she carried a bit of weight around her midriff. Her face appeared to have been badly lacerated but whether this had been caused by the crows who'd pecked at her eyes or by something else, Wesley couldn't be sure. Her body was so discoloured that it was hard to envisage what she'd looked like in life and as Wesley watched her being attended with such delicate care he felt a deep sadness. Whoever had put her there had stripped her of her clothes . . . and her identity.

'I can tell you a couple of things before the post-mortem,' said Colin, rousing Wesley from his thoughts. 'There's trauma to the head and I don't think we can blame wildlife for those wounds on her face. I think someone's mutilated her – stabbed her face repeatedly.'

'Are those marks on her neck?'

'I was coming to that,' said Colin. 'I think she might have been strangled with a ligature.'

'What kind of ligature?'

'Far too early to say, Wesley. But judging by the pattern of bruising, it could be something like a rope.'

From the first diary of
Lemuel Strange, gentleman

4th September 1666

As Frances had ordered, John had brought another horse to the town for my use and he rode behind on an inferior mount.

The horse was not the best of steeds but adequate for the journey, which was but two miles or slightly more along a rough, steep lane with high hedges concealing all view of the land beyond.

We came to a handsome gate topped by a pair of fine carved lions which lay beside a tiny chapel falling to ruin and as we approached the house I had little recollection of the place that, to my infant self, had seemed as large as a palace. Now, as it came into view at the end of the long track, I realised it was a mere manor house, little larger than the home of a prosperous farmer. It was built of stone behind a cobbled courtyard where I dismounted, looking for Frances whom I had expected to greet me after my long journey. But my hostess was nowhere to be seen so it was the servant who led me into the great hall and told me to wait.

I took a seat next to the large stone fireplace which bore the arms of our present King's grandfather, King James, on a carved mantel, and it was a full half-hour before Frances appeared. I would not have recognised her for in her grief she had become thin and drawn and her hair was peppered with grey beneath her linen cap. When I rose to greet her I noted that her eyes were red-rimmed from crying.

'They killed him,' were her first words to me. 'The devil is the father of lies and they are his servants.'

10

Neil didn't like being watched while he was working, although on community excavations open to the general public he'd become used to it over the years. People unconnected with the world of archaeology seemed to find his job fascinating and they'd stare at excavations for hours from behind the safety fences erected to stop anyone venturing too near the trenches.

As the builders watched him pick his way through the debris in the cellar he guessed it wasn't archaeology that interested them. Rather it was the prospect of finding more human remains and the chance to down tools while the discovery was investigated.

Wesley had made the request and he reckoned it wouldn't take long to have a quick look, although as the house had once belonged to Jackson Temples there was a chance that his search might turn up something major that would bring all work to a halt for the foreseeable future.

'Does anyone know anything about that patch of land that's been dug up near the gate?' He'd asked the builders once but he thought he'd try again now he felt he'd got them on side. But again his question was met with silence until eventually the man he'd heard the others address as 'Glen' spoke.

'The boss wants to put a reception building down there. He's had that architect round to discuss it. Ms Compton – black woman; very tasty,' Glen added with a wink and his colleagues nodded in agreement. Neil concluded that Ms Compton had made quite an impression.

'There's no reception building on the plans I've seen.'

'It's a new idea. That's why Mr Hamer's not here. He's gone for a meeting with the Planning Department.'

'I wasn't told about this.'

The men shrugged as one.

'When's he due back?'

'Your guess is as good as mine.'

'I saw a digger down there. You've started on the foundations?'

'Some of the lads made a start,' Glen said nervously. 'Then the boss told 'em to fill in the hole again while he sorts out the planning permission.'

'Well, that site's not to be touched until I've had a chance to discuss it with my colleagues and if you have any trouble with Hamer you refer him to me,' Neil said, trying to hide his annoyance. 'Now let's see what we've got in this cellar.'

All the builders followed him down the cellar steps, glad of a chance to down tools for a while, and watched him, mouths agape as though they anticipated some dramatic and gruesome discovery.

Once in the main cellar he cleared away a rusty bike with its front wheel missing and various pieces of household detritus that might well have been there in Jackson Temples' day. For the first time he felt uncomfortable at the thought the killer might have owned these things and touched them.

He was alert to any sign of makeshift graves in the

cellar but the floor was bare earth and, to his expert eye, it seemed undisturbed. He turned to the builders.

'Somebody made a call to the radio station – said some bones had been found and someone told them to keep it quiet. Anyone know anything about it?'

There was an awkward moment of silence, then the builders cleared out of the cellar. Neil had never seen anybody move so fast.

Danny Brice had remembered the biscuits. Bert liked biscuits. His rheumy old eyes always lit up when he saw the packet.

He was wearing Kevin's coat as usual; the red leather jacket that had been its owner's pride and joy until events dictated that he no longer needed it.

'Is that you, Kevin?' had been Bert's first words when he'd answered the door on his first visit. 'Your father told me you'd had an accident. He said you were dead.' He snorted with derision. 'He always was a liar. And a bloody prig.'

Danny knew he and Kevin had looked so alike they were often taken for brothers rather than lovers and even though he knew the deception was wrong, it had seemed cruel to disillusion the old man who'd looked so joyful at the reunion. 'I'm very much alive, Granddad,' Danny had heard himself saying with a reassuring smile. 'It's good to see you.'

It had seemed strange to be addressed as Kevin but from that moment on there'd been no going back. And now it was too late to tell the truth.

With the biscuits in his hand Danny approached the front door of the retirement bungalow on the edge of Stokeworthy. It was a village where, in the not too distant past, everybody had known everybody else's business, but now many of the properties were holiday lets or second homes. Besides, Bert's bungalow was shielded from its neighbours by a high hedge of leylandii, planted to provide privacy, something Danny was grateful for.

He'd gained the old boy's confidence and now he even had his own key, having helped himself to the spare hanging from a hook on the side of the kitchen cupboard.

He let himself into the bungalow, calling out Bert's name. Then 'Granddad. You there? It's me. Kev.'

When there was no answer Danny assumed Bert had dropped off to sleep as he sometimes did so he called out again, listening for a reply. But all he could hear was the relentless ticking of the grandfather clock in the corner of the hallway.

Feeling uneasy, he pushed open the glazed living-room door and saw Bert Cummings slumped in his old armchair, his eyes closed as though he was sleeping. Then Danny saw the red gashes on the old man's fawn sweater, and smelled the metallic scent of blood.

11

Ever since they'd cleared up their last major case – an investigation that had taken the team up into the wilds of Dartmoor – Rachel had developed a fresh enthusiasm for her imminent marriage to farmer Nigel Haynes. She'd made the decision to come to terms with the attraction she'd felt for Wesley Peterson, who'd showed no sign of straying from his wife, especially once he'd learned of her cancer diagnosis. For a while Rachel had nursed a barely acknowledged dream that one day things might change but she was a realist by nature.

After a couple of hours off work with Gerry's permission spent in pursuit of the perfect wedding shoes in the pricey shops of Moat Street, she'd called in at the florist's by the market to see if there was any word of Linda. To her disappointment only Jen was there, looking harassed and saying she hadn't had time to go round to Linda's cottage because she'd had a wedding and two funerals to cope with on her own. However, she'd phoned Linda many times, making frantic calls to both her mobile and landline and leaving a number of messages. *Where are you? Please pick up.* So far all her calls had gone unanswered.

A couple of weeks ago Rachel had paid an evening visit to

Linda's cottage to discuss her floral requirements because the demands of work meant that she'd had no time to call in at the shop. She'd been surprised that her florist had chosen to live alone in an isolated spot and, despite all efforts to steer the conversation round to the personal to satisfy her natural curiosity, Rachel had failed to learn much about the woman's private life. All she'd gleaned about Linda Payne was that she was single with no children or pets and came originally from London.

Linda seemed to be a woman who put all her energies into her business . . . and her hobby of amateur dramatics. During their meeting she'd spoken enthusiastically about her latest role. She'd been chosen to play the lead in the Harbourside Players' ambitious production of *The Duchess of Malfi*, which she'd told Rachel was a tragic Jacobean bloodbath with plenty of dead bodies littering the stage by the time the curtain came down. She hadn't thought it would be Rachel's cup of tea as it would remind her too much of work. In spite of her guarded nature, Rachel detected that Linda had a dark sense of humour.

Rachel had knocked on many doors in the course of her police career and she'd always prided herself on having a sixth sense for trouble. She felt it now as she approached Linda's cottage; a tingle of fear that worsened when she saw that the front door was slightly ajar. Habit made her put on the crime-scene gloves she kept in her coat pocket before pushing it open.

The front door led straight into the living room and as she walked in, calling out Linda's name, the only sound she could hear was birdsong outside the windows. It was four thirty, not yet dark, but the room was gloomy because the curtains were drawn across. She didn't touch them because her training had taught her never to interfere with a potential crime scene and she checked downstairs before making her way up the narrow stairs, calling Linda's name again and receiving no reply.

At first the disturbance wasn't obvious. On Rachel's previous visit she'd noticed that the place was fastidiously neat and now only a few tell-tale signs – a drawer in the sideboard downstairs left half open and a trio of books lying on the rug by the coffee table – betrayed the fact that someone had been in there, invading Linda Payne's private space.

Rachel peeped in the main bedroom and saw nothing amiss. Then, feeling she was intruding, she left Linda's inner sanctum and made for the small bedroom she used as an office.

A row of files stood neatly on the shelves and she fought the temptation to take them down and examine their contents. Most appeared to be connected with the florist's business, though she scanned the labels for anything of a more personal nature. She saw nothing until she spotted three files lying untidily on the desk. The first was labelled 'diary', which Rachel thought looked promising. However, when she opened it she was disappointed to find a small book of ancient appearance containing fragile pages filled with indecipherable handwriting in faded ink. She left it where it was and turned her attention to the second file. This was labelled 'paintings' and it turned out to be empty – as was the third labelled 'family'.

Once she'd completed her brief search she left the cottage, ensuring the door was locked behind her, and as she walked to the car she had the uneasy feeling that she was being watched.

12

When Wesley saw Rachel's name on his caller display he answered his phone at once.

She spoke before he had a chance to say anything. 'I've been round to Linda Payne's house and I'm sure something's wrong. The door was ajar and I think she's had an intruder.'

'A burglar?'

'Whoever it was left a brand-new TV. I think we should be treating her as a missing person.'

Wesley could hear an uncharacteristic note of panic in her voice.

'Can you describe Linda?'

'Why?'

'While you were out we had a call from a birdwatcher at Bereton Lake. He spotted a body in the water. A woman. Late thirties. Blond.'

There was silence on the other end of the line while Rachel took in the information. 'That could be a description of Linda,' she said after a few moments.

'Would you be willing to come and have a look at the body – just in case it's her?'

There was a moment of silence before Rachel spoke. 'OK. I'll do it.'

'Sorry to land this on you when you're supposed to be having the afternoon off.'

'All part of the job,' said Rachel, trying not to feel sorry for herself. 'Do you want me to come to the hospital or ...'

'Yes. I'll meet you there.' He paused. 'It might not be her, you know.'

'I've an awful feeling it is. Do you know how she died?'

'Colin's doing the PM first thing tomorrow.'

'But what does it look like? Could it be suspicious?'

'Colin's initial thought was strangulation ... and there's a head injury too.' Wesley hesitated. 'There's something else. There are lacerations on her face and Colin thinks they might be stab wounds. If he's right someone's tried to disfigure her.'

Half an hour after Wesley's departure another call came in and DC Rob Carter made his way to Gerry's office.

'I've just taken a call, sir. Male claiming he found a man dead in one of those old people's bungalows in Stokeworthy. Rang off before he could give a name.'

'Dead? Natural causes?'

'He said there's blood.'

Gerry Heffernan had his feet up on his desk, a picture of relaxation. He leaned back in his chair and glared at Rob, the newest recruit to Tradmouth CID, as though he held him personally responsible for this latest outrage.

'Thanks a bunch, Rob. We've already had one suspicious death today. Is someone out there trying to keep us in work or what?'

Rob stood there, unsure how to respond.

'Did the call come from a mobile? Can we trace who it belongs to?'

'No, sir. It was made from a landline belonging to the address he gave.'

Gerry rolled his eyes. 'Send a patrol, will you? And if the caller's telling the truth we'd better get a team down there pronto.'

Rob scurried back to his own desk to set things in motion. It was one of the best desks in the office, next to the window with a panoramic view over the Memorial Gardens to the river beyond. In summer the river bustled with craft, large and small, but now out of season there were fewer boats, only a few yachts making the most of the stiff breeze and the Queenswear ferry which plied to and fro whatever the time of year.

Gerry stalked out of his office calling for attention. 'It never rains but it pours. As well as the dead woman in Bereton Lake it appears we might have got ourselves another suspicious death over in Stokeworthy. Anonymous call. Patrol's on their way so we should know more soon.' He looked round. 'Where's Inspector Peterson?'

'Meeting Rachel at the hospital, sir,' Trish Walton said. 'The dead woman in Bereton Lake matches the description of her missing florist so she's volunteered to ID her.'

Gerry grunted, feeling lost without Wesley's input. Over the years they'd become a double act; a formidable one, he hoped. He lumbered back to his desk but before he could sit down his phone began to ring. It was the patrol. They'd attended the Stokeworthy address as instructed and found an elderly man on the premises with stab wounds to his chest. The scene had been sealed off and the CSIs called.

Gerry told the sergeant on the line to arrange house-to-house enquiries and said he'd be there as soon as he could.

From the first diary of
Lemuel Strange, gentleman

4th September 1666

I was given ale and a bowl of stew from the kitchen which I consumed gratefully, for I was hungry from my travels and had eaten nothing at the inn while I waited. Frances sat facing me and I hoped she would order the fire to be lit for, although it was summer, there was a chill in the air.

She seemed not to notice the cold and ate nothing, sipping at her ale as though she barely tasted it. When I had finished eating I poured more ale from the jug the servant had left and offered some to my cousin's widow but she refused and stared into the empty fireplace as though she was content to sit in silence.

But I was longing to hear the tale she had to tell.

'My cousin Reuben,' I said. 'How did he die?'

'I have no wish to speak of it,' she replied. 'What they did to him is too terrible to contemplate.'

Then she began to weep bitter tears and I watched her, not knowing what to say to give her comfort.

13

Wesley saw the initial look of horror on Rachel's face vanish to be replaced by the professional mask of the experienced police officer she was. Then she gave a businesslike nod. It was Linda Payne all right. She recognised her in spite of the vicious wounds to her face and the fact that she'd been in the lake for a couple of days at the mercy of the elements and the wildlife.

'It's always more difficult when it's someone you know,' he said sympathetically as they left the mortuary.

'The truth is, I liked her, Wes. Although there was always something . . . guarded about her.'

'As though she had something to hide?'

'I just assumed she was one of those private people – the type who doesn't tell you all their business until they get to know you really well. But maybe I was wrong.'

'What do you know about her?'

'Not much. She said she'd never married but she didn't mention any other relationships. She might not have thought it was a suitable subject to discuss with a prospective bride.'

'Probably not.'

'Apart from her business most of her time seemed to

be taken up with amateur dramatics – the Harbourside Players. She had the starring role in their next production but now I suppose it'll be the understudy's big opportunity. They're doing *The Duchess of Malfi*.'

'Ambitious for an amateur company.'

'It's run by a professional theatre director who's decided to spend his twilight years in Devon.'

'But he couldn't leave the day job behind.'

'Some people can't. Think of all those ex-cops who become private eyes or go into the security business. The Harbourside Players did *Hamlet* last year, you know, and *Julius Caesar* the year before. The productions get very good reviews, although most of the stuff they do isn't really my cup of tea.'

Rachel paused for a moment, as though she'd just remembered something that might be important.

'Linda was strangled. It could be a coincidence, but that's how her character dies in the play.'

'Or it could be relevant. I think we need to speak to her fellow actors as soon as possible.'

As they walked back to the police station side by side, saying little, Wesley received a call. It was Gerry to tell him that an elderly man had been found dead in a bungalow in the village of Stokeworthy, apparently the victim of a violent attack. Once Wesley had told Gerry about Rachel's positive identification of Linda Payne's body, he broke the news about the Stokeworthy murder to Rachel who looked resigned to the inevitability of her wedding preparations being disrupted by two murders.

'Could this Stokeworthy murder be connected with the recent burglaries? The victims were all elderly.'

'Too early to say. Look, you were supposed to be taking

the afternoon off so why don't you go? Gerry wants me over at Stokeworthy but I'm sure you've got things to do.'

His phone rang again and when he saw the caller was Neil he killed the call, telling himself he was too busy.

'Everything OK?' Rachel sounded concerned.

'It was Neil. Probably just rang for a chat about that skull.'

'Maybe you should have found out what he had to say.'

Wesley suddenly wondered whether she was right. Perhaps more bones had turned up – but even if they had, they weren't going anywhere and he had two recent corpses on his hands.

'I'll call him later if I have time. Why don't you get off home?'

'I feel guilty leaving you when—'

'Don't. The team are down at Linda's cottage and there's not much we can do until we know more. I'll tell Gerry you left before his call about the Stokeworthy murder came through. See you tomorrow morning. It'll be an early one.'

Rachel kissed him on the cheek, something he hadn't expected, and as she walked away he wondered whether he'd done the right thing. They were dealing with two separate murders and perhaps even the reopening of a historic case so they needed all the help they could muster. But it was the time when most people were leaving work and Rachel, who was looking exhausted, would be more productive after an early night.

However, he couldn't allow himself the same luxury. He picked up the car at the station and drove straight out to Stokeworthy, a small, pretty village dominated by its medieval church, its stone-built pub and its village hall. The bungalow where the elderly victim had died lay on the edge of the settlement in a small street of council bungalows built in the 1950s in brick that might have been chosen deliberately to clash with the older parts of the village.

The street was filled with police vehicles and rubber-necking neighbours, their faces shining with interest as though this was the most exciting thing that had happened there in years, which it probably was.

Wesley parked some way away and walked to the cordon, showing his ID to the sergeant with the clipboard who ticked off his name and lifted the tape to allow him to walk through. He could feel the neighbours' eyes watching him as he donned the crime-scene suit he'd been given and he wanted to know if they'd been spoken to. If they'd displayed as much curiosity when the killer had arrived, the case might be simple to solve.

He entered the house, stepping carefully on the metal plates put down to protect any evidence left on the floor, and found Gerry in the living room, watching Colin Bowman as he examined the dead man. CSIs flitted all around them taking photographs, samples and fingerprints in their well-choreographed ballet of forensic investigation. Wesley stood by the door, taking in the scene.

It was an elderly person's room furnished in the style of the 1950s. The style was back in vogue but Wesley knew there was no conscious fashion choice here; these were things the occupant had possessed all his adult life, possibly from the time he'd set up home after his wedding, an event captured in a framed black-and-white picture standing proudly on the mantelpiece of the tiled fireplace. The upholstery was worn and shiny in places and the layer of grime on the scattered knick-knacks told Wesley the house lacked a woman's touch. As well as the wedding photograph, there were pictures of a girl, a daughter perhaps, in various stages of development. There were also newer pictures of a dark-haired child – possibly a grandson – taken in some large city built of glass and concrete. It could have been America, Australia or Canada; it was difficult to tell because modern architecture gives everywhere an identical look.

From the evidence he'd seen so far he guessed that the dead man, who'd been named as Bert Cummings, was a widower, alone in the world since his wife passed away, leaving only distant offspring who were in no position to offer day-to-day care. Wesley felt a sudden rush of sadness at the thought of this lonely life ending in fear and violence. From what he could see, Bert had been stabbed a number of times although he could see no defensive wounds on the old man's arms, suggesting he hadn't put up a fight.

When Gerry spotted Wesley, a look of relief appeared on his face. 'Bad business, Wes. Vicious attack.'

'Neighbours see anything?'

Gerry snorted. 'They all had an attack of blindness and deafness at the appropriate moment. Amazing how often that happens, isn't it? We're widening the house-to-house visits to cover the whole village. Someone might have been awake but I'm not getting my hopes up. Lots of second homes and people out at work.'

'No chance of CCTV round here I don't suppose?'

'Chance'd be a fine thing.'

'Time of death?'

Gerry glanced at the pathologist, who was bending over the body, deep in concentration. 'You know what Colin's like,' he said, lowering his voice. 'He claims he can't be accurate but when I pressed him he reckoned sometime this morning – between eight o'clock and eleven. The anonymous call came in at two thirty.'

'Not our killer then?'

'Unless he had a fit of conscience and decided it was wrong to leave the old boy lying there.' He looked at his watch. 'I'm told his carer's due to come in at five to give him his dinner.'

'When was the last visit?'

'According to the agency she called this morning at eight to give him breakfast and leave him some sandwiches for lunch. They're still there, which fits with Colin's timings.'

'Apart from his killer she was the last person to see him alive so we'll have to speak to her.'

'Trish is seeing her later.' He sighed. 'Colin'll do Bert's PM after Linda Payne's first thing tomorrow. We've set things rolling so why don't we get some rest before the onslaught? Get home to Pam.' Gerry grinned. 'And your beloved mother-in-law.'

The mention of Della made Wesley's spirits sink. But she needed looking after while she recovered from injuries sustained in a car accident connected with one of his previous cases so he hadn't uttered even the slightest complaint to Pam, although recently he suspected that he'd been spending more time at the office than was strictly necessary. Now his workload had just increased dramatically he'd no longer need to make up excuses.

'How is the old girl?'

'Don't ever let her hear you calling her that. In her mind she's still eighteen – won't stop trawling through internet dating sites.'

'Is she still stuck in that wheelchair?'

A frown appeared on Wesley's face. 'Yes. She'll be with us for a while yet.'

Della wasn't the easiest of house guests and her strongly voiced opinions didn't always match Wesley's own – but since she was Pam's mother he could hardly ask her to leave.

He ignored Gerry's suggestion and worked late and when he arrived home something made him hesitate before getting out of the driving seat. He'd arranged to meet Grace the following lunchtime and he wondered whether, with so much work on, he should put her off. But what she'd said about seeing someone from her past and needing his advice had intrigued him. Or was it that he just wanted to see her again? He couldn't be sure.

14

The following morning Wesley felt overwhelmed. As well as the prospect of a tough day ahead at work, Della had been particularly irritating at breakfast, insisting that Pam make scrambled eggs for her even though she had to get to work and ensure the children were ready for school. He'd been glad when Pam told her she was having toast like everyone else but Della had sulked so he wasn't looking forward to returning home that evening. Della's sulks could last for days.

In clement weather he liked to walk to work because trudging up and down the steep hill into Tradmouth a couple of times a day served just as well as the gym sessions he had no time for. Today, though, he took the car because he had two murders to deal with and the rain was falling in horizontal sheets, veiling the town and the river beyond in grey mist.

When Rachel greeted him at the CID office door she seemed to be in a surprisingly good mood. 'The boss says we're using this as an incident room for both cases. I know it's not ideal but we're bringing in back-up from Neston so at least we'll have some more bodies.' She realised what she'd said and put her hand to her mouth. 'I could have put that better, couldn't I?'

'You seem more cheerful today.'

'I feel so much better after a good night's sleep. Good job you made me go home early last night – I feel ready to face the world again now.' The corners of her mouth twitched upwards in a sad smile. 'Anyway, keeping busy's probably the perfect cure for pre-wedding nerves.'

'Don't know what you're worrying about. All you have to do is turn up looking beautiful.'

She lowered her gaze and he thought he detected a blush. Perhaps his words were ill judged but they'd left his lips before his brain had had a chance to censor them.

He looked at his watch. 'I've got Linda Payne's post-mortem in half an hour.'

'I can't imagine who'd want to kill her, Wes. She was a nice woman. Jen said she'd been very good to one of their regular customers when her mum was burgled – went round to the old lady's with some flowers – on the house.'

He couldn't think of anything appropriate to say so he made for Gerry's office, stopping every so often at desks to check whether anything new had come in. But although extensive house-to-house enquiries had been made in Stokeworthy nobody had seen or heard anything suspicious around Bert Cummings' bungalow at the relevant time. As for Linda Payne, she was last seen at a rehearsal for *The Duchess of Malfi* on Monday evening. She'd left straight afterwards to drive home and she'd seemed her usual self. No hint of fear, nor mention of anyone who might want her dead.

An hour later Wesley was standing beside Gerry in Tradmouth Hospital's mortuary. In the new mortuary at Morbay Hospital where Colin sometimes worked, the facil-ities were state-of-the-art, allowing the police to stand some way away behind a glass screen, but here at Tradmouth they couldn't avoid being close to the action and Wesley tried to avoid looking at the body on the steel table while Colin went about his work, keeping up a running commentary for the benefit of the microphone hanging above his head.

'She was in her late thirties. Slightly built. Looked after herself although I suspect she enjoyed a drink or three. In good health – until someone strangled her,' he said with a smile looking directly at Gerry. 'She'd never given birth. And there are abrasions to her fingers, both old and recent.'

'She was a florist,' said Wesley.

'Then they could have been caused by rose thorns. Occupational hazard. No sign of violent sexual activity although of course I can't rule out consensual sex; the water will have destroyed any evidence of that sort of thing.'

Wesley was relieved when the pathologist asked his assistant to finish off and turned his attention to his audience.

'What's the verdict, Colin?' Gerry asked. 'Cause of death?'

'The head wound probably left her stunned but the actual cause of death was strangulation. As I suspected her killer used a rope which has left a distinctive pattern of marks on the flesh.' Colin hesitated. 'I've been having a good look at the wounds on the face and as far as I can see they were made with a sharp blade, probably serrated down one edge. He made a hell of a mess.'

Wesley noticed Gerry had turned pale. Then he spoke almost in a whisper, as though he was thinking out loud. 'Jackson Temples rendered his victims unconscious with a blunt instrument, before strangling them with rope and mutilating their faces with a knife.'

'Isn't Jackson Temples safely locked up?' said Wesley.

'Life sentence with a recommendation that he serve at least thirty years. He's out of the frame but the similarities can't be ignored, can they?' Gerry turned to Colin, trying to regain his composure. 'Anything else you can tell us?'

'Fortunately, in spite of the water I found a couple of fibres adhering to the neck which appear to be a natural material so it's possibly an old-fashioned hemp rope rather than the man-made stuff they use on most boats these days. We'll know more once the lab have done their work. My money's on it having come from a boat – but I'm afraid that hardly narrows it down around these parts.'

'Like you say, natural rope's rarely used on yachts these days,' said Gerry, the experienced sailor. 'So it could be from an older boat – or something left in an old boat yard.'

'That's possible.'

'What about time of death?'

'You should know better than to try and pin me down on that one, Gerry. The only thing I can say is that she died roughly four hours after she'd eaten – give or take a couple of hours.'

'She went to a play rehearsal on Monday night which, according to witnesses, started at seven and lasted two and a half hours. If she'd eaten beforehand, attended the rehearsal then driven straight home her killer might have been waiting for her there,' said Wesley, recalling what Rachel had said about her visit to Linda's cottage before her body was found. The front door had been unlocked and there'd been signs of an intruder.

'That might fit,' said Colin. 'I've sent samples off so I might have more for you in due course.'

Wesley thanked him and moved to leave but Gerry hung

back. He and Colin were old friends and they liked to pass the time of day over a cup of Colin's specially chosen tea and the special stash of superior biscuits he kept in his office.

Wesley, however, had other things on his mind. He wanted to take a look at Linda Payne's cottage for himself, although he would have preferred to have done so before the CSIs had been in and scattered their metal plates, fingerprint powder and markers all over the place. Once a crime scene had been processed it lost its special atmosphere; that tantalising imprint of the last souls to inhabit the place.

He also wanted to talk to Linda's fellow Harbourside Players. The fact that the character she was playing had also been strangled with a rope suggested a connection to the production and he'd heard that amateur theatre could throw up all kinds of jealousies and resentments. The stab wounds to the face hinted at bitter hatred but could her murder really have been a result of theatrical rivalry? Though the idea seemed far-fetched, after so many years in the police he had learned that people often behave in surprising ways.

He left Gerry with Colin and walked back to the station, so preoccupied that he didn't see Neil waiting for him at the entrance until he was a few feet away.

'You haven't been answering your phone. I've been trying to get hold of you,' Neil said accusingly. 'When I called Pam yesterday evening she said you weren't home.'

'She told me you'd called but I didn't get back till half ten last night. Two murders.' For a moment he felt a pang of irritation that Neil expected him to be at his beck and call. 'You haven't found any more skulls, have you?' he said, half joking.

'Not yet.' Neil sounded disappointed. 'But you know that call to the radio station – someone saying they'd found bones? Well, when I mentioned it to the builders they were very cagey so I reckon some of them know something. It wouldn't surprise me if more bones are found in that house. They've only stripped half the building – who knows what'll turn up when they do the rest. Jackson Temples used to live there. Think they might belong to some undiscovered victims?'

Wesley hesitated, unwilling to commit himself. 'When human remains are found in a house that once belonged to a killer it's hard to imagine the two things aren't connected, I suppose.'

'I've arranged to have some geophysics equipment taken down to the cellar. The floor doesn't appear to have been disturbed recently but I'd like to rule out any unexplained burials and it shouldn't take long. Hopefully we'll be in and out before the developer even notices.'

'Thanks, that might save the police a job.'

'No problem. Me and the conservation officer are keeping a close eye on the place 'cause I wouldn't put it past Joe Hamer to cut corners heritage-wise. Not that there'll be much left from Temples' day once the builders have devastated the place.' There was a long pause. 'I believe that the skull's been sent to a hot new forensic anthropologist called Jemima Baine in Exeter. She used to work at the Centre for Anatomy and Human Identification at the University of Dundee. They're acknowledged experts in the field so we're lucky to have her.'

'You've met her?'

Neil grinned. 'A few times.'

'How's Lucy?' Wesley asked, suspecting Neil's enthusiasm for Jemima Baine wasn't just due to her professional skills.

'She's helping out on a university dig at the moment – Roman stuff outside Exeter. Mind you, she's missing the archaeology up in Orkney.'

Wesley said nothing. He and Pam liked Lucy. She'd been a steadying influence on their old friend but if things were cooling off and she was thinking of returning to Orkney there was nothing they could do about it.

Neil headed off towards the car park leaving Wesley feeling uncomfortable. If it did turn out that the skull from Strangefields Farm was connected to Jackson Temples then a whole fresh investigation would have to be started and he knew it might well fall to him to interview the man in prison.

That wasn't something he was looking forward to.

15

When Gerry finally returned to the office after half an hour of tea and gossip at the mortuary, he agreed with Wesley's suggestion that they both visit Linda Payne's cottage. It was possibly the scene of her murder – unless she hadn't made it home that night and her killer had waylaid her en route. There'd been no evidence on her body to tell them where she died: no trace evidence; no fibres from carpets or minute samples of soil or plant life. The killer had disposed of the clothes she'd been wearing and the water had done the rest. A search had been instigated for her clothes but there were so many places to dispose of them in the area; places they were unlikely to ever be found.

He drove down the narrow lane, afraid an agricultural vehicle might come looming round one of the many blind bends at any moment. As he drove he noticed Gerry clinging to his seat, his knuckles white as though he was aboard a roller coaster, which did little for his confidence.

When they reached their destination they found several police vehicles parked outside. The forensic team were hard at work, dashing any hopes Wesley had nursed of being alone in the place to absorb its atmosphere. He looked at his watch. He'd arranged to meet Grace at one o'clock, something he'd mentioned to nobody: not Pam, not Gerry, not Rachel, not Neil. It almost felt as though he was harbouring a guilty secret.

After donning the appropriate protective clothing, Wesley strolled from room to room, taking in his surroundings. It was a small cottage, tastefully furnished and painted in the sort of expensive chalky shades that weren't available at your local DIY store. Linda Payne had been a woman of taste, but then the fact that she'd been a florist and amateur actor hinted at a well-developed creative side. Gerry had often observed that you can learn a lot about how someone died from how they lived and on this they were of one mind.

As Wesley looked around he noticed a script lying on the coffee table in the living room and picked it up with gloved hands.

'It's her play script,' he said to Gerry. '*The Duchess of Malfi*. It has all her stage directions and notes on it so I think we can assume it's the one she took to rehearsals, although we'll have to check.'

Gerry caught on quickly. 'So she dumped it here when she got in from the Arts Centre, which means she made it home and met her killer here. Either he called after she arrived or he was waiting for her.'

'There's no sign of a break-in?' Wesley looked enquiringly at one of the CSIs, a small ginger man wielding a fingerprint brush, and received a shake of the head in response.

'Nothing obvious. Unless whoever it was had a key,' the CSI suggested.

'He's after your job, Wes,' Gerry quipped, making the CSI turn an unattractive shade of red.

'He's got a point,' Wesley said with a reassuring glance

at the CSI. 'It might have been someone she knew well, or a relative. According to Rachel she never mentioned her family.'

'Which means we need to dig deeper. No man is an island ... or woman in this case. Who said that?'

'John Donne.'

'Well, he was right.'

As Wesley looked round he noticed the half-open drawer in the sideboard. 'Rach reckons someone searched the place.'

'So our man kills her then looks for something.'

'Or she walks in on him while he's at it.'

'What was he after, Wes? And did he find it?'

Wesley didn't answer. He was already halfway up the stairs, making for the bedrooms. Rachel had told him that Linda had used the smaller of the two rooms as an office and that was where she'd seen the most evidence of an intruder.

He looked first in Linda's bedroom: a feminine room where the ornate iron bed was neatly made with a sumptuous velvet bedspread and matching cushions. A large teddy bear lounged against the cushions like a louche Victorian gentleman in an opium den.

The door to the richly carved antique pine wardrobe stood ajar and Wesley opened it wider. The clothes inside had been pushed aside and the shoes stored at the bottom in neat transparent boxes – how Pam would have envied that level of organisation – had been tipped out onto the wardrobe's wooden base.

Wesley suspected that the chest of drawers had been searched too, as had the bedside tables, and whoever was responsible had shoved everything back willy-nilly. The room was in a state most people would have regarded as normal. If it hadn't been for Rachel telling him about Linda's obsessive neatness, he might not have found it suspicious.

He crossed the tiny landing to the bathroom, which was as gleaming and clutter-free as a showroom display, suggesting Rachel's opinion of the dead woman had been spot on.

The white painted shelves in the small office occupied the whole of one wall. Neat box files stood there, uniform as soldiers on parade, except that some had been taken down and now lay on the desk.

He opened the file marked 'diary' and took out the thing Rachel had described as a 'scruffy old book'. But Wesley recognised it as something far more interesting. As he turned the pages he could barely make out the handwriting but the odd word leaped out at him and his heart began to beat faster when he caught sight of the date – April 1685.

If this book was genuine it was an important historical find. The question was, how had Linda Payne got hold of it?

From the first diary of
Lemuel Strange, gentleman

4th September 1666

Frances was a young woman when Reuben married her, some twenty years his junior. At the time I thought her new husband's riches had attracted her to him and in the past I have been ashamed of this first assumption, especially when their son, William, was born and she proved herself a devoted mother. And yet in my heart I have always nursed a suspicion that all was not well with the marriage.

Frances is the only daughter of a Colonel Bartholomew who fought for Parliament in the late war – as did many men of Tradmouth, I understand. Reuben himself favoured Master Cromwell's cause but that is a matter best forgotten now that we have the late King Charles's son upon the throne of England.

Frances had said little since her strange utterings about the devil and her refusal to speak about the manner of Reuben's death. Once my hunger was satisfied I attempted once more to engage her in conversation. I asked her whom she accused of being Satan's servants but she became agitated and began to weep.

'They destroyed him,' she said. 'And they would not tell where he lies dead.'

16

Wesley was sorely tempted to pocket the ancient-looking book and go through it at his leisure but he knew he had to stick to procedure so he left it in place to be recorded with all the other evidence. At least that way he'd know it would be kept safe.

As he drove back to Tradmouth from Linda's cottage, Gerry sat beside him in the passenger seat, unusually quiet. When Wesley told him about the diary and its possible date he mumbled something about not getting sidetracked.

'I had a quick look at it and saw the name Strangefields,' Wesley said, unable to get it out of his mind. 'I told the CSIs to bag it up and bring it in as evidence. We can't ignore the similarity between Linda Payne's death and the Temples murders.'

'I agree, Wes. But one thing's certain. Temples is behind bars so it can't be him.'

'There's also the empty "family" file. What do we know about Temples' family?'

'His mother died when he was small and his dad remarried but soon got divorced. Temples lived with his dad at Strangefields Farm until the old man died and he inherited the property.'

'Had Temples any siblings?'

Gerry looked unsure of himself. 'None that featured in the inquiry.'

'What about the stepmother?'

'She shoved off after the divorce and never showed her face again. She was never even mentioned.'

'Odd.'

'Not really. If you were the stepmother of a serial killer you'd decide to keep your head down too. Wonder where she is now. Mind you, if I was her I'd have changed my name.'

'Might be worth finding out.' Wesley looked at his watch. 'I've got to do something this lunchtime. I'll see you in an hour.'

'Where are you off to?'

'I need to go to the bank and pick up one or two things for Pam.' In all the time he and Gerry had been working together this was the first time he'd told him a deliberate lie and he felt a creeping nag of shame. Then he justified his action by telling himself that a full explanation would take too long. Besides, he didn't want his meeting with Grace to become the focus of Gerry's notorious Liverpudlian wit; or for it to get back to Pam, who could so easily get the wrong idea.

He walked away, aware of Gerry's eyes on him. He knew he wasn't a good liar – and Gerry was a good detective.

He was relieved to find Grace waiting for him as arranged, leaning on the rail next to the cannon at the end of the esplanade, gazing out onto the grey waters of the river where boats were bobbing at anchor, some protected by tarpaulins against any coming rough weather. She had her back to him so he stopped a few yards away and watched her, thinking how much she'd changed since they'd last met. She was wearing an expensively cut beige trench coat which flattered her slender figure, and black court shoes: a businesslike outfit which made her look like a city lawyer. Her jet-black hair had been straightened and tied back into a neat ponytail. When he'd known her it had been curly. Natural.

'Hello, Grace.'

She swung round, startled. Then she smiled. 'Long time no see. How are you?'

'Fine.'

She stepped towards him and when he kissed her on the cheek he caught a whiff of her perfume as she held onto his arm longer than he was expecting. 'Good to see you again, Wes. I had lunch with your sister.'

'So you said.'

'She hasn't called you to arrange a meal? She said she was going to invite both of us round one evening.'

He shook his head. 'I'm dealing with two murder cases at the moment so I'll have to work late most nights until they're wrapped up. I'm afraid the timing's lousy.' He made a show of examining his watch. 'I can't be long. I've got a post-mortem to attend in an hour. The chip shop's this way. It's not far.'

He walked down a side street, past the queue of cars waiting to board the lower ferry, and she walked beside him, trotting on her high heels to keep up. The clouds over the river looked ominous.

The queue at the chip shop was mercifully short so they were soon back on the embankment, seated on a wooden bench looking out over the river.

'Don't drop any food or you'll be mobbed by gulls,' Wesley warned as he helped himself to a fat chip. Grace was eating hers hesitantly as though it had been many years since she'd indulged in such an ad hoc meal and she wasn't quite sure of the etiquette. 'I'd eat quicker if I were you. They're watching us – just waiting for their chance.'

She eyed the nearby gulls warily. 'I've never liked birds.'

'Well, this lot have all attended assertiveness classes so watch out,' he said with a grin, realising he was enjoying teasing her; cracking through that polished exterior to reveal a glimpse of the human woman beneath.

'How are your mum and dad?' he asked.

'OK. I hear your mum's retiring at the end of the year.'

'That's right. She says she'll miss her patients but not the paperwork.'

They made small talk about their respective families while they ate but as soon as they'd finished Wesley asked the question at the forefront of his mind. 'You said you'd seen someone from your past and you wanted my advice.'

Grace stood up to deposit her chip paper and Wesley's in a nearby bin and he had the impression that she was giving herself time to gather her thoughts. Eventually she sat down again beside him.

'His name was Dale Keyes and he was a client of my partnership. He was developing a warehouse near the Isle of Dogs – luxury apartments; high-end; million plus.' She paused and Wesley waited for her to continue. 'He went on holiday in Thailand a couple of years ago and he was on a ferry that sank. It was in the news at the time. Three Britons killed . . . including Dale.'

'Sorry. Don't recall.'

She hesitated, looking down at her fingers before wiping the grease off with a neatly folded tissue from her coat pocket.

'We had an affair. Started off as a bit of fun. No strings. Dale was very charming. Great fun to be with. And I was working bloody hard at the time so . . . '

'It became serious?'

She didn't answer for a few moments.

'He left owing my practice a lot of money. He claimed some woman who worked for him had ripped him off so he had a cash-flow problem.'

'Did you believe him?'

'I did at the time but I'm sure there were things he never told me. Although perhaps it was better that I didn't know because since then I've heard he sailed close to the wind business-wise.' She bowed her head so that he couldn't read her expression. 'I fell for him, Wes. Call it an aberration if you like but even successful architects have their Achilles heel.' She looked up and gave him a sad smile, as though she regretted her vulnerability, the breach in her armour of professionalism.

'Is it worth it?'

'What?'

'The hard work?'

'Don't tell me you don't work hard too.' She gave a mirthless smile. 'Only I probably earn a hell of a lot more than a detective inspector. Don't get me wrong, Wes, I love my job. There's nothing like that feeling of satisfaction when a project comes to fruition and the clients are thrilled with the result.'

'Let's get back to Dale.'

'This is going to sound stupid but I think I've seen him here in Tradmouth. He was getting off the higher ferry the day after I arrived here and I called out to him but he either didn't hear or he was ignoring me.'

'Are you sure it wasn't just someone who looked like him?'

She shook her head. 'It was Dale, I'm sure of it. He hurried away towards the town and I tried to follow him but I lost him near the library. I think he must have slipped down one of the little side streets.' She paused. 'I wondered whether he might have taken the opportunity of the ferry tragedy to fake his death and escape his debts. Or maybe he wanted to get away from someone unpleasant he'd got on the wrong side of.'

'Isn't it more likely you made a mistake?'

She shook her head again, more vigorously this time. 'I've always been good with faces. Don't you remember?' She grinned. 'I reckon I'm one of those super-recognisers. Don't the police use them sometimes?'

'It's been known. You haven't seen him since?'

'I've been looking out for him, but no.'

'You don't have a photograph of him by any chance?'

She took out her phone and scrolled through images until she found a picture of a good-looking man in his thirties with a shaved head and a confident smile. Wesley was sure he'd never seen him before.

'As I said, things are busy at the moment but if I get a chance I'll make some discreet enquiries about Dale Keyes. That's the best I can offer, I'm afraid.' He checked the time again. 'I need to get back. Are you staying in Tradmouth for long?'

'I'm here for a series of meetings with Joe Hamer, the developer, and the council. Joe's decided to have a flashy new reception building on the site and the plans have to be approved. Then I'll be coming back regularly to check on the project.'

'In that case I'll probably see you soon. I'll let you know if I manage to find anything out.'

As he walked off down the embankment he wondered whether her alleged sighting of Dale Keyes had just been an excuse to get back in touch, something she thought might intrigue a man who'd chosen detection as a career. Perhaps the whole thing had been a ruse to get his attention – or to satisfy her curiosity. The Grace he'd once known hadn't been a liar but he had the feeling she'd changed a lot in the intervening years, almost as if she'd become a different person.

Pam Peterson had used her lunch hour to drive into Tradmouth, and she'd been relieved to find a free parking space by the library. She needed to buy a present for her mother's birthday, something unusual, because Della didn't do 'ordinary'.

There was a shop on the embankment she'd hoped might have something suitable and, as she was hurrying there, checking her watch, she spotted her husband with a woman whose stunning elegance made her feel dowdy in her working clothes. He was sitting on a bench with her, chatting and sharing fish and chips, their heads bent together in an intimacy that made her heart lurch.

Pam forgot all about Della's present and ran back to her car.

17

'What have you been up to?' were Gerry Heffernan's first words when Wesley returned to the police station.

Wesley felt the blood rushing to his face. Was it so obvious that he'd lied and met an old flame instead of carrying out mundane lunchtime errands? 'What makes you ask that?' As soon as the words left his mouth he knew they sounded defensive.

'You're breathless. Been running a marathon?'

'I was in a hurry to get back, that's all.' He could see the scepticism on Gerry's face. 'I ... er, bumped into an old friend. Someone I knew in London when I was a teenager. Ended up having fish and chips on the front and a bit of a catch-up.' He tried his best to make it sound casual.

'Well we wouldn't want to get in the way of your social life, would we?' There was an uncharacteristic hint of sarcasm in Gerry's voice.

'Sorry. I know we've a lot on.'

'Good mate, was he?'

Wesley didn't correct him. 'At one time. Hadn't we better get back to the hospital?'

Gerry checked the clock on the office wall. 'Two

post-mortems in one day. I'm sure Colin's killing 'em to keep himself in work.'

They walked to the hospital. It was nearby and the parking was awkward so it wasn't worth driving. Gerry said nothing on the journey, which was unusual, and Wesley wondered whether something was bothering him.

'Something wrong, Gerry?'

The DCI didn't reply but his open face always betrayed his every emotion and Wesley sensed that he was preparing to share a confidence. Then before he could speak they'd arrived at the mortuary entrance where one of Colin's assistants greeted them at the door and led them through to the post-mortem room where Colin was waiting, gowned up and ready to make his initial observations.

Bert Cummings had taken Linda Payne's place on Colin's stainless-steel table. Wesley could see a cluster of bloodless knife wounds on his pale naked body but the expression on the corpse's face was remarkably peaceful.

Colin kept up his usual commentary and by the end of the proceedings they knew that Bert Cummings had been stabbed eleven times in all. His attacker must have lost control, Colin said, because there was no sign that Bert had tried to defend himself. He might even have been asleep in the chair when the attack took place.

The pathologist frowned. 'I think the murder weapon has a blade with a sharp point that widens out to a couple of inches and is serrated at one side.'

'Sounds like a sailor's knife – the kind you use on yachts,' said Gerry.

'It's possible.'

'Could it be a similar weapon to the one used on Linda Payne's face?' asked Wesley.

Colin thought for a moment. 'It certainly looks very similar. But I'll have to run more tests.'

Gerry looked at Wesley and frowned. 'It can't be the same perpetrator, surely. Linda was knocked out and strangled. This poor bloke was stabbed.'

'Two murders within days of each other, Gerry. We can't rule out a connection.' Wesley turned to Colin. 'Could a woman have done it?'

'It's possible.'

'What about Linda Payne's murder?'

'As the head injury probably rendered her unconscious, or at least stunned her, strangulation wouldn't have been difficult. I couldn't rule out a strong woman capable of transporting the body to the nature reserve – or even the possibility that she was killed near where she was found. Any signs of a vehicle being used?'

Wesley shook his head. 'When she was killed it hadn't rained for a while so our CSIs didn't find any tracks. However, that spot's perfectly accessible by car and some marks were found on the bank consistent with a body being dragged to the water.'

Colin nodded. 'The level of violence used in both cases certainly suggests a man but if a woman has enough hatred ... Hope I'm not being sexist,' Colin added with a smile.

'So that leaves the field wide open,' said Gerry.

Wesley had never seen his boss look so close to despair.

Danny Brice was shaking. After finding Bert like that and the effort of calling the police he needed something to calm him down. He'd returned to the squat in Neston, trying to behave as though nothing had happened and hoping nobody would notice the bloodstains on the red leather jacket he'd kept as a souvenir of Kevin – all he had left of him.

He needed to lie low because he knew he'd left his prints and DNA all over Bert's bungalow, which meant it would only be a matter of time before they'd come looking for him.

From the first diary of
Lemuel Strange, gentleman

5th September 1666

I spent the night in some discomfort for the bed was hard and the chamber cold as a tomb. I rose at sunrise for I could not sleep and after I had dressed I went to the hall where I had sat with Frances the previous night.

I had thought to see servants about their business but there was nobody and I was obliged to go to the kitchens where I found John in conversation with the cook, a fat slovenly woman with a bold stare and a filthy apron such as my wife would never have permitted in our own household.

I bade them good morning and enquired for their mistress but I received a sullen greeting in return and no word of when Frances would break her fast. Realising I would learn nothing if I was not bolder, I asked John what had happened to his master, saying I did not wish to distress his mistress by speaking of the matter in her presence.

At first the pair said nothing but after a while the cook broke the silence.

'The master was most brutally done to death, sir, by two who were his servants. It was Harry the groom who did the evil deed at the behest of my lady's maidservant Bess Whitetree. Bess is a devil in the form of an innocent maid, sir. As God is my witness she made fools of us all.'

Then John spoke. 'There is talk on the quayside that London is consumed by a mighty fire, sir. Some sailors have seen it.'

I smiled. 'That news must be a falsehood for London is a great city. The fire will have consumed but a few low dwellings. I would hear more of my cousin's murder,' I said, thinking he desired to distract me from my purpose.

18

The link between Linda Payne's murder and Jackson Temples' MO nagged at the back of Wesley's mind. Jackson Temples, who'd killed and mutilated young women with no apparent motive ... other than a love of killing.

The incident room was buzzing with activity. Linda Payne's contacts were being traced, interviewed and eliminated but so far none of the team's enquiries had thrown up anything helpful. However, it was early days and there were people Wesley wanted to speak to himself; particularly Linda's assistant, Jen, and the Harbourside Players.

When he sat down at his desk he found a brown envelope lying on top of the house-to-house reports he'd asked to see. When he tore it open he found it contained the report on Bert Cummings' bungalow he'd been promised earlier in the day. The CSIs had finished their examination of the premises and once Wesley had read through their findings he was disappointed to see that Gerry's office was empty.

'Where's the boss?' he asked Trish, who was standing with her hands pressed to her back as though it was aching.

'Gone to see the chief super,' she said. 'Should be back any moment.'

Deciding not to wait for Gerry's return, Wesley called for

attention. Everyone stopped what they were doing, apart from those who were on the phone, and turned to face him.

'The report on Bert Cummings' bungalow has just come in and you'll all be pleased to know we've got a finger-print match.'

Danny Brice could have kicked himself for being so care-less. Although a lot of people he'd hung around with in the past had said the police were useless, he knew they had all sorts of fancy scientific ways of getting every scrap of evidence from a crime scene. And Bert's bungalow was a crime scene – he'd realised that as soon as he'd seen the wounds on the old man's chest.

The squat above the empty shop on the edge of Neston town centre was short on luxury but there was electricity and running water. Its last incarnation had been as a whole-food store which had relocated to more central premises a year ago. Since then it had remained unoccupied, although the previous owners hadn't bothered turning the water off so when Stag had got in through the dodgy back door and did something mysterious with the electricity meter, the place was good to go.

Danny was wary of Stag and his girlfriend, who was posh and judgemental, damning anybody by calling them bour-geois or, worse still, suburban. However, they'd offered him a roof over his head when they'd seen him begging in the town centre with Barney and they'd made a fuss of the dog. Danny suspected it had been Barney rather than himself who'd been responsible for his place in the squat but he said nothing and kept his head down.

He stroked Barney's head and the dog looked up at him adoringly. It was good to have someone who loved you and even better when that love was unconditional. Barney was of mixed stock, a touch of Labrador here and a hint of Jack Russell there, but this lack of pedigree didn't matter to Danny. It was personality that counted; and loyalty. Danny had been loyal to Kevin, the man whose name he'd assumed, although that had been easy because he'd loved Kevin more than he'd ever loved any human being before. Then Kevin had betrayed him by walking into a car one rainy night in Toronto. Once Danny had realised his lover was dead he'd fled from the scene in panic because a lifetime of dodging authority had made him wary of involvement. He'd gone back to the room they'd shared and packed up his things, knowing it was time to go home to England. There had been nothing he could do for Kevin; his Canadian adventure was over.

He liked Devon because he'd once lived with foster parents in Topsham and he'd been happy there; possibly the happiest he'd ever been during his turbulent childhood. Knowing Neston's reputation for alternative lifestyles, he'd headed there to seek out a squat with people who didn't ask too many questions. Then he'd looked for the grandfather Kevin had spoken of so often; the only member of his family he'd felt close to after his parents had reacted badly to the news that he was gay. Since his parents had thrown him out at the age of seventeen, the real Kevin had only spoken to his grandfather on the phone long distance, which meant that Bert hadn't seen him for years, and luckily he'd accepted Danny without question.

When Danny had been treated as a much-loved grandson, a pleasure he'd never before experienced, he'd seen no harm in maintaining the deception if it made the old man happy. Besides, Bert was an interesting man who'd once been a teacher and for only the second time in his life – the first being with the real Kevin – Danny had felt as though he truly belonged.

He could have taken advantage of the situation and helped himself to any cash Bert left lying around but as he came to know the old man better, he rediscovered the conscience he'd forgotten he possessed. He'd enjoyed his visits to Bert's bungalow and was always careful never to go while his carers were there. Then came the dreadful day when he'd found Bert dead with marks of violence on his wasted body.

Danny kept thinking of the person he'd seen at the bungalow door a few days before he made his terrible discovery. But he couldn't go to the police. The less he had to do with the police the better.

19

Wesley took the seat opposite Gerry, watching the DCI's face and thinking that he looked strained, somehow older. He'd been looking that way since Linda Payne's body was found, as though the discovery had revived bad memories.

'So who is Danny Brice?'

'In care for most of his life. Mother had a drug problem and father was a ship that passed in the night. Couple of convictions for shoplifting in his teens then he went off our radar until now, when his prints have turned up all over Bert Cummings' bungalow.'

Wesley thought for a moment. 'One of the carers we've spoken to said Bert talked about his grandson, Kevin, visiting. Trouble is Bert had also told her that Kevin had been killed earlier this year. Car accident in Toronto. She thought it was a sign of Bert's mind going so she took no notice.' He took out his notebook and scribbled something down. 'I'll get someone to check it out. What about the other elderly people who've been burgled? Any sign of Brice's prints on their premises?'

Gerry shook his head.

'If the grandson wasn't a figment of Bert's imagination, my money's on him being Danny Brice and if Bert found out he wasn't who he said he was . . . We need to trace Brice as a matter of urgency. Any idea where he could be?'

'Afraid not. There's no up-to-date picture of him in the records so we don't even know what he looks like nowadays. He's no relatives – although as he was in foster care in Topsham for a while it might be worth checking there. I'll get someone onto it.'

Gerry shuffled some of the papers on his desk, as though he was trying to distract himself from the overwhelming amount of information that was coming in.

'What's wrong, Gerry?'

'Nothing.'

Wesley knew this was a lie so he waited.

Gerry gave a deep sigh. 'It's the Linda Payne case and this skull they found at Strangefields Farm. I thought the Temples case was ancient history but Linda's MO seems identical and that's really worrying me. Someone could be out there copying him – maybe someone obsessed with the original case.'

'I've been bringing myself up to speed on Temples,' said Wesley. 'He never confessed to any of the murders, did he?'

'Didn't need to. The evidence was overwhelming. All the girls' clothing was found at Strangefields, obviously kept as trophies. Then there was Carrie Bullen, the one who got away. She identified him.'

'We need to speak to her.'

'She killed herself a year later which as far as I'm concerned means she's another of his victims.'

'It might be helpful to speak to her family.' Wesley paused. 'And I think we should have a word with the man himself.'

Gerry's eyes widened.

'You think the skull belongs to Gemma Pollinger, don't you?'

Gerry gave a reluctant nod.

'Temples needs to be interviewed but you don't have to do it, Gerry. I can take Rach. If he's killed women it might be good psychology to include her. It'll be interesting to see how he reacts.'

'He not only killed them, Wes, he destroyed their faces – beautiful lasses they were and all.'

'Where's he being held?'

'Gumton Gate near Manchester. Category A.'

Wesley looked at his watch. 'Pity. Dartmoor would have been more convenient.'

'Not high enough security these days. He's a dangerous man.'

'Even so, he couldn't have killed Linda Payne.'

'You didn't see the paintings he did of his victims,' said Gerry with a scowl. 'I wouldn't put anything past him.'

At that moment one of the DCs seconded to the investigation gave a token tap on Gerry's open door. He was middle-aged with a beer belly and eyes that had seen it all before.

'Thought you'd like to have a look at this, sir,' he said before placing a photograph album on Gerry's desk. 'The search team found it in the loft at Linda Payne's cottage.'

Wesley thanked the man and picked up the album, flicking through the faded snaps of a younger Linda with an older woman he assumed was her mother. However, when he turned the final page he saw a teenage Linda with a short skirt and long wavy hair. She was standing outside a building Wesley recognised as Strangefields Farm and a much taller young man in his twenties had his arm around her shoulders.

He stared at the picture for a while before passing the album to Gerry. 'Is this who I think it is?'

'Well, well, well. Her name didn't come up in the original investigation but it looks as though our Linda Payne was one of Jackson Temples' girls.'

20

Joe Hamer, in common with many developers Grace Compton had worked with, was demanding. He'd changed his mind again about the design for the proposed reception building at Strangefields Farm. He wanted it larger and she'd had to explain gently that they'd pushed the planning authorities to the limit as it was. He'd also told her that someone from the County Archaeological Unit was making waves because he'd seen the new plans and discovered something on an old map that might be historically significant. The archaeologist was insisting on trenches being dug on the reception building site which would hold up the work and, according to Hamer, time was money. Grace had heard that phrase many times before and she knew the situation needed to be dealt with by charm and flattery so she smiled sympathetically and said the sooner the archaeologists started, the sooner they'd be out of his hair.

As she left the meeting her thoughts turned to Wesley Peterson. She was impatient to meet him again and curious to see Pam, the woman he'd chosen to marry; curious and maybe a little jealous, although she'd never admit that, even to herself. She'd made her choice years ago and her work had left little room for serious relationships – until she'd met Dale Keyes, the man she hadn't been able to get out of her mind.

She made her way along the embankment, stopping by the bench where she and Wesley had eaten fish and chips earlier that day. She ran her fingers over the wood, which felt damp and cold beneath her touch, wondering if her sighting of Dale had just been a pretext to see Wesley again. Now time had passed she was beginning to think she must have been mistaken because if Dale Keyes hadn't died in Thailand he would surely have been in touch. She'd once heard that everybody has a doppelgänger somewhere so it was possible she'd seen Dale's; a doppelgänger with the same dress sense and the same way of walking.

She walked on by the river, breathing in the seaweed-scented air and listening to the calming slap of water against the pontoons. She could see the hills rising above the town, lush and green, and the view out to sea framed by castle-topped cliffs. This place was very different from London with its traffic and crowds and for the first time she understood why Wesley had chosen to make the move.

She'd noticed some expensive clothes shops in the town along with a selection of interesting art galleries so, as her meeting had finished early, she decided to treat herself to an hour of retail therapy, a distraction from work before heading back to the hotel to send emails and pore over plans.

She passed the square inner harbour she'd heard people call the 'boat float', careful to stay away from the unfenced edge and the sheer drop into the water. Small vessels were bobbing there on the high tide as though they were trying to escape their moorings but since maritime matters bored her she hurried towards the shops of Moat Street, down the little alleyway by the Arts Centre where she'd last seen the man she'd mistaken for Dale Keyes.

She glanced around nervously, half expecting to see him waiting for her in a darkened doorway, but there was no sign of him and when she reached Moat Street she began to scan the shop windows, eager for a distraction from the irritations of work and Joe Hamer's grandiose ambitions.

Then she saw him. He was standing inside one of the street's many art galleries talking to a tall blond woman with a face like a horse. Grace stood in the street for a while watching and hoping he wouldn't turn and see her. He had more hair than when they'd been together and he'd now acquired a small beard, but she was as certain as she could be that it was him.

She sensed that it would be wise to go before she was seen. If he'd chosen to 'die' then he might be trying to escape something more unpleasant than the money he owed to her partnership.

Suddenly her certainty wavered. What if she was mistaken? But even if she was right she didn't feel ready to confront him just yet, so instead she hurried away.

From the first diary of
Lemuel Strange, gentleman

5th September 1666

'When are Bess and Harry to come before the judge at
the Assizes?' I asked.

John and the cook made no answer and I surmised
that there was more of the tale to tell. The cook wiped her
hands on her apron and looked away as if she could no
longer bear to hear the sorry story of her master's violent
death. John meanwhile shifted from foot to foot and
looked as fearful as a child threatened with a beating by
his schoolmaster.

'Speak up, man,' I said. 'If the trial be at Exeter I
shall attend to ensure my kinsman is avenged by the law
of the land. I feel it is my duty.'

I spoke the truth for although I had little love for my
cousin, I wished to see justice done and the felons hanged
as is only right and proper.

For a long while the man did not answer and I knew
he was hiding something from me. I asked him again to
say his piece and when he finally spoke it was in a low
voice I could barely hear.

'There will be no Exeter trial, sir. For Bess and Harry are dead already. Justice has been done. Our justice. And yet ...' He looked at the cook, who lowered her eyes like a coy maid.

'What?' I asked, impatient at the man's reticence.

'It is said in the town that they still walk. That they do not lie peaceful in their graves and will return to torment us all.'

21

It was six thirty and Wesley had already warned Pam that she was unlikely to see him before ten.

Gerry too had made a call to Joyce. Wesley had wondered whether their relationship would last after she'd turned down his proposal of marriage the previous month. She'd made the excuse that Gerry's daughter, Rosie, would disapprove of another woman taking her dead mother's place. But Kathy Heffernan had been dead for some years and, in Wesley's opinion, Rosie Heffernan was a selfish young woman who used her late mother's memory to retain control over her doting father. Though Gerry might be tough with his team, as far as the women in his life went he was a pussycat, and Rosie took advantage.

Wesley liked Joyce. Before Gerry had met her during an investigation he'd been floundering, balancing his chaotic domestic existence with the job. He'd relied heavily on Kathy and some men – indeed some women – struggled on their own.

Gerry had suggested a takeaway from the Golden Dragon and a young constable drafted in from Uniform to help with the inquiry was sent out to fetch the order. From the look on the boy's face, he thought the task beneath him but he didn't argue as Rachel handed him the list she'd made of everyone's requirements. She was a natural organiser, which was why she made such a good sergeant.

While Wesley was waiting for his food he sat at his desk studying the large whiteboard which almost covered the far wall of the office. One side was dedicated to Linda Payne and the other to Bert Cummings and Wesley wondered whether there could really be a link between their two cases. As far as he could see the two victims weren't acquainted and had nothing in common. If it weren't for the fact that they'd been killed within days of each other – and Colin's observation that a similar weapon might have been used – it would have been assumed that the investigations were separate, never to be connected.

On an easel in the centre Gerry had placed another whiteboard, this time bearing pictures of the skull found at Strangefields Farm. The name Jackson Temples stood out in large black letters, together with an oversized question mark. Wesley stared at the board with its comments and photographs, including the one they'd found of the killer with a young Linda Payne. He was deep in thought until Trish Walton's voice broke the spell.

'The Harbourside Players are having a rehearsal tonight at the Arts Centre. If we want to see them all together . . . '

'Thanks Trish. Good idea.' He imagined the director would resent the intrusion, especially as the leading role would have to be recast, but that wasn't Wesley's problem. The Harbourside Players had, presumably, been the last people to see Linda alive – apart from her killer.

As the team ate the Chinese takeaway at their desks, the smell of food wafted over the office. It would probably linger until the following day but if the chief super complained, Gerry could be relied on to tell her that criminals weren't brought to justice on empty stomachs.

Once the takeaway containers had been disposed of Wesley glanced at Rachel's desk, where she was trawling through statements from the elderly burglary victims, looking for anything they'd missed that might connect the culprit with Bert Cummings' murder.

She must have sensed she was being watched because she looked up and smiled. Wesley went over to her. 'Anything new?'

'Bert's carers have been spoken to again. One of them said he used to teach her at Neston High School but before that she thought he'd taught at some private school. His subject was maths and she reckoned he was very clever. Apart from him insisting that his dead grandson, Kevin, had been visiting him, she said nothing unusual had happened in the weeks leading up to his death.'

Wesley gave her a weary smile. 'I'm going to speak to Linda Payne's fellow thespians. They're rehearsing tonight.'

'They've all made statements, haven't they?'

'Yes, but they didn't tell us much. Everyone in the company liked Linda and there was never a cross word. No back-biting, no jealousies or disagreements, which sounds too good to be true.'

'You don't believe them?'

'I want to speak to them individually – find out what makes the group tick. Fancy coming with me?'

'Doesn't the boss want to go?'

'I haven't asked him.'

'Afraid they'll be offended by his cutting wit?'

'Something like that. Any whiff of pretentiousness and

he won't be able to help himself. And as you once moved in the world of amateur theatricals ... '

'That was a long time ago and I've got a mountain of paperwork but ... ' She stood up. 'OK. Lead on.'

'Macduff?'

'That's a quote from the Scottish play. Don't tempt fate.' She laughed and snatched her jacket off the back of her chair.

'What are you doing about your wedding flowers?' Wesley asked as they walked the short distance to the Arts Centre next door to the police station.

'Jen claims she can still do them, although I'm having my doubts.'

Once they reached the Arts Centre the fresh-faced young man on the reception desk told them the Harbourside Players were rehearsing in room twelve. They made their way down a corridor lined with pale wooden doors and, without bothering to knock, Wesley pushed the door open and found a dozen or so people sitting in a circle, scripts in hand.

The man who rose to his feet as they entered was in his late sixties with the lined face of a habitual smoker and grey hair tied back in a neat ponytail. He wore a pork-pie hat and a scarf draped artistically around his neck. He possessed the nervous energy of someone who rarely relaxed; someone who always liked to be in charge of some new project or other.

'This is a private rehearsal.'

The words were said with authority. You have no right to be here: get out. Wesley immediately put him right and watched the man's expression change from challenge to solemnity.

'You should have let me know you were coming,' the man said with a hint of reproach. He held out his hand. 'Lance Pembry. Director.'

Wesley shook his hand and Rachel did likewise. 'We're sorry to disturb your rehearsal, Mr Pembry, but we need to speak to everyone about Linda Payne. I take it you've all heard the news?'

'Of course. A constable visited me yesterday ... as I was one of the last people to see her. We've already given statements.' He looked round the group for support and a few people nodded nervously.

'I know. I've read them. But I'd like to get a few things straight.' He looked round the group. 'Who would you say knew her best?'

The actors looked from one to the other, as though nobody wanted to admit to being Linda's friend. Eventually a woman raised her hand. She had dark, almost black, hair and a generous mouth which formed itself into a nervous smile.

'We had a lot of scenes together – I'm playing her serving woman, Cariola – and we used to get together to go through our lines. My name's Pauline Howe by the way,' she added, waiting for Rachel to write it down in her notebook.

A youngish man put his hand up next. He was tall and had a pointed beard that made him look a little diabolical. His dark complexion hinted at black ancestry somewhere in his family tree and his eyes were a deep brown. He was handsome and Wesley guessed that he knew it.

The young man introduced himself as 'Rich Vernon. Playing Ferdinand, Duke of Calabria ... the Duchess's brother. The villain of the piece, I suppose you could say. Linda was fantastic. Really nice.'

112

Wesley recognised a platitude when he heard one and there was a distinct lack of sincerity in Vernon's voice. He hoped his performance as Ferdinand was more convincing.

'Who's playing Bosola, the character who orders the strangulation of the duchess and Cariola?'

A wiry middle-aged man raised a nervous hand.

'And the executioner?'

A thickset man with a shaven head raised his hand. Wesley thought he looked familiar, then he remembered that he'd seen him aboard the passenger ferry – one of the crew.

'You know the play, Inspector.' Pembry sounded surprised.

'It's one of my wife's favourites.' He hesitated, smiling. 'Although I must admit that after a day at the police station all that murder doesn't appeal too much as a form of entertainment.'

A couple of the cast laughed nervously.

Wesley looked at his watch. 'I realise now's not a convenient time—'

'You're right, Inspector. It's not convenient. 'We're having a read-through before Pauline takes over Linda's part, just to get her used to the lines.'

'I appreciate that.' He looked round the company hopefully. 'So if you let Sergeant Tracey know when you'll be available, we'll endeavour to speak to you all at a more suitable time.' He saw Pembry relax, as though he'd had a stay of execution, but the director's relief was premature. 'Although now we're here we might as well seize the opportunity of speaking to you, Mr Pembry. And then Ms Howe if it's not too much trouble. Is there somewhere we can talk in private?' Wesley had turned on the charm, so reasonable that Pembry would have appeared churlish if he refused.

'Can we carry on with the second scene of act five?' said a woman sitting next to 'Bosola'. I need some practice with the lines.'

'That's a good idea, Monica,' Pembry said pointedly, his eyes on Rachel as though he was assessing her suitability for a role. He turned back to his actors. 'Carry on and I'll be back soon.'

Wesley followed Pembry to an office a couple of doors away. The director took a seat behind the desk with the confidence of innocence.

Wesley had Pembry's routine statement in the document case he was carrying and he sat there studying it for a while before he asked his first question. Pembry had said he'd been with everyone else when Linda left the Arts Centre after the last rehearsal she'd attended and that had been the last time he'd seen her. Wesley wondered whether this was true.

'You knew Linda well?'

'Ours was a working relationship, Inspector. I came here from London a couple of years ago after a long career in the professional theatre. My wife has always loved Devon so when the time came for me to retire . . . ' He sighed. 'I thought it was only right to give something back to the community I'd chosen to join so I set up a company that would tackle challenging productions and rise to the highest standards. My actors are amateurs but I'm constantly amazed at what they can do with proper guidance. I must say I'm finding it as satisfying as working in the London theatre.'

'Was Linda talented?'

'She wouldn't have been given the title role otherwise. As I said, I insist on the highest standards.'

'The rope you use in the production – where did it come from?'

'Linda brought it in. I think she mentioned it came from her shop, although I can't be sure.'

'Would anyone else know?'

Pembry shrugged his shoulders theatrically.

'Did you ever see Linda away from rehearsals?'

'You're asking if I was having an affair with her.' He glanced at Rachel. 'The answer to that question is certainly not. There's no casting couch in the Harbourside Players, Inspector.'

'I'm sure there isn't, sir. Did Linda have any particular friends in the company? Anyone she saw outside rehearsals? Apart from Pauline Howe?'

He shook his head. 'Not that I'm aware of.'

Wesley thanked him for his time and asked him to send Pauline in. They'd learned nothing from the director and he was starting to feel despondent. Perhaps there was nothing more to learn there.

After a token knock Pauline entered the room, hovering nervously near the door before taking a seat as requested. She looked tense, picking at a jagged fingernail. Wesley smiled, hoping to put her at her ease.

'What do you know about Linda's background?' he began.

'She used to live in London but about eighteen months ago she said she got sick of city life and decided to move here. She opened her own florist's shop in Tradmouth. It was very successful.'

Wesley wondered whether there'd been a hint of envy in her last statement. Perhaps Pauline had been irritated when Linda boasted of her success. Linda had been the alpha female, the leading lady, while Pauline had played the serving woman. Now it was up to him to get her to reveal all.

'Did she mention any family?'

'No.'

'Did she have a man in her life – or men?'

'I saw her going off with Rich Vernon a couple of times. Now she might have been giving him a lift home but ... well, he lives in Tradmouth. Walking distance.' She raised her eyebrows.

This was something that hadn't been mentioned in the cast's bland statements and Wesley felt like a hunter who'd suddenly caught the scent of his prey. 'You think they were involved?'

'I wouldn't like to say. I'm only telling you what I saw.'

'Tell us what happened when you last saw her.'

'She left on her own but ...'

'But?' Rachel prompted.

'Someone was waiting for her and they walked off together but I couldn't see properly because it was dark. But Rich had left about five minutes earlier and ... well, it was just a figure in the shadows but it certainly looked like him. Right height and build.'

'He's younger than Linda,' said Wesley.

'So?' A smile played on Pauline's lips.

'Is there anything else you can tell us?'

'I don't think so. We really weren't that close.'

Wesley suspected there was something she was keeping back but he thanked her and looked at his watch. Rich Vernon could wait until tomorrow. Let him sweat.

116

22

It was almost ten o'clock by the time Wesley arrived home. The children would be in bed because it was school the next day and he hoped Pam would have a bottle of wine open and a glass ready. Then he remembered that Della was still installed in their spare bedroom and would probably have helped herself to his share of the wine, and his brief feeling of optimism faded.

He let himself in with his key and stood in the hall for a few seconds, listening as the cat, Moriarty, greeted him, tail raised and purring loudly. He picked her up and she enjoyed the attention for a while before wriggling free and dropping elegantly to the floor. He could hear the TV in the living room. The news had just started and from the tone of the newsreader's voice he could tell it was doom and gloom as usual. When he pushed the door open Pam looked up, but there was something guarded about her greeting and he wondered what was wrong. Della was slumped in the armchair by the window with a half-empty wine glass in her right hand, her two metal crutches propped up beside her.

'You're late,' she said before Pam had a chance to open her mouth.

Pam ignored her mother and stood up. 'Good day?'

'Not really. We're a bit overwhelmed with these two murders.'

'Have you eaten?'

'Had a takeaway in the office.'

'Your sister rang. She's invited us to dinner. Wants to know which night suits us best.'

'Not good timing I'm afraid.'

Della grunted. 'I've offered to babysit.'

'Thanks, Della but—'

'Pam told me about the skull at the Temples house.'

He'd been doing his best to put work out of his mind and Della's words caught him off guard.

'I'm surprised that frightful place hasn't been knocked down.'

'It's Grade Two star-listed so demolition isn't an option.' Wesley realised his answer was sharp but, after the hard day he'd just had, his patience with his mother-in-law was wearing thin.

'I used to work with one of his victims, you know.'

This captured Wesley's attention. 'One of them taught at your college?' Before her recent retirement Della had taught at a further education college where, in Wesley's opinion, she'd become a little too friendly with her students. 'I thought the victims were all teenagers.'

'Gemma was. She'd just left that posh private school near Neston – didn't bother staying on to do her A levels and got a job in admin at the college instead. She was nothing to look at, poor girl, but I don't suppose Temples worried about that. She was female and that's enough for some men.' She glared at her son-in-law as though she held him personally responsible for the failings of his sex.

Wesley ignored her and sat down next to Pam. She seemed unusually quiet and when he asked in a whisper if she was all right she didn't reply. He went to the kitchen to fetch a wine glass and as he reached for the half-full bottle of red wine on the coffee table in front of him, Della leaned forward and held out her own glass to be refilled.

'So you worked with Gemma Pollinger?' he said as he poured her drink. 'The girl whose body was never found.'

'That's right. I was on the teaching staff so I didn't have anything to do with her but Hattie who worked in the office got to know her quite well. I think she treated Hattie as a sort of mother figure, seeing her own family were a strange bunch. She boasted to Hattie that she had a new boyfriend who was an artist. Then one day she never turned up at work. Hattie didn't work out that the artist boyfriend must have been Jackson Temples until it was on the news.'

Wesley frowned. Like Jacky Burns, until the fishing boat had brought her skull up from the deep, Gemma's remains had never been found, which meant her family had been denied the chance to lay her to rest. To top that her brother had committed suicide soon after she went missing. Tragedy had followed tragedy. The thought of what her parents must have gone through made Wesley shudder.

'Hattie said Temples must have flattered poor Gemma by asking her to pose for him,' Della continued. 'But it seemed he had worse things on his mind than painting young girls in the buff.'

'I'd like to speak to Hattie. Do you know where I can find her?'

Della's eager expression suddenly turned solemn. 'She died. Heart attack. She was only two years older than me.'

Wesley made sympathetic noises, trying to hide his disappointment. It was looking increasingly probable that the skull from Strangefields Farm belonged to Gemma Pollinger but the woman who might be able to supply him with more information about her was dead.

'Jackson Temples used to pick up girls at the Green Parrot in Morbay, according to the papers,' said Della with a distant smile. 'I went there a couple of times myself. It was a bit of a dive.'

'Weren't you a bit old for that sort of thing?' said Pam sharply.

'You're as old as you feel,' Della snapped back before draining her glass.

Pam ignored her mother and looked at Wesley suspiciously. 'Are you sure you can't make Maritia's dinner? She said she's inviting an old friend of hers from London called Grace. She said you'd remember her.'

Wesley felt the blood rushing to his face. He hadn't told Pam about his impromptu lunch with Grace and it was probably too late to correct the omission now. He knew if Della got wind of it she wouldn't be able to resist stirring up trouble, just to relieve the frustration of being immobile.

'I remember her,' he said, trying to sound casual. 'I'm afraid you'll have to give Maritia my apologies. I'll be working late for a while, sorry.' He felt relieved as he said the words.

'That doesn't stop me going by myself.'

Wesley smiled a smile that he suspected had turned into a grimace of pain. 'Of course. If you want.'

He'd had his suspicions about Grace's motives and he hoped she wouldn't make mischief when she got his wife alone and exaggerate what had happened when they'd met. But he had other things to worry about. One of them was Gemma Pollinger and the possibility that they'd found her at last.

23

The following morning Rachel called Jen Barrow. She needed to talk to her about Linda's business dealings – and at the same time she intended to make sure that, in Linda's absence, her wedding flowers were still on track. The subject had been preying on her mind all night and she wondered if she was in danger of becoming the kind of obsessive bride she'd always thought she'd never be – a Bridezilla trampling over everything and everyone in her rush to get to the altar.

When Jen answered her mobile Rachel thought she sounded cagey, as though there was something she was hiding. She hoped it had nothing to do with her flowers.

Then she realised that Jen just sounded exhausted, as though she'd just hauled herself out of bed, and when she said she was still at home Rachel immediately told her she was coming round to speak to her, ending the call before Jen could object. Rachel had a niggling suspicion that something was wrong and she wanted to know what it was.

Jen's small terraced house stood on a narrow street near the market; a dark street where the sun rarely reached, and patches of moss dappled the painted facades of the more neglected houses. Jen's house, however, was freshly painted, one of the neater properties in the row, and Rachel took a deep breath before pressing the doorbell.

It was a while before Jen answered and when she did Rachel was struck by how tired she looked, as though she'd been up all night worrying about some intractable problem. Rachel guessed that Jen was probably in her late thirties. She was statuesque rather than fat, with bobbed dark-blond hair, a perfect nose and a neat chin, although in Rachel's opinion there was something about her looks that fell short of beauty. Today the dark circles beneath her eyes stood out against the pallor of her skin and the off-white top she wore drained her face of colour and made her look ill.

'Sorry to bother you, Jen,' said Rachel as she was led into a small, bland living room where the predominant colour was beige. The thought popped into her head that if Jen lay down on the pale sofa she might disappear into the background. There were mirrors all around the room, maybe in an attempt to make the place look bigger, and Rachel couldn't help noticing that Jen kept glancing at her reflection.

'I'd like to talk to you about Linda's business.'

'What about it?'

'Is it doing well?'

'Well enough.'

'I'd like someone to look over the shop's accounts. It's routine in a murder case.'

'I haven't got them.'

'Are they at the shop?'

'I don't know. Linda dealt with all that.' Jen began to pick at a large square plaster on her left hand. Rachel had seen her wearing it before when she'd visited the shop but she guessed cuts and scratches were an occupational hazard for a florist, especially if she was under pressure and prone to carelessness.

'What's her accountant's name?'

'I don't know that either,' she said quickly. 'Like I said, Linda dealt with that side of things.'

Rachel sensed her questions were making Jen nervous but she didn't press the matter.

'We need another meeting about the flowers,' said Jen.

Rachel recognised the deliberate change of subject. 'Of course. I'll call into the shop when I have a free moment.'

When she left she saw relief on Jen's face, as though some terrible burden had been lifted from her shoulders. Rachel had seen that same relief on the faces of people who had something to hide from the police and all of a sudden she wanted to get hold of those accounts.

Danny Brice had always had the instincts of a magpie. Shining things attracted him and as soon as he opened the door to the empty shop below where he slept his eyes were drawn to something glistening on the dusty floor, lying in the corner as though it had been kicked there and abandoned.

He picked it up and held it to the light that trickled in through the filthy windows. The marks on the yellow metal told him it was no cheap trinket.

He smiled at Barney and dropped the thing into his pocket as the dog wagged his tail.

From the first diary of
Lemuel Strange, gentleman

5th September 1666

'Why are the spirits of those who murdered my cousin so unquiet? Could it be that they had no trial?' I said. 'We are not savages in this land. A man is entitled to a fair trial before a jury of his fellow citizens.'

John bowed his head. ''Twas justice, sir,' he said with a hint of defiance. 'They did the master to death and hid his poor body to cover their crime.'

'What reason had they to kill their master?'

'Wickedness, sir. That and the gold they took from my master's chest in his chamber. The mistress said they took a great deal and a ring of great value that belonged to her was found in Bess's chamber.'

I asked if the rest of the treasure had been found and was told it had not, although men had searched for it diligently. The felons must have concealed it in a good hiding place and, with them dead, John was afraid it might never be found.

I enquired then if my cousin had other enemies and John and the cook exchanged sly looks.

'Master Treague of Neston believes the master betrayed his father in the late war between Parliament and our King's father. The old man was imprisoned by Cromwell's men and died of the fever in gaol so Master Treague vowed to be avenged on the master. But fear not, for Treague was in Bristol when our master died, so Bess and Harry's guilt is certain.'

When I enquired about Reuben's debts I was told the mistress was in sore distress and feared her creditors would soon be demanding payment.

I dismissed John, intending to go in search of Frances, when a messenger arrived with a letter from my wife saying that our house was in grave danger as flames could be seen at the end of the street. A great fire began at the King's baker's house, she said, and had spread, consuming all the houses and churches in its path. Many were fleeing to the country to seek refuge, and she was making the journey to Devon to join me. This news concerned me for, with our London house in peril from the fire, I too might be about to face great losses.

24

Jemima Baine was the kind of forensic anthropologist who'd look good on TV, Neil thought; the ideal woman to give archaeology a more glamorous image. Her glossy auburn hair tumbled down over the shoulders of her pristine waxed jacket and she pushed it back with the cleanest hands he'd ever seen on someone connected with his professional world.

'I've taken a look at your skull,' she said, her eyes on the small digger that had just started to scrape the earth away from the trench Neil had ordered to be dug near the gate, on the exact location of the feature marked 'chapel' that he'd spotted on the early map. Another trench was being opened where the earth had already been disturbed. Thanks to the yellow digger's previous efforts the soil there was soft, allowing two of his colleagues to do the honours with spades.

Neil and Jemima walked away from the noise of the digger's engine so they could talk in relative peace.

'What's the verdict?' Neil asked.

'It's undergoing tests, so we can't know anything yet, but I think your first instincts were right. It's a young female but I suspect it's over seventy years old.' She hesitated.

'I understand it was found in the house of a convicted murderer.'

'That's what rang alarm bells. I have a friend in the local CID who's been showing a great interest. I've done a geophys sweep on the cellar in case of any undiscovered burials down there but there was nothing untoward,' he said, sounding slightly disappointed. 'One of the murderer's victims was never found and as the skull belonged to a young female ...'

'You thought it might be hers. A reasonable assumption, I suppose.' Jemima paused and took a deep breath. 'I found something interesting while I was examining the skull. There was a cut mark near the base – possibly made with something like an axe.'

'A beheading?'

'Or the head was removed after death. It isn't a deep mark and could have happened post-mortem. If we found the rest of the body I'd be able to tell you more of course.'

She fell silent, watching the digger as it moved the soil from the trench some way away.

'If the tests confirm the skull is old there's one explanation I can think of,' said Neil. 'A few years ago I came across a burial just outside a churchyard. An outcast from society had been buried in unhallowed ground.'

'I think I know what you're going to say,' said Jemima.

'The skull was removed after death and placed by the individual's knees to stop him rising from his grave: a deviant burial.'

Jemima nodded slowly but before she could say anything one of Neil's colleagues standing by the newly dug trench raised her hand and the digger driver cut the engine. She began to wave at Neil excitedly. Something had been found.

25

While Wesley sat in the office going through the file on Gemma Pollinger's disappearance his mind was elsewhere, thinking of Grace.

The woman he'd met the previous day had been a different person from the girl he'd once known. Harder, colder and more cynical; perhaps even ruthless. He wondered fleetingly whether something had happened in her life to bring about the alteration but he had no time to indulge in amateur psychology. People change. And yet he'd never believed they changed fundamentally.

He forced himself to concentrate on the Pollinger case. Gemma had last been seen at the Green Parrot club on a Saturday night in August 1996. She had been on her own but two girls who'd known her from her school days said she'd mentioned that she was leaving early to meet someone, although she didn't say who. It sounded like Gemma was a plain, awkward girl who'd found it hard to get boyfriends which, in Wesley's opinion, would have made her more vulnerable if a man like Jackson Temples had paid her the attention she craved. Her parents and brother had been unable to add anything useful and the constable who'd spoken to them had noted that the brother seemed particularly distressed. Wesley knew that, sadly, the brother had killed himself shortly after Gemma's disappearance. He didn't yet know whether Gemma's parents were still alive but if they were, knowing their daughter's fate might bring them a small crumb of comfort in the never-ending nightmare they must have been living for more than two decades.

Around the point Gemma had disappeared the police had begun to connect the murder of Nerys Harred, whose body had been washed up near the castle, with the attack on Carrie Bullen, but a link to the disappearance of Jacky Burns hadn't yet been firmly established. Local girls had become cautious when they went out at night, but it wasn't until Carrie regained consciousness and told the police what she knew about Jackson Temples and Strangefields Farm that people knew who to fear.

As Wesley examined the file he knew that if he was to make any progress he needed to speak to Temples himself. They needed to find out how he knew Linda Payne and whether she'd been another of his girls; one that had escaped unharmed – until now.

Gerry's voice interrupted his thoughts. 'Come on, Wes, let's go and give Rich Vernon a wake-up call. Paul says he works behind the bar at the Marina Hotel. Lives in. Let's get down there.'

'I've spoken to the governor at Gumton Gate and told her we'll go and see Jackson Temples tomorrow. It's a five-hour drive but if we set off first thing we won't have to stay the night.'

'Well, I've got no objection to you staying overnight. It'll give Rach a nice little break from her wedding stuff.' There was an innocence in the DCI's words which showed that he had no idea what had happened last time he and Rachel had gone up north together to interview a suspect. Although Gerry was a good detective he was inclined to believe the best of people he knew and liked. 'But it's up to you. I'm off to a press conference at five. They're gathering like vultures and the last thing we want is for them to get wind of the similarities between Linda's death and the Temples murders before we're ready to release any details. If that happens all hell's going to break loose.'

Wesley knew Gerry was right. The thought of a copycat killer would send the area into panic and the press would think all their Christmases had come at once. He looked at his watch. 'Let's hope we find Rich Vernon in. Maybe we should call ahead.'

'And lose the advantage of surprise?' Gerry said with a wicked grin. 'That young man wasn't telling the truth and I want to know why.'

The Marina Hotel wasn't far from the police station so they walked, arriving in the plush reception area of the modern building within ten minutes of starting out. When Gerry asked the receptionist where Vernon's room was the young woman in the navy-blue suit drew herself up to her full height and looked as though she was about to refuse. When Wesley stepped forward with his most charming smile she seemed to thaw and said she'd ring through.

'We'd rather you didn't, love,' said Gerry, putting out his hand to stop her lifting the receiver. 'We'd like to surprise him. Where can we find his room?'

The defeated young woman muttered directions. The staff quarters were in the older wing, well away from the comfortably appointed guest bedrooms. After a few false turns down thickly carpeted corridors, they found the room at last. There were no thick carpets here, just shabby linoleum and scuffed doors.

On the way Wesley had been wondering where Grace's room was and whether he'd bump into her. Part of him wanted to but the other part – the one that knew he should avoid trouble and temptation at all costs – dreaded the prospect. Then he reminded himself that she would be working; consulting with her client about the design for the reception building she mentioned: the place where Neil intended to sink his trenches.

Gerry rapped on Rich Vernon's door and Wesley heard noises from within the room, as if someone was getting out of bed and hurriedly pulling on some clothes.

'Hang on. Won't be a sec,' was the cheerful call from beyond the door. Wesley suspected he wouldn't be quite so cheerful once he found out who it was.

The door opened to reveal a sleepy Rich Vernon wearing a thin cotton dressing gown that flapped open to reveal the grey T-shirt and boxer shorts he'd obviously slept in. The previous day, with his dark looks and mildly diabolical beard, Wesley had thought he was the sort who'd be perpetually surrounded by a whiff of danger but now he had the bleary-eyed look of a man who'd just woken up in shabby hotel staff accommodation after a late night; just another ordinary man in his late twenties earning a living behind a bar.

'Mr Vernon. Sorry to disturb you,' Wesley lied. 'OK if we come in and have a chat?'

Rich Vernon stood to one side to let them in before checking the corridor. It might not be good for his job prospects if the police were seen to come calling.

'Sit down,' said Rich, gesturing towards the unmade bed.

Wesley and Gerry remained standing but Rich pulled the duvet over the grubby sheets and slumped down, looking up at them expectantly.

'We'll come straight to the point, Mr Vernon,' said Wesley. 'What was your relationship with Linda Payne?'

'You mean on stage or in real life?'

'Don't try to be clever,' Gerry growled. 'You know exactly what Inspector Peterson means.'

'OK, sorry. We were friends. That's all.'

'You saw each other outside rehearsals?'

Vernon began smoothing the bedclothes, giving himself time to think – to come up with an answer that would get the police off his back. 'Sometimes.'

Wesley waited for him to elaborate. In his experience no interviewee could resist filling a silence.

'Linda was an attractive woman. We were both unattached and she invited me to her cottage to go through our lines. Lance goes mad if you're not word perfect. We began to spend a bit of time together. Nothing heavy and no strings attached. We'd both had bad experiences in the past so we kept it casual.'

'You used to stay at her cottage?'

'Occasionally. But working here made it difficult. I have to arrange my shifts round rehearsals so rehearsal nights were our only chance to spend the night together.'

'So did you spend the night with her after the rehearsal she attended on Monday evening?'

'No. She said she couldn't.'

'You were seen with her after the rehearsal.'

'Who by?'

'Is it true?'

There was another long silence. Then he took a deep

breath. 'OK. I waited for her outside the Arts Centre. I was hoping . . .'

'For a bit of how's your father,' said Gerry with a knowing grin.

'If you want to put it like that. I waited for her in a shop doorway she'd have to pass on her way to the car park and when I stepped out, she pretended to be shocked. But I could tell it was an act. She'd been giving me the come-on all night.'

'You must have been disappointed?' said Wesley.

'Wouldn't you be?'

'We're not talking about me. How did you feel when she turned you down?'

'Exactly what you said – disappointed. But that doesn't mean I killed her.' The last words sounded anxious, as though he'd just realised how his words might be interpreted.

'Tell us exactly what happened,' said Wesley. He glanced at Gerry, hoping the DCI would resist the temptation to put too much pressure on the man. In Wesley's opinion more would be gained by getting him to relax. To his relief Gerry stayed silent, his eyes fixed on Vernon's face.

'I told her I didn't start my shift until eleven the next morning so why didn't we go for a drink – or buy a bottle and go back to hers; we've done that a few times. But she said she couldn't. She had things to do.'

'What things?'

'No idea. I thought we were getting on well. Up till then she'd seemed only too keen, believe me.'

'She hadn't given any indication that something was wrong?'

'Not really.'

'Did she mention anything that was bothering her ... however small?'

He considered the question for a while before he answered. 'She said sometimes the shop takings didn't tally and she wondered if her assistant might have been dipping her fingers into the till, but she didn't like to accuse her because it could have been a mistake. Maths wasn't her strong point. Apart from that though ...'

Wesley and Gerry looked at each other.

'Did she mention it to her assistant?' Wesley asked.

'Don't think so. It was just a suspicion. She didn't have any proof.'

'Anything else?' said Gerry.

Vernon didn't answer for a few moments. Then he leaned forward as if he was about to share a confidence. 'I've sometimes wondered whether she and Lance knew each other from when she lived in London. She worked in a florist's near Leicester Square – theatreland. Used to talk about all the actors and theatre people who used to come in and buy flowers and all the bouquets she delivered to stage doors. When I first joined the Harbourside Players I got the impression it wasn't the first time Linda and Lance had met. Not that they said anything.'

'He's married, isn't he?'

'Since when did that stop anybody?'

'Surely you would have noticed if they'd been meeting.'

'Not necessarily. She was the discreet type and some women like to keep their lives in compartments. I was her bit of fun on my evenings off. Other nights I'm stuck behind the bar here so anything could be going on.'

'Can you think of any reason why anyone would want to kill her?'

He looked at Wesley as though he'd asked a particularly stupid question. 'Of course not. Linda was great. Hadn't an enemy in the world.'

'Did she ever mention Jackson Temples?'

'The serial killer? No. Why?'

'What about anybody from her past who'd turned up recently?'

Rich Vernon gave the question some thought, as though Wesley's words had resurrected some elusive memory.

'Over the last couple of weeks she'd been a bit ... distant in rehearsals. Lance had to tell her off a couple of times. Told her she needed to pull her socks up.' He paused. 'And she said something a bit odd last week. I didn't give it much thought at the time, but I was talking about a film I'd seen at the Arts Centre – *The Rise of the Zombies* it was called – and I asked her if she wanted to see it.' He paused. 'But she said she'd had enough of the undead recently.'

'Are you sure that's what she said – the undead?'

'She said people rise from the grave in real life so why watch a film about it.' He hesitated. 'I thought she was joking – only now, looking back, I'm not so sure.'

26

'Anything come in on Bert Cummings?' Wesley asked as he and Gerry walked back to the police station.

'Everyone who's been in contact with him has been traced and interviewed and there was nothing that rang any alarm bells.'

'Do you think there could be a connection to Linda Payne's murder?'

Gerry shrugged. 'I think it's more likely to be linked to this spate of burglaries. If Bert challenged an intruder high on drugs ... '

'Danny Brice?'

'Who knows?'

'But the burglaries seem highly organised. Hardly the work of some junkie in need of a fix.'

'You're right, Wes. And according to Colin the poor old boy was probably asleep when he was stabbed. Which brings us back to the same question: why go to the trouble of killing him? Even if he'd woken up Bert wouldn't have posed much of a threat.'

Wesley fell silent for a few moments, deep in thought. Then he spoke. 'We've been regarding Bert as an innocent victim, a harmless old man who was targeted by a heartless thug. What if there's more to it than that? I went over the possibilities last night when I couldn't sleep.'

'I know exactly what you mean,' Gerry muttered with feeling.

'It was a frenzied attack and I'm starting to wonder whether the stabbing was symbolic. Maybe to send some kind of message?'

'He was a retired teacher.'

They'd reached the police station and neither man said anything as they climbed the stairs to the CID office. When they arrived Wesley followed Gerry into his office and sat down.

'Are we both thinking the same thing, Wes?' said Gerry, keeping his voice down. 'There's so much of it in the news these days. Historic cases – the flapping of chickens coming home to roost.'

'You think he might have abused some of his pupils?'

'We've got to consider the possibility.'

'We've absolutely no evidence and before we have any, I'm reluctant to sully the man's reputation. *De mortuis nil nisi bonum.*'

Gerry shook his head. 'We've got to speak ill of the dead in our job, Wes, or the only murders we'd solve would be the ones where the victims were fully paid up saints. Where did he used to teach?'

'At Neston High School, I think.' He realised that if he hadn't been dealing with the Linda Payne case his research into Bert Cummings' background would have been more thorough and he felt annoyed with himself.

He returned to his desk and found a file lying on the top of his pile of paperwork. It contained Danny Brice's details and his photograph was attached to the first page with a rusty paperclip. The boy whose face stared back at him was good-looking, what some in the past might have called a pretty boy. He had longish dark hair and even features and his eyes were a bright cornflower blue. There was something open and innocent about his face – which would be a considerable asset for anyone planning to embark on a criminal career. But, according to records, Danny Brice hadn't put a foot wrong for over six years, which suggested that either he'd turned his life around or that he hadn't been caught.

'Sir, I've just been to see some of the burglary victims as you suggested.' Wesley looked up and saw Trish standing by his desk with a sheet of paper in her hand. Her face was animated, as though she'd made an exciting new discovery. 'I managed to speak to three.'

Dark-haired, sensible Trish was a reliable, if unimaginative, detective. She and Rachel were close friends, sharing a house and, probably, confidences, though from Trish's manner towards him he was sure Rachel had never shared their now-distant moment of temptation up in Manchester.

She sat down on the spare chair and leaned forward. 'When they were first interviewed the only visitors they mentioned were carers, relatives and friends who'd come round in the week before the burglaries. But when I took more time to speak to them over a cup of tea they all said they'd had a visit from a woman from Social Services – all long skirts and scarves, one described her as. She'd carried a clipboard and checked their houses for safety and asked questions about the carers; what time they came and so on. She'd called round a couple of weeks before the places were burgled so nobody thought to mention it.'

Wesley saw that Trish was looking pleased with herself and suspected there was more to come.

'I contacted Social Services and they told me that no visits had been made to those addresses. The woman flashed an ID card at the victims but they can't remember the name, which isn't surprising because they glimpsed it so briefly. Mind you, it probably wouldn't have done much good if they had been able to read it. What's the betting the name was false anyway? I think she might have been doing a recce. Taking a look around the place to locate the valuables for when she broke in later on. So if she is our burglar and she broke into Bert Cummings' place and panicked when she saw him sitting in the armchair . . .'

Wesley caught her meaning right away. 'Surely she'd just get out of there if she saw him and there's no evidence of a burglary. There was some good jewellery that most likely belonged to his late wife and it was still in the bedroom.'

Trish seemed reluctant to abandon her theory. 'The burglar might have panicked.'

Wesley didn't reply. As Trish returned to her own desk he put his head in his hands. Even though they'd brought in back-up from Morbay and Neston to deal with the two cases their lack of progress was frustrating.

He opened the file on Gemma Pollinger's disappearance he'd been studying earlier, hoping for inspiration. Temples had freely admitted that he'd met the dead girls at the Green Parrot club and that they'd modelled for him – but he'd sworn they'd all left Strangefields Farm alive. He'd even tried to put the blame onto another artist called Jonny Sykes who, he claimed, had been living there at the time of the murders. However, no witnesses had seen Sykes and no trace of him was ever found, so it was assumed that Temples had made him up to deflect suspicion from himself.

The jury had decided he was lying and Wesley hoped that after all this time he might be ready to admit the truth. With luck, he might even be able to tell them why someone had copied his MO when they'd killed Linda Payne.

When he took the file through to the DCI's office Gerry was on the phone but he signalled him to sit. Wesley could tell the call was annoying him and after a few seconds he saw him slam down the receiver.

'And have a nice day to you too,' he hissed at the phone, taking out his frustration on the inanimate object.

'Who was that?'

'Linda Payne's bank. I've been trying to point out to some numbskull in a call centre miles away that we need access to her account and that we've got a warrant. Apparently the computer keeps saying no. When there was a branch in Tradmouth we could just walk in and have a word with the manager but now everything's done online . . .'

Gerry's face had turned red and Wesley feared for his blood pressure. 'Oh brave new world that has such problems in it.'

Gerry looked up and grinned. 'Our Rosie keeps telling me I'm a dinosaur. She might well be right.'

Instead of replying Wesley shoved the Gemma Pollinger file across the desk. Gerry took out the photograph of the girl and studied it. It was a school photograph and the girl in the purple uniform looked uncomfortable, as though she didn't like having her picture taken.

'She's what my old gran would have called homely,' Gerry said, glad of the distraction. 'She's the only one of the victims Temples never painted in the nude.'

Wesley looked surprised. 'Really? Then how do we know she was there?'

'Her clothes were found at Strangefields Farm, hidden in one of the old barns with the other victims' stuff. He destroyed a lot of forensic evidence when he dumped his victims' bodies in the river but he couldn't resist keeping the clothes as souvenirs. There was a piece of metal piping with their blood on it in that barn as well – the pathologist reckoned he'd used it to knock them out. Then there was the knife he used on their faces. Suppose he thought they'd never be found. Turned out to be his big mistake.'

'It guaranteed his conviction.'

'That and his paintings of Nerys, Jacky and Carrie.' Gerry paused. 'I don't envy you and Rach having to interview him. He gave me the creeps and those paintings were downright weird. He painted them naked with ropes around their necks, laid out as though they were dead. Said it was art. He used to go on about the undead. Revenants – reanimated corpses. Like I said, weird.'

'What about the other girls – the ones who went there and got out unharmed?'

'The paintings he did of them were quite ... conventional; a mixture of nudes and portraits. Most of his models were identified at the time – they were all local girls so they weren't hard to find. There were a couple of nude paintings of girls who weren't located and they were taken to Morbay too just in case they turned out to be victims. But nobody else was reported missing so they were probably just young lasses who were too embarrassed to come forward.'

'Do you think Temples was trying to convince the jury that he wasn't responsible for his actions?'

'Playing the insanity card. That's what my boss thought at the time. Only I wasn't so sure and the jury didn't buy it. You'll be able to judge for yourself tomorrow.'

'He never painted Linda Payne?' Wesley asked, thinking of the photograph found in her loft.

'Her name didn't come up in the investigation at all.'

'What happened to the paintings?'

'The ones of the victims were brought in as evidence but I don't know what happened to the others. Hopefully someone put them on a bonfire.'

'Some of the girls who survived gave evidence at his trial, didn't they?'

'That's right. Five came forward. They were called for the defence and everyone was keen to save them embarrassment so they gave evidence from behind a screen.'

'I'd like to speak to them.'

'We can try to trace them, although they could be anywhere after all these years.'

'I'd like someone to speak to Carrie Bullen's family too. Before she killed herself she might have told them something she hadn't shared with the police.'

Gerry nodded slowly. 'Rather you than me.'

Wesley left the office and stood by the doorway, watching Rachel typing into her computer, deep in concentration. Coming face to face with Jackson Temples wasn't something he was looking forward to.

From the first diary of
Lemuel Strange, gentleman

5th September 1666

My wife wrote that the stench of burning fills the air and every man and woman is come away laden with goods to save and even the sick are carried in their beds. Houses are being pulled down but the fire overtakes faster than this is done. Carts rumble in the streets removing goods from one house to another and my wife has taken some of our belongings to her father's house in Islington and some she has told the servants to bury in our garden against the flames.

I would write to her to stay with her father but I fear she has already departed to join me here in Devonshire. She has no liking for her father's new wife and I suspect this is the reason for her journey rather than a wifely desire to be with me.

It was difficult to guess Frances's feelings when I broke the news of my wife's imminent arrival. Her face was like a mask and I wondered what turmoil of emotion surged within. She has suffered much and I hope my wife will not add to her troubles for she can be most critical of others and their households.

My conversation with Frances that evening was awkward until there came a thunderous knocking on the door. John looked most concerned as he went to answer and when he returned he was pale as a ghost.

'It is Master Sumner,' he said. 'And he wishes to speak with the mistress.'

Frances rose, staring ahead like a prisoner approaching the gallows. 'Tell him I cannot see him,' she said in a hoarse whisper.

'He says the thing must be done soon or we will never sleep safe in our beds.'

At those words Frances began to weep.

27

Wesley had agreed to pick Rachel up at seven thirty the next morning. When the alarm clock shattered the quiet Pam rose too and they both made their way downstairs in silence, trying not to wake Della and the children. This was their time alone; their chance to say their goodbyes. After feeding Moriarty Pam made scrambled eggs on toast even though Wesley had offered to grab breakfast at a motorway services on the way. When she put the plate in front of him he thanked her, whispering, 'I'll miss you,' as he took her hand and gave it an affectionate squeeze.

She didn't reply and the rest of the breakfast was eaten in silence. All the words had been said many times before but it was unlike Pam to brood.

'Something wrong?' he asked as he stood up.

'Should there be?' Her words were sharp and he flinched as though she'd slapped him.

'Of course not,' he said, wondering if she'd somehow found out about his long-ago lapse with Rachel, something he'd regretted ever since. Besides, nothing had actually happened and there was no way she could know about the temptation he'd felt.

'I'll call you tonight,' he said as he snatched up his car

146

keys from the hall table. He hesitated. 'I'm not looking forward to meeting Jackson Temples. I've been bringing myself up to speed on his crimes and—'

'People still call Strangefields Farm "the murder house",' Pam said quietly. 'The kids I teach say the place is cursed and they weren't even born when it happened.'

'Old superstitions die hard,' Wesley said before kissing her goodbye, a kiss she didn't return.

She stood at the door in her dressing gown and as he drove away he saw her in his rear-view mirror staring after him. He felt uneasy, hoping her cancer hadn't returned; her last test had been clear but it was the only reason he could think of for her subdued behaviour.

He picked Rachel up at the cottage she shared with Trish Walton. It was a small, two-bedroomed place of indeterminate age with salmon-pink walls and an incongruously modern glass front door. Rachel answered his knock almost immediately as though she'd been waiting in the hallway. As she shut the door she shouted goodbye to Trish who appeared at the top of the narrow staircase already dressed for work. They weren't the only ones with an early start. Even Gerry had promised to be in the office before eight.

Unusually there were no hold-ups on the motorway and at two thirty-five, after stopping for a sandwich at the motorway services, they arrived at HM Prison Gumton Gate. The prison was situated in the hinterland between the conurbations of Manchester and Warrington and was Category A, high security and reserved for the worst offenders – like Jackson Temples.

The governor was expecting them so, after the customary searches and confirmation of their identities, they were led to her office. Wesley wanted to know everything there was about the man they were shortly to face.

The governor was a tall, capable-looking woman in her fifties with short grey hair and a sensible black suit. The only hint of frivolity was a cheerful brooch in the form of a yellow cat; Wesley wondered if she removed it when she wanted to appear more serious and authoritative. Her handshake was firm and when she'd invited them to sit she clasped her hands together and leaned forward as though she was preparing to share a confidence.

'Jackson – or Jack as he likes to be called – is one of our more interesting guests.' Wesley noticed a hint of a smile and suspected that a sense of humour lurked behind the austere exterior. She probably needed one in her job.

'I understand he's always protested his innocence.'

'You're quite right, Inspector. He's never admitted his guilt.'

'There was a question mark over his sanity at the time of his trial.'

'All the psychiatrists who've examined him say he's as sane as you or me. He knew exactly what he was doing, and the fact that he's always refused to confess hasn't helped his case. Neither has the fact that he attacked one of my officers. He claimed he was trying to defend another prisoner at the time but that contradicts what my officer told me.'

'You believed him?'

'The officer in question has an exemplary record. Temples was sentenced to thirty years minimum for a reason.'

'You've been told that a skull's been found at his former home?'

'Presumably his missing victim?'

'It's being analysed but an archaeologist friend of mine is keeping an open mind. He thinks it might have been buried for some time, possibly even centuries.'

The governor frowned. 'Let's hope it's the girl whose remains were never found, then at least her family will have some closure.'

'You're convinced of his guilt.'

'I go by what the courts decide, Inspector. That's my job. But yes, I think the jury made the right choice in the Temples case. There was plenty of evidence and the testimony of that girl who survived clinched it.'

'Her name was Carrie Bullen. She couldn't remember the actual attack. The last thing she recalled was being with Temples in his studio. Loss of memory is common after trauma, I believe.'

'Didn't she kill herself?'

'That's right.' Wesley thought it was time to change the subject. 'I understand he expressed certain unusual interests at the time of his trial. Revenants – corpses coming back to life to torment the living.'

The governor smiled again. 'Zombies and ghosts are quite an obsession of his. He reads everything he can on the subject in the prison library. In fact that's where he spends most of his time. He's writing a book.'

'Crime novel, is it?' It was the first time Rachel had spoken and the governor's smile widened.

'How did you guess? Only it's not the blood-and-gore serial killer stuff you'd expect. It's quite gentle actually – Agatha Christie-style village murder set in the nineteen fifties. He gave me a copy to read and I must say I rather enjoyed it – once I'd forced myself to forget who wrote it. I was pleasantly surprised.'

149

So was Wesley. 'Anything in it about the undead?'

'Quite a lot. The plot hinges around an old lady who claims to have seen a neighbour who died a few weeks previously. The neighbour's long-standing enemy in the village is found dead and the old lady insists the corpse is responsible. Quite a good plot actually. He's sent it off to agents.'

'Is that allowed?'

'I don't think there are any hard and fast rules about it but I must say if it was accepted I wouldn't feel happy about it. Mind you, it wouldn't surprise me if a publisher considered it good for publicity. I hear there's nothing like notoriety for getting to the top of the best-seller lists.'

Wesley didn't comment but he guessed she could well be right. 'Is there anything we should know before we interview him? Any subjects that make him angry or ...'

'If you get him onto the subject of the undead you'll start off on the right foot.'

'I'll remember.'

Ten minutes later they were sitting in the windowless interview room reserved for police interviews and meetings with lawyers. The room smelled of stale dinners, suggesting the kitchens weren't far away. It made Wesley feel claustrophobic and one glance at Rachel told him she wasn't comfortable there either. But he knew prison wasn't meant to be a place of comfort – not even for the representatives of law and order.

The door opened and Wesley stood up. The man who walked in, followed closely by a burly prison officer, was smaller than Wesley had expected and more slightly built. His dark hair was long and peppered with grey. At one time he would have been handsome but he carried too much weight around the middle and his face had the pallor of one who rarely sees sunlight. His mouth was wide and his eyes were a dull grey. He didn't look like a killer but then killers rarely did. If they did then, as Gerry had often observed, the police's job would be a lot easier.

'To what do I owe this pleasure?' Temples asked, his gaze focused on Rachel.

'We'd like a chat, that's all.'

'Two police officers don't come up all the way from Devon to pass the time of day. Has there been a development? New evidence?' He sat down and crossed his legs, apparently relaxed. But Wesley could see his nervous fingers pulling at the fabric of his grey sweatshirt.

Wesley had heard that question before and it had always been asked with eager hope. But Temples sounded unenthusiastic, as though he was going through the motions.

'Yes, there has been a development. Strangefields Farm has a new owner who's renovating the house and building an upmarket holiday village in the grounds. The builders working there made a discovery.'

'Dry rot?'

Wesley didn't react to the man's feeble attempt at humour. 'Worse than that. They found a skull.'

Temples looked at Wesley accusingly. 'It must have been planted. I know what you lot get up to.'

'You're denying that it belongs to Gemma Pollinger, the girl whose remains were never found?' said Wesley.

'Of course I am. I told the police who the killer was but they never listened.'

'You accused an artist called Jonny Sykes, who also had a studio at Strangefields Farm. You claimed he vanished without a word around the time the last girl went missing but the police found no evidence he was ever there – or that he even existed. Not even any of his paintings.'

'His paintings were there all right only the police mistook them for mine. Jonny used to copy my style – hadn't an idea of his own. He definitely existed. I even gave a description.'

'Which was so vague it could have fitted anybody. The other girls who modelled for you never saw him. The ones who got out alive,' he added.

'He worked in a studio at the other end of the house. That's why they never saw him. Besides, he didn't usually go in for portraits. Landscapes were his speciality.'

Temples half rose from his seat, glowering over Wesley who was relieved when the prison officer ordered him to sit and he obeyed without question.

'Let's get back to the skull,' said Wesley. 'How do you explain the fact that it was found in your former home?'

'I can't. I don't know anything about it.'

Wesley suspected he was lying. 'It was in the cellar, in a cupboard near the stairs. You see our problem, Mr Temples: you're a convicted killer and human remains are found in your former home.'

'It was an old house. Lots of people have lived there over the years. I hardly went down to that cellar except to get rid of junk I didn't want.'

'So you're blaming a former occupant?' said Rachel with disbelief, earning herself a scathing look from the prisoner.

'I'm not blaming anybody. My grandfather moved in after the war so this skull you're talking about could have been there before then. You're making lazy assumptions. The police always do.'

'Not in your case. The evidence against you was

overwhelming. The girls' clothes; the metal piping you used to render them unconscious; the rope you used to strangle them; the knife you used to mutilate their faces . . . '

'That evidence was planted. I was innocent.' Rachel received another hostile look. 'Have you finished? I've got things to do.'

'I'm afraid not,' said Wesley. 'There's been another murder.'

'Well I've got a cast-iron alibi this time,' Temples said with a smirk. 'You can ask anybody here. They'll vouch for me.'

Wesley ignored him and carried on. 'A woman was murdered a few days ago. Knocked out, strangled with a rope and her face mutilated with a knife. Her naked body was found in water – the lake at Bereton Nature Reserve. Someone's copying you, Jack. How do you feel about that?'

'They say imitation is the sincerest form of flattery, Inspector. Only it isn't me they were imitating because I didn't do it.'

'I wouldn't have thought you'd have much of a taste for old clichés, Jack. You being an author. The governor told us about your book.' He looked at Rachel. 'We're impressed.'

'When you're in here you have a lot of time on your hands. And as for clichés, I regard them as a form of shorthand. An easy way of expressing a point when you're talking to the ignorant.'

Wesley let the insult go unchallenged. 'I understand you have a particular interest in revenants – corpses who return from the dead.'

The dullness in Temples' eyes suddenly vanished. 'It's always been a fascination of mine. Most people have no knowledge of the subject apart from what they see in zombie movies. And zombies are part of Haitian folklore;

nothing to do with Devon.' He looked directly at Wesley. 'Are your people from Haiti by any chance? Is that why you're so interested?'

Wesley shook his head. He had no desire to share any details of his family's roots with a killer. 'My degree's in archaeology and I came across a number of what we termed deviant burials while I was studying, usually individuals who had met violent deaths or were outcasts from society.'

Wesley knew he had Temples' attention.

'They used to cut off the heads and placed boulders on the graves. Sometimes they'd cut out the hearts and burn them.'

'You didn't do any of those things to your victims. Weren't you afraid they'd come back and haunt you?'

The fervour in Temples' eyes vanished in an instant. 'Perhaps they would have done ... if I'd killed them,' he said quietly.

'Does anybody write to you in here?'

'Sometimes.'

'Anybody who wants to know about your crimes?'

'It happens. People can be very ghoulish. I get a lot of letters from ladies. Even proposals of marriage.'

Wesley noticed Rachel wrinkling her nose in disgust. He wished she hadn't shown such disapproval. Nothing would be gained from alienating the prisoner.

'Anybody you correspond with regularly?'

'One or two.'

Wesley resolved to ask the governor about the letters. If somebody had become obsessed with Temples' crimes, it might be a suitable place to start if they were searching for a copycat.

'How do you know Linda Payne?'

Temples straightened his back, suddenly alert. 'What about her?'

'Please answer the question.'

'Linda went away to London with her mother when she was small. She's my half-sister.'

This was something neither of them had expected. But it explained the photograph – and the secrecy about her background.

It was Rachel who spoke first. 'I'm sorry to have to tell you Linda's dead. It's her murder we're investigating.'

The little colour left in Temples' face drained away and his shock was palpable.

'Who knew you were related?'

'Not many people, I don't suppose. It wasn't something she boasted about. How did she . . . ?'

'Someone copied your MO.'

Temples buried his head in his hands and when he looked up Wesley saw tears welling in his eyes.

'Tell us about her,' said Wesley gently.

'My mother died when I was young and my father married again and his new wife had Linda. Then when my dad and the wife split up she went to London, taking Linda with her. Linda always used her mother's maiden name – Payne – and I didn't see her all the time she was growing up. Then one day she turned up at the farm out of the blue and said she'd fallen out with her mum so she'd come to find me – her long-lost half-brother.'

'When was this?'

'Nineteen ninety-six.'

'So she was there around the time of the murders? Why wasn't she called to give evidence at your trial?'

'She'd left before the girls started disappearing. Her

bitch of a mother found out where she was and she turned up and whisked her back to London. Linda was only fifteen and her mother didn't want her involved with me – thought I was bad news. I haven't seen her since then; neither of them even came to my trial.'

'Her name never came up in the investigation.'

'She was only young and I guess her mother did her best to keep her away from all the fuss. The last thing the old bitch would have wanted was for the press to get wind of the connection so she made sure they lay low.' Temples paused. 'To tell you the truth it upsets me to talk about Linda.'

'So you were close?'

'I wouldn't say so. But blood's thicker than water, isn't it?' He pressed his lips together in a stubborn line. The subject was closed.

They reported back to the governor before they left, breaking the news of Temples' half-sister's murder.

'My guess is that someone found out who she was and took revenge on her brother through her,' she said, echoing Wesley's own thoughts. The contents of the file labelled 'family' had been taken from Linda's cottage, suggesting the killer hadn't wanted them to discover Linda's true identity.

Before they left they were provided with details of everyone who'd corresponded with Jackson Temples while he'd been incarcerated there. As the electronic doors shut behind them and they found themselves once more in the world of the free, Wesley was engulfed by a feeling of relief. Nevertheless, he thought he'd connected with Temples through his sympathy at Linda's death and their shared interest in the past and slowly things were becoming clearer in his mind.

Then he heard Rachel's voice. 'It's almost five o'clock. Do you think we should stay up here tonight or drive back?'

Even though he'd warned Pam that he'd probably be away for the night he knew he should opt to drive back. However, it was rush hour; the time when the motorways were often transformed into giant car parks.

'Taking the traffic into account we'll face long delays if we leave now. I've been hearing horror stories of the journey taking eight hours or more so why don't we get some rest and set off first thing in the morning?'

His words sounded reasonable. But he couldn't forget what happened last time he'd been up north alone with Rachel and a small inner voice told him to get in the car and keep driving.

Instead he heard himself saying, 'I saw a Premier Inn on the way here. We could try there. And we'll need something to eat.'

Rachel nodded, with an almost imperceptible smile.

'We need to find out what part, if any, Linda Payne played in Temples' crimes all those years ago. And I want to know if any of the women who've been writing to Temples has been getting ideas about proving his innocence.'

'If there's a murder with the same MO they'll assume we'll think we got the wrong man and reopen the case.'

'Exactly,' said Wesley as he unlocked the car.

28

Wesley and Rachel agreed that they needed a drink so they made for the pub next to the hotel.

'This place reminds me of a barn,' Rachel said as they walked into the large empty bar.

'Well, you grew up on a farm so you should know.'

His words made her smile. After the tensions of the day they needed to wind down so once they'd eaten Rachel ordered a large glass of Pinot Grigio and Wesley a pint of bitter.

The beer was indifferent but he drank thirstily, as did Rachel. When her glass was empty she pushed it towards him.

'Another?'

She nodded and when he got back from the bar he saw her fidgeting with the beer mat in front of her, staring at it as though it was the most fascinating thing in the room. When he put the wine down in front of her the spell was broken and she looked up.

'You OK?'

She didn't answer. Instead she picked up the glass and drank.

'Is it Temples? Did you let him get to you?'

She shook her head. 'I can't believe women write to him. Actually propose to him.'

'No accounting for taste.'

She took another large gulp of her wine.

'Remember last time we came up north together?'

Her question made Wesley uneasy. 'I thought we'd agreed to put that behind us.'

'I know but . . . it's difficult.'

'Look, Rach, I—'

'I know what you're going to say. You love Pam and the kids and—'

'What about Nigel?'

He saw that her eyes were brimming with tears and he experienced a sudden urge to comfort her. But he sat quite still, nursing his beer.

'What about him?' she said, looking away.

He scanned the room, hoping no one was watching. Then he told himself it wouldn't have mattered if they were. Nobody knew them there. They were an anonymous couple and, for all anyone knew, they were together.

She looked at him, uncertainty in her eyes. 'We could always buy a bottle of wine – take it back to the hotel.'

'We should probably call it a night. We've got an early start in the morning.'

'It's Saturday night, Wes. I feel like making the most of my freedom.'

Wesley drained his glass and stood up. 'It's tempting but . . . '

Reluctantly she stood too and followed him out. They walked back to the hotel in silence and parted on the corridor. Their rooms were next door but one to each other. Too close, Wesley thought as he shut his door behind him.

A couple of minutes passed before he heard a soft tapping on the door. Even though he knew it wouldn't be wise to answer, he did.

'Can I come in?'

He stood aside, his heart beating fast. 'You should go, Rach,' he said gently.

'I need to talk to you.'

'What about?'

She made for the bed and sat down. Wesley took the armchair near the window.

'I don't know if I'm doing the right thing marrying Nigel.' She hesitated. 'I keep thinking about us together – you and me. I'm sorry. I know it's stupid but I can't help it.'

'Nigel's a good man. He'll make you happy.'

Wesley made his way over to her and when she stood up to face him he took her in his arms and kissed her cheek. He told himself it was a brotherly gesture, though if he'd been honest with himself he would have realised it was nothing of the kind. Then he thought of Pam. Temptation was all very well but he had a family and Pam's illness had brought home to him how much he really cared for her. Besides, he and Rachel had to work together and he'd witnessed office dalliances that had turned toxic. He took his arms from her shoulders and stepped back.

'You should go.'

She sighed. 'You're right. I know we should be sensible. But it's tempting to play with fire, isn't it?'

He ignored the remark. The last thing he wanted was a post-mortem about what had been said. 'What are you going to do about the wedding?'

She considered his question for a few moments. 'I'm

fond of Nigel and we come from the same world. He understands me. He doesn't even mind the job taking over.'

'Is fond enough? Can you see yourself growing old with him?'

'I could ask you the same about Pam.'

He hesitated. 'And you know what the answer would be.'

She gave him a sad smile. 'I'll go.'

'See you in the morning,' he said, trying to sound professional. 'We've got a killer to catch and it's time we found out more about Jackson Temples' fan club.'

From the first diary of
Lemuel Strange, gentleman

6th September 1666

When Frances retired to her chamber last night I
enquired of John as to the meaning of his words. What
was this thing that must be done soon and why?

At first I thought he would not answer then he spoke
and his words seemed to me most curious.

'They must be stopped from walking, sir, or else they
will return to torment us, for thus it is with evil souls.'

'You speak of Bess and Harry?' I asked for he had
spoken no names.

'The killers of my master and the tools of Satan
himself,' he replied with the fire of certainty in his eyes.

I asked him when this terrible deed would be
performed and he said it would be that night and I could
witness it if I so wished. I told him I had no desire to
be present at such an abomination and he left the chamber
muttering of demons and evil spirits. The encounter
disquieted me and I wondered what Frances thought of
the savagery that was about to be wrought on her behalf.

I was soon to have my answer when, to my surprise,

John knocked upon my chamber door not long after I had retired for the night, saying that the mistress wished me to go with her and her young son to the ruined chapel by the gates.

29

Danny Brice tied the string to Barney's collar. It was time to go walkies and, with his newly found wealth in his pocket, he might even treat them both to some bar food: a burger for himself and sausages for Barney. He tickled the dog's chin and was rewarded with a look of devotion that warmed his heart.

Stag and Roberta had gone out again, which was a relief. He never felt comfortable when they were there, whispering in corners, watching him. They had secrets and he wished he knew what they were – and whether they were planning any surprises for him. He'd sensed a coldness about them, perhaps even a ruthlessness, that made him afraid. Or maybe he was imagining things; since Kevin died nothing had been right, as though there was a gaping hole where his heart should be. Close to tears, he stroked Barney's soft coat and felt a sliver of comfort, although he knew nothing would be good again.

He stood up and tugged at the makeshift lead. It had started to rain outside so he shoved on his beanie and fastened his leather jacket – the real Kevin's jacket. It still smelled of Kevin and Danny slept with it every night. It had become his single most important possession.

He reached the pub on the corner and made for the small bar round the side. Not many pubs had separate public bars and lounge bars these days but this one was a relic of times past. The public bar had a battered lino floor and still smelled of tobacco even though the smoking ban had been in force for a decade. Its walls were mustard yellow and its clientele exclusively male. Danny had sold things here in the past, no questions asked, and besides, Vera, the elderly barmaid, had a soft spot for Barney.

He thought it must be his lucky day because as soon as he walked in he saw the man sitting in the corner alone. After buying a half of the cheapest bitter he went over and sat down beside him, waiting for Barney to settle on the grubby floor beneath the table before he spoke.

'I've got something you might be interested in,' Danny said, taking the bracelet from his pocket and passing it to his new companion under the table.

'Where did you get it?' The question was asked in a whisper.

'Found it.'

'I'll give you twenty.'

'Fifty. It's gold.'

'Thirty and that's your lot.'

'Done.'

Danny went back to the squat feeling pleased with his small triumph.

It was about time life dealt him some good luck.

On Sunday morning it was Rachel's turn to drive and the first part of the journey passed in silence. It was Wesley who spoke first, just as they passed the sign to Stoke on Trent.

'Fancy stopping for a coffee when we reach Gloucester services?'

'Let's see how we feel when we get there.' There was an awkward pause before she spoke again. 'I'm sorry about last night. I didn't mean all that to come out.'

'Nothing to be sorry about. Let's forget about it,' he said. 'Friends?'

'Friends.' She revved the engine to overtake a BMW.

After a couple of minutes Wesley broke the silence. 'Do you think Temples knows who's copying his MO?'

'You're thinking of the people who've been writing to him.' She thought for a few moments. 'Some people say there's something sexy about the power killers have over their victims but I can't see it myself. Let's face it, Wes, we've come across a lot of killers in our job and once we get them into the interview room most of them are pathetic.'

'Did you think Temples was pathetic?'

'No. I felt there was something ... unhealthy about him. Twisted.'

'Perhaps that's what he wanted us to believe. I think he was playing games with us but his reaction to the news of Linda's death was real enough.'

Once the conversation had returned to murder the atmosphere in the car lightened.

'Talking of Linda, her assistant, Jen, seemed a bit evasive when I asked her about the shop's accounts.'

'Think she's been cooking the books?'

'If she was afraid of Linda finding out, it would give her a motive for murder.'

'Rich Vernon said Linda mentioned something about the shop takings sometimes not tallying. Why don't you go and see Jen when we get back? Say you want to discuss your wedding flowers.'

There was a long pause. 'Yes, I'll still need flowers, won't I?'

Wesley and Rachel arrived back in Tradmouth shortly after lunch and, while Wesley made straight for the station, Rachel walked to the market where she found Linda Payne's shop open to catch the Sunday cemetery trade. Jen was taking her obligations to her late employer seriously.

When she pushed the shop door open the bell jangled loudly, startling her and making her jump. She hadn't realised she was so nervous about visiting the premises with their memories of the woman she'd last seen lying on Colin Bowman's mortuary table.

She'd expected the sound of the bell to bring Jen hurrying out of the back room to greet the newly arrived customer but there was no sign of her so Rachel stood for a while breathing in the scent of the fresh flowers that bloomed in buckets all around the shop. Even though she was there on police business she couldn't help admiring the colours and assessing each variety's suitability for her wedding bouquet. As nothing had been finalised yet it was still preying on her mind.

One display caught her attention. She'd seen it before but it hadn't really registered until now. In the far corner stood five tall containers wrapped in coils of rope that looped from vase to vase giving the display of tumbling silk flowers a nautical theme.

She called out Jen's name and a few seconds later the woman herself appeared in the doorway behind the counter wearing an apron that bore the name of the shop above a stylised rose.

'Hello, Rachel. What can I do for you? Have you come about your wedding flowers?' Jen sounded harassed, as though the situation was beginning to overwhelm her.

'Can we have a chat? Somewhere private?' Rachel looked at her hopefully and eventually Jen took the hint and switched the sign on the door to Closed before leading Rachel into the small room at the back of the shop. She'd been there before to discuss her floral requirements with Linda and little had changed. The mugs still stood upside down on the little stainless-steel draining board and boxes of oasis, ribbons and other tools of the florist's art stood stacked by a tall filing cabinet in the corner. An apron matching the one Jen was wearing hung from a hook behind the door; Linda's apron that she'd no longer need dangling there as though she could return any moment.

'Would you like a cup of tea? I've just boiled the kettle.'

Rachel accepted Jen's offer, watching as she took a pair of tea bags from their box on the shelf above the sink. Jen was very quiet as she poured the boiling water into the mugs and stood with her back to Rachel waiting for the tea to brew.

'Is something wrong?' Rachel asked after a long and awkward silence.

'No . . . well only about Linda. I still can't believe anybody would do that to her.'

'I know. It's hard.' Rachel was experienced in family liaison work so she was good at empathy, even though the effort sometimes left her drained.

'She was always so full of life.'

'You've been asked this before but have you remembered

anything – something she said or someone who came into the shop to see her? Anything at all.'

Jen shook her head, her eyes focused on the floor.

'A colleague of mine spoke to one of her fellow actors in the Harbourside Players. He said she mentioned something about the undead. Zombies. Does that ring a bell? Did she ever mention seeing someone she'd thought was dead?'

The florist shook her head again, more vigorously this time. 'No. Linda wasn't into that sort of thing, or not as far as I know.'

'There was also a suggestion that you'd been taking money from the till.'

Jen looked affronted. 'I don't know where you heard that but it's not true.' Rachel could hear the hurt in her voice, the pain of the wrongly accused. 'I borrowed a tenner once when I was short but I put it back a couple of days later.'

'Would Linda have noticed?'

Jen took a deep breath. 'She might have done but she never said anything.'

Rachel suspected the 'borrowing' hadn't been a one-off thing but she decided not to press the matter. She left a few moments before she asked her next question. 'Have you ever heard of Jackson Temples?'

Jen frowned. 'I know the name but ... '

'He lived round here – killed three women.'

Jen shook her head. 'I used to live up north but I think I heard about it on the news. Why?'

'Linda was his half-sister.'

A look of shock passed across Jen's face. 'She kept that quiet – still, you would, wouldn't you?'

Rachel eyed the filing cabinet in the corner, wondering whether the missing accounts were in there. She could have asked directly but she'd developed a relationship with Jen and was reluctant to upset her again without any solid evidence.

'By the way,' Jen said as though she'd read her mind. 'I've found those accounts.'

She walked over to the filing cabinet in the corner and took out a pink file which she handed to Rachel. 'I'm sure they're all in order,' she said as Rachel took them, feeling a stab of guilt.

30

Wesley would ideally have taken Rachel with him to see Gemma Pollinger's father – she was good with grieving relatives, having the right blend of sympathy and practicality. However, she was out, so he took Trish instead.

The families of Nerys Harred and Jacky Burns had already been spoken to and someone was due to visit Carrie Bullen's sister in Appledore the following day. So far none of the relatives had been able to supply any new information and Gerry feared that all they were doing was reopening old wounds. But it had to be done.

They'd only just discovered Timothy Pollinger's whereabouts – a nursing home on the outskirts of Exeter. According to the constable who'd been given the task of tracing the family, Pollinger's wife had died fifteen years ago, cause unknown. With her daughter murdered and her son having committed suicide, Wesley suspected a broken heart might have had something to do with it.

It was Sunday and when they entered the building the smell of stale roast dinners lingered in the air, reminding Wesley of his visit to HM Prison Gumton Gate the previous day.

They found Pollinger alone in one of the lounges, propped up in a tall winged chair upholstered in a blue wipeable material. An oxygen cylinder hissed gently by his side and he held a small plastic mask in his right hand.

After Wesley had reassured the care assistant who'd shown them in that he wouldn't tire the old man out, she left and he took a seat facing Pollinger's chair. The man's face was ash-pale but his darting blue eyes were the sort that missed nothing.

'We're sorry to have to bother you, Mr Pollinger,' Wesley began.

'I know why you've come. You've found her, haven't you?'

Wesley suddenly felt guilty that he couldn't tell the man he could finally lay his daughter to rest.

'We haven't. I'm sorry. But I'm hoping you might be able to help us. There's been another murder – very similar to—'

The old man turned his head away and put the oxygen mask to his face.

'I know it's hard for you but is there anything you can tell us about the time Gemma disappeared? Anything, however irrelevant you thought it was at the time, that would help us build up a picture.'

When Pollinger spoke again his voice was surprisingly strong. 'There were things I didn't say back then 'cause I didn't want to upset the missus.' He hesitated and Wesley sat on the edge of his chair, willing him to continue. 'Our Gemma wasn't easy. She fell out with us and used to go off God knows where. Disappeared for days on end sometimes. She had a job so she thought we had no right to tell her what to do. We tried our best but ... At first the missus hoped she'd gone off of her own accord. Then they found her clothes and necklace at that place and we knew we'd never see her again.' There was a lack of emotion in his voice; perhaps over the years all his tears had been shed.

172

'She was close to your son, I believe.'

Pollinger made a noise that sounded like a snort of derision. 'Close? Thick as thieves they were. Graham was ... easily led. He'd do anything she told him and I reckon he used to cover for her. He knew where she was all right but he never told us, not even when his mum was sick with worry. We gave her everything: best schools; riding lessons; anything she wanted. She threw it back in our faces.'

Wesley could tell his daughter's behaviour still hurt, even after all those years.

'While Graham was working for me I knew where he was. That changed once madam had him at her beck and call ...'

'You ran a business supplying Calor gas to yachts,' said Trish, who'd looked up the details of the case.

Pollinger smiled as he recalled happier times. 'Amongst other things. We used to deliver the supplies by boat and the business did well. Had four men working for me including Graham. He wasn't the brightest but, even so, I would have left the business to him if he hadn't ...'

'I'm sorry,' said Wesley quietly.

'Gemma had such a hold over him that he must have thought he couldn't carry on without her.' Tears were welling in his eyes now as he put the oxygen mask to his face again. 'Gemma wasn't easy but she didn't deserve that. Obsessed with that bloody artist, she was. Wouldn't listen to reason.'

Wesley looked at Trish. It was time to go and leave the father with his memories.

As they drove back to Tradmouth he felt a deep sadness, as well as fear. When you were a parent you were a hostage to fortune. All you could do was your best.

31

First thing on Monday morning Neil stood by the side of the trench staring down at the section of wall they'd uncovered the previous day, along with a few pieces of interesting medieval pottery. It wouldn't be unusual to build a chapel in such a place in medieval times because the lane opposite the gates would have been one of the ancient routes into the port of Tradmouth and journeys would have been arduous and fraught with danger. Finding such a chapel on the way would have given medieval men and women a chance to pray for good fortune in their business dealings or an opportunity to give thanks for a safe journey – a kind of spiritual filling station. There was however still the question of how the place had acquired the name Dead Man's Lane. Had it once been a place of fear rather than comfort? Neil's research had confirmed that there was no burial ground near the chapel and the town gallows had stood on the main road to the east so that wasn't the explanation. He'd have to keep searching for the answer.

His colleagues were experienced archaeologists who could safely be left to their own devices now that the digger had scraped off the top layer of soil. The second trench, the one that had already been partly excavated by the builders, was coming on nicely, although his team had yet to reach the bottom of the disturbed earth. Remembering the call to the radio station, his gut feeling told him there was something down there, which was why he'd given the order to dig slowly and carefully.

He scanned the soil inside the trenches for any more tell-tale signs of building materials and any change in the colour of the soil that would indicate a floor or a robbed-out wall. It had been a while since he'd felt this excited about a commercial dig and he tried to ignore the fact that, even if they had found the remains of an unknown medieval chapel, their prize might still be destroyed when the foundations for the nasty glass reception building were dug.

The skull still nagged at the back of Neil's mind like an unanswered question, frustrating, irritating. Jemima Baine had promised to get back to him with the results of her analysis as soon as possible but the process was slow and he was feeling impatient.

He heard someone calling his name and when he looked round he saw that his colleagues who'd been digging in the disturbed trench had jumped out and were staring down into the hole. He made his way over, picking his way carefully across the uneven earth.

'What have we got?'

'Bones. Look human,' was the answer.

Neil took out his phone. 'I'd better call the cops. Any sign of a skull?'

'Not yet.'

'Then carry on digging.'

Wesley checked his phone as soon as he reached the station and found a message from Neil. Human remains had been discovered and it looked as though something was missing – namely a skull.

He returned the call straight away.

'I had a word with the workmen and they've admitted that they came across the bones last Monday when they started digging the foundations for the new reception building.' Neil tutted. 'Jumping the gun before planning consent was given. Naughty. When they told Hamer what they'd found he told them to fill the hole in again and say nothing, only one of them had a conscience and called the radio station.'

'Why not us?'

'Don't think he likes the police much.'

'What does Hamer have to say for himself?'

'Haven't seen him.'

'Do you think the skull Glen Crowther found in the cellar could belong to the skeleton?'

'Can't say for certain yet but you don't find too many headless skeletons, do you?'

'I'll send someone over.'

'Can't you come yourself?' Neil sounded disappointed.

Wesley looked at his watch. There was a lot to do but this was something he couldn't resist. Half an hour later he was standing by the trench gazing down at the bones lying stark against the red-brown soil.

'Our friend with the digger said he found a couple of clay pipes near the bones along with the remains of a Bellarmine jug. He's now handed them over, I'm glad to say. They're in that tray over there.' He took a deep breath. 'In my professional opinion, judging by what was found in the grave, I'd say the bones are old – possibly seventeenth century or thereabouts. And it looks as if the grave had

176

been disturbed long before the digger got to work, probably years ago by someone digging a drain – which might explain how the skull came to be in the house.'

'So the ground might have been dug up in Temples' day?'

'My money's on it being a lot earlier than that. Remnants of the drain look Victorian.'

'Hope you're right.'

Neil shrugged. 'Jemima will confirm it in due course.' He pointed at the headless skeleton. 'That damage to the ribcage looks as though it was done post-mortem. I think someone removed the heart as well as the head.'

Neil saw Wesley shudder.

'It seems colder up here than it does down in town.'

'Views are good though.'

Wesley looked around, his attention caught by the words on the signpost just visible through the gates. 'Dead Man's Lane. Any idea how it got the name?'

'No, but I've heard the developers have applied to the council to get it changed back to its original name – Hall Lane.'

'You can't erase history,' said Wesley before returning to his car.

As Neil walked to the gate and watched his friend drive away the sun emerged from behind the clouds, and the shadow of the signpost was cast on the wall of the derelict cottage on the opposite side of the lane. By some freak of the light the shadow took on the shape of a figure, a hanged man dangling from a gallows. Neil stared for a few moments until the sun went behind the clouds and the figure suddenly vanished.

32

The brief visit to Neil's dig had provided Wesley with a welcome distraction from the case – and from his unease about Pam's distant manner at breakfast that morning. She'd hardly said two words to him and the possibility that she'd had disturbing news from the doctor that she didn't feel ready to share kept flitting through his mind as he entered the CID office.

To his disappointment nothing new had come in during his absence. He'd nursed a hope that the appeal for information the press office had put out on the local TV news the previous night might yield something but the only calls received had been from attention-seekers and the lonely who had no information but who needed a listening ear.

Their investigation into the two murders was moving too slowly for his liking. They needed a breakthrough and there were several people he wanted to speak to if he could find them, especially the girls who'd gone to Strangefields Farm to pose for Temples and emerged unscathed. One name in particular caught his eye: Jane Webster, who'd given evidence for the defence at the trial. She'd been in the sixth form when she'd met Temples, by all accounts a clever girl who'd started studying medicine at Bristol University by the time the case came to court. He'd asked someone to trace her current whereabouts, hoping for the best.

He also kept thinking of Carrie Bullen, the girl the press called 'the one that got away'. Unlike Jane, Carrie had been attacked and her experience at Temples' hands had left her so traumatised that shortly after the trial she'd taken an overdose of sleeping tablets and had never woken up. Even though Temples had been safely behind bars by then, nobody was able to protect her from her own feelings. Trish and Paul had set off for Appledore to visit her sister first thing that morning, but he wasn't getting his hopes up that she'd be able to tell them anything new.

Wesley sat down at his desk and made a list, just to get things straight in his mind. The governor of Gumton Gate had given him details of the people who'd corresponded with Temples and one of the DCs had been given the task of tracing them all.

Then there was the suspicion of Linda's fellow actor, Pauline Howe, that Linda and the director, Lance Pembry, had known each other in London. This might have been guesswork on her part but if there was history between the pair it needed to be followed up as well.

'Any thoughts on the Bert Cummings case?'

Gerry's voice broke Wesley's train of thought. He turned and saw the DCI standing behind him.

'I've asked someone to find out what they can about his background.'

Gerry sniffed. 'That's the thing with the elderly – they all have a lot of history, some good, some bad. Every time I go to a funeral someone gets to their feet and says the little old lady who spent all her time making tea for the Mothers' Union was an ace decoder at Bletchley Park during the war or the old boy who sat in the corner of the bar making a half of bitter last all night flew in the Battle of Britain. We underestimate the old at our peril, Wes. Besides.' He grinned. 'We'll all be old one day.'

'Bert taught maths, I believe.'

'I hated my maths teacher although I don't suppose he was murdered because someone once got one out of ten for their quadratic equations.'

Wesley smiled. Gerry was right. Either Bert's murder was connected with theft or it was personal, and if it was connected with something in his past they were bound to come across the information sooner or later. Secrets never stayed buried for ever.

They were interrupted by Trish who'd just arrived back and had made straight for Wesley's desk, still wearing her coat.

'Sir, Paul and I have seen Carrie Bullen's sister, Jodie.'

Wesley thought he could detect a slight blush at the mention of Paul's name and he wondered if the journey to the other side of Devon had rekindled Trish and Paul's former feelings for each other. But station romances were none of his business – not unless it affected their work.

'And?'

'When I told her about the similarity between the attack on her sister and Linda Payne's murder she asked if Temples was out of prison. I told her he wasn't. He's in the clear this time.'

'Did she say anything interesting?'

'She talked about Carrie's suicide. Said she was beautiful and the disfigurement of her face had been a constant reminder of what happened. In the end she just couldn't live with it.'

'Did she tell you anything we don't already know?'

'I asked her if Carrie had told her anything that hadn't come up in the investigation and the answer was no.' Trish hesitated. 'But . . . she claims to be a psychic.'

Wesley saw Gerry roll his eyes.

'She said she'd "seen" the attack on Carrie.'

'Seen? How?'

Wesley ignored the sceptical look on Gerry's face. 'What did she claim to see?'

'She said she saw Carrie laughing, even though she was tied up and couldn't move. And she said she could smell oil paints. Then she felt a pain . . . here.' She touched the top of her head. 'And she saw a rope like a hangman's noose.'

'She got all that by sitting through the trial,' said Gerry.

'And she said her attacker had a sweet smell – like perfume.'

'Aftershave?'

Wesley turned to Gerry. 'Was that mentioned at the trial?'

Gerry shook his head.

'Anything else?'

'She said she could feel hatred. Not lust or . . . just hatred. And jealousy. Then she said: "What if it wasn't Temples?"'

'Psychic? Sounds like a load of rubbish to me,' Gerry tutted. 'The evidence against Temples was overwhelming. It was him all right.'

Wesley wondered whether the boss's involvement in the original case was colouring his judgement. He preferred to keep an open mind.

'What if Jodie was lying and Carrie did tell her something before she killed herself?' he said.

Gerry snorted. 'That would mean she's protecting her sister's attacker and that wouldn't make sense.'

Wesley looked at Trish. 'You met her. What do you think?'

'I don't know. Who can tell what goes on in other people's minds?'

From the first diary of
Lemuel Strange, gentleman

6th September 1666

It seemed that half the town of Tradmouth was gathered there near the gates to the hall, many with flaming torches to light the scene.

I had noticed the little chapel there on my arrival, half fallen to ruin, and it was here that we stopped and the crowd fell silent and parted to let us through. It was a dark night and, with the moon vanished behind thick cloud, the leaping flames alone lit the spectators. I could see their faces twisted with hatred and anticipation which made me fear that much cruelty would be performed there that night.

I held fast onto Frances's arm but she did not acknowledge me as she stared ahead. Her gaze was focused on the spot where two men made ready with spades. I could see two patches of bare soil where the earth had been recently disturbed and I realised the men were preparing to dig there. Soon other men joined them, also with spades, and they began to shift the soil with practised ease.

I was close enough to see into the gaping holes they were creating and to my horror my worst fears were realised. In the torchlight I saw limbs inside these graves. Two bodies, unshrouded, naked and stinking.

I attempted to persuade Frances to abandon her vigil and leave that terrible place but she shook her head and said, 'It must be done else they will walk and make us all suffer for their sins.'

33

Rachel had just received bad news. Jen Barrow's latest email had been apologetic but this hadn't softened the blow. Jen had made the decision to shut the shop for a while and she was contemplating getting away from Tradmouth, destination unspecified. The shock of Linda's murder and the responsibility of coping on her own had proved too much for her, she said, and she couldn't say when she'd be back. She ended with the words 'sorry to let you down'.

Rachel's spirits sank further when she saw the number of other emails waiting in her inbox. When she started to trawl through them she spotted one from a detective constable based at Neston Police Station headed *Albert Cummings – information*. As soon as she'd read it she called Trish over.

'Come and have a look at this.'

Glad of a distraction from her paperwork, Trish hurried over.

'There was an incident when Bert Cummings was teaching at Fulton Grange – that private school on the other side of Neston which closed down a few years ago.'

'I thought he taught at Neston High School.'

'He must have worked at Fulton Grange before that. A

boy punched him because Bert put him in detention when he wanted to go to an art club. Cummings lost a couple of teeth – had to go to A and E.'

'Was the boy charged?

'Apparently not. For some reason it was never made official.

'So how come it's on record in Neston?'

'It's not, or rather not officially. The DC who emailed me only found out about it because he was talking about Cummings' murder to his brother-in-law who said he remembered him from his schooldays. He said the boy who attacked Bert had a history of making trouble and left soon after the incident.'

'What about Cummings?'

'He stayed on at Fulton Grange for a few more years then when the school got into financial trouble he took a job at Neston High where he worked until his retirement. He was popular and no other incidents were reported. Cummings had been giving the boy low marks and told him off for persistent disruptive behaviour so there was bad feeling between them. We've been assuming Bert didn't have an enemy in the world but now we've found one.'

'How old would this boy be now?'

'In his forties?'

'Do we have a name?'

'Jonathan Kilin.'

Rachel went over to tell Wesley. She had the feeling he'd want to know right away that Bert Cummings had at least one old enemy who might have wanted him dead.

34

Wesley asked one of the DCs drafted in from Neston to trace Jonathan Kilin. Anyone who'd borne a grudge against Bert Cummings had to be considered as a suspect.

He also wanted to speak to Jane Webster, one of the girls who'd given evidence for the defence in Jackson's trial. He was anxious to hear another side of the story. But he needed to be patient while the team tracked her down.

It was eight o'clock by the time he arrived home. He'd warned Pam that he probably wouldn't be back till bedtime so he'd been hoping she'd be pleased to see him back so early. But as he poured himself a glass of wine she seemed distant and the uneasiness he'd felt earlier returned.

'Are you OK?'

'Of course I am.'

'You haven't been to see the doctor or . . .'

'I told you, I'm fine.'

It was obvious she was in no mood to confide in him so he began to tell her about the case, feeling the urge to fill the awkward silence. He'd just poured himself another glass, trying to clear his mind, when Della clattered into the room on her steel crutches. Over the past couple of weeks she'd been able to abandon her wheelchair for short periods; hopefully a sign she was on the mend.

'You're back then.'

'Good evening to you too, Della,' he said. Although he found his mother-in-law's constant presence wearing, he suddenly realised she might be in possession of some useful knowledge.

'Della. Didn't you teach at Neston High at one time?'

She lowered herself carefully into the armchair, propping her crutches against the arm. 'I taught there two years when I was fresh out of university but a lot of water's passed under the bridge since then. Why are you asking?' Her question was cautious as though she feared Wesley was trying to rake up some unsavoury incident from her past.

'Did you know a school called Fulton Grange?'

She wrinkled her nose in disgust. 'That posh boarding school where poor Gemma Pollinger went. It was a bastion of privilege. I was glad when the place closed down.'

'Know anyone who taught there?'

Della thought for a few moments. 'As a matter of fact I do. My friend Stephen who taught with me at the college worked at Fulton Grange for a while before it closed.'

'I'd like to speak to him if that's possible.'

She eyed him suspiciously before whipping her phone from her pocket and selecting a number. After a brief conversation she turned to Wesley. 'Stephen says he'll be happy to have a chat tonight if you want to pop round. He lives in a converted lighthouse near Little Tradmouth Head.' She levered herself out of her seat with her crutch. 'He's expecting us. That wine'll be waiting for you when you get back.'

'You're coming too?'

'I haven't seen Stephen for a while and I'm going stir crazy here.'

Wesley knew he had no choice. Della was going to sit in on the interview whether he liked it or not. He promised Pam he wouldn't be long and when he held the passenger door open for Della he saw a look of triumph on her face. He wouldn't have put it past her to mislead him just to relieve her boredom and he hoped it wouldn't be a wasted journey. He made her promise to leave all the questions to him. The last thing he needed was for the conversation to veer off course.

After a fifteen-minute drive they arrived at the light-house. It was an isolated spot and Della told him that Stephen Kelly, who hadn't yet retired, lived alone there with his two cats. He was a popular, gregarious man, she explained. It was just that there were times when he pre-ferred to be alone with nature, his books and his music.

Wesley let Della make the introductions and shook the man's hand, before they were welcomed in. Stephen had the look of an academic, tall with a shock of grey hair and a mouth that turned up at the corners giving him an amiable expression. He also seemed glad of the company. Perhaps over the years solitude had lost its allure.

'When you were working at Fulton Grange did you know a teacher called Bert Cummings who taught maths?' Wesley asked once the pleasantries were over.

'Yes indeed. I heard about his murder. Terrible business. Have you any idea who's responsible?'

'That's what we're trying to establish,' said Wesley, reluctant to admit that they were floundering in the dark. 'What kind of a man was he? Was there ever any gossip about him?'

Although Wesley's strict churchgoing parents had always taught him that slandering others behind their backs was wrong and such misgivings tend to stick, in his job gossip was a useful tool. Gerry always said you could learn a lot from tittle-tattle.

'Wasn't he attacked by a burglar?'

'Please. I wouldn't ask if it wasn't important.'

Stephen sat down in his armchair and a large tabby cat leaped onto his lap. Wesley saw that Della was listening in silence, keeping her promise not to interfere. He hoped her co-operative mood would last.

'Bert Cummings was quite strict,' said Stephen. 'The kids respected him and he never had to raise his voice. He was one of the old school which meant he probably disapproved of my more progressive teaching methods, although he was always too polite to show it. He was a lot older than me, of course, so we didn't socialise or anything like that. He had a daughter and a grandson in Canada but I heard the daughter died of cancer and more recently the grandson was killed in a motor accident. Tragic.'

'You haven't mentioned Jonathan Kilin.'

Stephen rolled his eyes. 'Kilin wanted to go to some art club but his behaviour had been appalling so Bert put him in detention and the boy just lost it. Thank God Kilin was never in my class. His parents were decent people as far as I recall and they were horrified by what happened. And I believe he had a younger brother at another school who was no trouble whatsoever. But you get that in families, don't you? A rotten apple, a quirk of nature. Kilin was clever, mind you. Probably the type who'd go far. They say a lot of captains of industry have psychopathic tendencies, don't they?'

'Any idea what happened to him?'

'The head asked him to leave and I heard his family moved away from the area. Sorry, that's all I know. I'll tell you who else was at Fulton Grange while I was teaching there – Jackson Temples, the serial killer. He was the art teacher's star pupil. She used to sing his praises.'

Wesley stared at him, stunned. This was information he hadn't come across before, though that was hardly surprising. A serial killer was obviously not the sort of old boy a school would boast about in its prospectus.

'What do you remember about him?'

'I never actually taught him. I just remember the art teacher talking about him in the staffroom.'

'Did Bert teach him?'

'He might well have done. They were there around the same time.'

Wesley was silent, his mind racing.

'One of Temples' victims was at Fulton Grange too,' said Stephen. 'Gemma Pollinger. Mind you, she was ten years younger than Temples so they weren't there at the same time.' His face suddenly clouded. 'She was in my class for English but she'd left school by the time it happened.'

'What was she like?'

'An average girl – not the sort you'd notice, although I heard she was very good at maths – one of Bert Cummings' protégées. Shame she left after her GCSEs and didn't take it any further.' He sighed. 'I suppose she got the attention in death she never got in life. The family were dogged by tragedy, you know. Her brother, Graham, killed himself soon after her disappearance. Jumped off a cliff near Littlebury. I taught him too. Not too bright, I'm afraid – easily taken advantage of. I always felt sorry for him.'

'I've spoken to his father.'

There was no mistaking the grief on Stephen's face. If he hadn't particularly mourned the unremarkable Gemma, he'd certainly mourned her brother Graham.

'Did Kilin and Temples know each other?'

'I wouldn't know. I think Kilin was a few years younger, but their paths might have crossed – especially as they were both into art.'

There was sincerity in Wesley's thanks as they left. Stephen had provided them with vital information and there was a lot to think about. Jackson Temples and Bert might have known each other from Fulton Grange, but could Temples be the link between the murders of Bert and Linda? And they had to find Jonathan Kilin. Could a boy who bore Bert a grudge all those years ago have returned to kill him?

As soon as they arrived home Wesley rang the incident room and spoke to one of the officers on the graveyard shift to see what progress had been made in the search for Jonathan Kilin. He needed to speak to him sooner rather than later.

35

Now a few days had elapsed, Grace Compton was starting to have doubts about her sightings of Dale Keyes. She feared she'd made a fool of herself in front of Wesley and the thought made her cheeks burn. Yet the man she'd seen had looked so like Dale that the two men could have been twins.

She'd been working in her hotel room with the plans for the holiday village laid out before her on the desk, but now the digital clock beneath the TV told her it was nine o'clock and she needed a drink; just a glass of wine in the bar downstairs, although with nobody to talk to she always ended up drinking too fast. There were times she wished she'd brought a colleague with her to Tradmouth because she hated drinking on her own, trying to ignore the surreptitious knowing looks and the curious stares. There were some places women hadn't yet achieved full equality and one of them was in a hotel bar drinking alone.

She looked at her phone, wondering whether to call Maritia, then decided against it. Maritia was a busy woman, and Wesley would be working on his case. The local TV news was full of the two recent murders – the florist and the retired teacher, trawling over every grisly detail. Reporters had even been hanging around Strangefields Farm in the hope of resurrecting interest in the murders that had happened there years ago. They hadn't yet learned about the skull and the bones that had just been discovered and if they found out the builders would probably be called upon to ward them off, which wouldn't suit Joe Hamer at all.

She was on her own in a strange town and to her surprise she found herself longing for those days of certainty when she and Wesley had gone to the church youth club together and life had seemed so simple; those days when home had been a place of security and the future had been full of possibilities.

She decided not to brave the bar but she needed a break from work so she grabbed her coat before going downstairs. A walk on the waterfront and some fresh air would clear her head.

She left the hotel and walked towards the centre of town. To her left the water lapped against the embankment, the streetlights reflected on the dark ripples in pools of sparkling gold. The tourist boats bobbed at anchor at the end of pontoons and yachts lay in darkness although some of them showed lights in the cabins, suggesting someone was on board.

There was something strangely calming about the presence of water and she stood for a while inhaling the salty air, ignoring the group of youths on a nearby bench braying as they ate their fish and chips. At that moment she envied their carefree youthful confidence.

She was about to return to the hotel when a figure emerged from the cabin of one of the yachts moored below where she was standing. She could see the man quite clearly in the glow of the nearby streetlight and her heart began to beat faster. There was no doubt about it this time – the way he moved; his unconscious habit of scratching his chin. It was definitely him. She was tempted to call out a greeting but something stopped her.

Then she told herself she had nothing to lose but her dignity – and there was a chance she might even get back the money he owed her. She summoned her courage and shouted out to him: 'Fancy meeting you here.'

He froze and stared up at her, a horrified expression on his face. Shakespeare's words 'a guilty thing surprised' summed it up perfectly, she thought.

'Grace. What the hell are you doing here?'

'Working. I heard you were dead.'

'I ... er ...'

He vanished into the cabin, bolting like a terrified creature pursued by a wolf. 'What about that money you owe me?' she called after him, her words swallowed by the breeze from the river as her heart beat faster.

He'd disappeared below and she didn't fancy the precarious leap onto the bobbing yacht. He hadn't wanted to speak to her but he owed her money – and an explanation. If he thought she was giving up that easily he could think again.

Then, to her surprise, he reappeared on the deck.

He stood looking at her for a few moments before reaching out his hand. 'Well what are you waiting for? Come aboard.'

Danny hugged Kevin's leather jacket around his thin body and shivered as Barney nuzzled up to him. Stag and Roberta had gone out again; he had no idea where. They always lowered their voices to a whisper when he was around and they never said what they were up to. He suspected they had a secret and he wasn't sure what they'd do if they thought he was spying on them so he kept his distance.

He contemplated going to the pub to enjoy the buzz and the warmth while making a half last all night. Barney was bound to want another walk, he thought, persuading himself that he was only going to the pub for the dog's benefit, though the truth was that he didn't want to be around when Stag and Roberta got back. If they discovered the bracelet they must have dropped was missing they might assume he'd taken it. And they'd be right.

He was on his way out with Barney on the end of his length of string when he noticed Stag and Roberta's door was ajar. He hesitated, feeling the pull of temptation. Then his curiosity got the better of him and he pushed the door open wider, hovering on the threshold and breathing in the smell of dirty bed linen mingled with stale marijuana smoke.

He began opening the drawers in the battered dressing table but all he saw there was Roberta's underwear, grey from over-washing. He looked through the contents of the huge shabby wardrobe in the corner, disappointed when he found nothing of interest. Then as he was walking back to the door the creak of a floorboard beneath the threadbare rug that half covered the dusty wooden floor made him stop. He squatted down and when he pushed the rug back he was surprised to see that some of the boards had been cut to form a small trapdoor in the floor. And the cuts looked fresh.

His ears attuned to the sound of the shop door downstairs, he levered up the boards to reveal the hiding place.

He sat back on his heels and stared at the cavity between the bedroom floor and the ceiling below.

Apart from in a jeweller's window he'd never seen so many shiny valuables in one place.

From the first diary of
Lemuel Strange, gentleman

7th September 1666

I will never forget what I saw that night: the putrefying bodies of the young man and maid hacked with knives and axes and the stench of their torn-out hearts burning on the fire the men had lit nearby. Once the heads had been removed they were placed between the corpses' legs with little ceremony and great stones found to lay upon the bodies.

'They will not return to torment us now,' Frances said as we walked back to the hall. I saw a look of triumph on her face. Her husband's murderers had faced justice. And yet I was uneasy.

'Where have they hidden the treasure they took?' I asked.

'John will continue to search tomorrow,' she replied.

When I retired to my bed I could not sleep. How I wish my wife had resolved to stay with her father in Islington so she could attend to my affairs and see what can be salvaged from the fire, but she will arrive soon and I am loath to tell her of the dreadful things I have witnessed in this place.

36

Wesley rubbed his eyes. He hadn't slept well. Jonathan Kilin's attack on Bert Cummings had been churning through his head. Could a schoolboy who'd once assaulted his maths teacher be connected in any way to his murder decades later? He was intrigued by the possibility that Temples and Bert might have known each other from Fulton Grange. Had he discovered the link between Bert's and Linda's murders? Or was the fact that Bert and Temples had both spent time at the same school irrelevant to the case?

Gerry turned up at eight thirty, lumbering into his office without acknowledging anybody. Wesley followed him in and waited until he'd taken his coat off before he spoke. He could tell by the DCI's expression that he was in a bad mood.

Wesley began with an account of his meeting with Stephen Kelly.

'If I murdered every teacher who'd ever put me in detention the streets of Liverpool would be littered with corpses,' was Gerry's immediate reply.

'Fulton Grange is a link between our murders. Temples went there and Bert taught there.'

'Did Linda Payne go there?'

'No, but I think it's worth pursuing.'

Gerry nodded. Any connection, however tenuous it seemed, was worth following up.

'Anything new come in?'

'That rope the Harbourside Players use in the play to kill Linda Payne's character has been sent off to the lab. They say the results should be through in a few days. It's an old hemp rope, the same type Colin said was used to kill Linda, so if the killer's connected with the play it could be the murder weapon.'

'Can't the lab get it done any quicker?'

Wesley didn't reply. He wished things would happen as quickly in real life as they did on TV dramas.

'Well there's no reason to let Lance Pembry know the results aren't through yet, is there?' said Gerry with a hint of mischief. 'Let's go and ruffle his feathers.'

'We can send a couple of DCs.'

'No, Wes, I need some fresh air.'

When they arrived at Lance Pembry's address in Stoke Beeching Wesley was surprised to find that he lived in a modern bungalow not far from the village centre. Somehow he'd imagined that a London theatre director would have chosen something with a lot more character as a retirement retreat: a pretty cob cottage in the countryside perhaps or maybe a Georgian sea captain's residence in Tradmouth. The austere 1950s architecture of the house hardly suggested artistic sensibilities.

When Wesley rang the doorbell and waited, Gerry shifted from foot to foot impatiently. After a few moments he leaned across Wesley and rang the bell again, more urgently this time. As the bell's echoing chimes faded

Wesley saw a shape behind the frosted glass. Then the door opened slowly to reveal a woman in a wheelchair. Her black clothing was relieved by a bright scarf around her neck and her long grey hair was pinned away from her face by a colourful hair slide. It was a striking face with strong features and she wore a look of displeasure as the two officers introduced themselves and showed their warrant cards.

'Lance is in his den in the garden. Go round the side,' she said as though she was giving orders to a pair of recalcitrant footmen. Her voice was mellifluous, a clear voice trained for the stage.

'You are ... ?'

'Mrs Pembry. Better known as Isobel Helling in happier times. Lance is my husband.' There was no mistaking the bitterness in her voice. If Rich Vernon's hints about Pembry and Linda had any basis in truth perhaps this wasn't surprising.

Wesley glanced at Gerry and saw that he was impressed. 'Weren't you in that series filmed in Tradmouth? *The Call of the Sea*. Didn't you play Mrs Cordwainer, the captain's wife?'

The woman's expression seemed to soften. 'How clever of you to remember, Chief Inspector.'

'Our whole family used to watch it because it was supposed to be set in Liverpool. That's where I'm from.'

'I'd never have guessed,' the woman said with an amused smile. Gerry had been in Devon for many years but he hadn't lost his Liverpool accent. She sighed. 'That was a long time ago. Things have changed a lot since then.' She looked down at her wheelchair. 'I don't get out of the house very much these days, never mind working.'

'Was it your idea to retire to this area?' Wesley asked.

'Yes. I fell in love with South Devon while I was filming

here. I'd have liked to live in Tradmouth itself but the town's all hills and different levels which of course is part of its charm. However, I'm restricted to a bungalow on flat ground, I'm afraid.' She pressed her lips together. 'You don't want to stand there listening to me feeling sorry for myself. Go through the gate to your right. It isn't locked.'

She manoeuvred the wheelchair backwards and shut the door in their faces.

'You heard what the lady said,' Gerry muttered before heading round the side of the house with Wesley in his wake.

Lance Pembry's den proved more impressive than either man had expected. It was a large brick-built studio standing well away from the house. Glass folding doors took up the entire wall that faced onto the long garden, making it a light airy space. They could see Pembry sitting at a large antique oak desk, poring over what looked like a play script, deep in concentration. When Wesley tapped on the glass he started and turned in alarm but as soon as he realised who was disturbing him his face became a mask of innocent calm, although his eyes betrayed his disquiet.

Pembry rose and opened a section of the door to let them in.

'Sorry to bother you, Mr Pembry,' said Wesley. 'Your wife told us where to find you.'

Pembry waved a hand in the direction of a sofa. 'Do take a seat. What can I do for you?' Wesley sensed mild hostility behind his polite words. 'Your colleagues took one of our props away for examination: a rope. When can we have it back?'

'As soon as we've finished with it,' said Gerry. 'Shouldn't be long – provided they don't find anything suspicious.'

Pembry sounded nervous and Wesley couldn't help wondering why.

'Linda Payne used to live in London. She worked at a florist's in theatreland. Did you know her back then?'

'London's a big place, Inspector.'

'She told her colleague that people from the theatres used to use her shop. You were a director. Perhaps you were one of her customers.'

A flash of panic passed across Pembry's face and Wesley thought he was about to lie, but to his surprise he nodded.

'Yes, I admit I did know Linda back in London.'

'How well did you know her?'

There was a long silence, as though he was deciding how much it was wise to reveal. When he finally spoke it was almost in a whisper. 'I might as well tell you the truth because I don't want you going and asking questions in London. The theatre world is an incestuous place and if it was thought I was a suspect in a murder inquiry ... I'd rather come clean – lay my cards on the table.'

'That would be wise, sir,' said Wesley.

'The inspector's right,' said Gerry. 'Tell the truth and shame the devil – that's what my old mum used to say.'

Wesley could have done without Gerry's mum's words of wisdom but he sat on the edge of the settee in silent expectation, waiting for the revelations to begin.

'My wife used to be a well-known actor – at one point her career was far more successful than mine. Then some years ago she was involved in an accident and her limitations frustrate her so she isn't the easiest person to live with. She insisted on moving here, which meant I had to give up London and the work I loved so much. I hate this bloody bungalow. It reminds me of everything I've sacrificed for

Isobel. What I was and what I've become: trying to make amateurs work like professionals is like herding the proverbial cats.'

Wesley was taken aback by the bitterness in his voice. He'd assumed he'd retired voluntarily and that he was making the most of his opportunity to be a major figure in the South-West arts scene. 'If you felt that way why did you agree to come here?'

'One word, Inspector. Guilt. Isobel and I had had an argument and in a fit of pique I picked the car up from the garage where it was being serviced before the brakes had been fixed. The mechanic tried to stop me but I was in such a foul temper that I didn't listen to him and I just drove off. I was known for being stubborn and arrogant in those days. Sometimes it proved to be an advantage. I demanded high standards and produced brilliant work, even though I say it myself. But on this occasion ...'

'What happened?' Gerry asked.

'When I drove the car home everything seemed fine so I thought the mechanic had been fussing for nothing. He even rang the house but I put the phone down on him and left it off the hook. How stupid was that? Then Isobel went out in the car that evening and the brakes failed – all my fault for not listening. I've been paying for my mistake ever since. And before you ask, no, I've never been able to bring myself to leave her – not after I'd done that to her. But ...'

Wesley knew there was more to come so he waited patiently, hoping Gerry's impatience wouldn't make him break the spell.

When Pembry finally spoke it was in the hushed voice of a penitent making his confession to a priest. 'I've had a lot of affairs over the years – in fact that's what Isobel and

I were arguing about when ... There have been a lot more women since the accident but I've been discreet. My marriage might be purgatory, Inspector, but I still can't bring myself to hurt Isobel.'

'Was Linda Payne one of the women?' Wesley's question was gentle.

Pembry nodded. 'Linda was attractive – bubbly – and we had fun in London. It was nothing serious but ...' He glanced in the direction of the door as though he expected someone to be eavesdropping. 'Anyway, one day she turned up at a casting rehearsal for a previous production. I'd heard she'd moved to Devon but it's a big county and I was shocked to see her. And pleased, I suppose. We started meeting. Just fun. Nothing heavy. Then she began to make demands. She wanted me to cast her in main roles and when I refused she hinted that she'd tell Isobel about our affair.'

'She was blackmailing you?'

'I didn't think of it like that at the time, but yes, I suppose she was.'

'Her death was convenient for you then,' said Gerry.

'It's hardly convenient having the police coming round asking questions. And it's been very inconvenient for the production. Pauline the understudy's still not off the book and we open in a fortnight.'

Gerry frowned. 'Off the book?'

'She doesn't know her lines,' said Wesley, relieving Pembry of the burden of explanation.

'Did Linda get the part of the duchess because she put pressure on you?'

'If I'm being honest I would have preferred to cast Pauline straight away but I felt I had no choice. I can't risk hurting Isobel any more than I have already. I ruined her life and I'll pay for that until one of us dies.'

'Hasn't stopped you getting up to hanky-panky though.' Gerry's words were blunt, as though he'd seen through the show of repentance and the dramatic statements and wanted to expose the man's hypocrisy.

Pembry's face turned a vivid shade of red that made Wesley fear for his blood pressure but he didn't answer.

'Where were you on the night Linda Payne died? What did you do after the rehearsal?'

'I went for a drink with George who's playing Antonio and Hugh from the Arts Centre. We just had one in the Angel and then I drove straight home. Left the pub around twenty to eleven and got back at eleven on the dot. I know that because the church clock was chiming. Isobel was waiting up for me and she'll tell you I didn't go out again that night.'

Before they left they asked Isobel to confirm his story which she did without hesitation, although Wesley thought she recalled the evening a little too readily – almost as though her answer had been rehearsed.

'Well, he's got a motive,' said Gerry as they got into the car to drive back to Tradmouth.

'And Linda Payne was a blackmailer as well as being Jackson Temples' little sister. What if Lance Pembry wasn't the only person she was putting pressure on?'

'Then I'd say we've just got ourselves a new line of enquiry.'

37

As soon as he returned to the station Gerry phoned the lab. He needed the results on the rope used in the production of *The Duchess of Malfi*. Lance Pembry was now a suspect; perhaps it appealed to his theatrical turn of mind to copy the MO of a notorious local killer. Information about Jackson Temples' crimes was readily available on the internet; there for everyone to see and, if they felt so inclined, emulate.

He'd told Trish and Paul to have another word with members of the cast to see whether Linda knew anything about anyone's private life which might leave them open to blackmail, even blackmail of the most subtle variety. Yet, to Wesley, the murder of Linda Payne didn't seem like a spur-of-the-moment act and Gerry agreed. Someone had gone to a great deal of trouble to copy Temples' crimes.

When Rachel told Gerry that Jen Barrow was thinking of leaving Tradmouth he wasn't pleased. She could be a witness, he said, and they needed to know where to find her. But as he was about to vent his anger Wesley entered his office with a sheaf of papers in his hand.

'I've been trying to trace the girls who modelled for Temples and gave evidence on his behalf. Trish has spoken to one who's now up in Scotland but she couldn't add anything to her original statement.'

'What about the others?'

'Still working on it. I've also been reading though the letters Temples has been receiving in prison. Some of them are pretty explicit.'

He handed the copies to Gerry who scanned them quickly, his eyebrows rising a little higher as he turned each page. 'Well, they're imaginative, I'll give you that.'

'And they're not afraid of providing their names and addresses either – which is convenient for us. The nearest one has an address in Neston and she seems to be running a campaign on Facebook to get his conviction quashed. Fancy paying her a visit?'

'Why not? If she's local she might have been around at the time of the original case.'

'Her name's Hayley Rummage and she lives on that new estate near the castle. I've looked her up on the PNC. Nothing known.'

'What about the others?'

'The next nearest one's in Sheffield. Then there's one up in Aberdeen and another in Belgium. There's even one in the States.'

'What do they get out of it?'

Wesley considered the question for a moment. 'Probably a fantasy thing. Sex with a strangler?'

'Each to his own, I suppose. Did he receive any letters other than fan mail? Any threatening revenge?'

'About fifteen years ago Gemma Pollinger's mother wrote begging him to say what he'd done with her body.'

'Did he reply?'

Wesley shook his head.

'Doesn't bear thinking about, does it?'

'There's something else that might be worth following up,' said Wesley. 'Rob's found a website that's selling Temples' work.'

'His art, you mean?'

'Before his arrest he was an up-and-coming artist who sold his work in galleries throughout the West Country. It was said at his trial that that was why he found it so easy to lure his victims back to Strangefields Farm to pose for him.'

'Nude.'

'Not all of them. He did a lot of portraits and conventional nude studies which, I guess, were left at Strangefields Farm. Only the nastier ones were produced at the trial and as far as I know they're still in the evidence store at Morbay nick.'

Gerry sighed. 'Temples always claimed he was just pushing the boundaries – pushed them a bit too far if you ask me and those lasses died as a result.'

'Well, someone's flogging his pictures for a fortune. Temples' notoriety has no doubt added to their value.'

'Can we trace the seller?'

'I've got Tom from Scientific Support working on it. I'd like to pay this Hayley Rummage a visit. We could send a couple of DCs but I'd like to meet her for myself. I'm curious.'

'Me too. I'd go with you if I didn't have a meeting with the press officer to discuss the latest statement.' He didn't look too pleased at the prospect. 'According to her they've got wind of a possible connection between our two murders and she's been under siege.'

Wesley noticed that Rachel was standing by the window, taking a well-earned break from her paperwork. She was gazing out at the view across the river and sipping a cup of coffee. She looked as though her thoughts were miles away. 'I'll take Rachel. I'd value her opinion.'

When he told Rachel his plans she swigged back what remained of her coffee and fetched her coat.

'I've read the letters Rummage wrote to Temples,' she said as they made their way to the car park. 'She must be a bit of a weirdo. What do we know about her?'

'No criminal record. But having the hots for a serial killer isn't regarded as an offence.'

It was four o'clock by the time they reached Hayley Rummage's address: a small modern semi on a new estate on the outskirts of the pretty Elizabethan town of Neston, eight miles upriver from Tradmouth. Wesley knew they'd find her home because Rachel had rung on ahead, although she hadn't told her the reason for their visit. Wesley hoped it would come as a surprise.

The woman who answered the door was in her forties with the intense look of a habitual worrier. Her short spiky hair was dyed ash-blond and she wore pair of thick-rimmed spectacles.

'What's this about?' she asked after they'd showed her their ID. The question was guarded, as though she had a guilty conscience.

When Wesley asked if they could talk inside she stood aside reluctantly to let them enter. The small living room was neat and soulless and Wesley and Rachel seated themselves on the corner sofa that dominated the space.

Wesley gave Rachel a small nod. It would be up to her to begin.

'Have you lived in Neston long, Ms Rummage?'

'Just a year. Why?'

'Do you work?'

'For a charity that helps offenders. Not the sort of thing you'd be interested in. What is it you want?' She was on the defensive and Wesley wondered why.

'We've been to visit Jackson Temples in prison,' said Rachel.

She blushed and her body tensed. Then suddenly she straightened herself up and looked Wesley in the eye.

'How is he?' There was a challenge in the question.

'He seems well. Did you know him before he went to prison?' He calculated that she would have been a teenager at the time Temples had committed his crimes. 'Did you ever go to Strangefields Farm? Were you one of the girls who posed for him?'

She shook her head. 'I've never actually met him.' It sounded as though this was a cause for regret. 'But it upsets me to think of him locked up in there deprived of all the freedom we all take for granted. For a man with his remarkable talent to be confined in a tiny cell for hour upon hour without daylight or—'

Rachel couldn't listen to this any longer. 'He murdered three women and was responsible for the suicide of a fourth. I wouldn't waste your sympathy.'

She shook her head again, more vigorously this time. 'You're wrong. He's innocent. He was framed by your lot. It's always happening.'

'Not true.' Rachel lowered her voice, affronted at the accusation.

'It is true. And it's been happening on your watch, Detective Sergeant.' She turned to Wesley. 'And yours, Inspector. I work for Rights for Prisoners and virtually all the ex-prisoners we deal with say they were wrongfully imprisoned.'

'Well, they would say that, wouldn't they?' said Wesley reasonably.

'It's that attitude that causes the problem.'

Wesley recognised in her the kind of intensity that robs a person of the ability to see the alternative point of view; the sort of intensity that, twisted, can create a fanatic or a terrorist. It was time to come to the point.

'You've been writing to Temples.'

'I do what I can to give him comfort in his situation. Is that so wrong?'

'From your letters you seem to be ...' He searched for the right word but in the end he opted for simplicity. 'You seem to be in love with him.'

'What's wrong with that? Love is better than the hatred he's been subjected to over the past two decades. Did you know he won't be considered for release because he refuses to confess? Does it ever occur to anybody that he might not admit to those murders because he didn't commit them?'

'There was the testimony of Carrie Bullen, the girl who survived,' said Rachel. 'She described posing for Temples before the attack.'

'But the attack left her with amnesia. She couldn't remember what actually happened, could she?'

'There was forensic evidence that all the victims had been at Strangefields Farm.'

'He was an artist. They modelled for him. He freely admitted that.'

'With a rope around their necks. The post-mortems revealed that an identical rope was used in their murders and the victims' clothes were found hidden on his premises.'

'I'm familiar with the details of the case,' she snapped.

'There was another artist working there called Jonny Sykes. Why was he never questioned?'

'Because no evidence was found that he ever existed.' Rachel sounded as though she was losing her patience. 'None of the girls who survived ever saw him and the jury concluded that he was a figment of Temples' imagination. A handy scapegoat.'

'Jackson said he cleared out taking all his stuff with him when the last girl went missing but the police made no attempt to find him.'

'There was an extensive search for him but nobody of that name who fitted the description Temples gave was ever found. Jonny Sykes didn't exist.'

'Then he must have been using a false name,' she shouted. 'It's no use talking to you. Your minds are closed.'

Wesley shot Rachel a warning look. It would do them no good to get embroiled in an argument with the woman.

'I'm afraid the nature of this case and the thought of those innocent victims tends to arouse strong feelings in the people who have to deal with the aftermath,' said Wesley quietly, giving Hayley Rummage his most disarming smile. 'But I can assure you I've never knowingly locked anybody up I didn't believe to be guilty. And we do have to think about those poor young women who've been deprived of the chance of growing old and having families of their own. They're my main concern. That's why Sergeant Tracey and I do the job we do.'

Hayley opened her mouth to reply but no words came out.

'I take it you're familiar with the details of the Temples case?'

She sniffed. 'I made it my business to learn all I could when I began writing to him.'

'Have you read the transcript of the trial?'

'Yes.'

'So you know what was done to the victims?'

She looked away as though she couldn't bear to face the uncomfortable reality of Temples' crimes. But Wesley intended to force her to confront it and after a few seconds she turned back to face him, her eyes glowing with defiance.

'I've spoken to one of the women who gave evidence on his behalf. She's convinced of his innocence too.'

Wesley and Rachel glanced at each other. 'What's her name?'

'Jane Webster. She's a GP here in Neston. You couldn't find a more reliable witness.'

'Which surgery?'

'Parr Court. She still uses her maiden name professionally.'

Wesley took a deep breath. Jane was a colleague of Maritia's and he cursed himself for not finding her sooner. Now by chance it seemed his luck was in.

'Have you ever visited a florist's shop in Tradmouth? The one opposite the market.'

Hayley looked confused by the change of subject. 'No. Never.'

'Have you ever had any dealings with the Harbourside Players? It's a drama group based at Tradmouth Arts Centre.'

'No. Why?'

'Do you know a woman called Linda Payne?'

'I've heard her name on the local news recently but I didn't know her. Why should I?'

She was starting to look uncomfortable – which was exactly what Wesley wanted. Rachel looked as though she was long-ing to jump in and say something but Wesley gave her an almost imperceptible shake of his head. As he seemed to have established some sort of rapport with the woman, he was going to be the one who did the talking for the time being.

'Linda Payne was Jackson Temples' half-sister, although it wasn't something she made widely known.'

Hayley's mouth fell open. 'I didn't know. She's never been mentioned ...'

'She was killed in exactly the same way as Jackson Temples' victims.'

A look of triumph appeared on Hayley's face. 'I think that proves his innocence once and for all, doesn't it? The killer's still out there.'

'Another possibility is that somebody's copying his MO. Perhaps somebody who's trying to prove Temples' innocence.' He tilted his head to one side, waiting for the implication to sink in.

'Well, don't look at me. I've never killed anybody.'

'People will go to any lengths for love, Ms Rummage. You proposed to Jackson Temples in your letters, which presumably means you love him enough to marry him. Or rather you love the idea of him because you've never actually met him, have you?'

She stood up, anger burning in her eyes. 'Get out,' she said, pointing at the door. 'I want you to leave. Now.'

'Can you tell us where you were last Monday – that was the night of Linda Payne's murder?'

For a few moments she didn't move and Wesley could see the fire of her righteous indignation ebbing away. Then she bowed to the inevitable and searched in the depths of a large worn denim bag that lay on the floor by the side of the sofa. She brought out a diary and once she'd found the right page she thrust it in Rachel's face.

'I was at a meeting all evening. Then I went for a drink with the others afterwards; didn't get back till midnight. You can ask anybody who was there.'

'If you give us the names we will,' said Rachel. 'Thank you for your time.'

After the names were provided they left, keen to get away.

'He's innocent, you know,' Hayley called after them as they walked to the car. 'One day soon you're going to realise you've made a big mistake.'

'Do you think she's capable of murder?' Wesley asked when they drove away.

'I don't think it, Wes, I know it.'

38

There was no time like the present, Wesley thought as he parked outside the surgery where his sister worked. He had wondered whether to contact Maritia but in the end he'd decided against it. If his visit to Dr Webster came as a surprise it could be to his advantage.

When he came face to face with the receptionist, however, he had second thoughts about the wisdom of his decision. The woman looked him up and down, clearly taking him for a malingerer.

'Can we speak to Dr Webster, please?' he said, showing his ID discreetly.

Rachel was standing behind him as though she was queuing to be seen and she too flashed her ID.

'Nothing to worry about. Just routine,' he added with a smile.

'She's with a patient.'

'In that case is Dr Fitzgerald available? I'm her brother.'

The woman eyed him suspiciously as though she suspected him of lying. 'She's out on call. You'll have to wait.'

Wesley and Rachel meekly took a seat on a plastic bench, knowing argument was useless. The man next to Rachel was coughing dramatically and she edged closer to Wesley. If you wanted to get sick this was the right place to come.

After a ten-minute wait an elderly woman emerged from one of the surgeries and the receptionist barked, 'Dr Webster's free now. Surgery Three.'

It took Wesley a few seconds to realise that she was addressing him and when he and Rachel stood up they received a hostile look from the coughing man. Nobody liked a queue jumper.

The woman sitting behind the surgery desk was in her late thirties, tall and slim with shoulder-length brown hair, a pleasant, sympathetic face and very blue eyes. She gave them a professional smile as they took the two seats on the patients' side of the desk.

'Doreen on reception tells me you're Maritia's brother.'

'That's right.'

The doctor suddenly seemed more relaxed now that Wesley's credentials had been established.

'You're a policeman, I believe.'

'That's right. Tradmouth CID.'

'Then how can I help you?'

'We're investigating the death of Linda Payne. You've heard about it.'

'I have indeed. Same MO as the Jackson Temples murders, I understand. And I'm guessing you want to speak to me because I gave evidence at his trial.'

Wesley was relieved that she'd caught on so readily. 'That's right.'

'All I can say is what I told the police at the time. I was a silly seventeen-year-old intent on smashing my parents' barriers. I went to the Green Parrot with two friends from school.'

'Which school?'

'Morbay Grammar. Temples approached me – said I was beautiful and he wanted to paint me. I was flattered and we went back to Strangefields Farm with him to be painted. We thought it was a great adventure and I felt so sophisticated, drinking and smoking dope with an artist. He chose to paint me rather than the others which gave me a lot of street cred with my friends, I can tell you.'

'And all of you got out unharmed?'

'We did.' She hesitated. 'In fact we were shocked when we heard of his arrest. The murders were in the news but all it said was that the girls had been to the Green Parrot and had gone back to Strangefields just like we had. There were three of us together so perhaps it was a case of safety in numbers. Even so, my parents went berserk when they found out where I'd been. They said it could have been any of us but . . .'

'But?' Rachel was on the edge of her seat, waiting for her to continue.

'At the trial there was talk of the dead girls posing naked, all tied up with nooses around their necks, but I didn't see any of that. OK, after he'd done a conventional portrait of me I agreed to pose nude, which I thought was really daring, and he did a quick sketch of me – a life study really. But he never touched me and I never felt as though I was in any danger. At the trial I could only tell the truth, couldn't I?'

'Hayley Rummage has been in touch with you?'

'Yes.' She smiled. 'She's a strange woman but I couldn't in all honesty tell her she was deluded. I saw nothing at Strangefields Farm to make me think Jackson Temples killed those girls, although he was intense and probably very weird so I might be mistaken. He might have behaved quite differently once he got those girls alone – but my gut feeling still tells me he was innocent.'

Wesley had rarely come across a better witness and he had more questions to ask.

'Temples claimed there was another artist there. A Jonny Sykes. He was never traced.'

'I never saw another man there but that doesn't mean he didn't exist. Strangefields was a big place. I saw those paintings at the trial ... the ones of his victims tied up with ropes. Temples didn't deny painting them but I did wonder whether they were the work of this Jonny Sykes and he was covering for him for some reason. Mind you, they were certainly in Temples' style.'

'Did you ever see anyone else when you were at Strangefields? A younger girl, for instance?'

She frowned. 'There was a girl there who was even younger than us. She brought Temples some beer on one occasion. I'm ashamed to say we didn't take much notice of her. We were too busy having a good time.'

'Did you tell the police about her?'

'Don't think so. They never asked so I didn't think it was important.'

'What about the girls who died: Nerys Harred, Jacky Burns and Gemma Pollinger? And the one who survived the attack. Carrie Bullen?'

'I never met them. And they didn't go to my school so I didn't know them. They were just names in the newspaper, I'm afraid. Sorry.'

Wesley stood up. 'Thank you for your time, Doctor. You've been very helpful.'

For a moment Jane looked unsure of herself. Then she

spoke again. 'When we were all sitting around drinking Temples told us a story about a man who once lived in the house. He said he'd come back from the dead and that he was still there.' She gave a nervous laugh. 'He was just trying to scare us, of course. It was all nonsense.'

When Wesley and Rachel left the room he glanced back and saw that she was sitting quite still, staring ahead lost in thought.

From the first diary of
Lemuel Strange, gentleman

15th September 1666

The fire, my wife tells me, raged four days and nights and our house is destroyed, which causes her much distress.

I met her on the quayside at Tradmouth for she sailed from London, having taken a wherry to Tower Wharf to find the ship of a captain of my acquaintance. The captain attested that London is burned and St Paul's is a miserable sight with all the roofs fallen.

Frances says we may make Strangefields Hall our home for as long as we wish and I am thankful, although my wife says only that Tradmouth is not London and she wishes to return. I tell her our home is gone and Strangefields is a good place and beg her to consider Frances's offer. She is, after all, a widow alone in the world apart from her son.

There have been no further sightings of Harry and Bess and all say their spirits are now in hell. I have not told my wife of what I witnessed that night.

The people round about now call the lane near where they lie buried Dead Man's Lane. Yet I like not this reminder of that terrible time.

39

Neil Watson hated meetings. He hated listening to planners and developers talking about foundations and profit margins. He always had the feeling he wasn't wanted there; that archaeological assessments – and, worse still, actual excavations – got in the way of making money. Even so, he always stood his ground because the past was too important to sacrifice for a fast buck – or a hideous reception building.

That morning's meeting at Strangefields Farm had been mercifully short because Grace Compton hadn't turned up. He had to admit that he felt a sneaking admiration for the architect – an attractive woman from an ethnic minority who could more than hold her own in the ruthless world of developers. And apparently she was an old friend of Wesley's which, he supposed, was a recommendation of sorts. He did wonder why Wesley had never mentioned her before, either recently or during their student days, but Grace also knew Maritia so perhaps she'd been more her friend than Wesley's.

When Neil had broken the news about the skeleton the atmosphere in the meeting had been tense – and that was before he'd mentioned the possible presence of a chapel on the site of the proposed reception building. He could almost smell the financial disappointment in the stale air of the old house which had been stripped of its oak panelling to allow the builders to do their work unhindered. After dodging with practised ease the vexed questions of how long the discovery of human remains would delay matters, he left, saying he had to get back to work.

He walked down the long drive towards the gates, his hands thrust into the pockets of the ancient combat jacket he always wore for work. He'd wondered whether he should have brought something smarter in his car to wear at the meeting but he couldn't be bothered. He was an archaeologist, not an accountant, and if they didn't like it that was their problem.

When he arrived at the trenches his team were so engrossed in their work that they barely noticed his arrival. He stood at the edge of Trench One and watched for a while before going over to the marquee to see if there was anything interesting in the finds trays.

He was examining an early eighteenth-century clay pipe when he heard someone shout his name, followed by the chatter of excited voices.

When he emerged from the tent he saw that everyone had assembled around the edges of Trench Two where they stood staring into the hole like children gathered around a toyshop window. 'What is it?'

'Come and see what we've found,' said Neil's second-in-command, a young woman with cropped hair and a no-nonsense manner.

The team parted to let him through and as Neil looked down he saw the first suggestion of a ribcage, clearly visible against the dark soil and half covered by a large stone.

After the discovery of the first skeleton he'd done

some research and concluded that the burial had all the appearances of the kind of ritual used to keep the dead from rising to plague the living, especially wrongdoers or outcasts from society. The revenant – the one who returns – had been part of everyday belief and folklore for centuries, even up to recent times, and he'd been excited at the possibility that he'd found evidence of that belief at the Dead Man's Lane site.

'Start exposing it. But be careful.'

His phone began to ring, the caller display telling him it was Jemima Baine. He answered, watching his colleagues as they worked away in the trench.

'I've got news about your skull,' Jemima said without any preliminary pleasantries. 'Estimated date is between sixteen fifty and sixteen ninety. And she was brought up in the South Devon area. By the way, the soil that was clinging to the inside of the skull has been analysed as well. The techniques are remarkably accurate these days and I always believe in being thorough.'

'And?'

'It matches the composition of soil found in the area just above Tradmouth where your skeleton was discovered. I'm running tests to match the skull with the bones.'

'All we need now is to find out why she was buried like that,' he said.

It took a couple of hours before enough of the second skeleton was uncovered to confirm that it was definitely human. But instead of the skull resting in the usual place, it was grinning out from between the corpse's legs.

40

Wesley felt a little disappointed when Hayley Rummage's alibi for the time of Linda Payne's murder was confirmed by her colleagues on the charity committee, although Gerry said he wouldn't have trusted any of them not to lie to the police on principle.

'Any luck finding Jonathan Kilin yet?' Gerry asked after Wesley had filled him in on his meeting with Dr Webster.

Wesley had to answer in the negative. Enquiries had been made and there was no trace of Jonathan Kilin. He had no criminal record so he wasn't on the police radar. At the time of the assault on Bert Cummings the Kilins had lived in a hamlet three miles from Tradmouth. Afterwards the family had moved away, destination unknown, and Jonathan had vanished from all official records.

Then there was Danny Brice, whose prints had been found at Bert Cummings' bungalow. All patrols were still on the lookout for him but so far they'd drawn a blank.

His phone rang and when he saw it was Neil he wavered for a moment, wondering whether to allow his friend to intrude on his working day. Eventually he yielded to temptation and answered.

'We've found another body.' Neil began without any introduction. 'Looks like a man this time judging by the pelvis.' Neil sounded excited and something told Wesley that this was no ordinary burial. 'There's a big stone on top of him and cut marks on the ribs just like the first . . . and we found his skull between his legs. Jemima Baine is going to take the bones away for examination once we've lifted them. She's certain they're archaeological so they're not your problem. She also says the first skull definitely dates from the late seventeenth century.'

'Glad that's cleared up,' said Wesley, thinking of Gemma Pollinger, relieved in some way that the skull wasn't hers.

'Anyway, I'm notifying you about the bones as per procedure along with the coroner. Want to come over and have a look?'

Wesley looked around the office. Gerry was talking on the phone and everyone else had their heads down, deep in concentration, just waiting for a lead. Now was as good a time as any. Besides, Strangefields Farm was just a short detour from home.

He knocked on Gerry's open door and the DCI looked up, motioning Wesley to come in and take a seat. From the expression on his face Wesley guessed that whatever he was talking about was something he hoped would move the case along.

'That was Neston nick,' Gerry said once he'd finished his call. 'Some of that jewellery from the burglaries has been offered to a jeweller in the town. He told the lad to come in first thing tomorrow then he called us. He recognised a couple of pieces from the list he was given. Good thing he was on the ball.'

'Let's hope this'll get that case wrapped up.' Wesley

thought for a moment. 'Although I'm still not convinced the burglaries are connected with Bert Cummings' death, I'm more intrigued by the Temples connection. Bert might have taught Temples all those years ago, and now Bert and Temples' half-sister have been killed within a few days of each other. It's too much of a coincidence.'

'Not sure if I agree with you, Wes. Danny Brice's prints were all over Bert Cummings' place and he's got a record.'

'Pinching a few valuables is a very different kettle of fish to murder. By the way, I've had a call from Neil. The skull Glen Crowther found is old – seventeenth century – so it definitely doesn't belong to Gemma Pollinger. And another skeleton's turned up at Strangefields Farm. That looks archaeological too but I said I'd go round and see to the formalities.'

Gerry rolled his eyes. 'OK. I know it'll make you happy.' He sighed loudly 'Paul's been trying to find out who's selling the Temples paintings via that website. And there's still no sign of Jonathan Kilin. Maybe he went abroad to find himself.'

Wesley experienced an overwhelming feeling of frustration. Tantalising snippets had been dangled in front of them only to lead nowhere. If they could find Jonathan Kilin and confirm that Linda Payne was murdered because of her connection with Jackson Temples, they might make some progress. But at that moment everything seemed as elusive as sea mist.

'I'll be off to Strangefields Farm then,' he said, wondering whether Grace would be there, surprised at how much he was looking forward to seeing her again.

He saw Gerry glance at the clock on the wall. 'It's six

o'clock. Why don't you go straight home after you've seen Neil? Early start tomorrow.'

Wesley didn't need telling twice, but as he turned to go Gerry spoke again.

'All Temples' victims' families have been seen and ruled out. If Linda's murder was a copycat . . . '

'What about friends of the girls?'

'The ones we could find have been spoken to and there's nobody who stands out.'

Wesley could read Gerry's thoughts. If anyone had a motive for taking revenge on Jackson Temples by killing his sister, it was the families of his victims. But this line of enquiry had hit a dead end – for now.

On his way to the car his phone began to ring. It was Maritia and she sounded worried. 'I understand you've been to the surgery to speak to Jane.'

'Word gets round fast.'

'Have you heard from Grace at all?'

When he answered in the negative she carried on, slightly breathless as though she'd been hurrying. 'I arranged to meet her for a quick lunch in Neston today but she never turned up. I've been trying to call her but her phone's switched off, which is strange if she's here on business. I rang the hotel too but they say she hasn't been there. I think something's wrong.'

'I'm on my way to the site where she's been working so I'll ask around and call you back if I learn anything.'

It took him twenty minutes to get to Strangefields Farm because of the rush-hour traffic; people who worked in Tradmouth and lived elsewhere leaving for the day. When he turned off Dead Man's Lane onto the drive he saw a green marquee to his right near where a group of archaeologists, supervised by Neil, were manoeuvring a large tarpaulin over a trench, covering it for the night to protect whatever was in there until they could resume work the next day.

Neil hurried to meet him and led him straight to the trench.

'We won't have time to lift them today,' he said. 'So we're covering the trench so we can start first thing tomorrow. I don't like to leave them there overnight but most of the team, including me, have got things on this evening so they can't stay late.'

Wesley asked his permission to climb into the trench and once he was in there he squatted down to examine the skeleton.

'Jemima's taken a look at it and she's as sure as she can be that it's a young male and that he's been there a long time. Probably centuries although she won't commit herself until the lab's done the relevant tests.'

Wesley smiled. 'Sounds as if she uses the same script as Colin Bowman. I'll leave you to it,' he said, straightening himself up. He stared at the bones, fascinated, suddenly regretting that he'd promised his sister that he'd go up to the house and see whether anybody could throw any light on Grace's whereabouts.

'The cuts on the ribs are clearer on this one, which is really exciting,' Neil continued as though he hadn't heard. 'Jemima says the marks are consistent with the heart having been removed – all part of the ritual.'

Wesley felt obliged to listen politely for a few more minutes, glancing surreptitiously at his watch from time to time. Eventually he escaped and drove up to the farmhouse, now surrounded by scaffolding which had gone up since his last visit.

When he went through the open front door he heard soft footsteps on the floor above his head. Someone was working late but he wasn't holding out much hope of finding anyone directly connected with the architect in charge.

But his luck was in. He walked through a hallway shrouded in plastic sheeting and saw a man in a suit standing by a makeshift table at the foot of the wide wooden staircase studying a clipboard. Motes of dust danced in a shaft of light streaming through a leaded window at the top of the stairs, creating a halo effect around the man's fair curls. But from the impatient look on his face Wesley had the impression that he was no angel.

'You're trespassing,' the man said, looking Wesley up and down as though he was some medieval peasant who'd intruded into the lord's private chamber.

Wesley showed his warrant card and the man grunted. 'What do you want?'

'A word with your architect, Grace Compton.'

'She hasn't been here all day. And before you ask I've no idea where she is.'

'I take it you were expecting her?'

The man glanced at his watch as though he was anxious to bring the conversation to a close. 'I was hoping she'd show her face today because there are things we need to sort out.' The man looked at a pile of architectural plans lying on a nearby table. 'But the building side of the project's going smoothly so I presume she's grabbed the opportunity to go back to London and catch up on other things. I'm sure she'll be back tomorrow. If that's all.'

'You said the building side's going smoothly – are there problems elsewhere?'

'Is that any of your business, Inspector?'

'It might be, Mr ... ?'

'Hamer. Joe Hamer. I wouldn't describe them as problems. Stupid superstition, that's all.'

He fell silent but Wesley knew he was longing to get something off his chest so he stood patiently and waited for him to elaborate.

After a few seconds Hamer spoke again. 'In the nineteen nineties this house was the scene of several murders. Most of the tradesmen are local and they've been listening to ridiculous stories.' A smirk appeared on his lips. 'They say things have been moved – tools aren't where they left them. One of the electricians said he heard a woman sobbing but if you ask me they've been playing tricks on each other. Even so, some of them are refusing to do overtime because they don't want to be here after dark.' He shook his head, exasperated. 'I'm surprised the locals haven't come with pitchforks and flaming torches to burn the place down before now.'

'You obviously think people will want to come here on holiday?'

Hamer suddenly looked more cheerful. 'By the time we've finished with the main house and the holiday village is built the place will be unrecognisable. We're changing the name – giving it a whole new identity. In a couple of years' time nobody will remember Strangefields Farm and Dead Man's Lane.'

Wesley, knowing the public's fascination with true crime, wasn't so sure.

'If you'll excuse me I need to lock up,' said Hamer, taking a set of keys from his pocket.

'You'd better let the person upstairs know you're going,' said Wesley.

'There's nobody else here. I'm on my own.'

'Well, someone's walking around up there. I definitely heard footsteps when I came in.'

Wesley saw the colour drain from Hamer's face.

41

Grace Compton had let Maritia down by not turning up to lunch and the conscience she thought she'd lost all those years ago was beginning to niggle at her like a troublesome tooth. She'd spent the night and all that day with Dale Keyes on his yacht and now she regretted that she'd ever mentioned his name to Maritia and Wesley. She'd assumed he'd disappeared to avoid paying what he owed her so she'd been angry with him. Now he'd had a chance to explain and the situation had changed completely.

He'd sworn to pay back everything he owed her and made it clear that his problems had only arisen because one of his employees had helped herself to the contents of his company's bank account before vanishing without a word. He'd informed the police but they'd been useless, even suggesting that he'd defrauded the company himself because they'd found no record of the woman ever existing. Her ID had been faked and her National Insurance number had turned out to belong to someone else altogether.

Dale had not only felt like a fool, he'd been ruined so when he was involved in the ferry accident he'd seen it as a chance to make a new start. On the ferry he'd met an Englishman he'd talked to in the bar the previous night; a man who'd told him in the drunken early hours that he had had no family and no ties. Despite Dale's frantic attempts to save him, the man had drowned on that doomed ferry journey and on impulse Dale had planted his own ID on his floating body before making his escape. Consequently he'd been listed amongst the dead.

Since his vanishing act Dale had been living in Spain under a fresh identity. He'd made wealthy contacts and a very successful living managing holiday properties for fellow Brits, all the time keeping well below the radar of the authorities without troubling the Spanish taxman. When Grace had first encountered Dale one of her fellow architects had described him as a wide boy, someone who'd land in shit and come up smelling of roses. It seemed he'd been right, but maybe she liked that in a man.

Because of Dale Keyes Grace's partnership had taken a bad financial hit; but now his fortunes had been restored and he'd promised to pay her what he owed – provided she didn't tell the authorities he was still alive and had returned to the UK on his yacht. He'd seemed so contrite that she'd agreed to keep her silence as long as he came up with at least a payment on account by the end of the week. If he didn't agree to her terms the 'dead man' would be dragged back to life, which was something neither of them really wanted.

She'd decided not to mention this new development to Wesley; he was a police officer who would never ignore wrongdoing. With Dale back on the scene, it might be wise to keep her distance from the Petersons from now on.

After returning briefly to the hotel to pick up a few essentials, she made her way back to Dale's yacht and knocked on the cabin door. Dale had promised food and she could smell something good.

'We've still got a lot to talk about,' he said as he poured her a glass of wine.

She took the glass and raised it in a half-hearted toast. 'Such as where you're going to get the money from.'

'I've got the money. No worries about that. Although it might take some time to get to you. Unless ...'

Grace waited for him to continue.

'I haven't told you the real reason I've come back to the UK. A friend of mine thought he saw the bitch who cleaned me out here in Tradmouth.'

'You've come looking for her?'

'Too right I have.'

'Have you found her?'

'Yes, and I'm going to make sure she pays back every last penny.' The determination in Dale's voice made Grace uncomfortable.

'I've waited long enough for the money so a few more weeks won't make much difference.'

'I always knew you were a reasonable woman, Grace.'

'It's not me you owe money to, it's my partnership.'

'Oh yes, your life's work.'

'I'm passionate about what I do. What's wrong with that?'

'Nothing at all.' He paused, as though something was bothering him; something he wasn't quite sure how to put into words. Eventually he spoke. 'You're not the only one who's recognised someone from their past, you know.'

'What do you mean?'

'There's a developer I used to work with while he was doing up a property in Kent – old place he was converting into flats. I saw him in Tradmouth, which means I've got to be extra careful it doesn't get out that I'm still in the land of the living. Fortunately I don't think he saw me.'

'Who are you talking about?'

Dale poured more wine into Grace's empty glass before answering.

'He's called Joe Hamer.'

'That's the client I'm working for.'

Dale Keyes swore under his breath 'Let's change the subject, shall we?' Dale raised his glass again. 'Here's to you and here's to architecture ... And getting back on an even keel.'

Grace sighed. She'd found Dale Keyes again and the strong feelings she'd once had for him had returned with a force she hadn't expected. She'd have to return to Strangefields Farm soon to resume work. But in the meantime, she intended to make the most of the surprise reunion.

Life was short.

42

Wesley's two cases were preying on his mind, even in the small hours of the morning when only night creatures should be wide awake.

Shortly after he'd arrived home from Strangefields Farm, Gerry had called to say that Colin had run more tests on the victims' knife wounds, as promised. The tests confirmed his initial observation that identical blades, sharp with one serrated edge, had been used on both Linda Payne and Bert Cummings. There had been a vicious anger behind both attacks and, now it seemed almost certain that they were connected, he was sure Jackson Temples was the link between the two victims.

Pam was fast asleep by his side and his mind raced as he lay listening to her soft breathing. He couldn't forget how he'd felt when he'd visited Strangefields Farm, as though he was being watched by something malevolent. He wondered whether the developer Joe Hamer had felt it too, although he imagined the man would never admit to anything so fanciful.

Wesley, however, kept an open mind about such things. He'd often come face to face with evil in the course of his working life and he knew that it could seep into the fabric of a place and remain for centuries. Jackson Temples had murdered three young women in that house – four if you counted Carrie Bullen. Jane Webster and Hayley Rummage might harbour doubts about his guilt but as far as Wesley could see the evidence proved otherwise. Perhaps the teenage Jane and her friends had just been lucky. Strangefields Farm was evil all right – and it was the last place he'd choose to spend a holiday.

He climbed out of bed, leaving Pam to sleep because she wasn't working that day and didn't have to get up until the children started clamouring for attention. He crept downstairs and was surprised to find Della already at the kitchen table cradling a mug of coffee in both hands, her crutches propped up against the nearby cupboard.

'You're up early,' he said.

'Couldn't sleep.' She looked him in the eye. 'Are you cheating on my daughter?'

Wesley stared at her, stunned, wondering whether she'd somehow found out about his moment of temptation with Rachel.

'Of course not.' He knew he was trying too hard to convince her; the sure sign of a liar.

'Pam saw you in Tradmouth. Sharing fish and chips. All very cosy – intimate, she said. Black woman – gorgeous-looking with expensive clothes. Who is she?'

Wesley felt as though a weight had been lifted from his shoulders. He'd assumed Pam's distant manner had something to do with her health – but all the time it had been simple unfounded jealousy.

'That was Grace. I must have mentioned her. She's a friend of my sister's and we knew each other when we were teenagers. She's an architect working on that new development at Strangefields Farm. I promise you she's always seen me as a sort of . . . brother figure. She wanted my advice about something, that's all.'

Della eyed him suspiciously.

'Maritia's planning a dinner while she's down here so Pam might get a chance to meet her.' He gave his mother-in-law a smile that he hoped looked sincere.

Della grunted. 'I suppose I'll have to take your word for it. Have you found out who killed Bert Cummings yet?'

'We're still trying to trace Jonathan Kilin. He seems to be the only person who ever got on the wrong side of Cummings. Everyone else we've spoken to has had nothing but good to say about him. Any coffee in that pot?'

He took a mug off the draining board and Della poured coffee into it while her son-in-law dropped a piece of bread into the toaster. Before he could sit down Della spoke again. 'Years ago when I taught at the high school in Dukesbridge a colleague of mine got married and I'm sure the photographer she used was called Kilin. I remember the name 'cause it was unusual.'

'You don't know where this photographer is now by any chance?'

'I think that's your job, don't you? But I can ask around if you like.'

'Thanks. That'd be a great help.' It was unlike his mother-in-law to be helpful so he reckoned she needed encouraging.

As he was preparing to leave the house Pam came downstairs in her dressing gown. He could hear the children squabbling in the background but she was ignoring them for the moment. He kissed her on the cheek.

'Della said you saw me with Grace the other day.'

She raised her eyebrows. 'That was the Grace your sister mentioned?'

'She wanted to meet because she needed my advice about something that was worrying her. See you later,' he whispered before leaving the house, telling himself the misunderstanding had been sorted out.

When he walked into the CID office, trying hard not to be noticed, Gerry was already addressing the troops. Once everyone had been allocated their tasks for the morning, Wesley followed the DCI into his office.

'Jonathan Kilin, the boy who beat up Bert Cummings – it's possible his father was a wedding photographer. I've had a quick look online but I can't find any mention of him. He'll probably be retired by now.'

'Put Trish onto it. She enjoys a challenge.'

As he turned to go he felt Gerry's hand on his shoulder. 'That jeweller in Neston should be opening his shop in half an hour. If our lad turns up at least we'll have made one arrest. And if he broke into Bert Cummings' place he could be his killer.'

Wesley still had the feeling that the murder and the burglaries weren't connected, but that didn't mean the thief couldn't provide useful information.

The small jeweller's shop stood down a narrow side alley off Neston's main shopping street, a picturesque thoroughfare with the arch of the town gate at its centre. Underwood's was a pleasingly old-fashioned shop with sparkling rings and gold necklaces brightening the small, dark windows. When Wesley pushed the door open a bell jangled and an elderly man bobbed up from behind the counter like a jack-in-the-box.

'Sorry, I was just taking some stock out of the drawer. You're from the police? I was told you'd be here.'

Wesley showed his warrant card, a little disappointed that his occupation was so obvious.

'I'm Tony Underwood, the proprietor. An inspector and a chief inspector: I'm honoured.'

'We like to get away from the paperwork from time to time,' said Gerry cheerily. 'And there is a bit more to this case than you've been told.'

Mr Underwood tapped the side of his nose. 'Of course. The lad said he'd come in first thing so if you'd like to wait in the back room ...'

Wesley led the way, hoping the lad in question hadn't been watching the shop and seen them enter. Mr Underwood brought them tea and as they drank he was aware of time passing. When ten o'clock arrived he began to suspect they'd made a mistake arriving so openly and he said as much to Gerry, who'd settled in an armchair exuding an air of zen-like calm.

'I looked round as we came in, Wes. There was nobody about. The lad's just a bit late. From the description Mr Underwood gave he didn't sound like an early riser.'

They heard the shop bell jangle and Wesley sat forward in his seat, suddenly alert, glad that Underwood had one of those voices that carry well so they could make out every word.

'You haven't told me where you got them.'

'My gran left them to me when she passed away. But what am I going to do with them? I'd rather have the cash.'

There was a long silence and Wesley imagined that Underwood was having a closer look at the items, using his jeweller's loupe to examine any hallmarks. It was a good delaying tactic.

'How much are they worth?' The young man was beginning to sound nervous, almost as though he'd started to suspect something was amiss.

'I'll give you fifty for the lot.'

This was the signal. As agreed Gerry waited in the back while Wesley, the faster of the two, nipped out of the back door and made his way round to the front. They didn't want the seller of the jewellery to get away if they could help it.

After a minute or so spent listening to the young man push Underwood's offer up from £50 to £70, Gerry calculated that Wesley would have reached his post. He strolled out from the back of the shop, trying his best to look casual, in time to see Underwood hand over the cash as agreed.

'Can I have a look at those?' he said as the shop bell jangled again. Wesley had arrived and was standing behind the young man, playing the part of a customer waiting his turn to be served. The two policemen were surprised to see that the lad had a dog with him, sitting patiently while his master conducted the transaction.

The young man's eyes widened in panic and he tugged at the dog's makeshift lead, preparing to make for the door. Wesley made a grab for the man's leather jacket but it slid from his grasp and before he knew it their quarry was getting away down the street. Wesley hurtled after the boy. But when he reached the main street there was no sign of him or his dog.

'He can't have got far,' said Gerry when he caught up with him and stopped to get his breath.

'Trouble with Neston is there are so many alleyways and lanes. If he knows the place he could have taken cover anywhere.'

'At least we know what he looks like.'

'And he's bound to have left his prints all over the jewellery.'

They returned to the shop and bagged up the shiny evidence. To Wesley's untrained eye, some of it looked good; gold and diamonds glittered in the evidence bag and his first thought was that Underwood's offer had been extremely mean. Still, that wasn't his problem.

They drove back to Tradmouth and a couple of hours later they knew the identity of the man who'd escaped them in Neston. Danny Brice's appearance had certainly changed since he'd sat for the mugshot they'd seen on the computer screen. But he'd left his fingerprints in Bert Cummings' bungalow – and they were all over the stolen jewellery too.

43

While Wesley was still stinging from his failure to apprehend Danny Brice a call came through from the lab. The rope used in Lance Pembry's production of *The Duchess of Malfi* had been examined and traces of DNA matching that of Linda Payne had been found. Not only that but the pattern of the rope matched the marks on the dead woman's neck exactly and the fibres matched as well. It appeared that they'd found the murder weapon and Wesley felt this was a step forward.

As well as Linda's, DNA from four other people had been found on the rope. There was Pauline Howe's, Linda's understudy, which was to be expected. Then there was that of Ossie Phillips, the man playing the executioner, as well as Rich Vernon's and Lance Pembry's.

Wesley selected his home number and was relieved when Pam answered after three rings. He came straight to the point. 'You know *The Duchess of Malfi* pretty well, don't you?'

'I suppose . . . ' She sounded surprised by his question.

'Can you tell me whether the actor playing Ferdinand would have any reason to handle the rope the duchess is strangled with?'

'Hang on, I'll get my copy of the play. It's in the spare room.'

He'd expected an instant answer but now he realised that it was a long time since their student days and memories fade. He walked over to the window and gazed out at the river while he waited patiently for Pam's verdict. Eventually he heard her voice again.

'As far as I can see Ferdinand never actually handles the rope himself. He leaves it to the executioner to do the dreadful deed. Is that helpful?'

'It might be. Thanks.' He paused, looking round at his colleagues in the office. 'Everything OK there?'

'Maritia's just texted me from work to say she hasn't been able to contact Grace but she's hoping to arrange the dinner for the weekend.' There was a short silence before she spoke again. 'I'm sorry about—'

'My fault. I should have told you I'd met her. I'll be home as soon as I can,' he said before ending the call. Grace's continuing absence made him uneasy but at that moment he had other things to worry about.

Gerry had just walked in, fresh from a meeting with the press officer to bring her up to date with the latest developments. Wesley followed him into his office and broke the news about the latest DNA report. 'To cut a long story short,' he continued, 'Rich Vernon doesn't handle the rope in the play but his DNA's all over the ends – in the same place as the actor's who performs the strangulation on stage. So is Lance Pembry's but he's the director so he might have been demonstrating. I'm not sure if it's relevant but I'd like to talk to both of them again.'

'Are we sure that rope's the actual murder weapon?'

'All they'll say for certain is that it's a match for the type of rope used.' Wesley hesitated. 'The lab had a look at the nineteen ninety-six forensic reports and they say it's similar to the rope used to strangle Jackson Temples' victims but not identical.'

'Lance Pembry said Linda provided the rope for the production. He thought it came from her shop, although he wasn't able to swear to it. I'd like to bring Rich Vernon and Lance Pembry in for an interview under caution sooner rather than later.'

Before Gerry could say anything Rachel appeared in the doorway. 'Any sign of Danny Brice yet?' Wesley asked hopefully.

'Not yet. But all patrols are on the lookout.'

'With that red leather jacket and the dog he shouldn't be hard to spot,' said Gerry.

Rachel looked impatient, as though she had important news to relay. 'Those Jackson Temples paintings – the ones for sale on the internet? We've got an address for the Jackles Gallery – and it's here in Tradmouth. Jackles: a combination of Jackson and Temples. Not very subtle.'

As Gerry stood up his chair creaked as though it was glad to be relieved of his weight. 'If we've got an address let's get round there and have a word with whoever's in charge – find out what kind of ghouls want a painting by a serial killer hanging on their living-room wall. No time like the present.'

The Jackles Gallery wasn't in the centre of town like most Tradmouth galleries designed to reel in the wealthier tourists. Instead the address turned out to be a private house in a terrace overlooking the river on the road to the castle. The glossy paint on the front door was fresh and the house, probably built for a retired sea captain, looked smarter than its neighbours. There was no reply when Wesley rang the doorbell and no sign of life behind the sheer white curtains at the windows.

'Let's have a word with the neighbours,' said Gerry.

Before Wesley could answer Gerry had knocked on the door of the neighbouring house, raising the heavy lion door knocker and letting it fall with a crash.

The door opened to reveal an elderly lady with steel-grey hair gathered back in a bun. At first glance she looked like an old-fashioned schoolmistress but then Wesley noticed the short denim skirt she wore over brightly striped tights.

'Sorry to bother you, love,' said Gerry. 'We're trying to get hold of your next-door neighbour. You don't know where we can find him by any chance?'

The woman shook her head. 'I don't have a neighbour. I'd feel a lot safer if I did.' Seeing Wesley's questioning look, she carried on. 'Nobody's been living there for the past six months. There was talk of it being made into a holiday let and I think I'd prefer that to an empty house.'

'Do you know who owns it?'

'Bayside Properties they call themselves but if you ask me it's a fly-by-night outfit. I've seen this man come here, sharp suits and a BMW – wouldn't trust him as far as I could throw him. And I saw a couple of girls too.'

'Girls?'

'Women then. When you get to my age everyone younger seems like a girl.'

When she invited them in Wesley was tempted to accept because her loneliness was almost palpable. But there wasn't time for good deeds so he thanked her and said they might be in touch.

He was about to walk away when she spoke again. 'I've got a key. Old Mrs Morton who used to live there gave me one and I never gave it back. You can have a look inside if you're interested.'

'Of course we're interested, love,' said Gerry, beaming.

She vanished into her house and came back with a key dangling from her fingers. She handed it to Gerry with a coquettish smile.

'Thanks, love. I could kiss you,' said Gerry, making the old lady giggle like a schoolgirl.

'Have you ever heard of the Jackles Gallery?' Wesley asked. 'It's an outfit that sells paintings, possibly from next-door's address.'

The old lady shook her head.

'You can leave it to us now, love,' said Gerry. 'We'll drop the key in as soon as we've finished.'

The woman's cheery smile told Wesley she was looking forward to this second encounter.

'We'll have time for a cup of tea when we've done,' said Gerry after she'd shut the door as though he'd read Wesley's mind. 'Who knows what we might learn. Never underestimate the Miss Marple effect.'

The first things that struck Wesley as they entered the house were the stillness and the fact that the place was spotlessly clean and newly decorated. The neutral colours gave it a bright, spacious look and Wesley could smell the distinctive scent of new carpets. When he pushed open the door to the front room he saw that it was sparsely furnished with modern, light-coloured pieces in the Scandinavian style.

'Looks pretty bare,' said Gerry, disappointed, as Wesley led the way through to the back of the house where they found another reception room as bland as the first. It had the feel of a recently renovated property, stripped of its character and waiting for an occupant to make their mark on it.

'Let's try upstairs.' Wesley was starting to feel their trip had been wasted and that the address was an empty property chosen at random to add authenticity. The Jackles Gallery might not even exist, apart from in cyberspace.

They started at the front in the unfurnished bedroom overlooking the river. The view alone would double the market value and Wesley couldn't help wondering why the property company had left it unoccupied. A row of white fitted wardrobes occupied one wall and Wesley opened one of the doors.

As soon as he saw what was inside he shouted to Gerry, who was gazing out of the window, watching a large yacht in full sail making its stately way upstream.

'Look what I've found.'

Stacked up inside the wardrobes he could see bright canvases, a mixture of landscapes, portraits and seascapes in oils with heavy, impressionistic brush strokes, best viewed from a distance but undoubtedly the work of a talented hand. Wesley heard Gerry gasp and he swung round to see the boss staring open-mouthed in amazement . . . or horror.

'Are they by Temples?'

'Either that or someone's made a good job of copying his style. And there's his initials in the corner – JT. He always signed his work like that as I remember.' Gerry turned away as though he couldn't bear to look at the things. 'Close that bloody door, Wes. I've seen enough of Temples' daubs to last a lifetime.'

'They're good. Not at all what I was expecting. Very tasteful and not a rope in sight,' said Wesley. 'He had quite a reputation as an artist before the case blew up. Made a good living from it. The kinky stuff – or experimental as he called it – was just a sideline.'

Gerry seemed eager to get out of that room with its

251

reminder of Jackson Temples' crimes. He mumbled something about having a look in the other rooms and shot out
but Wesley lingered because he wanted to have a closer
look at the paintings. He opened the wardrobe door again
and squatted down, examining each picture carefully but
concentrating on the portraits.

There were portraits of attractive young women and he
recognised Jane Webster posing modestly in a pale-blue
dress. There was another of Jane too, a conventional nude
study which captured her youthful beauty.

He carried on examining the paintings and recognised
Jacky Burns and Nerys Harred, their flawless features
familiar from the files he'd spent so much time studying.
But again these were conventional portraits: nothing disturbing and certainly no sign of ropes. Perhaps Temples
had kept that for when he knew the girls better and they'd
become more relaxed with him.

He saw Carrie Bullen with her beautiful heart-shaped
face in an off-the-shoulder top, her bare shoulders providing a faint hint of nudity, and there was a picture of Gemma
Pollinger, posed in profile, again fully clothed. She had a
snub nose and a prominent chin.

He called through to Gerry. 'Weren't all the portraits he
did of his victims taken as evidence?'

Gerry appeared at the door. 'Only the kinky ones with
ropes.' He thought for a moment. 'I think they took a few
pictures of a couple of girls they hadn't been able to trace
and all, just in case. At one time the basement at Morbay
nick looked like the storeroom of an art gallery. Only the
rope ones were produced at the trial; the others weren't
regarded as evidence.'

'I want to know who brought them here and is selling

them, and how they got hold of them. Next stop Bayside Properties, I think.'

'After we've had our cup of tea next door. There might even be biccies,' said Gerry. 'The paintings were probably left at Strangefields Farm and someone took them once the investigation was over – the stepmother perhaps, Linda's mum.' Gerry turned his face away, concealing his emotion. 'I don't want to look at them, Wes. Close that door, will you?'

They made their way to the second bedroom at the back of the house where they found more paintings – and something else. Wesley slipped it into an evidence bag and held it up for Gerry to see. It was a woman's scarf, floral and bright, and as he picked it up he caught a whiff of perfume. He was sure he'd smelled that perfume before but he couldn't remember where.

'Better ask if it belongs to anybody at the property company,' Gerry said before leaving Wesley to continue his study of the paintings. The one at the top of the pile featured a youthful Linda Payne. Like the rest it was impressionistic in style and she was dressed in a gingham summer dress and a cardigan that made her look like a schoolgirl.

There were no more pictures of girls in the wardrobe near the windows. Instead there was a selection of landscapes and pictures of Tradmouth, the kind so popular with the tourist market.

As he continued going through the pile it struck him that some of the paintings were subtly different, as though somebody had made a great effort to copy Temples' style with slight variations in the brush strokes that only a trained eye would see. Some paintings bore the initials JT in the bottom right-hand corner, but others were just signed with the letter J.

'I think some of these might not have been painted by Temples,' said Wesley.

'Why do you say that?'

'When I was in the Art and Antiques Unit at the Met I picked up a lot by watching the experts. There are subtle differences in the style. And besides, they're only signed with one initial. Temples signed his work with both.'

Wesley was beginning to wonder whether Temples had been telling the truth and there really had been another artist at Strangefields Farm. Perhaps Jonny Sykes hadn't been a figment of Jackson Temples' imagination after all.

From the second diary of
Lemuel Strange, gentleman

4th April 1685

For nineteen years I have written no account of my deeds, for the business of my life and the running of Strangefields Hall on Frances's behalf has kept me from the leisure I enjoyed in London. Even the death of our good King Charles in February and the accession of his brother, James, has had little effect on us here at Strangefields.

Frances trusts me absolutely to run her estate and, after the untimely death of her son William of the fever but two years after his father's murder, I am now sole heir to the property which now prospers with all Reuben's debts paid. Frances herself inherited a great fortune from her father on his death last year and Strangefields has a new wing and is a goodly house.

My own son, born a year after my wife's move here to Devonshire, has grown to be a fine young man and studies the law at Oxford while our daughter Jane is to marry a young man who owns much land nearby. Devonshire is now our home and that is why I find the reports which have lately reached my ears most unsettling.

Yesterday a sailor accosted me on the quayside in Tradmouth with a tale so strange I would have accused him of being a lying rogue, were it not for the solemnity of his demeanour. He told me he had seen my cousin Reuben, the late master of Strangefields, with his own eyes in a Plymouth tavern. When I asked him how he could be certain he replied that he had once worked at Strangefields and knew the brother of the maidservant, Bess Whitetree, who was hanged for her master's murder. Reuben Strange's face, he said, was one forever in his memory.

44

Joe Hamer stood amidst the dust and debris of Strangefields Farm and stared at the object in his hand with distaste. Glen Crowther had found it behind some panelling upstairs and he'd brought it to Joe with a grin on his face, as though he was expecting a reward. But Joe couldn't work out what would make Crowther think he'd be interested in a scruffy old book filled with handwriting that was impossible to read. He'd been tempted to throw the thing in the skip outside with the rest of the rubbish, then something had stopped him.

The rumour that the place was cursed flashed through his mind and he was struck by the possibility that this object might be the source of the curse, hidden behind ancient oak panelling in an upstairs room. He'd heard of such things being discovered in other old houses: bottles filled with nails, mummified cats and written curses in concealed places. The workmen claimed to have heard things; even the detective inspector had said something about footsteps. On the other hand old houses creak and he was sure that Strangefields' bad luck hadn't come from a supernatural source. It was a man who'd brought death and suffering to the place, not ghosts and witchcraft.

He deposited the book on the windowsill amongst the builders' unwashed mugs and examined his phone. Grace Compton still hadn't turned up but that wasn't necessarily a bad thing, as architects sometimes got in the way.

He heard a voice calling his name and rolled his eyes. If that bloody archaeologist was looking for him, the news wouldn't be good. The discovery of human remains along with the foundations of some old building near the gates had held up work for too long already. Watson had mentioned the possibility that executions might have taken place in the grounds which, given the recent history of the place, wasn't something he'd be putting in the brochure.

'Can I have a word?' said Neil.

'Of course.' Hamer was trying his best to hide his annoyance.

'I just wanted to tell you we've lifted the skeleton.'

'So you've finished down there?'

'Not yet.'

Neil paused, enjoying the look of suppressed anger on the developer's face. 'There could be more human remains.' He looked around as though he was hoping another skull would appear any second. Then he spotted the old book nestling between the tannin-stained mugs. 'What's that?'

'Just some old rubbish.'

Neil picked up the book and flicked through it, his face betraying his excitement. 'Mind if I keep it?'

Then he rushed out of the front door without waiting for a reply.

It was three o'clock by the time Wesley and Gerry arrived back at the station.

As Gerry predicted, the neighbour had been able to give them some interesting snippets of information. As well as the suited man and the women she'd described as 'girls' she'd seen a van parked outside there several times. It had a logo on the side, a flower she thought, but she hadn't been able to see it properly and hadn't thought to make a note of the registration number.

Sometimes the neighbour had heard noises through the walls as if somebody was moving things about, although as the walls were thick she hadn't been able to hear voices.

'No doubt she had a glass to the wall,' said Gerry as they'd left her house. 'I know I would have done. A van with a flower on it – I'm thinking Linda Payne was flogging her half-brother's paintings on his behalf . . . or maybe her own.'

'But how would she get access to the property?' Wesley looked at his watch. 'Rich Vernon and Lance Pembry are being brought in. Let's see what they've got to say about that rope.'

'We still don't know if it was the actual murder weapon.'

'I've asked the lab to conduct more tests.'

'Will we have the results by the time we interview Pembry and Vernon?'

'Even if we haven't we don't have to let them know that, do we?'

'You're learning, Wes,' said Gerry, giving his inspector a hearty slap on the back.

'In the meantime let's visit Bayside Properties and while we're there we can tell them their house is out of bounds for the foreseeable future.'

Gerry frowned. 'You go with Rach. I've got a meeting with the chief super. She's quibbling about the overtime budget again.'

Wesley's lack of sleep was beginning to catch up with him so he was happy to leave the driving to Rachel. She drove to Morbay via Neston because the car ferries were always busy at that time of the day and pulled up outside the offices of Bayside Properties at four o'clock on the dot.

The office's faded UPVC frontage had the slightly seedy look of a building that had been modernised some years ago with every expense spared. They pressed the entry-phone by the front door and waited to be buzzed in.

The interior was every bit as shabby as the outside, Wesley thought as he stepped over the threshold just as a man was emerging from a door behind the reception desk. He was portly with combed-over hair and perspiration stains on the armpits of his pale-blue shirt even though the office wasn't particularly warm. When they showed their ID he looked nervous and Wesley couldn't help wondering why.

The man introduced himself as George Horrocks, the manager, and when he shook their hands his palms were sweating so much that Wesley had to resist the temptation to wipe his hand on his trousers.

Wesley came straight to the point of their visit. 'What do you know about the Jackles Gallery?'

The man looked confused and a trickle of sweat dribbled onto his lips. 'Nothing. We don't deal with any art galleries.'

'My colleague didn't say it was an art gallery,' said Rachel.

The man looked even more flustered. 'I just assumed . . . '

'Your company owns a property in Tradmouth. Number six Castle View Terrace.'

'If you say so. I don't know all our properties offhand. It's my secretary's day off and I'm not up to date with—'

'This one's been modernised but it's unoccupied and

being used by a company or individual to store paintings. Can you tell us who's renting it?'

Horrocks invited them through to his office. When Wesley glanced back at the secretary's desk he saw a pile of files there and a box of tissues beside the computer. A word with the desk's occupant might be helpful, he thought. Secretaries saw a lot and knew more than their bosses imagined. He took the scarf from Castle View Terrace – now encased in an evidence bag – out of his pocket.

'Recognise this?'

For a second Horrocks looked puzzled. 'It looks familiar. I might have seen my secretary wearing something similar. Why? Where did you get it?'

Wesley didn't answer the question. 'If we could have those details of the property . . . '

Once in Horrocks' office he made a great show of rummaging through his filing cabinet and eventually he pulled out a file. 'Number six Castle View Terrace. Here we are. Currently unoccupied. Nobody's renting it.'

'Then where do the pictures come from?'

'Left by a previous tenant?' Horrocks suggested nervously.

'Someone's using that address. Could it be one of your staff?'

'Absolutely not.'

'Who else works here?'

'Just me and my secretary,' he said with a nervous grin. 'But I'm sure she won't know . . . '

'Even so, I'd like a word with her. Can you give me her name and contact details?'

When Horrocks provided the information, Wesley caught Rachel's eye. Horrocks' secretary was Pauline Howe, Linda Payne's former understudy. Now the new Duchess of Malfi.

45

Danny hadn't been so frightened since he'd found Kevin's granddad lifeless in his chair with those terrible bloody wounds. He'd been afraid then that he'd get the blame even though he'd had nothing to do with it.

Kevin had often talked of Granddad Bert. How he'd been a teacher and how he'd told Kevin all sorts of things and taken him fishing when he was a boy. Kevin said that his granddad had never known he preferred boys to girls but he'd intended to tell him one day because Kevin knew he'd understand. Danny was sure Kevin had been right because the Bert he'd come to know had had a twinkle in his eye and hadn't possessed a bigoted bone in his body.

Even though he wanted the bastard who'd killed Bert found as much as the police did, he knew he was the one they suspected. He'd fallen into their trap at the jeweller's and only just managed to escape. He'd taken off Kevin's red leather jacket because it was too noticeable, folding it carefully so only the black lining showed and carrying it over his shoulder before dodging into an alleyway.

Barney, however, wasn't so easily disguised so he'd returned to the squat, hoping Stag and Roberta wouldn't be there. It was time to move on before they found their hoard was missing. Perhaps he'd find a place in Morbay or possibly Plymouth or Exeter; somewhere bigger where he could get lost in the crowd. Now Bert was dead he had no reason for staying around.

He started packing his meagre possessions into his rucksack. It was time to go.

Just as he'd finished a sound from the empty shop below made him freeze. He put a reassuring hand on Barney's head, praying he wouldn't bark. They were back and he knew he had to get out fast.

Wesley needed to speak to Pauline Howe but when they'd called at her address there had been nobody at home.

On his return to the CID office he noticed that the evidence bags containing the stolen jewellery from Neston were lying on Rob Carter's desk. Rob was busy listing all the pieces and matching them with the burglary reports.

'Any sign of Danny Brice?' he asked as he passed.

Rob looked up, glad of the distraction. 'Not yet. He'll have gone to ground.'

Wesley left him to his tedious task and found Gerry in his office, surrounded by paperwork and looking desperate.

'Tell me some good news, Wes,' he said as he raised his head. 'I sent someone round to bring in Pembry and Vernon for questioning but neither of them was in. I said to try first thing tomorrow – drag them away from their breakfast.'

Wesley sat down. 'Rachel and I paid a visit to the property company that owns the Jackles Gallery.'

'If you can call it a gallery.'

'Well you'll never guess who works there – Pauline Howe; Linda Payne's understudy in the play. I don't believe in coincidences and neither do you. Besides, I'm sure she owns the scarf we found at Castle View Terrace.'

'Apart from knowing Linda, I can't think what connection she could have to Jackson Temples, unless she was one of his models. Mind you, her name never came up in the original case.'

'We won't know unless we ask her.' He checked the time. It was coming up to six. 'She wasn't in when we called round and she's not answering her phone.'

'We'll pay her a visit tomorrow. Think we should be treating her as a suspect? She wouldn't be the first understudy to resort to murder to get the plum role.'

This wasn't what Wesley had in mind but no possibility could be ruled out. He was about to leave Gerry's office when Neil rang. Wesley felt grateful for the distraction from police work.

'Wes. I've found something at Strangefields Farm. It was hidden behind some panelling they were removing for restoration.'

'What was?'

'It appears to be some sort of diary.'

'Is it connected with Jackson Temples?'

'It looks old; long before Temples' time. Possibly late seventeenth century.'

There was a lengthy silence before Wesley spoke. 'Something similar was found at the cottage of our murder victim. It's in our evidence store.'

Wesley had had so much on his mind that he'd almost forgotten about the little book from the file marked 'diary' at Linda Payne's cottage and now he wondered whether that had come from Strangefields Farm too; whether she'd found it during her time there and kept it out of curiosity – or maybe retained it as a relic of times past. He'd wanted to read through it then show it to Neil but the investigation had kept getting in the way.

'I could bring it round to yours tonight. I'll make a copy for you to read at your leisure if you like.'

'That'd be good.'

'Could you get a copy made of the other one?'

Wesley hesitated. 'I'll try. But things are pretty full on here at the moment so I can't promise anything.'

Intrigued, he told Gerry he was going home to think things over and get an early night. Gerry raised no objection and said he was about to do the same because Joyce hadn't seen much of him over the last few days.

Wesley had been checking his phone at regular intervals to see if Grace had been trying to call because her lack of communication was starting to worry him. It was in the back of his mind that a Jackson Temples copycat might be emerging from the shadows to pursue a sick re-enactment of his crimes. Though he told himself there was probably an innocent explanation for Grace's absence, this didn't stop his imagination working overtime.

When he arrived home he found Pam in the kitchen.

'My mother's been doing some detective work,' she said as she opened the fridge door. 'Go and ask her what she's found out. I haven't seen her so pleased with herself in ages.'

Wesley did as she suggested and when he walked into the living room he saw Della sitting there with a smug smile.

'Pam tells me you've got some information for me.'

'It wasn't hard. Just a matter of making a few phone calls. I've traced Mr Kilin, the photographer. He's retired and living in Modbury, not that far away.'

'How did you find him?'

She tapped the side of her nose. 'Teaching mafia. I have a former colleague in Modbury who's a bell-ringer.'

'What's that got to do with it?'

'Ken Kilin's taken up ringing in his retirement.'

Wesley was rendered temporarily speechless. Then he gathered his thoughts. 'What about his son, Jonathan?'

'Kilin's only got one son as far as she knows. Christopher. Married with kids and living in Exeter.'

Wesley's hopes plummeted. Then he remembered Stephen Kelly saying that Jonathan Kilin had had a younger brother so maybe Della had found the right man after all.

There was only one way to find out.

46

Soon after Della's revelation the previous evening Neil had appeared on the doorstep. Wesley had been glad to see him; during his time in the Met he'd known officers who'd had no friends outside the force and he'd vowed never to let that happen to him. Besides, chatting about archaeology, the subject he and Neil had studied together, had helped to take his mind off his problems at work.

Neil had brought Lucy round with him, which pleased Pam, and after the couple had left Wesley went to bed and lay beside his sleeping wife with the case churning around his brain. Eventually he'd fallen into a fitful sleep around two in the morning, dreaming of Jackson Temples painting Pam's portrait. She was naked apart from a noose around her neck and Wesley was watching behind a glass screen which he couldn't break to get to her. He woke sweating, his heart pounding, only to find Pam beside him slumbering peacefully, safe and sound.

When he rose at quarter to six, bleary-eyed and yawning, he knew he'd drunk too much wine with Neil and Lucy the previous evening; with friends it was always tempting to lose count, especially with Della urging him to open another bottle. But at least it had been a temporary distraction from the case, as well as the growing unease he was feeling about Grace.

He hadn't had a chance to make a copy of the diary from the evidence store so he'd felt guilty when Neil produced a photocopy of the one from Strangefields Farm. The sheaf of papers lay tantalisingly on the dressing table as he showered and pulled on his clothes, trying not to disturb Pam, and eventually he yielded to temptation and took them downstairs. He spread them out on the kitchen table and as he began to study them he realised that Neil's 1666 diary from Strangefields appeared to have been written by the same hand as the one from Linda Payne's cottage, which made it probable that Linda had found hers there too. He imagined the teenage Linda discovering the mysterious little book and keeping it as her personal treasure; deciphering the handwriting, relishing the story it told, enjoying a secret glimpse into history.

Fortunately, before he could get beyond the fifth page, he checked the time. Gerry wanted them to make an early start and if he didn't get a move on he'd be late so he put the copy to one side and grabbed himself a bowl of muesli for breakfast.

When he arrived at the station he requested a copy of the book from the evidence store while he still remembered, knowing that if he delayed, the investigation would drive it from his mind.

In the CID office he found Gerry waiting for him. Unlike himself, the boss seemed wide awake.

'Keeping you up, Wes?' he said when Wesley stifled a yawn.

'Sorry, Gerry. Late night. I've got news. I think Jonathan Kilin's parents are living in Modbury and I'd like to speak to them. Jonathan was good at art and Temples always claimed there was another artist at Strangefields Farm called Jonny Sykes. They went to the same school . . . '

'You think Sykes might be Kilin? Surely if they were at the same school Temples would have known his real name.'

'Maybe he changed it. Or Temples didn't know him at school – I didn't know everyone a few years below me.'

Gerry thought for a moment. 'Follow it up if you must but remember we need to speak to Pauline Howe. We can return that scarf and see what she knows about the paintings at Castle View Terrace. And don't forget we're due to have a word with Rich Vernon and Lance Pembry this morning.'

'Neil came round last night. I told you about the strange burial he found at Strangefields Farm, didn't I?'

'And I said unless we need to investigate, I don't want to know.'

The phone on Gerry's desk rang and after a short conversation he looked up at Wesley with the look of a hungry man who'd just been presented with a plate of tempting food.

'The patrol dragged Vernon out of bed and he's just arrived downstairs. A car's picking Pembry up in half an hour. Best to catch them first thing before they've had a chance to wake up,' he said with a wicked grin.

Wesley was about to leave Gerry's office when the DCI spoke again. 'Do you think Linda's murder's connected with the Harbourside Players?'

Wesley didn't reply. The idea of some internecine war between rivals in an amateur drama company somehow didn't convince, although he acknowledged that the theatrical manner of Linda's murder might appeal to Lance

Pembry, a man familiar with the techniques of illusion and misdirection.

Rich Vernon was waiting in the interview room; not the windowless one they used for serious suspects but the more comfortable version reserved for witnesses and people they invited in for a more informal chat.

Vernon looked as though he'd dressed in a hurry, and he seemed more nervous than he'd been when they'd last met at the hotel. Wesley, however, didn't read too much into this; police stations often had that effect on people.

'We've had the rope used in the production examined,' Gerry began. 'Our experts say it's the same type as the one Linda Payne was strangled with. In spite of her body being immersed in water our forensics people managed to find minute traces of rope fibre on her neck. It matches your rope so we're working on the assumption that it was the murder weapon.'

Vernon frowned. 'That's impossible. All the props are kept at the Arts Centre and I swear to you that rope's never gone missing. Honestly.'

'Do you handle the rope in the play?'

'No. The duchess is strangled on my orders. I don't do it myself.'

'Then how do you explain the fact that your DNA was found on it?'

Vernon sat with his mouth open for a couple of seconds. 'I ... er, don't know. I can't think.' Suddenly his face lit up. 'Yes, I remember. We were messing about and I was holding it, demonstrating how the scene should be done. Light-hearted ... you know.'

'A light-hearted strangling?' said Gerry. 'Is there such a thing?'

'Lance told Ossie Phillips, the bloke who plays the executioner, off for being too timid. Ossie said he didn't feel comfortable strangling someone because a cousin of his was strangled years ago. It freaked him out.'

Wesley and Gerry exchanged glances. This was something new.

'Do you know the cousin's name?'

Vernon shook his head. 'He never talked about it. All I know is that he was a kid when it happened. Don't suppose you ever get over something like that, do you?'

'Mr Phillips never mentioned this when he gave his statement. Did the murder happen locally?'

'Like I said, he never talked about it. Anyway, I took the rope and demonstrated on Linda. We didn't think anything of it.'

'Did you know Linda was related to Jackson Temples?'

The look of shock on Vernon's face told him the answer was no.

'Who else in the cast might have known?'

'I've no idea. All I know is that she never mentioned it to me.'

Gerry gave Wesley a nod and he left the room, announcing his departure to the machine that was recording the proceedings at the end of the table. After running upstairs to ask one of the team to check out Vernon's story, he returned to find the suspect looking more nervous, as though he feared he'd just incriminated himself.

However, he stuck to his story and ten minutes later a constable brought in a message. Another member of the cast had confirmed Vernon's story. Ossie Phillips had been agitated at the rehearsal. The stage strangling had revived bad memories.

'Before you go, Mr Vernon, can you tell us whether Lance Pembry ever handled that rope?'

'I suppose so. He's the director.'

As soon as Vernon had gone a call came through to tell them Lance Pembry had arrived in reception and five minutes later the director was sitting in the seat Vernon had recently vacated. He looked a lot more confident than the other man had done and answered their questions with apparent honesty. Yes, he'd demonstrated the strangling scene because the 'executioner' hadn't approached it with enough enthusiasm at first then he'd seemed upset and he'd said something about a cousin. He remembered his 'Ferdinand' demonstrating how it should be done at the final rehearsal before the 'duchess's' disappearance, confirming Vernon's story. Pembry had a habit of referring to his cast by the names of their roles; perhaps it was easier for a director than remembering their real names. The 'executioner's' distaste for his task had resulted in him almost losing his part. Pembry didn't sound as though he had much sympathy with the man who'd lost his cousin in such a dreadful way.

'Were Pauline Howe and Linda friends?'

'Yes, I'd say so. They did a lot of talking in corners when Linda should have been thinking herself into the role.' He glared at Gerry. 'If you ask Pauline about it for heaven's sake don't upset her. She's shaky enough on her lines as it is.'

'We'll be gentle,' said Gerry with heavy sarcasm.

'You asked my wife to confirm my alibi?' Pembry suddenly sounded a little anxious.

'We asked the two people you were drinking with too. Everybody backs up your story.'

A smug expression appeared on Lance Pembry's face. 'There you are then.'

'You still admit to having had an affair with the dead woman – and that she was blackmailing you.'

'I wouldn't call it blackmail exactly ... '

Gerry stood up and his chair scraped loudly on the floor. 'Thank you, Mr Pembry. You're free to go.'

For the first time Pembry looked uncertain, as though he hadn't expected to be let off so lightly. But Wesley sensed they'd found out all they could from him for the time being. And they were both impatient to speak to Pauline Howe.

From the second diary of
Lemuel Strange, gentleman

7th April 1685

*I made no mention of the sailor's words to Frances or to my
wife but they came to me again as I lay awake that night.*

*I went down to the quay the next day and supped
with my sailor at the Star, hoping to learn more of
the matter. He told me he had heard tell that Bess
Whitetree had spurned Reuben's unwelcome advances
when she was maidservant to Frances and that Harry,
being Bess's sweetheart, had borne his master some ill
will, although he swore they were both God-fearing young
people who would never steal or kill. My sailor spoke
much about the enmity between Reuben and Master
Treague of Neston who had made vile threats against
him and vowed revenge on him for betraying his father to
Parliament in the late war and causing his arrest and his
sorry death in prison. I had been told of this many years
ago but I had little understood the depth of the hatred
Master Treague had for Reuben until now. My sailor
called Reuben a Puritan hypocrite but, after what I'd
learned, I had no desire to defend his memory.*

Last night I made mention of the sailor's tale to Frances, expecting her to call him a liar, but instead she wept and my wife had to comfort her. I suspect something is amiss but I know not what it is.

47

Cities and towns are anonymous places where you can lose yourself if you wish, hidden in plain sight amongst the crowd. Yet even though Neston was a town, it was relatively small and Danny knew it would be easy for Stag and Roberta to find him. That was why he decided to head for Stokeworthy.

The village was surrounded by woods and farms and, according to Bert, the food the church collected for the local foodbank was stored in the village hall, along with donations for a monthly jumble sale. He'd seen the hall and he reckoned it'd be simple to get in undetected, giving him access to food and a change of clothes. The church too was left unlocked during the day and that was somewhere Stag and Roberta would never think to look for him. He also had a vague recollection that there was something called sanctuary which meant you couldn't be arrested if you were inside a church. Besides, churches were peaceful and they made him feel safe, as though they provided a protective shield against the world and its dangers.

He'd taken the bus from Neston to Tradmouth first thing, getting off at the pub where the lane branched off to Stokeworthy and walking the rest of the way. He had the seventy quid from the jeweller, along with what he had left from the money Bert had given him, which would keep him going for a while if he was careful. Kevin's red leather jacket was stuffed in his rucksack because it was too recognisable and he reckoned that he could find something else to keep out the cold amongst the jumble sale stuff in the village hall. The important thing was not to be caught.

When he reached the village he saw that Bert's bungalow was still festooned with police tape so he hurried past and crouched behind the churchyard wall to make his plans. The police would have finished there now and he still had the key so if he was careful he could have a comfortable bed for the night and nobody would be any the wiser. He'd have to wait until dark and in the meantime the church had a chapel with big tombs that would provide perfect cover for a time, and a bell tower where nobody ever went apart from the bell-ringers.

After checking nobody was around he headed for the church door. When he was halfway down the path between the gravestones he turned his head and saw something that made his heart lurch. A little white van was driving slowly past Bert's bungalow, slowing down to look, so he shot into the shadow of the church porch and pressed his body against the cold stones.

It was Stag and Roberta. And he was afraid they'd come looking for him.

Once they'd finished with Lance Pembry Wesley and Gerry set out for Morbay together. The chief super had asked Gerry to update her on developments but Wesley suspected he was trying to avoid her because he had so little to report. They were still chasing shadows and Wesley was starting to despair.

They'd asked someone to find out about the death of Ossie Phillips' cousin. First though they needed to speak to Pauline Howe. However, when they reached the offices of Bayside Properties they were in for more frustration because Pauline had phoned in sick that morning. Once again Wesley tried the number that Horrocks had provided and once again there was no answer.

'We'll just have to surprise her. Hope she hasn't got anything catching,' said Gerry as they walked to her address.

In Wesley's opinion Pauline's sickness was a little too convenient and he said as much to Gerry, who nodded in agreement.

Pauline Howe lived in a flat on the first floor of a large white stucco villa, a relic of Morbay's glory days as the jewel of the English Riviera when discerning travellers flocked there to enjoy sun, sea and sand at a time when abroad was reserved for the super-rich. The property looked as though it had been recently modernised and there was a neat row of bells next to the glossy front door. Wesley pressed the one marked 'Howe' and after a few seconds a disembodied voice asked who was calling. There was a long gap before they heard the buzz that meant the door lock was released and Wesley wondered whether she was making herself decent to receive them or just playing for time.

She was fully dressed when they arrived at her flat and to the untrained eye she displayed no sign of illness. However, her manner was cautious, as though she feared saying something indiscreet.

'We've been trying to contact you, Ms Howe,' said Wesley.

'I don't answer my phone if I don't recognise the number.' She sniffed. 'Too many nuisance calls.'

'Your boss, Mr Horrocks, said you weren't well.'

'Just a headache,' she said quickly. 'I've taken some pain-killers and I'm feeling better now.'

She was twisting a strand of hair in her fingers, a sign that she was nervous about something. Wesley produced the scarf he'd found at Castle View Terrace.

'Is this yours?'

She hesitated for a moment as though she was consider-ing denying it. 'Er, yes. Where did you find it?'

Wesley handed her the scarf but he didn't answer the question.

'We'd like to talk to you about Linda if that's all right.'

'I didn't really know her that well. I only saw her at rehearsals.'

Wesley was used to people lying to him and Pauline wasn't good at it ... which didn't bode well for Lance Pembry's production.

'Have you lived in the area long?'

'No. I came here from up north about eighteen months ago. I wanted to live near the sea.'

'Do you live alone?'

'Yes. Why?' She sounded defensive.

'You're not ... in a relationship?'

'No.' There was a finality about the reply. Don't enquire any further.

'How long have you worked for Mr Horrocks?' Gerry asked.

'About eight months. I'm on the lookout for something better if you want the truth.'

'What about before then?'

'I temped for a while. I really don't see what that has to do with Linda's murder.' She was beginning to look flus-tered and Wesley watched her face carefully.

'What made you join the Harbourside Players?' he asked. He kept the question light, as if they were having a pleasant conversation.

His tactic seemed to work because she seemed to relax a little. 'It's the first time I've done any acting since school but I've always been interested. I used to have a job in a theatre box office.'

'Whereabouts was that?'

'Manchester . . . where I used to live.'

'You lived there for a long time?'

'Yes.'

'But you didn't like it enough to stay?'

'I needed a change of scene.'

'You haven't got a northern accent,' said Gerry accusingly as though he suspected her of letting the side down.

She shook her head but offered no explanation.

'How do feel about taking on Linda's role in the play?' said Wesley. 'I imagine it's quite a challenge.'

'I'm still shaky with my lines.' She pointed to the well-thumbed copy of the script lying on the glass coffee table in front of her.

'Lance Pembry wouldn't have entrusted you with the part if he didn't think you could do it.'

This raised a smile, the first one Wesley had seen.

'Lance was the reason I went for the audition. I knew his reputation as a director and I couldn't believe he'd bestow his talents on an amateur company like that. It was too good an opportunity to miss. I was so lucky to get the part.'

'Lucky that Linda died?'

Wesley shot Gerry a look. He was making progress and the last thing he needed was for his boss's bluntness to set things back.

'No, I didn't mean . . . I was lucky to get any part and to be made understudy. I never dreamed I'd be playing the duchess. Honestly.'

'Did you know Linda Payne was once in a relationship with Lance Pembry?'

'I suspected there was history between them, yes.'

'Do you think that's why she got the part?'

'I don't know.'

She fell silent but Wesley waited, sure she had more to add. Eventually his patience was rewarded.

'To tell the truth she really wasn't that good. Some of the others used to get exasperated with her. And she used to be quite high-handed with people who didn't have the star parts.'

This was a very different picture of Linda Payne to the one they'd heard previously but people were often reluctant to admit that the recently dead were anything other than saints.

'You included?'

She shrugged. 'I always got on fine with her.'

'Lance Pembry said Linda supplied the rope that's used in the production. The one that's used to strangle the duchess and Cariola.'

She nodded. 'That's right. She said she'd found it in her shop. The previous owner was a keen sailor and it was amongst some old stuff that was left in the back. She used some of it for a display and brought some in for the production.'

Wesley remembered seeing the nautical display in Linda's shop but he hadn't linked it to her murder until now. It looked as though she might have provided the means for her own death.

'Have you ever visited six Castle View Terrace in Tradmouth?'

She hesitated. 'Yes. It's one of the properties we deal with.'

'That's where we found your scarf. When were you last there?'

Pauline looked uncomfortable. 'I'm not sure.'

'The address is being used to store pictures and there's a website linking it to somewhere called the Jackles Gallery – does that name ring any bells?'

She didn't answer.

'We had a look round the premises and found a number of pictures there painted by a man called Jackson Temples. I'm sure the name must be familiar to you. He murdered three women back in the nineteen nineties at Strangefields Farm just outside Tradmouth. The case was notorious at the time.'

Pauline lowered her eyes and said nothing.

'How did the pictures come to be there?'

'I don't know.'

It was clear they weren't getting anywhere. Wesley glanced at Gerry and stood up. 'Can I use your bathroom?'

It was a request he'd never known anybody refuse. When he left the room he closed the door behind him; this was his opportunity to find out more about Pauline Howe and instead of making straight for the bathroom he tried the door opposite and found himself in a bedroom.

He'd been curious about her private life since she'd given such evasive responses to his questions about her relationships and he began to examine a group of framed photographs on a chest of drawers in the corner. Most were of Pauline in recent times, one posed in front of the entrance to the Royal Exchange Theatre in Manchester. But there was one of a group of laughing girls and at first he couldn't make out whether Pauline was among them. Then suddenly he experienced a jolt of realisation. The girl with the short hair was Pauline all right and he recognised one of the girls with her too: Hayley Rummage, the woman who was determined to establish Jackson Temples' innocence, had her arm around Pauline's shoulder – girls on a good night out.

'You know Hayley Rummage?' he asked when he returned to the living room.

'You've been in my bedroom.'

'I'm sorry. But this is a murder inquiry.'

Pauline sighed. 'OK, I met Hayley when I was up in Manchester.'

'You know about her campaign – Jackson Temples?'

Pauline nodded. 'That's the kind of thing she's always been involved in – injustices.'

'Are you involved?'

When she didn't reply Wesley asked his next question. 'You knew that Linda was related to Jackson Temples, didn't you?'

She gave a reluctant nod. 'I mentioned Hayley's campaign to Linda and that's when she confided in me. Up till then she'd kept it very quiet for obvious reasons.'

'You agreed to store the pictures for her.'

'She knew I worked for a property company and she said she'd got hold of some paintings done by her brother. She wanted to sell them and a friend was helping her. There was no room to keep them in her cottage so she paid me to store them. The friend had set up a website and I told her the house was empty and it would be OK to keep them there for a while. I'm sorry I didn't tell you about it before, but I wasn't sure if it would get me into trouble.'

'Does this friend of Linda's have a name?'

'Jonny. Jonny Sykes. She said some of the pictures were his.'

48

Danny continued to watch from the shelter of the church porch. If he didn't keep an eye on Stag and Roberta they might find him and that was the last thing he wanted.

They drove slowly past Bert's and brought their van to a halt outside another bungalow eight doors away but, as Bert had only spoken about his immediate neighbours, Danny didn't know who lived there. He saw Roberta open the passenger door while Stag stayed in the van. She looked around, as though she was making sure nobody was about, straightened her back and marched purposefully to the bungalow's front door. She was carrying a large tote bag and she looked smarter than usual in her long skirt and jacket, as if she'd dressed up for the occasion. He thought he'd seen her in those clothes before, calling on Bert a few days before his death. Bert had said his visitor had been a lady from Social Services so Danny concluded that he'd made a mistake and no more was said about it.

But this time he was sure and he watched Roberta knock on the door with a confidence he hadn't expected, as if she had every right to be there. When the door opened he was surprised when she was invited in immediately like a welcome guest.

Now he had to decide what he was going to do about it.

One thing was certain: Linda Payne was in no position to explain the nature of her relationship with the mysterious Jonny Sykes. There was no record of his existence and he seemed as elusive as the ghosts who reputedly haunted Strangefields Farm. And yet it seemed Jackson Temples hadn't been lying; Jonny Sykes existed and Wesley's suspicion that a good proportion of the paintings at Castle View had been the work of another artist influenced by Temples' style had been proved right.

Wesley tapped the keys on his computer and brought up an email that had arrived half an hour ago; something he'd been meaning to look at but hadn't yet had the opportunity to do. He'd asked an officer at Morbay Police Station to photograph the Jackson Temples paintings they had stored in their basement and once he'd scrolled through the attachment he called Gerry over. 'I'm beginning to think we should have asked to see these earlier.'

By the time he'd finished speaking Trish had joined Gerry and was peering at the screen. As he scrolled down he heard Trish gasp.

'The victims are here – Nerys Harred, Carrie Bullen and Jacky Burns,' she said with disgust. 'All trussed up like Christmas turkeys. Sick.'

Wesley couldn't help agreeing with her. In these particular paintings the girls were bound hand and foot with ropes around their necks, arranged in a hangman's noose, and their heads were bent back in a posture of submission – or ecstasy. These girls weren't models as Jane Webster and her friends had been – they were victims.

'There are none of Gemma Pollinger.'

'She was the last victim. Maybe things escalated and he went even further with her so he decided to destroy the evidence. Why did he paint these particular girls like this and not the others?'

'Maybe they were the only ones willing to go along with it,' said Trish matter-of-factly. She fell silent for a few seconds and studied the pictures. 'Have you noticed the victims are all exceptionally beautiful and the same physical type? Long dark hair and heart-shaped faces. Maybe he had a thing about destroying beauty.'

Wesley nodded. What she said made sense.

'There are a few nudes too – nothing too alarming,' he said, scrolling down through the images. Then he stopped. 'This is Linda.'

The three of them stared at the screen. It was definitely a young Linda Payne but this time she was naked, posed like the Rokeby Venus on a chaise longue, gazing at her reflection in a mirror. The effect was erotic in a tasteful way.

'This isn't by Temples,' said Wesley. 'It's only signed with a J. This is by Jonny Sykes.'

'I think you could be right, sir,' said Trish as though he'd just performed a spectacular conjuring trick.

'If Jonny painted Linda like that what's the betting they were close. And if she was telling Pauline the truth, it means he's still around and they were in contact.' He thought for a moment. 'What if Jonny was afraid Linda would tell someone he hadn't been a figment of her brother's imagination? She'd told Pauline about him after all.'

'But Pauline can't have told Hayley or she would have used it as ammunition to get the case reopened.'

'Pauline probably didn't realise the significance of the name.'

The phone on Wesley's desk rang and he answered it. 'Call for you, sir,' said the voice on the other end of the line. 'Someone by the name of Danny Brice and he says it's urgent. He thinks there's going to be a murder.'

Grace had told Joe Hamer she had urgent business in London so she could spend a couple of days with Dale on his boat and, as there had been no frantic phone calls, either from Hamer or her London office, she presumed she'd got away with her minor deception.

A few months ago she would never have done anything so reckless – something that might jeopardise the reputation of the Compton Wynyard Partnership – but meeting Dale Keyes again had made her forget everything outside the warm, intimate world of their newly rekindled relationship. She regretted that she'd ever mentioned his name to Wesley. If the police had caught up with him it could have ruined everything, but she wasn't to know at the time.

She knew her moment of irresponsibility had to come to an end and she should face the inevitable and get back to work. Besides, Dale hadn't returned to the boat the previous night as he'd promised and all sorts of possibilities had started to run through her mind, some humiliating, some worrying.

Eventually worry triumphed as she recalled the words he'd said before they parted. 'I'm going to get back what's mine but it shouldn't take long. I'll be back before you know it.'

She tried Dale's number and again there was no answer. Then she made a decision.

Wesley Peterson would know what to do in the case of a missing person. However, when she called him all she heard was his voicemail message.

From the second diary of
Lemuel Strange, gentleman

10th April 1685

I found my sailor once more in the Star where he had taken much drink with his fellows. I demanded of him the name of the tavern where he had seen my cousin alive for an idea had started to form in my mind, a thing so terrible I scarcely liked to acknowledge it.

After I was satisfied that all was well at Strangefields I resolved to ride to Plymouth on the morrow. But that night something happened to prevent it.

I retired to bed and sank into a fitful sleep. Then in the early hours I was roused by the dogs barking. Hearing sounds from Frances's room I rose and lit a candle, fearing robbers had come, but when I reached her door I heard lowered voices. In all my years at Strangefields I had never once suspected Frances of entertaining a lover and yet there was a man in her chamber in the depths of the night.

When I opened the door a strange scene greeted me. A man very like my cousin Reuben, though much aged, stood before me and for a moment I thought I must be mistaken. Then I suddenly saw the truth. Reuben had not died as everyone had thought. He had fled the wrath of his enemy, Treague, who would surely have killed him, and left the town to believe him murdered by his servants.

I guessed from the terror on Frances's face that she had not been privy to this deception and when Reuben saw me he stepped back in shock. It was then I saw he had a pistol. And it was pointing at my chest.

49

Wesley had asked DC Rob Carter to find out all he could about Ossie Phillips' cousin, the one he claimed had been strangled. Eventually he came up with an answer and it wasn't one Wesley had expected. As soon as Rob found out that Ossie's mother's maiden name had been Burns, the pieces of the puzzle fell into place. Ossie Phillips was the cousin of Jacky Burns. This discovery was sufficient reason for Wesley to ask for him to be brought in for questioning.

As Ossie worked aboard the passenger ferry, he wasn't hard to find and an hour later Wesley and Gerry were sitting opposite him in the interview room.

Ossie was being interviewed under caution but he'd refused the services of a solicitor. According to him, he didn't need one.

'Jacky Burns was your cousin,' Wesley began. As soon as he said the victim's name, Ossie turned his face away.

'Yes. But I don't like to talk about her,' Ossie muttered, his voice cracking as though he was on the verge of tears. 'It upsets me.'

'I'm afraid you've got no choice,' said Wesley. He glanced at Gerry, who was staring at the man as though he was watching for a mistake, a slip-up in the act.

Ossie took a deep breath. 'Me and Jacky used to be close . . . until she started going round with that . . . artist.' He almost spat out the word. 'I told her he was bad news but she was flattered.' He buried his head in his hands and Wesley waited patiently for him to continue. After half a minute he looked up and Wesley saw his eyes were wet with unshed tears. 'When Lance made me pretend to strangle Linda it brought it all back – how they said Jacky died. I just couldn't do it.'

'You've still got the part, haven't you?'

'After that first time I got over it. Told myself it wasn't real. It was just a play.'

'Did you know Linda Payne was Jackson Temples' half-sister?'

Ossie's mouth fell open and a thin trail of dribble trickled from the corner. He wiped it away with his sleeve and shook his head vigorously. 'No. I'd no idea. She never mentioned it and I don't blame her. That man was evil and even if I had known about Linda I wouldn't have blamed her for what he did. Why would I?'

'You were obviously fond of Jacky?'

He nodded. 'She was a lovely kid – until she got in with Temples. Really beautiful she was – like an angel.' He looked Wesley in the eye. 'But I never harmed Linda, I swear on my mother's life. I could never kill anybody. Honest.'

'You said you went straight home after the rehearsal, which means you haven't got an alibi for the time of Linda's murder.'

'I can't help that. My partner was away visiting her mum.'

After a few more questions Wesley ended the interview and told Ossie he could go, but to make sure they knew where to find him.

'What do you think?' he asked as he and Gerry climbed the stairs to the CID office.

'I believed him,' said Gerry.

'Me too.'

'Although if he found out about Linda's true identity somehow – maybe from Pauline – he might have just lost control and ...'

Wesley shook his head. 'No, Gerry. I don't think Linda's death was a spur-of-the-moment thing. It was well planned.'

'But we've got to remember that Ossie's in the Harbourside Players – he's used to putting on an act. He has to be on our suspect list.'

Wesley couldn't argue with that.

The interview with Ossie Phillips wasn't the only thing on his mind though. He kept thinking of Danny Brice's call. The lad had been on the run since their encounter at the jeweller's so contacting the police seemed an odd thing for him to do, and when he'd asked Wesley to meet him at Stokeworthy church he'd sounded frightened.

He told Gerry he needed to see what Danny had to say because there was a chance he might have information about the murder of Bert Cummings. He didn't intend to go to the meeting alone, but as Gerry had things to do he decided to take Rachel with him. He trusted her judgement.

They borrowed a pool car to drive the three miles to Stokeworthy and when he reached the village he parked near the church gate, thinking how peaceful the place was. A quintessentially English village with a church, pub and village hall; hardly the sort of place most people associated with murder – apart from in the pages of the cosier sort of crime novel.

They walked up the church path and when he pushed at the heavy wooden door it opened with a creak that announced his arrival like a fanfare. Wesley shut the door behind him and waited for his eyes to adjust to the gloom before making his way slowly down the aisle with Rachel by his side. There was no sign of Danny Brice and he was starting to think the call might have been a trick, maybe to throw them off the scent. Then when he reached the handsome painted rood screen he saw a movement in the side chapel to his right, a figure emerging from behind a grand table tomb topped by an effigy of a knight. He recognised Danny Brice at once and raised his hand in a gesture of reassurance.

'Danny. You wanted to talk. Maybe it'd be best if we went back to the station.'

Danny walked slowly towards him, his dog, Barney, trotting obediently to heel. He looked remarkably meek for a wanted man, not what Wesley had been expecting at all.

'Thanks for coming.'

Wesley had never been thanked by a suspect before but he hid his surprise and gave Danny a small smile of acknowledgement. 'I want to tell you where I got that stuff from.'

Wesley and Rachel looked at each other. The man was clearly in a confessional mood and he felt reluctant to break the spell by hauling him back to the interview room. That could come later.

'Go on.'

'It was under a floorboard at my squat. There's this couple who live there – Stag and Roberta – and it was in their room.' He looked round as though he was afraid of being overheard. 'I've just seen her going into a house round the corner all dressed up with one of those things round her neck . . . like she was official.'

'A lanyard?'

Danny nodded.

'Where does she work?'

'She doesn't. Neither of them do. That's why I thought it was odd.'

Wesley had been puzzled by Danny's words but slowly the jigsaw was starting to fit together. Some of the elderly burglary victims had said they'd been visited by a lady from the council a week or so before their valuables were stolen but nobody had connected these visits with the burglaries – and certainly not to Bert Cummings' murder. Now Wesley couldn't wait to follow it up.

'A couple of days before he died Bert said a lady from Social Services had come to see him. Said she'd asked all sorts of questions about his security. I saw Roberta near his house around that time. Do you think it could have been her pretending to be from the council?'

'Do they know the jewellery's gone?'

'Don't know. I wasn't going to take the risk so I've moved out.'

'We've been looking for you. Where have you been?'

Danny shuffled his feet. 'Here and there. I never harmed Bert. I wouldn't.' He sounded desperate to be believed. 'I . . . I knew Kevin, his grandson,' Danny continued. 'We were . . . together. When I turned up at Bert's the first time he thought I was Kevin and I went along with it 'cause I didn't want to upset him.' He glanced towards the altar nearby. 'As God's my witness, I just found him like that and called your lot. Honest.'

Wesley's instincts told him that Danny was telling the truth – and that his fear was genuine.

'Do you think Stag and Roberta killed Bert? If he caught them stealing . . . '

When Wesley didn't answer the question, Danny spoke again. 'And there's something else. It's probably nothing.'

'Let me be the judge of that.'

'Something odd happened when I took Bert on the ferry across the river the week before he died. He didn't get out much and he wanted to do it so I borrowed Stag's van and took him into Tradmouth. He was on the ferry, all happy like, when he suddenly looked like he'd seen a ghost. I asked him what was wrong and he said it was nothing but I could tell something had upset him 'cause he wanted to stay on when we got to Queenswear and go straight back to Tradmouth. I think he saw something on that ferry – or somebody.' The words came out in a rush, as though he'd been brooding on the incident during his time as a fugitive.

'Who was it? Who did he see?'

'Haven't a clue. Do you think it might have been Roberta? Or Stag? What if he was scared of them and he never told me?'

'Come to the police station and look at some pictures – just to see if you recognise anyone. We'll give you a lift to Tradmouth.' He looked at Rachel, who was standing by his side, her eyes fixed on Danny as though she was afraid he'd make a run for it. But she could see Wesley had developed a rapport with the suspect so she was wise enough to stay silent.

Wesley assumed the worried look on Danny's face was because of his imminent trip to the police station. He was soon to realise he was wrong.

'When I came in here I saw Stag's van parked at the end of Bert's street. Like I said, I saw Roberta go into one of the bungalows while he waited outside. I think an old woman lives there on her own. What if they killed Bert and they're planning to kill the old girl too?'

There was an urgency about Danny's words that told Wesley he needed to act. It could be a ploy but somehow he didn't think so. He called for a patrol car to take Danny in, telling him to wait in his car with Rachel and Barney in the meantime until it arrived. If Danny wasn't lying, he had to investigate.

Following Danny's directions, he walked the short distance to the bungalow Danny had described but when he arrived there was no white van in sight. He took his warrant card from his pocket and knocked on the door, which was opened by a small birdlike woman with a shock of white hair. She was leaning on a Zimmer frame and she looked him up and down suspiciously.

Wesley introduced himself and asked her whether a woman had just called. The answer was yes. A very nice young lady from the council had just been round to check her house was safe.

When Wesley asked her to see whether any valuables were missing she told him to wait and disappeared into a back room, returning a few minutes later with a look of triumph on her face. Her jewellery was all there, she said.

'Have you a spare front-door key?' Wesley asked, earning himself another wary look. 'Please, it's important.'

'It's under the plant pot outside.'

'Did you tell the woman who's just visited you where it is?'

The woman's watery blue eyes widened. 'Why shouldn't I? She wanted to make sure I was safe.'

Wesley told her to move her key somewhere else. He now knew how the burglaries had been committed so neatly.

He returned to the car just as the patrol pulled up. Danny was sitting in the back of his car beside Rachel, fondling Barney's ears, so he reckoned it was safe for them to take him in themselves. Even so the patrol's presence wasn't wasted. He instructed them to pick up Stag and Roberta as a matter of urgency.

As he was about to drive away his mobile rang and he saw Grace's name on the caller display. He needed to get back to the station so he killed the call. He'd ring her back later.

When he reached the station he settled Danny in the interview room with a cup of tea and a bowl of water for Barney before hurrying upstairs to the CID office. Gerry was pacing up and down impatiently and the solemn expression on his face told him something was wrong.

'A man's body's been found,' he said. 'And it looks like another murder.'

50

Wesley had been intending to return Grace's call only for events to overtake him. A man's body had been found at Knot Creek, with no ID and no phone. Two lads had been mending their motor boat at low tide when they spotted the body face down in the mud a few yards from the shore and called the police.

It was a short distance by boat from Tradmouth to Knot Creek but it took longer via the winding country lanes. Wesley and Gerry arrived just as the tide was beginning to turn and for the CSIs it was a race against the incoming water as they photographed the corpse *in situ*. In the end they yielded to the inevitable and moved the dead man to the bank to allow Colin Bowman to make his examination.

'When the call came in my money was on a drowning,' said Gerry as they stood watching. 'You know the old legend, Wes: every year the river claims a life. There's been two this year already. That drunk who fell off the embankment in Regatta Week and the rowing boat caught in that storm last month.'

'But?'

'Once the officer who was first on the scene noticed the stab wounds we knew different.'

At that moment Grace rang again. This time Wesley answered, ready to point out politely that he was in the middle of a case so he hadn't time to chat. But as soon as she spoke the worry in her voice told him it wasn't a social call. 'You know I told you about Dale?'

'What about him?'

'I told Maritia a little fib. I haven't been in London for the past few days. I've been staying with Dale on his yacht.' She'd lowered her voice as though she was making a confession and her words gave him a jolt. The man sounded like bad news and he felt hurt that she'd misled him.

'He went out last night,' she continued. 'Said he was going to see someone who owed him money and he wouldn't be long. Only he never came back and his phone's switched off.'

'Are you sure he didn't just lose interest?' Wesley knew his words were blunt but it was a question that needed to be asked.

'Of course I'm sure,' she snapped. 'He'd have said something. We're both adults. I think something's happened to him.'

Wesley looked at the body lying there surrounded by police photographers and the forensic team, the centre of everyone's attention. 'Can you describe him?'

As she began to speak he saw Colin squat down to examine the corpse. He listened while she went into impressive detail about the clothes Dale had been wearing when she'd last seen him: chinos, denim jacket, checked shirt. They were all there, draped sodden on the corpse in front of him.

The man matched her description of Dale Keyes exactly but he felt reluctant to tell her. Then he realised he had no choice.

'Er ... a man's body's just been found in the river.' He heard a gasp on the other end of the line. Perhaps his words had been too brutal.

'You don't think it's Dale?'

'We're not sure, but would you be willing to have a look at the body?'

She fell silent for a few seconds. Then, 'OK. Will you be there?'

'Promise.'

To make things easier for her he said he'd pick her up from wherever she was, but she said it wasn't necessary; she'd drive over straight away. It would only take twenty minutes.

An hour later she still hadn't arrived.

It was the easiest money Stag and Roberta had ever made. The only time they'd feared things might go wrong was when she'd visited Bert Cummings. He'd had a few nice pieces of jewellery belonging to his late wife but Roberta had recognised him at once. He'd taught her maths at Fulton Grange, although she'd hardly been his star pupil.

She always used a different name when she made her visits, of course, but she'd had to bluff it out when Mr Cummings told her she looked familiar and asked if she'd once been one of his pupils. After that she'd got out quick and the incident told her it was time to move on and try another part of the country. If they were careful they couldn't fail.

In a few days, once the old lady had had time to forget about her visit, they'd do their last job in South Devon and, although they knew it was premature, it felt like an occasion for celebration. Danny and that dog of his weren't at the squat which meant they had the place to themselves, and their feeling of imminent triumph acted as an aphrodisiac so they made straight for their room where they made love on their mattress. When they sold the stuff they were going to have cash and life felt good.

Once they'd dressed, Roberta experienced a miser's urge to gloat over the treasure they'd accumulated so far. There were some nice pieces in their hoard and she felt a thrill of excitement as she levered up the floorboard. Then when she looked into the hiding place her elation turned to despair.

'The stuff's gone. That little scrote Danny must have helped himself. How did he know it was there? You didn't tell him, did you?'

Before Stag could reply there was a thunderous knocking on the door.

'Let's get out of here,' Roberta hissed.

But by the time they started gathering their things together it was too late.

51

At one thirty Grace still hadn't turned up and Wesley had started to worry. He tried to convince himself she'd changed her mind about the identification, something that can be daunting even for an experienced police officer. Although if that was the case surely she would have let him know.

The body of the man they believed to be Dale Keyes had been taken to the mortuary and a team had been sent to his yacht. Wesley had also asked Rob to go to Grace's hotel to look for her and if she wasn't there, he was to try Strangefields Farm.

In the meantime Danny Brice had given a formal statement and they had two prisoners waiting in the interview suite. He'd asked Trish and Paul to conduct the interview with Stag while he and Rachel questioned Roberta. As Rachel walked into the windowless room where the woman was waiting for them with the duty solicitor, Wesley saw a look of grim determination on his colleague's face. Rachel Tracey didn't like people who took advantage of the vulnerable and neither did he, only she wasn't as good as he was at hiding her disapproval.

'I'll need your name and address,' Wesley began.

'Roberta Georgina Felicity Onslow-James,' the woman

replied with a hint of a smirk before reciting the address of the Neston squat. 'And I'm denying everything.'

'You visited a Mrs Ethel Smith in Stokeworthy earlier today.'

'No comment.'

'We found a lanyard amongst your possessions – Neston Social Services. They say they've never heard of you.'

'No comment.'

'Did you ever visit Bert Cummings, the man who was found dead in Stokeworthy?'

'No comment.'

The interview continued for another ten minutes by the end of which Wesley was heartily sick of hearing those two words. As they left the room Roberta called after them.

'You can't prove anything and you know it. You'll have to release us.'

Wesley turned to face her. 'We've got the jewellery.'

She rolled her eyes. 'That little toe-rag Danny told us he'd taken it. He boasted about how he went round these old people's houses offering to do odd jobs. Said they were never careful where they left their cash and jewellery. It's him you should be arresting, not us.'

She sounded so convincing that for a split second he was almost tempted to believe her. Then he thought about Danny and knew she was lying.

He shut the door behind him just as Paul and Trish were emerging from the room next door looking pleased with themselves.

Resisting the temptation to share their discoveries in the corridor, they made their way upstairs to the CID office and headed for a small conference room where they wouldn't be disturbed.

It was Paul who spoke first. 'He's come clean to the lot, sir. Says it was all Roberta's idea. She pretended to be from Social Services and once she'd gained the victims' trust she found out where they kept their keys and their valuables. Then Stag went back at night and helped himself to anything he could lay his hands on.'

'She was cool,' said Rachel. 'No comment all the way.'

'According to Stag she comes from a wealthy family,' said Trish.

'In that case they'll probably pay for a clever barrister who'll put all the blame on Stag ... or Danny Brice.'

'We won't let that happen,' said Wesley but he felt anger welling up inside him because he knew Rachel could be right.

'Why would a woman who had her advantages in life turn out like that?' said Trish in disbelief.

'Some people are just born bad,' Rachel replied.

Wesley checked his watch. 'Let's break the news to Gerry. At least that's one of our cases solved.'

They would leave Paul and Trish to tie up the Stag and Roberta case and make sure they had enough evidence to charge them; the last thing they wanted was for Roberta to wriggle out of the charges on a technicality. But before Wesley left the room he had another question for Paul.

'Did you ask Stag about Bert Cummings' murder?'

Paul frowned. 'He swears that had nothing to do with him and Roberta. He says they might be thieves but they're not killers.'

'Did you believe him?'

Paul considered the question for a few moments. 'I think I did. What about Roberta?'

'I think of the two of them she's the more ruthless,' said Rachel.

Wesley made for Gerry's office with Rachel by his side.

'How did you get on with our friends from Neston?' Gerry asked as they came in.

'The man's confessed to burglary but the woman won't talk.'

'Women are made of tougher stuff, Wes. I found that out years ago. A team's going over Dale Keyes' yacht and I've got someone looking into his past. Apparently he was a property developer until his company got into big trouble – something to do with an employee who cleared out his company bank account. Anyway, he was involved in a ferry disaster in Thailand, believed dead, but it turns out he's been living in Spain for the past couple of years and doing very nicely for himself. There's evidence that a woman was with him on the yacht. We need to find out who she is and make sure she hasn't suffered the same fate.'

Wesley wasn't prepared for the flurry of panic he felt inside when Gerry put his fears into words. Last time he'd spoken to Grace had been three hours ago. According to Rob Carter she wasn't at her hotel or at Strangefields Farm and he had a gut feeling that she was in danger.

It was time to come clean with Gerry but he didn't want Rachel to overhear.

'If we could have a word in private . . . '

Rachel got the message and left the office.

'I know who's been living on Keyes' yacht.'

Gerry waited for him to carry on.

'Her name's Grace Compton and she's an old friend of mine from London. She's an architect and she's down here

307

working on the new holiday development at Strangefields Farm. She used to know Keyes.'

'Know as in hanky-panky?'

Now Gerry had put it into words it sounded sordid, almost a slur on his memories of the girl he'd once been fond of. 'If you want to put it like that, yes. Anyway, like everyone else she thought he'd died in that ferry accident so she was surprised when she spotted him here in Tradmouth. It looks as if they got together again ... not that she confided in me.'

'Where is she now?' Wesley could hear the concern in Gerry's voice.

'That's what I want to know. She agreed to come and identify his body but she never turned up. She's not at Strangefields Farm or at her hotel.'

'Then we need to find her.'

'All patrols are on the lookout for her car. Her mobile's off but if she switches it on we'll be able to locate it.'

Gerry looked him in the eye. 'You're worried about her, aren't you?'

'Yes.' He thought for a moment. 'Do you think Dale Keyes' murder could be linked to Linda Payne's – they were both found in water ... ?'

'Multiple stab wounds. Colin'll be able to tell us whether the same weapon was used.'

'Keyes has no connection with Jackson Temples, has he?'

'Not that we know of.'

Wesley looked out of the window and saw clouds gathering over the hills above Queenswear. After a while he spoke again. 'Temples was telling the truth about another artist being at Strangefields Farm with him. Jonny Sykes existed.'

'We tried to find him at the time. No joy.'

'Sykes might not have been his real name. I'm think-ing of Jonathan Kilin. He and Temples went to the same school and were both into art. They weren't in the same year but that doesn't mean they didn't know each other.' Wesley flopped down into the seat next to Gerry's desk. 'I was going up to Modbury to talk to Kilin's parents but with Grace missing . . .'

Suddenly he had an idea. Grace and Maritia had been close as teenagers so there was a chance that Grace might have sought out her old friend in time of trouble – or at least told her where she was.

He punched out his sister's number, half expecting to hear a disembodied message telling him she was unavaila-ble, but to his surprise she answered after two rings.

'It's my day off,' she explained, making him feel guilty about having lost track of the hours she worked at the surgery. 'I've been trying to call Grace but her phone's switched off.'

His heart sank. 'When did you last speak to her?'

'A couple of days ago. She said she was going back to London for a few days and she'd be in touch when she got back.'

She'd lied to Maritia as well but he wasn't giving up hope.

'I'm afraid she didn't tell you the truth. She met a man she thought had died in Thailand and they were seeing each other again. His name was Dale Keyes and a man answering his description has been found dead. We're treating it as murder.'

There was a stunned silence and he could almost pic-ture the look of shock on his sister's face. 'Surely you can't suspect Grace.'

'We don't know where she is at the moment. She hasn't

been in London – she's been staying on Keyes' yacht with him and she called me this morning to say he was missing. Then a body turned up in Knot Creek.'

'Drowned?'

'He appears to have been stabbed a number of times ... similar to that elderly man in Stokeworthy a few days ago. Grace said she'd come to the mortuary to identify him but she hasn't turned up and I'm getting worried. Is there anything she said to you – anything at all?'

'I'm thinking ... I'm thinking.' She sounded exasperated with herself, as though there was something she was trying to recall; something she'd ignored at the time which might prove important now. 'I'm sorry, there isn't. Is there any sign of her car?'

'It's not in the car park at the hotel. I've asked Traffic to go through their number plate recognition system but if she's gone off the main routes ...'

'Let me know when she turns up, won't you?'

He promised but with each minute that passed he was feeling more and more uneasy. He kept telling himself there was no evidence that Grace was in danger even though it was a possibility he knew he had to consider.

He'd just rung off when Rachel walked into the CID office and he was surprised to see that she wasn't alone. Danny Brice was with her, looking sheepish amongst so many police officers. She came over to Wesley's desk, Danny hanging back as though he longed to be somewhere else.

'You said you wanted Danny to look at some photographs. I thought it'd be better to bring him up here.'

Wesley gave Danny an encouraging smile. 'They're on that board over there,' he said, pointing to the large white-board bearing pictures of all the people who'd featured in

310

the investigation so far. 'Do you recognise anyone? Perhaps someone you've seen near Bert's house – or on the ferry.'

The actual crime-scene pictures were on another board nearby. Wesley wished he'd had time to cover them up but Danny gave them a swift glance before obeying Wesley's instructions.

He studied the photographs for a while before turning to speak to Wesley. 'Yeah. I recognise that one.' When he pointed to one of the photographs Wesley hid his surprise.

From the second diary of
Lemuel Strange, gentleman

10th April 1685

My cousin held the pistol steady.

'What do you want?' I asked. 'Why have you returned?'

'I want what is mine. My wife and son.'

'Your son is dead.' I heard Frances utter these words with no hint of the grief I knew she felt.

'I know that now. Terrible news to greet a man on his return to the land of the living.'

'Why did you disappear leaving all to think you dead?'

He grabbed Frances roughly by the arm. 'I saw a chance to flee my debts and an enemy who had sworn to kill me. It was a simple matter to change my name and take a ship to Holland where I have prospered as I never did here in Devonshire. I returned to do business with a merchant in Plymouth but when I heard of my wife's inheritance ...'

'You have no right to that,' I said, angry on Frances's behalf. 'You abandoned her to your creditors

312

and allowed her to think you dead. If I hadn't come to her aid . . . '

I heard a sound behind me and turned to see my wife, standing open-mouthed. I shouted to her to fetch John and as she ran down the staircase in her nightgown Reuben fired his pistol and Frances screamed loud enough to waken the dead. By God's good mercy his shot missed and I lunged forward to grapple him to the floor. The pistol fell from his hand but he fought fiercely, although his age gave me the advantage. When John arrived in the chamber Reuben realised he was outnumbered and exhaustion overcame him. John pinned his arms behind his back but, being a man of few words, he expressed no amazement at his late master's strange resurrection. Rather he looked to me for instruction.

52

'You would have seen him on the ferry,' Wesley said. 'He works aboard. His name's Ossie Phillips.'

His mind was racing. Ossie Phillips' DNA was found on the rope which might have killed Linda Payne. Now he was beginning to wonder whether Bert Cummings had been afraid of him for some reason.

However, Danny Brice was soon to dispel his suspicions. 'Yeah. Bert said hello to him and asked him how he was doing. He used to teach him at Neston High School, he said.'

'So he wasn't the person Bert seemed worried about?'

'Oh no. He was pleased to see him. But then he saw someone else. Don't know who but he was rattled all right.'

Wesley had an idea. 'Could the person he saw be someone else he used to teach?'

Danny shrugged. 'If he was, the man on the ferry didn't recognise him.'

'Then if he wasn't at Neston High then he might have been at the other school where Bert taught – Fulton Grange.'

Wesley knew he was taking a gamble. With Grace missing he knew he should be concentrating on finding her but what he wanted to do wouldn't take long. He thanked

Danny and shot into Gerry's office. When he told Gerry what he was planning the DCI looked crestfallen. He relished any opportunity to get out on the river but the amount of paperwork in front of him meant he was trapped behind his desk for the time being.

As Wesley was on his way out of the office he caught sight of the photographs on the noticeboard. With everything that had happened, he'd almost forgotten about Linda's assistant, Jen Barrow. She'd told Rachel she was thinking of going away for a while because she was so upset by Linda's murder and, according to Rachel, she hadn't been answering her phone. But what if she hadn't gone away? What if something had prevented her and she'd met the same fate as her employer?

'Anyone tried to contact Jen Barrow recently?'

Gerry looked up. 'Rach has but she's had no luck.'

'I'm wondering whether she knows more than she admitted about Linda's death and she's left because she's frightened the killer would come after her? The two women worked together. They must have talked – passed the time of day. Maybe Linda told her something and she didn't think it was important enough to mention it when we were questioning her but later she realised its significance.'

'If that's the case she might have been right to get out of the area. I only wish she'd kept us informed.'

'Unless . . . unless the killer's already caught up with her.'

'I know, Wes. That's worrying me too. I keep coming back to Linda's link with Jackson Temples. I don't think we can ignore the possibility that Ossie Phillips decided to take revenge on Temples' half-sister for the murder of his cousin. He's admitted that he and Jacky Burns were close.'

Wesley took a deep breath. What he was about to say might sound like heresy to Gerry, whose opinions were coloured by his involvement in the original case, but he couldn't keep his thoughts to himself. 'What if Temples didn't do it? What if he was innocent?'

He saw Gerry frown with disbelief and shake his head. 'He was guilty as hell, Wes. All the evidence pointed to it. The jury only took an hour to reach their verdict.'

Wesley didn't bother to reply. Instead he joined Danny at the office entrance.

'Someone's phoned the hostel. They've got a place. As long as we know where to find you you'll be released on bail,' said Wesley. 'Thanks for your help.'

'I'm not in danger, am I?'

Wesley felt he couldn't tell a lie. If the killer thought Danny had seen him or her at Bert Cummings' bungalow or on the ferry, he might be a target. 'Call me if you're worried about anything ... anything at all,' he said as he handed Danny his card. 'You've got your phone?'

When they reached the police station entrance they went their separate ways and Wesley stood watching until Danny disappeared round the corner, feeling somehow responsible for him. Stag and Roberta were in custody but he wasn't sure whether Danny might be facing a threat from another source.

He walked the short distance to the passenger ferry landing stage and when it docked he waited until the passengers had disembarked before stepping aboard. Unlike Gerry, he wasn't good on boats but he breathed in the diesel-scented river air, telling himself the nausea he felt was all in the mind. When he felt less queasy he made his way round the deck, searching for Ossie Phillips. This would be an informal chat. He could always arrange for him to be brought to the station later if necessary.

Wesley found him collecting fares down below and, with his cheerful banter to his passengers, it was difficult to imagine him being cast as the 'executioner' in Lance Pembry's production.

'Hello, Inspector,' he said warily. 'What can I do for you?'

'If I could have a word.' Ossie looked worried but Wesley was quick to reassure him. 'Nothing to worry about.'

'I'll have to finish this first. Give me a minute,' said Phillips with the confidence of an innocent man.

When Wesley offered his fare Ossie waved it away. 'Police, fire, ambulance and the lifeboat crew get it on the house.'

Once Ossie had completed his task he came back. 'Now what did you want to ask me? Is it about Linda? 'Cause I've already told you everything I know.'

'It's not about Linda this time. Do you remember seeing this man on the ferry a couple of weeks ago?' He handed him Bert Cummings' photograph. 'He was with a young man.'

Ossie's eyes lit up. 'That's Mr Cummings. I was in his class at Neston High – used to like the old boy. Right upset I was when I heard about him.'

Wesley was on the point of asking him whether he remembered Della but he thought better of it.

'Mr Cummings was strict but you could talk to him; not like some,' Ossie continued. 'He said the lad was his grandson. It was nice they seemed so close.'

Wesley didn't feel inclined to enlighten him. 'The young man told us Bert might have recognised someone while he was on board. He said he seemed upset and wanted to go straight back to Tradmouth.'

Ossie sat there on the wooden bench, frowning in concentration. 'I remember I said hello, asked him how he was and all that, but I didn't have time to hang around. When I saw him again I realised he hadn't got off but there were a lot of passengers on that day so I was too busy to talk to him again. But . . . '

Wesley had a feeling that he was about to learn something important. He held his breath and waited.

'I could be wrong,' Ossie said. 'But I think I saw Mr Cummings speaking to someone. The grandson had gone to the toilet over there.' He pointed in the vague direction of a toilet sign at the other end of the cabin. 'And Mr Cummings went up to this person and said something. I thought he looked a bit rattled and by the time the grandson came back the person had gone up on deck. She got off at Queenswear.'

'It was a woman?'

Ossie considered the question for a few moments. 'I'm saying "her" but it could have been a "him". It was raining and they had their hood up so I couldn't see their hair or face, but from the way they walked . . . '

'So when this person left the ferry Bert Cummings stayed on?'

'That's right. The grandson stood up to get off but Mr Cummings pulled at his sleeve and he sat down again. If you ask me, Mr Cummings looked scared.'

'Can you describe this person?'

'Tallish, wearing jeans and a navy-blue waterproof jacket with the hood up; just ordinary. And when I collected their fare she – or he – had their head bowed so I didn't see the face.'

'How old?'

'Couldn't really tell. Sorry.'

Wesley took four photographs out of his pocket: Linda Payne, Pauline Howe, Jen Barrow and Roberta. 'Could any of these be the person Bert spoke to?'

Ossie studied them closely. 'It definitely wasn't Linda or Pauline 'cause I know them from the Harbourside Players. As for the other two I can't tell. Like I said, I didn't really get a look at their face – and I can't put my hand on my heart and say it wasn't a him. Sorry.'

Wesley tried to hide his disappointment. 'Would you recognise this person if you saw them again?'

Ossie shook his head again. 'Sorry.'

His fellow passengers were standing up, ready to disembark, but Wesley had no business in Queenswear so he didn't move while Ossie rushed up on deck to help with the docking.

He gazed out of the window at the water. The sun had emerged from behind the clouds, making the surface of the river sparkle with diamonds of light. When his phone began to ring the noise made him jump. It was Neil and he felt a sudden rush of optimism. If Grace had turned up at Strangefields Farm, he might have seen her.

'Read that diary yet?' was Neil's first question.

'Haven't had time to finish it yet. Sorry. There's been another murder.'

'Who?'

Wesley was about to tell him but he stopped himself. In Grace's absence, the dead man hadn't been formally identified yet and when he was, there would be relatives to inform as soon as they could be found. 'Not sure yet. Is this just a social call?'

'We've just found a third skeleton. Another deviant

burial the same as the others. Looks like another male – probably older this time.' There was a short silence before Neil carried on talking. 'You know that other diary I gave you a copy of?'

'What about it?' The ferry had set off again and the motion brought on another bout of queasiness.

'It explains the first two bodies – the young man and woman – but there's no reference to an older man at all. You said the one you've got at your police station might have been written by the same person?'

'It's possible. Sorry, Neil, things are busy here but I've asked someone to make a copy of it and I'll try to take a look when I've got a minute.' Much as Wesley would have liked to discuss Neil's find, he had more pressing matters to think about. 'You haven't seen Grace Compton up there recently, have you? The architect.'

'Is that what she calls herself? Have you seen the nasty little boxes she's designed for the holidaymakers? They're going to cost a bomb. And that reception building's a monstrosity—'

'Have you seen her?' Wesley interrupted.

'Someone said they saw her car on the lane earlier.'

'What time?'

'Sometime this morning, I think.'

'Sure it was her car?'

'I wasn't paying much attention so I might have got it wrong. Or it might have been yesterday. Sorry. Mind on other things.'

Neil could be oblivious to the world outside archaeology during an exciting dig but, even so, Wesley found his vagueness frustrating. 'Was Grace alone? Or with someone else?'

'No idea.'

'Who saw her?'

'Can't remember but I can ask around if you like. Are you coming to see our new skeleton? We're about to lift it so if you want to see it *in situ* you'll have to get a move on.'

Wesley said he hadn't time and ended the call, wishing Neil had been more specific about the sighting of Grace.

When the ferry docked in Tradmouth he said goodbye to Ossie Phillips, gave him his card and told him to get in touch if he remembered any more. As he disembarked he made a decision. It would do no harm to call in at Strangefields Farm on his way to Modbury to see Jonathan Kilin's parents. It would make Neil happy if he could show off his thrilling new find and while he was there he could ask if anybody else had seen Grace.

When Grace opened her eyes she could see sunlight between the slats of the boarded-up window. Her head throbbed as if a hundred tiny builders were hard at work in her brain with drills and hammers so she closed them again.

She'd been on her way to keep her appointment with Wesley when she'd received the text from Dale. *Sorry. Got held up. Meet me. Urgent.* He'd signed off with a kiss, which was just like him. He'd always been a charmer; that was why he'd managed to get away with so much. She'd felt a wave of relief. After speaking to Wesley she'd been certain he was dead – that she'd lost him a second time – and the text had made her giddy with joy.

He'd instructed her to drive to the little derelict cottage near the T-junction on Dead Man's Lane and to leave her car behind the building, well concealed behind overgrown bushes and out of sight of the road. She knew the cottage because Joe Hamer had shown an interest in acquiring it but hadn't been able to contact the owners – although she wasn't sure whether she'd believed him. There were a lot of things about Hamer she wasn't inclined to enquire into too closely.

As she'd parked she'd heard the archaeologists' voices carrying over the light breeze. But they'd been hidden behind the high Devon hedge on the other side of the lane so they'd been oblivious to her arrival, which had suited her fine. As far as Hamer knew she was in London and the subterfuge had made her feel like a naughty schoolgirl bunking off lessons.

When she'd tried the cottage door she'd wondered why the place hadn't been bought up and renovated years ago, maybe as a second home. Perhaps the address, Dead Man's Lane, had put off potential purchasers.

She'd also wondered why Dale had chosen to meet in such a place. Who was he hiding from and why? She'd checked the ground floor and found it empty but with signs of recent habitation: used plastic coffee cups and food wrappers. Then she'd climbed the half-rotten stairs, feeling a thrill of excitement as she anticipated the reunion. A door had been standing ajar and when she'd pushed it open she'd found herself in a small upstairs room with a boarded-up window and daylight trickling through a hole in the ceiling, open to the sky because half the roof slates were missing.

She could hear the soft cooing of pigeons in the rafters and in the dim light she could see that the room was roughly furnished with an old armchair and a double air bed. Her phone had told her she had another text and as she'd read it she smiled. *Just popped out. Left wine.*

Suggest you make a start while you're waiting. Got big surprise. Won't be long.

As soon as her eyes had adjusted to the gloom, she'd spotted the bottle of wine and a pair of wine glasses standing on a dusty bamboo table in the corner of the room. As instructed she'd opened the screw top and poured herself a drink before settling down in the armchair to wait. That was the last thing she remembered before she'd woken up with a thumping headache and a feeling that her limbs didn't belong to her.

She guessed the wine had been drugged. What was more there was no sign of her phone – or of Dale.

53

Wesley picked up a car and drove to Strangefields Farm. As soon as he reached the gate Gerry rang, asking where he was.

'Strangefields Farm. I want to ask whether anyone's seen Grace. I'm worried about her.'

'Traffic's just told me their cameras spotted her car on the main road out of Tradmouth soon after she called you.'

'Near the turnoff for Dead Man's Lane?'

'Not far away.' He paused. 'If our body is Dale Keyes and she was shacked up with him it doesn't bode well.'

Gerry's words echoed Wesley's fears but he tried to focus and told the boss about Ossie Phillips' statement. 'He thinks Bert recognised someone on the ferry – someone who made him decide to stay on rather than getting off at Queenswear as planned.'

'He didn't tell Danny Brice who it was?'

'No, but when Danny got back from his visit to the toilet he thought something had upset him. Perhaps Bert knew something about this mystery person and he was killed to stop him talking.'

'There is another possibility we keep ignoring, Wes. If Jonathan Kilin punched Bert there might have been more to it than a simple argument about a detention. You hear so much about child abuse these days. Maybe Kilin had a good reason for doing what he did and if Bert had done it to others, there might be plenty around who'd be out for revenge. Perhaps it was one of his victims he saw on the ferry.'

Wesley thought for a while before answering. 'There was never the remotest suggestion that Bert was like that. I've spoken to one of his colleagues and if there'd been any suspicions at the time it would surely have got around.'

Gerry's suggestion made him feel uncomfortable because it didn't seem to fit with the Bert he'd heard about, although he knew some abusers were cunning enough to present an innocent face to the unsuspecting world so it wasn't something he could rule out entirely.

He parked on the pitted drive near where the archaeologists were working, some standing around with clipboards recording measurements and taking pictures while others worked inside the trenches, deep in concentration. He guessed they were in the process of lifting the skeleton and he couldn't resist going over to watch. Neil was supervising proceedings and as soon as he saw Wesley he beckoned him over to stand by his side and look down at the bones.

'You'll dine out on this in archaeological circles,' said Wesley.

'True,' said Neil smugly. 'Look at the size of that stone they put on the abdomen to weigh the body down. Someone was determined he wouldn't get up again.'

'Have you found out who saw Grace?'

He turned and called over to a dark-haired young woman with a clipboard. 'You saw the architect, didn't you, Sally?'

Sally looked up from her work. 'It was this morning – around ten thirty. I saw her car belting up the lane.' She suddenly looked less sure of herself. 'At least it looked like hers but I can't be absolutely sure. It was going so fast.'

Wesley thanked her before driving up to the house. Sally might have been mistaken, or perhaps Grace had been making a flying visit and was long gone. After asking the builders if they'd seen her and receiving a negative reply, he had a quick look in the outbuildings where he found nothing apart from rusty farm machinery and rubbish.

As he drove out of the gates the weak sun emerged from behind the clouds and when he was halfway down the lane he received a call from the station to tell him that Jonathan Kilin's parents had been contacted and were expecting him to call that afternoon. He experienced a sudden rush of optimism. It was time they had some luck. Jonathan Kilin might have nothing to do with the case but his instincts told him that Kilin's history with Bert Cummings had to make him a suspect. And he was still wondering whether Kilin, the young art lover, might have changed his identity to become Jonny Sykes. If anybody knew what had become of him it would surely be his family.

He returned to the CID office and was pleased to find the copy of the diary from the evidence store he'd requested earlier lying on top of his computer. After eating a quick sandwich at his desk he stuffed the diary into his pocket and set out for Modbury at two thirty, taking Rachel with him. He asked her to drive because he wanted to read the copy of the little 1685 diary on the way, realising it might be the only chance he'd get. Linda Payne had considered it important enough to store carefully in its own file. Besides, he thought a complete change of focus might clear his head.

He deciphered the ancient handwriting, realising with growing excitement that the story appeared to be a continuation of the one told in Neil's 1666 version and something, perhaps a faint echo of the events described in the diary, triggered a flicker of recognition at the back of his mind. But they were nearing their destination so he put the copy of the diary on the back seat. At that moment history wasn't his priority.

'How are the wedding plans going?' he asked as they reached the outskirts of Modbury, breaking the amicable silence. Over the past few days Rachel had hardly mentioned her forthcoming nuptials, not even to bemoan her lack of flowers, and he felt the need to take his mind off the nagging worry that was increasing with each passing moment.

'With Jen deciding to go AWOL I've had to find another florist in Neston. More expensive than Linda but ... Maybe the boss was right. What would it really matter if I carried a bouquet from the supermarket? Who'd really notice ... or care?'

'Quite right. The day's about you and Nigel.'

She fell silent, concentrating on the road ahead.

Then she spoke again. 'I'm still a bit worried about Jen.'

'She told you she was going away – and after what happened to Linda I can't say I blame her.'

There was another silence. Then he spoke again, thinking aloud.

'Dale Keyes had an employee – a woman – who cleared out his company's bank account. He let everyone believe he was dead to escape his creditors.' He paused. 'Including my friend Grace.'

A sceptical smile appeared on Rachel's face. 'Friend?'

Wesley felt his face burning. 'We've known each other since we were kids and her connection with Dale Keyes worries me. If he was involved in something and he told her about it – or if she witnessed something she shouldn't ...'

He didn't tell her that all sorts of dreadful scenarios were flashing through his head: Grace's lifeless body being found at low tide on the river bank; Grace trapped somewhere by Linda Payne's killer. He tried to put it out of his mind but he couldn't. He was on his way to Modbury on what could be a wild goose chase while he could have been searching for her and he felt helpless.

They arrived at the Kilins' address just after three and when Rachel rang the bell the door opened almost immediately to reveal a man in his forties. He was tall and athletic with fair hair, jeans and a collarless shirt. His face was pleasant with even features and grey eyes. He reminded Wesley of someone but he couldn't think who.

The man held out his right hand. 'Chris Kilin. I had the day off work so I thought I'd come and keep my parents company.' There was a hint of criticism behind his words, as if he suspected they'd come to give the Kilins a hard time. Wesley knew it would be up to him to convince him otherwise.

Chris led them into a light, spacious living room where an elderly couple sat like bookends at either end of a large leather sofa. The man rose when he saw Rachel, a gesture of old-fashioned chivalry, and shook hands with both of them as they introduced themselves.

'I'll make a cup of tea,' Chris said before hurrying out of the room with a backward glance, as though to make sure his parents were comfortable.

'We're sorry to bother you, Mr and Mrs Kilin,' Wesley began.

'Ken and Emma, please.'

Wesley smiled. The use of first names was a good sign. 'I'm Wesley and this is Rachel. You were told we're from Tradmouth. You lived near there once, I believe?'

'Barnton – a small village a couple of miles outside.'

'I know it,' said Rachel.

'A friend of my mother-in-law remembers you taking the photographs at her daughter's wedding,' said Wesley.

'I've taken so many wedding pictures in my time, they all blend into one, I'm afraid.' He looked as though this was a cause for genuine regret.

His wife meanwhile was looking increasingly nervous as she fidgeted with the neckline of her sweater and Wesley gave her a reassuring smile. 'We're sorry to intrude like this but we're investigating the murder of a former teacher at Fulton Grange School. I believe your sons were pupils there.'

'Only our eldest, Jonathan. Chris went to Tradmouth Comprehensive.'

'Why was that?' Rachel asked.

There was a long silence and Wesley suspected the subject was a sensitive one. To his surprise it was Emma Kilin who answered.

'Jonathan was a difficult child, Inspector. We thought the more sheltered atmosphere of a private school would suit him better whereas Chris ... well, Chris was an easygoing boy who'd thrive anywhere. However, it turned out to be the wrong decision. Jonathan hated the school and made a lot of trouble.'

'He punched a teacher.'

'His maths teacher had put him in detention when he wanted to go to an after-school art class. Art had become an obsession, you see – it was something we used to argue about constantly. He was very bright and we thought he should concentrate on all his school subjects, not just art. On this occasion he lost his temper and lashed out at Mr Cummings. We were devastated of course and we felt we had no alternative but to remove him from the school.'

'You sent him to Tradmouth to be with his brother?'

She shook her head. 'We tried to home school him for a while but that didn't work out so we moved away. By that time he'd lost all interest in school and he was determined to become an artist. He had a high IQ but he was troubled.'

'Did you seek help?'

'I'm sure people would these days but back then we saw it as our failure, although in contrast Chris has always been the easiest of sons. He's married with three little ones and he's an IT manager. How could two boys brought up in the same way be so different?'

'It's a mystery, but it happens.' said Wesley. 'You'll have heard about Mr Cummings' murder.'

She gave a little nod. 'Of course. It's a terrible thing to have happened. But surely you can't think it's anything to do with Jonathan.' She sounded worried, eager to leap to the defence of her lost son.

'We have to follow every lead, Mrs Kilin – Emma. I'm sorry.'

'When did you last see Jonathan?' Rachel asked.

At that moment Chris entered the room with a tray of steaming mugs and he spoke before his parents could reply.

'We haven't seen him since he left home. That was nineteen ninety-five – almost twenty-five years ago.'

'He said he was going and didn't want anything more

to do with us,' Ken Kilin said sadly. 'He said someone he knew was setting up some sort of studio and that's where he was going.'

'What was this person's name?'

'I don't know. Jonathan wasn't one for bringing friends home.'

'Was it someone he knew from Fulton Grange?'

'He never said. He rarely spoke to us.'

'You don't know what happened to him?'

'Don't think we didn't try to find out,' said Emma. 'We made every effort to look for him but it was as though he'd vanished off the face of the earth. We even hired a private detective, didn't we, Ken?'

'I'm sorry,' said Wesley. To this couple their son's rejection of them must have seemed like a bereavement.

'He was such a bright boy. He could have had a brilliant future ahead of him.'

'In art?'

'Not only art. I think the whole art thing was just his way of defying us. He had a scientific brain too and he was very good at maths. I think that's why he resented Mr Cummings. Before the ... incident he'd told Jonathan off for messing about in a maths lesson and put him in detention, but Jonathan only did it because the others couldn't keep up with him and he was bored. Jonathan never liked being made a show of.'

'Have you ever heard the name Jackson Temples?'

'He was that serial killer,' said Ken Kilin.

'He had a studio in a farmhouse he'd inherited outside Tradmouth. Could he have been the person Jonathan went to work with?'

The Kilins looked at each other.

'There was no mention of Jonathan's name in the news-papers. If he'd been there surely . . .'

'Could he have changed his name?'

'It's possible,' said Chris. 'He told me once that he wanted to go away and become a different person.'

'Could he have used the name Jonny Sykes?'

There was a long silence. Then Chris spoke again. 'When I was reading *Oliver Twist* for English one day he told me Bill Sykes was his favourite character – he liked the scene where he killed Nancy.'

Wesley could see the pain on the parents' faces and Chris had seen it as well because he said, 'I'm sorry. We can't cover up for him any more.'

Ken nodded sadly. 'I don't know where we went wrong.'

'You probably didn't,' said Wesley, looking at Chris.

'Would you have a look at these pictures and tell us if you recognise anyone?' said Rachel, taking a sheaf of photographs from the file she'd brought in and handing them to Ken.

Ken sifted through them, passing them to his wife, but when he came to one he froze. Emma was leaning over to see the picture and he heard her gasp.

'This is him. This is Jonathan. I'm sure of it.'

'He's changed after more than twenty years but Emma's right. This is definitely him.'

Ken handed the picture back to Wesley and when he showed Rachel her eyes widened in surprise.

'He's using the name Joe Hamer now and he's a property developer building a luxury holiday village just outside Tradmouth. He appears to have made a success of his life if that's any consolation.'

'Hamer was my maiden name.' A sad smile appeared

on Emma Kilin's lips. 'I never expected him to follow that particular path but as long as he's happy . . . '

'That's all anyone can wish for their children,' said Wesley.

He looked at Chris and saw his face had clouded. 'I can't get over that he's been doing all this but hasn't bothered contacting us to let us know he's all right. In a way this makes everything worse.'

Ken Kilin was still sorting through the photographs, refusing to meet his son's eye. Wesley saw him stop and stare at one of the pictures, then at another. Eventually he spoke, holding one of the photographs up for Wesley to see. 'I recognise her. She was at Fulton Grange. Striking girl.'

'Her name's Roberta. Was she friendly with Jonathan?'

'Not that I'm aware of. I remember her because she was in a school production of *The Tempest* we went to see. She played Miranda, and I remember taking her photograph for the local newspaper. She was a cheeky little madam as I recall.'

Wesley held out his hand for the pictures, assuming Kilin had finished. Instead he passed them to his wife. She too flicked through them and when she came to one she frowned.

'Someone you recognise?'

'I don't know. I thought this one looked familiar – but different somehow.' She shook her head. 'I think I must be mistaken.'

When she passed the picture to Wesley he said she was right. She was mistaken.

54

Grace was desperate to pee but she couldn't move and even though she'd tried her best to work the rope that bound her hands free it was tied so tightly that the knots hadn't budged. Her head ached from the drugged wine and tears pricked her eyes, hot and uncomfortable. She'd always hated confined spaces and she was struggling to breathe in the fetid air that smelled of bird droppings and worse. The soft cooing of pigeons in the rafters above her sounded smug, almost mocking.

She'd made some mistakes in her life but this was the worst of them. This was Devon, a county of fields, woods and open spaces, and there was nobody out there to hear her scream. She began to mouth the words of a prayer from her childhood, one she'd recited with Wesley at Sunday school. Then she screamed anyway. At least she could tell herself she'd tried.

On the way back Wesley said they should stop at Strangefields Farm and Rachel agreed with him. They could bring Gerry up to date with developments later.

As Rachel drove up the potholed drive he battled the temptation to see how things were progressing at Neil's dig;

but some things were more urgent. When they arrived at the house he came across Glen Crowther. He looked sheepish at first but once he learned that they weren't there to see him he directed them to the great hall with the eagerness of a party host who was keen to impress.

Once there they found Joe Hamer leaning over a set of plans laid out on a trestle table with a pen in one hand and a phone in the other. He was talking to someone and he didn't sound happy.

The pen hand hovered over a notebook and he was drawing frantically, making rapid marks, unconsciously creating human forms. Wesley could see life and movement in his doodles, the work of a talented artist.

'She said she was going back to her London office but you're saying you haven't seen her,' he barked down the phone. 'This isn't good enough. There are things here that need sorting out.'

Wesley stood listening for a few moments, certain he was talking about Grace. He had a sudden desire to leap to her defence except he knew that if Hamer thought she'd been unprofessional, then he had every right to complain.

'Mr Hamer. We need a word,' Wesley said once the man ended the call with a violent jab at his phone.

'Can't it wait?' He sounded exasperated, as though a visit from the police was the last thing he needed.

'It can't, I'm afraid. We've been talking to your family.'

The colour drained from Hamer's face and he froze as though he'd seen some horrific vision from his past. 'I don't know what you mean.'

'We know who you are, Jonathan. You should have told us the truth right away.'

It was a few seconds before he spoke. 'What would have

been the point?' he said almost in a whisper. 'That was in another life and Jonathan Kilin was a loser.'

Wesley picked up the notebook he'd been doodling in. 'I've seen some of the paintings you did while you were here in the nineties. You have quite a talent.'

'So I used to be told but there's no money in art unless you're extremely lucky or well connected. It's something I dabbled in when I was younger ... until I put away childish things.'

The biblical quote was spoken with scathing irony, perhaps as a reaction to the mention of his parents; a rejection of all they stood for.

'Was this when you used to be Jonny Sykes?'

Hamer shrugged.

'That's three identities you've used. Are there any others we should know about?'

'No, that's it.' There was a challenge in his eyes. 'OK, I've got a past. I've done things I'm not particularly proud of.'

'Like murder?'

Rachel gave Wesley a look which told him she thought he'd gone too far.

'No. I swear I've never murdered anybody.'

'We need to talk properly down at the station,' said Wesley. 'Either you can come voluntarily or I can arrest you.'

'What for?' The question came out as a squeak.

'You knew this house very well before you bought it, didn't you? You lived here in the nineteen nineties when Jackson Temples owned it. How did you get to know him?'

The man looked frightened now and Wesley knew he had to keep the pressure on. 'How did you meet Jackson Temples? And don't bother lying. We still have unidentified fingerprints on file we can compare with yours.'

Hamer sank down onto the dusty window seat and put his head in his hands as his shell of confidence cracked. Wesley waited for him to speak.

'We met at an artists' studio someone set up in a disused barn at Tradington Hall. He'd been a few years above me at school but he didn't recognise me and I didn't want him to. That school was something I'd rather forget. Anyway, we got talking and he told me he'd inherited this farmhouse and he wanted to set up an artists' community here. Some community – there were only the two of us. We worked at different ends of the building so we were quite independent of each other.'

'He brought girls back.'

'Women found him attractive, although I always thought he was a bit ... weird. He was one of those people who always have a whiff of danger about them if you know what I mean. He used to pick up girls at a club in Morbay – telling them they were beautiful and he was desperate to paint their portraits. It proved a very effective chat-up line.'

'You painted them as well?'

'I mainly stuck to landscapes and seascapes. I was awkward with girls in those days. Didn't have Jack's charm.' There was a long pause. Wesley thought he looked troubled, as though he was remembering something disturbing. 'I was in a pretty dark place back then. Drugs.'

'Sex?'

'Not then but Jack got plenty. He used to say that painting someone's portrait created an atmosphere of intimacy. He mostly did conventional portraits and nude studies but he ... chose certain girls – just a few – to push the boundaries as he called it. He used to call them his "special girls" and they were stunningly beautiful – way out of my league, or so I thought at the time.'

'They were the ones he painted with ropes?'

'He said he wanted to explore the wilder side of his nature. Used to read de Sade and he went on about creating his own version of the Hellfire Club. Do what you will.'

'What did you think?'

'I was pretty unconventional back then but to tell you the truth some of the things he used to do and say made me uncomfortable. I wanted to be a serious artist and I thought his . . . weird tastes were a distraction. It didn't take me long to reach the conclusion that we wanted different things.'

Wesley saw that Rachel was listening intently, barely able to hide her disapproval.

'He used those women. Humiliated them,' she said, breaking the spell. 'And you did nothing to stop him.'

Wesley shot her a look, wishing she hadn't interrupted Hamer's flow of memories. It seemed she'd got the message because she stepped back.

'What happened to make your arrangement with Temples stop?'

'One of Jack's "special girls" was found nearly dead; she was in a coma for a couple of months. Then another was found dead and they said she'd been strangled with a rope – just like in Jack's paintings. I told myself it couldn't have anything to do with him at first but when another of his girls went missing I got scared. Eventually I cleared out my stuff and went to London because I didn't want to get involved.'

'You think he killed them?'

'Who else could it have been, because I know it wasn't me? Then when the girl came round from her coma and pointed the finger at Jack . . . well, the whole thing brought me to my senses. I came off the drugs, gave up all thought of being an artist, went to London and got myself a job with a property company. Then I began my own business, changed my name and tried to forget the whole affair. It made me sick to think about it.'

'Until this place came on the market.'

'It was a business opportunity. That's all. It's the ideal spot for a holiday village.'

'Where did he get the ropes?'

'He said they came from an old yacht; some bloke was throwing them away.'

Wesley paused. 'You said you weren't into painting portraits but I've seen a couple I think are yours. A young Linda Payne in a gingham dress.'

A fond look appeared in his eyes, as though he was reliving a happy memory. 'Jack's little sister Linda turned up one day after she'd had a row with her mum. Unlike Jack, she was lovely.'

'I've also seen the nude painting you did of her. The Rokeby Venus.'

'That wasn't like Jack's pictures,' he said defensively. 'I wanted to capture her essence.'

'You saw her as your muse?'

'I suppose so. And I felt a bit . . . protective of her.'

'Mixed feelings then?'

His face reddened. 'Yeah, well . . . but I didn't want her involved in what Jack was doing so I tried to keep her away from all that.'

'He didn't paint her with ropes?'

'She was his sixteen-year-old sister.'

'Fifteen.'

'She told me sixteen. Look, Jack might have been sick but he wasn't that sick.'

'Were you and Linda lovers?'

He shook his head. 'It never got that far. I wasn't very confident with girls in those days.'

'When you were a student at Fulton Grange you assaulted your maths teacher Mr Cummings.'

Hamer looked surprised at the change of subject. 'That's not something I'm proud of now. Cummings made me angry and I wanted to kick out and hurt him. Like I said, I was troubled back then.' He paused. 'I heard he was dead, but I promise you it had nothing to do with me.'

'He was stabbed in a frenzied attack. I'll need to know where you were at the time of his death.'

'I didn't harm him. Why would I? My parents were so mortified by what I did that they felt they had to move away. That's the sort of person I was then but I've changed.'

'Do people change that much?'

'I've channelled all that aggression into something more constructive, more socially acceptable.'

'Jackson Temples said he thought you'd killed the girls. Only by the time he was arrested you'd disappeared without trace and nobody believed you existed. Most of the girls never saw you.'

'I've told you, I worked at the other end of the house and Linda was the only girl I painted. She was whisked away by her mother well before it all blew up so she wasn't even called to give evidence.' The troubled expression appeared again. 'I got out quick and erased any sign that I'd been there, apart from my paintings. I couldn't take them with me.'

'Why didn't she tell anyone that Jonny Sykes existed when it came up at the trial?'

'Even if her mother hadn't kept her well away Linda knew I had nothing to do with killing those girls so why would she drag me into it? I imagine she thought Jack had done it just like everyone else did.'

'There are some paintings for sale on the internet – yours and Jackson's.'

He took a deep breath. 'It was Linda's idea to sell them. I should have mentioned before that I met her when I came back here. She'd noticed that the house was up for development and she came up to see what was going on. We recognised each other at once. It was ... good to see her again.'

'Why didn't you tell us?'

'And incriminate myself? I heard about her murder and I thought it better to keep quiet. I don't know who killed her so what help would I have been?'

'Where did you find the paintings?'

'Here at the house. I was surprised they were still here. The police left the more ... conventional ones because they were only interested in the ones that could be used as evidence at the trial. Linda knew someone who worked for a rental company and she asked if we could store them in an empty house while the building work was going on here. I set up the website. There's been a lot of interest in Jack's paintings – ghouls I expect.'

'You've been passing your work off as Jack's.'

'The website doesn't actually say they're all by Jack but my style in those days was similar to his and people draw their own conclusions.' He shrugged. 'It might not be completely honest but it's not illegal. And if weirdos want to own something painted by a murderer ...'

'What was Jack's attitude to Linda?'

'He said she was a bloody nuisance – cramped his style. I'm sorry she's dead. I really liked her. But I don't know who killed her.'

'She was killed in the same way as Temples' victims.'

Hamer stared at him, horrified; the sort of horror that's hard to fake – but not impossible. 'I didn't know. Why hasn't it been on the news?'

'We've tried to keep those details out of the media.'

'Do you think it was someone who'd found out who she was – someone who took revenge on Jack by killing his little sister? Hurting him? Only he and Linda weren't close so I doubt if her death would upset him that much.'

As Hamer fell silent Wesley had an idea. He took the photographs he had with him out of his pocket and spread them out on the table. 'Do you recognise any of these people?'

It was a few moments before Hamer could bring himself to look. Then he sighed deeply and picked the photographs up one by one, shaking his head at each. Suddenly he stopped and took a picture between his thumb and his forefinger. Wesley saw a flicker of puzzled recognition in his eyes before he shook his head and passed on to the next.

From the second diary of
Lemuel Strange, gentleman

IIth *April* 1685

My wife said we should call the constable but I knew Reuben had committed no crime worthy of taking before the magistrate and his claim on Frances's inheritance was certain in law, for a wife's property belongs to her husband. Yet I could not allow his deception to go unchallenged for it had caused the death of two innocents at the hands of the mob.

So it was that later that day I sent John to spread the word in the port that my cousin lived, knowing it would be but a short time before the news reached the ears of Bess Whitetree's kinsmen. Then, with John's help, I lured Reuben to the wine cellar, saying I had some good bottles of claret to show him, and locked him in there to await the agents of justice.

Frances was trembling when they arrived and I showed them to the cellar. As they dragged him out of there he ordered them to unhand him but soon he was begging for mercy. I told him that mercy was something he hadn't shown to Bess and her sweetheart and he flew at me in a rage but was held back by Bess's brother who was carrying a rope upon his person.

I never saw what they did to my cousin but when they buried his body close to where Bess and Harry lay, Frances watched, weeping bitter tears.

55

Roberta was still being held in a cell beneath Tradmouth Police Station, awaiting her appearance before the magistrate the following morning. Stag was somewhere nearby but she had no idea where or what he'd told the police. If he'd had any sense he would have pushed all the blame onto Danny, but she'd found out years ago that men were weak and couldn't be trusted.

She rose from the blue plastic mattress that smelled of disinfectant and banged on the cell door. If she made enough noise someone would come. Someone would listen to what she had to say.

When the custody officer peeped in she put her face close to his and whispered, 'Tell your Inspector Peterson I've got important information for him and I'm willing to do a deal.'

'What information's this?' The officer sounded sceptical, as though he'd heard it all before.

'Tell him it's about the murder of the old man. Only I want something in return.'

The grille in the door shut with a sharp snap. But she was sure the message had got through.

*

Grace tried to relax her limbs. She'd always believed that there was a solution to every problem and she needed to think. The thing around her neck was a rope, she was sure of that, and the thought made her shudder. She'd been too engrossed in her own concerns to take any notice of the archaeologists' talk of hangings and strange burials on the site of the proposed reception building she'd designed. Should she have viewed it as an omen? Was that to be her fate – to meet her death by slow strangulation?

She fought back tears as she looked around. If she could somehow wriggle out of the noose and shuffle over to the window she could loosen those rotten battens and get at the glass. She took a deep, calming breath then, with a great effort, she manoeuvred herself until she was lying on her stomach. She buried her head in the foul-smelling mattress, pressing her whole body down and trying not to inhale as she inched down the bed. The rope was against the nape of her neck now, then against the widest part of her skull, catching her hair and making her wince with pain. Then suddenly she managed to free herself. The rope had been tied around the mattress in the hope that it would pinion her there but it hadn't worked and she allowed herself a moment of triumphant rest. Now there were only the ropes around her wrists and ankles to deal with.

She dropped to the floor and slithered over to the window, glad she was a regular at her London gym. The slats covering the windows were half-rotten and easy to nudge aside with her elbows once she'd hoisted herself into a standing position.

The next part would be the hardest. As soon as she was satisfied that she'd cleared a good area of window, she closed her eyes and jabbed at the filthy glass with her elbow.

As it shattered and she pulled her arm away, the fabric of her cashmere sweater snagged on the jagged glass and she felt it scratching her flesh. She had to get this right or she was in danger of cutting herself badly.

She turned her back to the window and positioned her tethered hands over the sharp edges, sawing to and fro, cautiously at first then more vigorously as she gained confidence. She could feel the rope fraying and loosening which gave her the courage to carry on even though her whole body was aching.

She had to get away. If her captor returned she wouldn't be allowed to live.

56

Joe Hamer, alias Jonny Sykes, alias Jonathan Kilin, had been brought in for questioning on suspicion of murder. But Wesley wasn't convinced they'd got the right man.

'If Temples killed those girls they must have been in cahoots,' were Gerry's first words when Wesley broke the news. 'My old governor always wondered whether Temples had an accomplice but when we found no evidence of the other artist . . . '

'If someone who knew what they were looking for had been allowed to examine those paintings more closely they might have realised.'

'We can all be wise with hindsight, Wes.' Gerry sounded irritated, almost as though he'd taken the criticism personally. 'Anyway, hopefully the case'll be cleared up in time for Rach's wedding.'

'You don't fancy Roberta and Stag for Bert's murder?'

Gerry suddenly looked unsure of himself. 'I reckon that's Hamer's handiwork and all. He had a grudge against Bert going back over twenty years.'

'According to him that's something he regrets.'

'People lie to us, Wes. It's an occupational hazard. Hamer must have been involved in the Temples murders.

If he wasn't up to his neck in it why didn't he stay and give evidence? An innocent man doesn't run off like that and even his parents thought he was a wrong 'un. Parents don't disown their own child like that without a damn good reason.'

'He rejected them, not the other way round,' Wesley pointed out gently. There were holes in Gerry's logic but he didn't feel inclined to enter into a long discussion.

'What about Dale Keyes?'

'He and Hamer were both property developers in the Smoke. Who knows what history they had between them? I've contacted the Met to see what they know about him.' He thought for a moment. 'Keyes was involved with this architect of yours so maybe he went up to Strangefields Farm and stumbled on something. When we find your ex-girlfriend we might learn more.'

'She's not my—' Wesley began before he thought better of it. There was no time to argue the niceties. He just wanted to know Grace was safe. Joe Hamer had sworn he had no idea where she was and Wesley had been inclined to believe him., Or perhaps he just didn't want to think of her falling prey to the man who might have been responsible, either on his own or jointly, for the Temples murders. As her phone was switched off he'd asked the tech people to trace her last position.

'Hamer's been waiting downstairs long enough. Want to sit in on the interview?'

'I'd love to,' said Gerry, rubbing his hands in anticipation. Wesley found himself wishing he hadn't suggested it, but it was too late now.

As Hamer sat opposite them, he seemed to have regained his confidence. Back at Strangefields Farm

Wesley had sensed a vulnerability but now the air of co-operation had vanished. It would be up to Wesley to bring it back.

'What would you like to be called?' Wesley asked. 'Jonathan, Jonny or Joe?'

'Joe will do. That's what I've been calling myself for years and I've kind of got used to it.'

'We still can't contact Grace Compton. Have you any idea where she is?'

'I've told you, no. I wish I had.'

'When I showed you those photographs you seemed to recognise one of them.'

The suspect had been fidgeting with an empty plastic cup that had once contained tea, but he suddenly stopped and looked up at Wesley. 'I was mistaken.'

Wesley produced the photograph again and waited while the man studied it carefully.

'There's something familiar about her,' Hamer said after what seemed like an age. 'But she's different. I can't put my finger on it.'

'Who does she remind you of?'

Hamer sighed and said a name. 'But it can't be her, can it? Anyway, this woman's a lot better-looking.'

'Tell me what you remember about her.'

'Temples never painted her in the nude, although she was more than up for it. Like I said before, he was particular. Only the prettiest got the nude treatment and only the most stunning became his "special girls".' He sat back in his seat and folded his arms. 'She used to follow Jack around like a little dog. Then when he told her to get lost she started disturbing me while I was painting and I had to be quite brutal.' He was smirking, as though he was beginning to enjoy the situation and Wesley caught a glimpse of the student who'd tormented Bert Cummings.

'How brutal?' It was the first time Gerry had spoken and Joe looked at him as though he was an interesting, albeit unpleasant, specimen he'd just viewed under a microscope.

'Not in the way you're thinking of. She came to my studio and I threw her out. Told her to stop bothering me.'

'And Temples?'

'He told her bluntly that she wasn't good-looking enough to model for him in the nude even though she'd offered to do anything he wanted, if you get my meaning. But she still hung round – wouldn't take no for an answer.'

'So you killed her to get rid of her.'

'Why would I do that? She was just a sad, pathetic teenager with a crush. I presumed Jack had snapped and killed her like the others.' There was a moment of hesitation. 'This is going to sound ridiculous but I thought I saw her in Tradmouth a couple of weeks ago. Gave me a jolt.'

'The woman in the picture we showed you?'

'Yes.'

'You said she looked different. Why did you think it was her?'

'Something about her was familiar and then I noticed she had this mark on her hand – a birthmark the shape of a heart. It was quite distinctive. Still, it couldn't have been her, could it?'

Wesley and Gerry leaned forward.

'I thought I saw the same woman yesterday as well.'

'Where?'

'On Dead Man's Lane – near that derelict cottage. I'm interested in acquiring the place but I haven't been able to find out who owns it. I was in the car and I only caught a glimpse of her.'

'You didn't stop?'

Hamer shook his head. 'Even if it had been her that was a time of my life I'd rather forget. Besides, I was sure I was mistaken. I must have been. If I'd said anything I'd only have made a fool of myself.'

Wesley wondered whether Hamer was trying to muddy the waters to deflect attention from his own possible guilt.

For the benefit of the tape, he announced he was leaving the room. He needed time to think. And he needed to find out whether the tech people had managed to trace Grace's phone.

57

It was almost six o'clock when Roberta asked to see Wesley, which was all he needed. They only had a limited time left to charge or release Joe Hamer but Gerry had agreed to let him stew for the time being while they contemplated their next move.

Wesley wandered into Gerry's office, hands in pockets, looking as despondent as he felt. Maritia had just called to see whether there was news of Grace and having to give her a negative answer had made him feel worse.

'The tech people say Grace's phone was in the Dead Man's Lane area when it was turned off earlier.'

Gerry looked at him enquiringly. 'Think Joe Hamer's keeping her somewhere?' He didn't say what he was really thinking – that she could be dead; murdered like Dale Keyes. She'd been with Keyes for the past few days so he'd presumably shared his secrets with her, if he had any. Up till now no connection had been found between Hamer and Keyes apart from their respective work in London, but he'd called the Met and they'd promised to dig deeper. If there was a link they'd find it.

'I don't know. We'll have another go at him later.' He slumped down in a chair and put his head in his hands.

'Once you've had a chance to calm down. It's not like you to let your emotions get in the way, Wes.'

'I've known Grace for years so of course I'm worried about her,' he said quickly. 'Roberta wants to see me. She says she's got some important information.'

'Off you go then. It'll take your mind off Grace. I've got to go and bring the press office up to date with the latest developments. They're saying it's like a siege in there with all the calls coming in.'

Ten minutes later Wesley and Rachel were sitting opposite Roberta in one of the interview rooms. Roberta didn't look like a woman who'd just been charged with theft and was under suspicion of murder. Instead she appeared completely relaxed and pleased with herself, almost smug.

'I have information but I want something in return.'

'What's that?'

'I want you to put in a word for me – say I've been very co-operative.'

'What about Stag?'

She shrugged. 'He's got nothing to bargain with. He didn't go to my old school.'

'Fulton Grange?'

'How did you know?'

'A photographer recognised you from when you played a leading role in *The Tempest*.'

'Hell, that was a lifetime ago. The place is now defunct, thank God. Abandon all hope ye who enter here.'

There was an intensity in Roberta's words that surprised Wesley. Fulton Grange had kept cropping up in this investigation from the beginning. The school where Bert Cummings had once taught maths had also been the alma mater of Jonathan Kilin, alias Joe Hamer, Jackson Temples and Gemma Pollinger, and now he had another former pupil sitting there in front of him.

'I can't promise anything until I hear what you have to say.' He tried to sound casual even though he was longing to lean across the table and shake the information out of her.

'Very well. I saw a girl I recognised from school. Why would that be of interest, I hear you ask. Well normally it wouldn't, of course, only this girl happens to be dead.'

'What's her name?'

'Gemma Pollinger. It was the talk of the dorm at school – I was a boarder at Fulton Grange.' She gave a mirthless grin. 'Made me the woman I am today.'

Wesley drew in his breath. He hadn't been sure whether to believe Hamer's claim that he'd seen a woman who reminded him of Gemma Pollinger but now there was a possibility he hadn't been lying.

'You're sure it was her?'

'I wasn't at first. She's improved a hell of a lot since I last saw her.'

'Why are you certain it was her that you saw?'

'When I first noticed her I couldn't place her. There was just something vaguely familiar about her walk . . . and her eyes. Then I spotted the birthmark on her hand and I knew exactly who it was. It was in the shape of a heart – just like Gemma's. Boy, had she changed. It's amazing what cosmetic surgery can do. But there are some things you can't change, aren't there?'

'You knew her well at school?'

'Not that well. She was a few years older than me and she left school at sixteen to take some boring job but I knew her because she was in the hockey team; changing rooms are intimate places.' She grinned. 'Everyone gossiped about her going to that artist's place – the one who murdered those girls – which was surprising because she was such a plain little mouse; not so little actually; she was quite tall. She was the last girl you'd imagine would get involved with something like that: bondage and weird sex so I heard.' She chuckled at the thought and shook her head. 'She must have been desperate for attention, poor cow.'

'What else do you remember about her?'

'She always tried to hang around with the best-looking girls, which was her big mistake because they just used her to show up how good they looked: plain friend syndrome. I don't think she knew how they used to laugh at her behind her back.'

'Kids can be very nasty.'

'There was a lot of bullying at Fulton Grange. You had to be queen bee or you went under.'

There was bitterness in her voice and Wesley wondered whether she'd been a victim of bullying herself – until she'd learned to cover her insecurities with an impenetrable shell. At that moment she placed her elbows on the table and her sleeve slipped back to reveal a fine tracery of scars around her wrists, like snail trails on the pale flesh.

'If you were at Fulton Grange you must have known Bert Cummings. Did he recognise you when you called on him?'

She sat back in her chair, looking pleased with herself. 'He did but I bluffed it out. I told him I was working for Social Services and he said he was pleased I'd become a useful member of society.' She grinned. 'I thought it was quite funny. Of course after that I had to give up the idea of robbing him. Far too risky.'

'Did you kill him?'

Her smirk turned into a laugh. 'Do me a favour. I'm not a murderer and neither is Stag. Why would I? He honestly thought I'd turned into Mary Poppins.'

'You must have been very surprised to see Gemma.'

'That's an understatement.'

Wesley leaned forward. 'Where did you see her? What was she doing?'

When Roberta told him, he looked at Rachel and saw her mouth had fallen open in shock.

'We need to have another word with Joe Hamer,' he said to her once they were outside in the corridor.

From the second diary of
Lemuel Strange, gentleman

17th April 1685

Frances raised no hand to save her husband and she has said nothing of the matter since that day.

It is a sennight now since it was done. I confess I acted in anger when I permitted the desecration of my cousin's corpse, just as the mortal remains of those two innocents had suffered that same terrible mutilation.

The townsfolk, led by Bess's brothers, performed the dreadful rites for they reasoned that Reuben was an evil soul who would return from hell to do harm to those who had meted out justice to him. I prayed nobody would inform the constable but I had no need to fear since it seemed all were agreed to keep silent upon the matter. For who can kill a dead man?

Reuben Strange is now truly gone from this earth. And he can never return.

58

By the time they set out for Strangefields Farm again it was threatening rain. Because Gerry couldn't be found Wesley asked Rachel to go with him, unsure whether he should take back-up as well. If his suspicions were correct the person he was looking for was dangerous.

Hamer said that he'd spotted her on Dead Man's Lane the previous day but he was sure she hadn't seen him. When Wesley told him he might not have been mistaken he seemed shaken, and puzzled as to how she'd accomplished her convincing vanishing act.

The rain clouds had dispersed and the evening sun was emerging from behind the clouds as Rachel brought the car to a halt on Dead Man's Lane beside the signpost. The hanging man shadow was there again and it seemed almost like an omen. As he got out of the passenger seat, he pointed it out to Rachel who muttered the word 'spooky' before taking a photograph of the phenomenon with her phone.

'How long's the cottage been empty?' he asked Rachel, hoping her encyclopaedic knowledge of local matters would provide the answer.

'For as long as I can remember. Word has it that it used

to belong to an elderly couple who died and there was some legal wrangle about ownership. But I don't know how true that is.' She paused. 'Can you hear something?'

Wesley stood still and listened. He could hear birdsong and the distant buzz of a power tool, possibly the builders working overtime at the house. Everything seemed normal, until he heard the sound of glass smashing followed by a faint tinkling as it fell to the ground. Then he heard a muffled shout; a woman's voice calling for help. Rachel had heard it too. She grabbed his arm and pointed to the cottage.

Wesley began to run towards the sound, his heart beating fast. After what Hamer and Roberta had just told him all their assumptions about the case had been turned upside down.

They could hear the voice more clearly once they reached the front door – a frantic, muffled shout from somewhere upstairs. And Wesley spotted a car parked behind the house, half hidden by thick greenery: Grace's car. He tried to shoulder-barge the door but it held fast.

He turned to Rachel. 'Neil's team's been working near the gates. They might have packed up by now but go and see if they've left a mattock lying around.'

Rachel shot off in the direction of the lane while Wesley circled the cottage, calling out to reassure Grace that help was at hand.

He found the broken window at the rear of the cottage, facing away from the road and overlooking lonely fields. There were battens fixed to the inside of the window so he couldn't see Grace but he could hear her through the small section of glass she'd managed to break. When he shouted up to her she called his name and he heard relief in her voice – mingled with terror.

After what seemed like an age he was surprised to see Neil appear, running ahead of Rachel with a mattock in his hands. A few of the team were working late while the rain held off, he explained breathlessly, trying to lift the latest skeleton they'd found before nightfall. At Wesley's signal he swung the mattock at the rickety back door and after a few blows the door panel gave way. Wesley reached inside to draw back the bolt which felt frustratingly stiff, as though it hadn't been used for a long time. He struggled with it for a while until Neil took over.

When the door finally burst open the three of them stumbled into the kitchen. The windows were boarded up so the house was dark but in the meagre light trickling between the slats Wesley could make out long-abandoned furniture, coated in a fur of dust and grime. He climbed the stairs, hardly aware of Rachel and Neil behind him, and when he reached the door of the room where Grace was imprisoned, he found it locked with no key in sight.

Neil still had his mattock and before Wesley could say anything he'd put a hole in the door, striking it again and again until there was enough room for Wesley to squeeze through.

The first thing he saw was Grace standing unsteadily near the window with tears streaming down her face and he instinctively rushed over and took her in his arms. The self-confident Grace had vanished and she was once again the shy fifteen-year-old girl he'd felt so much for. He held her close while she sobbed out her relief.

'He's going to kill me,' she whispered.

'Who?'

'I don't know. I haven't seen him. He lured me here with a text from Dale's phone and left a bottle of wine, which must have been drugged. When I came round I was tied up and I don't know what he's planning to do.'

Wesley reached for his phone. They definitely needed back-up.

But as soon as Wesley had made the call he heard the sound of a car coming to a halt on the drive outside. A few seconds after the engine died there was a noise downstairs: the click of a key in a lock. Since the front door was still intact Wesley hoped Grace's captor wouldn't realise she wasn't alone. The element of surprise would give them the advantage. He put his finger to his lips and the others got the message. All eyes were focused on the broken door and it seemed an age before a shadow appeared at the top of the stairs and they heard someone swearing under their breath.

'What have you done, bitch?' the newcomer shouted as she pushed the door open.

'Jen.' Rachel had gasped the name before she could stop herself.

'Gemma,' Wesley corrected. 'Gemma Pollinger, you're under arrest – the false imprisonment of Grace Compton will do for starters.'

Ignoring Wesley, the woman stepped further into the room, tense like a cat preparing to spring. Her face was twisted with hatred as Grace edged closer to Wesley for protection. He felt in his pocket for his handcuffs, knowing the back-up would take time to arrive. He could see something dangling from Gemma's hand – a rope. If they hadn't arrived in time Grace would have met the same fate as Linda Payne.

Suddenly Gemma dropped the rope and pulled something from her coat pocket. The light was dim so it took

Wesley a second or so to realise it was a pointed knife with a serrated edge down one side: the very weapon Colin Bowman had described.

Without warning she lunged at Neil, who was standing closest, and Wesley cursed himself for not anticipating what she'd do. Neil cried out and the mattock he was holding dropped to the floor with a crash.

Wesley made a grab for Gemma but he was too slow. The woman escaped his grasp and hurtled down the stairs. Neil was on the floor now, clutching his stomach and groaning, and Grace, emerging from her state of shock, threw herself to her knees beside him, ripping off her cashmere cardigan and using it to stem the bleeding.

Wesley watched the soft pale fabric turn a glistening scarlet as he knelt beside Grace, murmuring words of reassurance but feeling helpless. He could hear Rachel calling an ambulance, speaking to the call handler with professional calm although there was a tremble in her voice. He prayed the ambulance would hurry because Neil was losing a lot of blood which was spreading over the splintery floorboards.

As Grace applied pressure to the wound Neil's eyes fluttered closed.

'Come on,' Wesley whispered in his ear. 'Don't leave us now.'

59

Time seemed to slow as Wesley bent over his unconscious friend, listening anxiously for the sound of the sirens which would herald the arrival of help.

He was torn between staying with Neil and pursuing Gemma Pollinger, who was out there somewhere, planning her next move.

Once the ambulance and the police back-up had arrived he rushed out of the cottage. A few members of the archaeological team had stayed late to lift the skeleton and were still working nearby and Wesley was suddenly struck by the dreadful possibility that, if they'd challenged her, Gemma might have launched an attack on them too. He ran through the gates, filled with dread, but to his relief he saw they were unharmed, packing up and piling boxes of equipment in their gazebo, oblivious to the drama that had been acted out on the other side of Dead Man's Lane.

He rushed across the uneven ground towards the open trenches and when he shouted out they turned to look at him.

'Have you seen a woman – tall, fair hair, blue quilted jacket?'

One of the men raised his hand as though he was

answering a question in class. 'She ran past a couple of minutes ago, making for the house in one hell of a hurry. We've packed up the skeleton. Neil's taking it to Exeter. Do you know where he is? He ran off a while ago with a mattock and we've not seen him since.' He looked round the group, who were looking increasingly lost without their leader.

'I heard sirens,' said one of the women. 'Is something going on?'

It wasn't a question Wesley felt ready to answer. 'I'll tell you later,' he mumbled before setting off towards the house, running as fast as he could manage, cursing his lack of speed. He'd heard the sound of power tools earlier which meant some of the workmen were still up there; surely if she tried anything they would be able to overpower her, he thought. And yet he knew an attack was the last thing they'd be expecting so they'd be unprepared.

Once he reached the house everything seemed normal and all he could hear was the sound of distant hammering. When Wesley dashed inside he came face to face with a startled electrician. Like the archaeologists, he was working overtime.

'Have you seen a woman?' He gave a brief description but the man looked at him blankly before scolding him for not wearing a hard hat. Health and safety mattered, the man reminded him with an officious bark.

Glen Crowther appeared at the top of the staircase. 'I saw someone heading for the old barn a few minutes ago. Called out to the stupid cow but she ignored me. It's a building site – she could get herself killed and with the boss not here . . . '

'Shut all the outer doors and don't let anyone in or out,' Wesley ordered before shooting out into the weak sunshine.

The barn was behind the main house, part of the old farm buildings as yet untouched by the building work.

He skirted the house and when he reached the barn he saw that one of the huge double doors was ajar. He squeezed through the gap and found himself in a large space full of rusting farm equipment and bales of rotting straw. The place smelled of decay and for a few moments he stood still and listened to the soft cooing of the wood pigeons nesting in the great rafters above his head. Just as in the cottage earlier they seemed to be watching and commenting on the unfolding drama like a Greek chorus.

Then all of a sudden he heard a crash as a pile of straw bales tumbled to the ground at the far end of the barn, sending up a cloud of dust. When it cleared he could see something hanging from one of the rafters, a human figure swinging to and fro, and he acted without thinking, hardly aware of rushing over to grab the woman's dangling feet, supporting her weight as she struggled for breath. His instinct to save life was automatic.

Gemma Pollinger had tried to hang herself.

60

'I hope there's an officer on duty outside her door.'

'What do you think I am, Wes? Daft? She's being watched day and night. We don't want her slipping off again, not after last time. How's Neil?'

Wesley didn't reply. When he closed his eyes he could still see his friend lying there as Grace fought to stem the bleeding. He was in Tradmouth Hospital too, in a ward not too far away from where Gemma Pollinger was recovering. He'd been in the ICU for twenty-four hours but now the doctors, pleased with his progress, had put him in the high dependency unit. A procession of Neil's colleagues had been to visit him, wearing the confused look of a flock of sheep without a shepherd, and Wesley had tried to reassure them that he was receiving the best of care and that he'd soon be back supervising the dig. In the meantime he promised he would make sure the builders didn't begin any work before the archaeology was completed.

'If she's up to talking we might as well have a word,' said Gerry, interrupting his thoughts.

Wesley nodded, careful not to betray the apprehension he felt. Gemma Pollinger had murdered five people and would have killed more if she hadn't been stopped. And without Grace's quick thinking he might have lost his friend.

They arrived at the hospital and made straight for the side ward where they found Gemma guarded by a uniformed constable. When they entered she was sitting up in bed listening to music through earphones and the normality of the scene jarred with the horror of what she'd done.

When she saw her visitors she took out the earphones and stared at the newcomers defiantly.

'You might be interested to know that the man you stabbed at the cottage is going to live,' said Gerry, relieving Wesley of the need to broach the subject. She looked away as though the news didn't interest her.

'Why did you try to kill yourself?' said Wesley softly.

She'd pulled her hospital nightgown up to her chin and as she shrugged her shoulders it slipped a little to reveal the marks of the rope around her neck.

'Because I couldn't face spending the rest of my life locked up.' Her voice sounded hoarse.

'Like Jackson Temples has,' said Wesley quietly. 'He had nothing to do with the deaths of those girls, am I right?'

'He deserved everything he got.'

'Why's that?'

She pouted like a spoilt child who couldn't get her own way. 'I asked him to paint me like the others. I told him I didn't mind all that kinky stuff with ropes but he laughed and said no thanks. I wasn't the type he was looking for.' She leaned forward, her eyes burning with fury. 'I watched them go into his studio preening and smirking; looking at me as though I was something they'd trodden in. I thought he'd notice me once they'd gone but he still treated me as though I didn't exist. I made him pay, that's all.'

'I still don't understand,' Wesley said. 'You're an attractive woman so why . . .'

She looked at him as though he was being particularly obtuse. 'Do you know what they used to do when I was at Fulton Grange? They used to wait for me after school and walk behind me calling me names. Ugly Gemma. Face like the back of a cow.'

'Children can be cruel.'

'They weren't children. They looked like women. When I couldn't stand any more I left school and got a job but whenever I went out there were still girls just like them – smirking and whispering behind my back. They thought they were better than me but I taught them different.' She gave a throaty laugh. 'They weren't so beautiful once I'd finished with them.'

She began to laugh, a sound that made Wesley shudder. He saw disgust on Gerry's face; the disgust of a man who'd seen this killer's handiwork at first hand.

Wesley had seen the picture Gemma's parents gave the police at the time of her disappearance and, although he could still see the resemblance, over the years Gemma had acquired a perfect nose, a sculpted chin, larger eyes and hair that was now the colour of honey. The one thing she hadn't thought to change was the heart-shaped birthmark on her left hand. That was what Bert Cummings had recognised and it had sealed his fate. If she'd realised Roberta had seen it, her life too would have been cut short.

'You had cosmetic surgery.'

'I didn't want to be invisible any more so as soon as I had enough money . . .'

'You stole the money to fund it?'

'At first I saved up for it then I began stealing from the petty cash wherever I worked. I spent years temping, helping myself to whatever I could to pay for the procedures. Then I got the job with Dale Keyes and I saw my opportunity.'

'You were the Jenny who worked for him. You cleared out his company's bank account.'

Her bitter smile gave him a glimpse of the original Gemma beneath the surgically altered exterior.

'Ten out of ten, Inspector. I'd had all my surgery by then but I'd borrowed a lot and run up huge debts. I paid them off with what I stole from Dale's business and I thought I'd got away with it when he was reported dead. I thought everyone would forget about me.'

'But you were recognised by someone he knew and he came here to look for you. He wanted to get back what you owed him so he had to die.'

Gerry had been sitting in stunned silence but now he spoke. 'If you'd changed so much how come Linda recognised you from the time she spent at Strangefields Farm?'

'She didn't at first, although she did ask me if we'd met before. I said we hadn't, of course.' She held out her left hand and he saw the birthmark standing out red between the forefinger and thumb. 'I should have had it removed but it never seemed important. I always wore a plaster over it at work, just in case.'

'Did you remember her?'

'Yes, but I thought she was only a kid so I didn't take much notice of her.'

'I don't understand why you came back to Tradmouth,' Wesley said. 'Why risk being recognised?'

'I didn't think I was taking a risk. It was over two decades ago and I think I've changed beyond all recognition, don't you? I was curious because I'd seen Jack's paintings for sale on the internet ... and I'd heard Strangefields was going to be made into a holiday village.' She gave a bitter laugh. 'Then I read online that there was a campaign to prove Jack's innocence and I wanted to know what was going on. I needed to find out what they were saying about me and whether anyone was suggesting I might still be alive. I went to a meeting and that's where I saw Linda – she stayed at the back of the room where she couldn't be seen. I recognised her from all those years ago and when I learned she had a florist's shop and was looking for an assistant it was as though it was meant. I'd worked in a florist's once, you see, and I knew that then I could keep a close eye on her and any developments in Jack's campaign.'

'Why did you kill her?'

She didn't answer immediately and when she finally spoke it was almost in a whisper so that Wesley had to lean forward to hear what she was saying.

'My plaster came off one day while I was washing my hands and she came into the room before I could replace it. She saw my birthmark and said one of the missing girls had had one exactly the same. She asked me straight out if I was her. I denied it of course but I knew she was onto me and it would only be a matter of time before she gave me away. She told me who she was and she said there was a group who wanted to prove Jackson's innocence. She even asked me if I was willing to help.'

She shook her head, as though she could hardly believe Linda's naivety.

'I copied her house key and took some rope from the

shop display – she'd taken some earlier for her play so she never noticed more was missing. It wasn't quite the same as the rope I'd used at Strangefields but it was similar enough and I knew it'd do the job just as well.' She looked as though she was reliving a happy memory. 'She always went to a play rehearsal on Monday nights so I went round to her house and waited for her in the dark. As soon as she came home I hit her, left her stunned, then I pretended to turn up and said I'd take her to A and E. Only I took her to Bereton Lake instead and finished what I'd started.'

'What about Dale Keyes?'

'One of his friends saw me in Linda's shop and followed me home. That's how Dale found me. I promised to pay the money back but I said I needed time to get it together. He gave me his phone number and told me to get in touch when I had the cash. I texted him and asked him to meet me at the creek because it was private but he had no idea what I had in mind. I presumed he'd told his girlfriend about me. That's why I had to deal with her too.'

'You didn't kill her right away.'

She swallowed hard. 'I wanted her to know that just because she's beautiful it doesn't mean she can trample all over other people. I wanted to destroy her face and I needed her to know what was happening and why.' The pitch of her voice was growing shriller with bitter emotion. 'I didn't expect the pills I put in the wine to wear off so soon.' She looked disappointed, annoyed with herself for miscalculating so badly.

'Dale never told her who you were. She was no threat to you,' said Wesley.

'I don't believe you,' she said like a petulant child.

'Let's get back to the Strangefields girls.'

She closed her eyes, smiling.

'At school I used to dream about getting a gun and shooting them all down. Only when I got to Strangefields and saw how Jack painted them I had a better idea. They deserved it. I wanted them to suffer like I had all those years, and I wanted him to pay for how he treated me.'

'You killed them at Strangefields?'

She shook her head. 'That would have been too risky. I sent them notes telling them to go to the cottage. They thought it was one of Jack's little games. The notes said not to tell anyone and they didn't. It was easy.'

'How did you move the bodies?' said Wesley. 'Surely you didn't put them in the river by yourself.'

She looked away. 'My brother, Graham, had access to my dad's firm's van and the motor boat. He would have done anything I asked him.'

'He helped you?'

She nodded slowly. 'After the first one went wrong – after Carrie Bullen survived.'

'Who drove Carrie to the river bank?'

'I did. I'd passed my test and I borrowed the van but after it all went wrong I knew I had to put them in deeper water. That's when I asked Graham to help me.'

'So he killed himself because he couldn't live with what he'd done?'

Wesley was surprised when she looked him in the eye. Her gaze was piercing, unblinking. He had to look away.

'His conscience began to get the better of him. He said he didn't want to help me any more and when he started talking about going to the police I said we needed to discuss it and why didn't we go for a walk. I got him to drive to Littlebury and . . . '

'You pushed him off the cliff?'

She paused. 'I had no choice. Anyway, after that I knew I had to disappear for good.'

'Tell us how you did it,' said Wesley.

'I left plenty of evidence at Strangefields to incriminate Jack then I picked up the bag I'd left at the cottage. My "going away" bag I called it. I'd got some money together – saved up and taken some from home – and some from Jack when he wasn't there.'

'Where did you go?'

'Up north at first – Leeds. Then I went to London. It seemed more ... impersonal. Best place to get lost in the crowd.'

'How did you know about the cottage?'

'It belonged to a relative of Jackson's and he had a key. I pinched it 'cause he never went near the place. Why would he when he had Strangefields? It was my private space. I was surprised to find it still in the same state when I came back.'

'Tell us why you killed Bert Cummings.'

'He saw me on the ferry and he came up to me; started staring at my face – then at my hand. Once I'd got rid of Linda I got careless about wearing my plaster. "It's Gemma, isn't it?" he said in that intense way he always had. He recognised my birthmark at once 'cause I'd been his star pupil at Fulton Grange. He told me he'd heard my dad was in a nursing home and didn't I think I should let him know I was safe ... as if I could care less.' She rolled her eyes. 'I'd seen a lad with him earlier and I couldn't take the risk of him telling anyone he'd recognised me so I found out where he lived and paid him a visit. It was for the best.'

'For the best?' Gerry said in a low growl. 'Who for?'

Wesley stood up, his chair clattering backwards over the

hospital linoleum. Gerry did the same, turning his head away from the woman in the bed.

'Keep an eye on her,' Gerry said to the constable on his way out.

61

As Wesley walked through the museum door he scanned the room for Joe Hamer. He hadn't seen the man since the case against Gemma Pollinger had been wrapped up and handed to the CPS and he was surprised that there was no sign of him. He'd been so sure he'd be there, showing off his generosity. Maybe he intended to make a grand entrance once everyone had arrived.

The exhibition about the Strangefields Farm excavation was taking place at Tradmouth Museum rather than Neil's preferred Exeter because Hamer, who was funding the whole thing, had insisted on it being held in the town where he was investing so much capital. It was hoped the new holiday village would provide a welcome boost to the local economy and Hamer was grasping every opportunity to get the town council and community on side.

After the truth about Gemma Pollinger had finally emerged, Wesley had spent some time talking to Hamer and the artist turned developer had been as surprised as everyone else at how events had played out because, like the trial jury, he'd been convinced of Temples' guilt. The shock of the murders had made him abandon the world of art so at least, he'd told Wesley, some good had come of it because his current life had made him a wealthy man. Wesley couldn't agree – as far as he was concerned, no good had come of Gemma Pollinger's crimes; only grief.

Gemma herself was awaiting trial but it seemed inevitable that the jury would find her guilty. Jackson Temples' case had gone to appeal and there was little doubt he'd soon be a free man.

Grace had returned to London and she'd told Wesley she was too busy to make the exhibition. Archaeology wasn't really her thing anyway. Wesley hadn't let her know how disappointed he was about her absence. But maybe she thought the exhibition would bring back bad memories of Dale Keyes, in which case she was right to stay away.

As Wesley and Pam entered the room their son, Michael, trailed slightly behind them. He'd been keen to come, the subject of executions and the walking dead being irresistible to a boy in his early teens, and Wesley was pleased he was taking an interest.

It was good to see Neil there with Lucy, even though he still looked pale and had lost a lot of weight during his stay in hospital. He was standing proudly beside the three faces, reconstructed by experts, who stared out from their glass case at the modern-day men and women of Tradmouth who'd come to gawp at them. Centuries ago those faces had been known in the town and their owners had walked down the streets and shopped in the market place. Now they were exhibits in a museum and Wesley couldn't help wondering how they would have felt about their strange resurrection.

Artefacts from Neil's dig were displayed in glass cases around the room and the walls had been hung with enlarged photographed extracts from Lemuel Strange's two diaries, written nineteen years apart, with clearly printed transcriptions alongside to make reading easier for the modern eye.

A small crowd had gathered around a plastic reconstruction of the damaged ribcages bearing marks where the hearts had been ripped out. The boulders that had been placed on the bodies also formed part of the display. In Reuben's case a broken millstone had been used but Wesley imagined it had served the purpose just as well. He watched Michael edge his way to the front of the throng to stare at the morbid display while Pam made a beeline for Neil and Lucy, greeting them with a kiss. Wesley left Michael to it and joined her.

'How are you feeling?' Pam asked anxiously.

'Not too bad,' Neil said, looking slightly embarrassed by this reminder of his mortality. He turned to Wesley. 'Have you heard Hamer's abandoned the plans for that reception building? It would have wrecked the foundations of the chapel. And, let's face it, it was quite hideous.' He grinned. 'I know Grace designed it but I've got to be honest. She's gone back to London, I believe.'

'That's right.'

'Pity. I liked her – even though we didn't always see eye to eye professionally.' He paused. 'And if it hadn't been for her ...'

Neil didn't have to finish his sentence. Wesley wasn't going to forget the events of that day in a hurry.

As he strolled round the exhibition he kept thinking of Gemma Pollinger, who'd returned from the grave and eliminated anyone she considered a threat to her new existence. He stopped to look at the faces of Harry the groom, surname unknown, and Bess Whitetree, lovingly reconstructed and so lifelike that he felt as though he might meet them in the street. The servants' unremarkable but open faces suggested honesty and innocence and Wesley wondered whether the expert who'd done the reconstruction had been influenced by their story. Reuben Strange had left clues to incriminate the hapless servants who'd offended him, Bess by spurning his advances and Harry by coming to her defence. Then almost twenty years later Reuben had returned to life and the community had exacted revenge on Harry and Bess's behalf, burying him near his victims at Dead Man's Lane and taking steps to prevent him returning to plague the living. To the people who'd lived back then, a kind of justice had been achieved.

Reuben's image sat apart in its own case. He was a lot older than Bess and Harry and Wesley thought he had the look of a hawk, a bird of prey waiting for an innocent victim. Again he wondered whether this effect had been created subconsciously.

'Hamer is coming, isn't he?'

Neil nodded. 'I saw him earlier and he said he'd be late. He's meeting his brother – bringing him along. He sounded a bit mysterious about it.'

Wesley said nothing. If the Kilin family were making the first tentative steps towards reconciliation, it wasn't something he felt inclined to gossip about.

He heard someone saying his name and turned to see Rachel approaching, hand in hand with her soon-to-be husband, Nigel, who looked awkward in the unfamiliar setting of the museum.

Wesley shook Nigel's hand. 'How's Danny Brice getting on?'

'He's doing well,' Nigel said. 'Taken to farm work and

doesn't even seem to mind getting up at stupid o'clock. I've let him have one of the farm cottages. Unmodernised but it's better than the streets.'

'And I'll soon be there to keep an eye on him,' said Rachel, giving Nigel's arm a squeeze.

Wesley saw the gesture of affection and felt an unexpected twinge of envy which he swiftly suppressed. All that was over, he told himself as he watched Pam with Michael, mother and son studying the exhibits, deep in conversation.

'See you soon then,' Nigel said before whisking Rachel off to the table where the cheap Prosecco was being poured into glasses by a harassed-looking member of the museum staff.

After they'd helped themselves to the free drinks, handing an orange juice to a disappointed Michael, Wesley led Pam over to the reconstructed heads. She stood staring at Harry and Bess for a while before saying, 'Poor things. Sometimes people don't realise the effect they have on others.'

It was Michael who spoke next, pointing accusingly at the face of Reuben Strange. 'He looks mean. Those things they did to the bodies ... do you think they really managed to stop their spirits walking?'

'Who knows?' Wesley took a sip of Prosecco and smiled.

62

Hayley Rummage was waiting outside the prison gates. She'd never actually met Jackson Temples but she knew she'd recognise him right away. She'd lingered over his photograph in the files she kept; the photo the papers had used at the time of his trial beneath the headline ARTIST CONVICTED OF RITUAL KILLINGS or in the more sensational red tops GIRLS SLAUGHTERED IN PAINTER'S KINKY STRANGLING SESSIONS. Only the papers had got it wrong and Hayley had been proved right all along.

Since the recent arrest she'd spoken to Dr Jane Webster, who'd told her she had a vague memory of seeing Gemma Pollinger at Strangefields Farm. She'd felt sorry for her because she'd heard that some other girls had been making fun of her with the cruelty of a pack of teenagers turning on an outsider. Now everyone knew that this, along with Jackson's rejection, had created a twisted hatred that ultimately led to murder. The authorities at the time had been so convinced of Jackson's guilt that no other possibilities had even been considered. But she, Hayley, had known better.

He was bound to be grateful for her faithful devotion to his cause and she was sure he'd be thrilled to find her waiting there for him. She was about to enjoy her moment of triumph and she closed her eyes, imagining what would happen next.

The prison gate would open and he'd emerge blinking from the gloom, gaunt from his incarceration, He'd search desperately for a friendly face, then he'd spot her and a smile would appear on his pale but handsome features. She imagined him hurrying towards her and, after a few moments of nervous hesitation, he would throw himself into her waiting arms. She could almost feel the embrace, the kiss, tentative at first then more passionate, sealing their future together now that his innocence had been proved beyond doubt.

She took her eyes off the prison gates momentarily to check her watch. Any time now.

After what seemed like an age, she saw the wicket gate open and a thin middle-aged man with the face of a sly weasel stepped out and looked around. She did her best to hide her disappointment when another stranger emerged after the first; a young man with a shaven head who was greeted by a woman Hayley took to be his mother.

Third time lucky. There he was, standing by the gate looking lost, his parcel of possessions tucked under his left arm. Hayley moved forward. This was her chance at last. As she trotted across the road she was almost run over by a glossy red sports car travelling too fast. But she was barely aware of her near miss – this was the moment she'd been anticipating for so long. She waved and smiled but he didn't look in her direction. Instead he seemed to be expecting someone and as the red car screeched to a halt he began to walk towards it. Perhaps he thought it was her. Perhaps he hadn't seen her standing there waiting for him.

She quickened her pace and eventually drew level with him, just in time to see a woman get out of the driver's seat.

'Jackson. It's me. Hayley,' she said, starry-eyed as a teenager approaching her pop idol for an autograph. When he looked puzzled she put it down to disorientation after his long imprisonment. 'We've won at last,' she said. 'I persuaded them to re-examine the case and—'

He was still frowning. 'Sorry, who are you again?'

'Hayley Rummage. I've been writing to you. Remember?' Her voice was becoming more high-pitched, more desperate. 'The campaign for your release was my idea.'

The red-car woman was standing by his shoulder. She was well groomed and wore a stylish leather coat that would have cost Hayley a whole month's salary. She made Hayley feel shabby and ill-prepared for the encounter. Perhaps she should have made more effort with her clothes – even put on some make-up – but she'd assumed freedom was the only thing that would matter to him.

At last Jackson Temples smiled. He had a lovely smile, just as Hayley had expected. 'Of course I remember. Thanks for thinking of me, er, Hayley. Much appreciated. It can get lonely in there, I can tell you. Er . . . thanks.'

He was shifting from foot to foot as though he was impatient to be away.

'Er . . . Sorry, I've got a lunch engagement.' He waved his hand vaguely in the direction of his new companion. 'This is my agent. She's just taken on the novel I wrote in prison. Nice to meet you, Hayley. Be lucky.'

Hayley Rummage watched him drive off, a tear trickling down her cheek and rage bubbling up inside her. After all she'd done for him he couldn't just abandon her like that. She wouldn't let him.

Author's Note

One of the most common questions a writer is asked is 'Where do you get your ideas from?' The answer is that ideas can come from anywhere but in the case of *Dead Man's Lane*, the initial notion popped into my head because of a chance meeting on Bayards Cove in Dartmouth, Devon. I was with my husband and we started chatting to a gentleman who showed us a photograph he'd taken on his phone – the shadow of a hanging man on the side of a cottage taken at a place called Dead Man's Cross, a crossroads on a hill outside the town which was once the site of public executions. Although the image is an illusion created by road signs at the crossroads, it has caused quite a sensation on social media and in the press and is now available for all to see on the internet. I refrained from telling the gentleman I was a crime writer and that he'd just given me the first germ of an idea for my next book.

Soon after this I came across a newspaper report saying two skulls had been discovered in the town of Totnes, both in carrier bags – one behind an empty shop and one on the banks of the River Dart. The skulls appeared to be over a hundred years old but their origin was a mystery – and I can never resist weaving a story around a mystery.

I'm a member of my local archaeology society and recently I attended a very interesting talk about 'revenants' (literally 'the returned') and the ancient belief that the dead could emerge from their graves to torment the living. The reanimated corpse appears to be a constant feature of folklore throughout many cultures, from Transylvanian vampires to Haitian zombies. Fascination with the 'undead' has inspired a host of films and books (the most famous perhaps being Bram Stoker's tale of Dracula) and since the first showing of *Night of the Living Dead* almost fifty years ago, the idea of a 'zombie apocalypse' has been popular amongst those who enjoy their entertainment with a frisson of terror.

Throughout history there has been a fear of the 'walking dead', a fear confirmed by archaeological discoveries. The placing of severed heads between a corpse's legs is found in Romano-British and Anglo-Saxon burials, possibly as a protection against restless spirits (or maybe evidence of judicial execution) but it is not until the twelfth and thirteenth centuries that 'revenant' stories become rife.

Fear of the dead returning to harm the living was very real to the medieval mind, as was the concept of a 'good death' (with the soul fully prepared for departure by the rites of the church) and a 'bad death' which leaves a soul restless and liable to return. In Geoffrey of Burton's twelfth-century 'Miracles of St Modwenna' two men arrive in the village of Drakelow in Derbyshire and die only to rise from their graves and terrorise villagers who then die mysteriously. This campaign of terror continues until most of the villagers are dead then the desperate survivors dig up the men's corpses, decapitate them, placing the heads between the legs, and remove and burn the hearts, after which the trouble ceases. Other tales of the returning undead include the notorious Alnwick vampire from the North-East of England, recorded by medieval chronicler William de Newburgh in the late twelfth century.

Archaeological evidence confirms that these gruesome tales had their roots in genuine fear and a number of what are known as 'deviant' burials have been discovered during excavations in Wharram Percy (a deserted medieval village in Yorkshire) as well as in many other locations (often in unconsecrated ground outside a churchyard). Sometimes a corpse was buried face down and sometimes, as well as decapitation and the burning of the heart, a boulder was placed on the body to prevent it rising from the grave.

The historical narrative of *Dead Man's Lane* takes place in the seventeenth century, around the time of the Great Fire of London, and research shows that even after the medieval period belief in the restless dead tended to linger, especially in isolated communities. In certain parts of the world, such as Eastern Europe, these beliefs continue well into modern times. Even in London in 1811 the body of John Williams, the man accused of the shocking Ratcliffe Highway murders, was buried at a crossroads (to confuse his spirit). In 1886 employees of a gas company digging up the road where Cannon Street Road and Cable Street cross discovered Williams' body and found that it had been buried upside down with a stake driven through the heart, which proves the story wasn't fanciful.

Until relatively recent times 'protection' marks (such as religious symbols) have been put on the thresholds of buildings and objects such as shoes hidden in vulnerable parts of a house to protect against evil. Fear of ill fortune has been constant throughout the ages and people will do everything in their power to keep it at bay. Just think, next time you touch wood, cross your fingers or refuse to walk under a ladder, you're joining in with this long tradition.

Even in our supposed 'age of reason' there is no sign of the public's latent fear of the returning dead – or their enthusiasm for zombies and vampires – waning any time soon.

Kate Ellis discusses her next Wesley Peterson mystery, *The Burial Circle*

On a stormy night in December, a tree is blown down on an isolated Devon farm. Only when the fallen tree is dragged away is a red rucksack found, caught amongst the roots that have been torn from the earth – and next to the rucksack is a human skeleton.

The discovery of the rucksack jolts some memories – a hitchhiker who went missing in 2008 was last seen carrying a distinctive red rucksack. And DI Wesley Peterson knows the half-forgotten cold case has suddenly become red hot.

Meanwhile, in the small Devon village of Petherham, Damien Lee, a famous TV psychic, is the main attraction at a supernatural weekend. The event is held at the Mill House, a guesthouse that was once home to the owner of Petherham's water-powered woollen mill, now reopened as a tourist attraction and the subject of a study by Wesley's friend, archaeologist Neil Watson.

The Mill House has a sinister history and, along with the mill itself, it was the scene of several mysterious deaths back in the nineteenth century. When the psychic dies in suspicious circumstances, Wesley discovers a connection between the dead man and the vanished hitchhiker. But was he responsible for her murder? Or has a shady organisation called The Burial Circle, set up in the reign of Queen Victoria and connected with those strange deaths over a hundred years before, been revived in the present day?

I have a keen interest in archaeology and, living in the North West of England, I've become familiar with industrial archaeology, especially the archaeology and history of textile mills. When I discovered that Devon (where Wesley Peterson investigates crime) also has an impressive industrial heritage, I couldn't resist including it in my latest novel, *The Burial Circle*. Petherham Mill's dark history and the strange events in Petherham village in the nineteenth century echo down the years – and bring Wesley one of his most frightening and dangerous cases yet.

The Burial Circle will be published in February 2020 and is available now to pre-order.

Have you read the other mysteries in the Wesley Peterson series?

For a full list of the novels and to find out more
visit Kate Ellis online at:

www.kateellis.co.uk
@KateEllisAuthor

Don't miss Kate Ellis's historical thrillers in the Albert Lincoln series